REVELATIONS

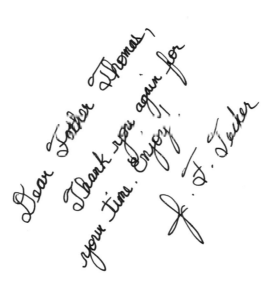

BY J.F. TUCKER

Dear Father Thomas,

Thank you again for your time. Enjoy.

J. F. Tucker

DORRANCE
PUBLISHING CO
EST. 1920
PITTSBURGH, PENNSYLVANIA 15238

Dorrance Publishing Co
585 Alpha Drive
Pittsburgh, PA 15238
Visit our website at *www.dorrancebookstore.com*

ISBN: 978-1-4809-2573-1
eISBN: 978-1-4809-2343-0

ACKNOWLEDGMENT

I would like to take the opportunity to thank the many people who helped make this book possible.

First, to my personal editors Linda Barbour and Michelle Sargent. Your insight and encouragement were invaluable in helping me get this book finished and into print.

Second, to my beta readers, Julie Backholm, Gina Selgrath, Jocelin Teachout, Andreea Harambas-Jamotillo as well as my brother Abelardo Flores and husband Jeff Tucker, for pointing out what worked, what didn't, and what readers want to see on the written page!

Third, to Theresa Jocson-Roley, Joseph Roley-Arzaga, Paul Ortiz Jr., Wade High and Monsignor Richard Duncanson who were kind enough to provide me with technical advice on subjects ranging from religion to computers.

Fourth, to Mark Jamotillo, for creating such a beautiful cover for my debut novel.

To Jared and Allison:

Without you, there would be no Jeremy or Alexis.

PROLOGUE

The Church is dying, thought the Devil with glee as he stumbled upon two teenage girls in Catholic uniforms arguing in front of their school's chapel. His eyes widened in surprise when he caught sight of the Archangel Michael watching them from a distance. The concerned look on the Archangel's face piqued his curiosity. The Devil moved in for a closer look just as the petite girl with fiery red hair poked her finger at the taller, brown-haired girl's chest. She looked like she was ready to pounce on the other girl at any moment. He rubbed his hands together eagerly, practically salivating at the prospect of a physical fight. However, his anticipation quickly turned to disappointment when the taller girl simply bowed her head and took the verbal blows being hurled in her direction, as if she were a punching bag. He felt cheated; he wanted this spineless and pathetic creature to be beaten to a pulp. Thus, he was genuinely shocked when the Archangel continued to keep a watchful eye over *her* rather than the red-haired girl, who had stormed off. After a moment of deliberation, the Devil formulated a plan. He smiled contemptuously at his newfound prey and said, "Taking your soul should be easy enough."

CHAPTER 1: THE BARGAIN

It was a bright and sunny June afternoon, as a large group of mourners huddled around a casket near the top of a grassy hill. Although there were a number of trees interspersed throughout the cemetery, none were close enough to provide any respite from the sweltering rays of the sun, which were mercilessly beating down on them. Many in the crowd were young and unaccustomed to being so close to death and its symbols. The boys fidgeted with their ties, while the girls twirled their fingers through their hair. They looked on while the Reverend James O'Brien, or Father Jim, as he was known by parishioners at Corpus Christi Catholic Church in Bonita, California, said prayers, expressed words of comfort, and sprinkled holy water on the casket.

Also in attendance was an old man who stood apart from the crowd as he took in the fruits of his handiwork. He wore a sweat-stained work shirt, well-worn shoes, and a frayed straw hat for the occasion; his weathered features complemented his ragged clothes. He assumed the few people that bothered to look in his direction probably thought he was a groundskeeper or a grave digger. It made him smile to think that they only thought of him as the hired help.

His smile, however, quickly turned into a sneer as soon as his eyes fell upon Father Jim. He nearly convulsed when the priest made the sign of the cross over the casket and said, "Eternal rest grant unto her, O Lord. And let perpetual light shine upon her. May she rest in peace. Amen. May her soul, and the souls of all the faithful departed, through the mercy of God rest in peace. Amen." While the mourners said, "Amen," the old man turned away from the crowd and spat on the ground.

As the casket was lowered, the old man felt something brush up against his leg. He looked down and saw a program with a teenage girl's picture on the front. He picked it up and read the girl's name, Avery Elizabeth Edwards, followed by the date of her birth and death under her youthful face. The girl in the casket had only been sixteen years old when she died. *So far, so good.* Everything was going according to plan. He folded the program and stuck it in his breast pocket.

When the service ended, the old man tried to surreptitiously listen in on the mourners' conversations. He was eager to learn what they knew and thought about Avery's untimely death. He struck gold when he came upon two notorious gossip mongers. One of the women, Melinda Lynch, was a stocky busybody who glittered like a Christmas tree as the sunlight hit the oversized jewelry on her arms, ears, and neck. He thought that the gaudy multicolored flower brooch pinned to her black jacket was a particularly nice touch. Her friend, Gloria Santos, was an even larger woman who reeked of some cheap drugstore perfume which, to his great amusement, had caused more than a few people to gag and cough in her presence. The old man looked up at the sky and grinned. *So, are these self-indulgent women the pillars of your Church?* He shook his head. *They're also rotten to the core.*

"Rumor has it that Avery was drinking when she drove that car of hers off the road," Mrs. Lynch said in a low, conspiratorial voice to her friend. Mrs. Santos audibly gasped as she shot her friend a look of shock worthy of an Oscar nomination. Mrs. Lynch put a hand on Mrs. Santos' arm, adding, "I heard she was using prescription drugs, too."

Mrs. Lynch motioned to her niece, Lea Meeks, a girl with perfectly styled blond hair, manicured nails, and a frozen smile, to come over. Lea dutifully complied and walked toward her aunt with a friend of Filipino-American descent, Cecilia Licad, who seemed to share Lea's fashion sense and haughty disposition. Mrs. Lynch pulled Lea toward her in order to form a close-knit circle and proceeded to pepper her with questions about Avery. Lea, for her part, was only too happy to fill her aunt in on what she knew.

"I caught Avery smoking in the girl's bathroom a couple of times," Lea said. "I don't think she cared who saw her. She bragged to me once about stealing drugs from her mom's medicine cabinet, and looked high half the time she was in class."

Mrs. Lynch shook her head while Mrs. Santos crossed herself. Mrs. Lynch asked Lea, "Did the administration do anything about it?"

"She got called into the principal's office a couple of times, but not for drinking or using drugs," Lea replied. "I don't think that she ever got in trouble for doing those things at school."

"Avery was skipping school and getting mouthy with her teachers," Cecilia chimed in. "Not exactly the smartest thing to do when your best friend is the principal's daughter."

"You mean ex-best friend," Lea said.

This time, Mrs. Santos looked genuinely surprised. "Did Avery and Alexis have a falling out? I thought those two were nearly inseparable."

"I'll say," Cecilia said. "They've been best friends since grade school. But someone told me that they had a pretty big blowout just before Avery died."

"About what?" Mrs. Lynch asked.

"It wasn't a secret that Alexis didn't like Avery's boyfriend," Lea replied. "She thought he was bad news. I think she might have also felt kinda left out. Alexis doesn't exactly have a lot of friends."

"Is Avery's boyfriend anyone we would know?" Mrs. Santos asked.

"Maybe," Lea replied. "I've seen him in church before. I think his name is Bobby." From the looks on their faces, the name didn't seem to ring a bell for either woman.

"Is he a student at Mater Dei?" Mrs. Santos asked.

Lea shook her head. "I think that he goes to one of the public high schools around here. Not sure which one though."

Mrs. Lynch's interrogation of her niece came to an abrupt halt as soon as she saw Father Jim walking by them. Mrs. Santos flagged him down with a wave of her hand. He smiled at them and said, "Good afternoon, ladies."

They responded in kind and invited him to join them as they commiserated about Avery's passing.

"It's such a tragic loss of life, isn't it Father?" Mrs. Santos said with great dramatic flair. "She had her whole life ahead of her, but I suppose God had His reasons for taking her so young."

Father Jim paused briefly and then said, "Death at any age is unfortunate, but particularly when it happens to someone so young."

"I heard she was…troubled," Mrs. Lynch said with a note of derision in her voice.

The priest furrowed his brow and clasped his hands firmly together as he locked eyes with Mrs. Lynch. Abashed, she turned her head away and took a step back as he said, "Even though God has a plan for each one of us, He lets us choose whether to follow Him or not. Luckily for us, He *never* abandons us, no matter how far we stray."

"How are her parents doing?" Mrs. Santos asked, in a transparent attempt to draw the priest's attention away from Mrs. Lynch.

"About as well as one would expect," Father Jim replied. "The loss of a child is one of the most devastating things that can happen to a person. I hope you will keep them in your prayers."

"Of course we will," the two older women said, almost in unison, while the two teenage girls nodded in agreement.

"Will you be going to the reception?" Mrs. Lynch asked tentatively.

Father Jim looked down at his watch and said, "Unfortunately, no. I have other business I need to attend to."

After exchanging a few more pleasantries with these ladies, he politely excused himself and walked away.

Once Father Jim was no longer within earshot, Mrs. Lynch turned to Mrs. Santos and said, "That girl will need more than the prayers of our congregation to save her. If you ask me, I think she went straight to…"

Mrs. Santos clucked her tongue with a disapproving "tsk, tsk," as she alerted her friend to the old man's presence. Mrs. Lynch gave him a disapproving look. He tipped his hat and flashed her a toothless grin. Her horror-stricken face made him smile even more broadly. He suppressed the urge to laugh as they quickly moved away from him. As he watched them recede into the departing crowd, he thought about how much he was going to enjoy seeing the looks on these ladies' faces upon entering his realm in the next life.

The old man then turned his attention to a light-skinned girl with long brown hair and brown eyes who was standing, silent and immobile, in front of Avery's now lowered casket. A hint of a smile spread across his face as he said her name under his breath, "Alexis MacKenzie Neil." After months of careful study, he felt that he knew a great deal about her and her family history, and had come to his own conclusions as to why this unassuming girl was garnering the attention of so high-ranking an angel. At the moment, she looked as lost and fragile as a china doll. *Such easy prey.*

Alexis' mother, Lisa Perez Neil, a petite Filipino-American woman in her early forties, was standing beside her. She put her hand on her daughter's shoulder and said, "*Anak ko*, it's time to go now." My child.

"Can you give me a few more minutes, please?" Alexis replied with a slight tremor in her voice. Lisa obliged with a nod and stepped sway.

A moment later, Avery's mother, whose gaunt features were hidden under a black veil, came up to Alexis and hugged her.

"I'm so sorry," Alexis said in a choked voice.

Mrs. Edwards shook her head as she placed her hands on either side of Alexis' face. With quivering lips, she said, "No one blames you for what happened. It was an accident. You were her best friend, and I know that you'd never deliberately do anything to hurt her." She took Alexis' hands in her own and said, "She's with God now."

Alexis nodded her head slowly as Mr. Edwards approached his wife from behind. He acknowledged his daughter's best friend with a slight smile before wordlessly leading his wife toward a car parked immediately behind the hearse.

Moments later, Alexis' father, Eric Neil, a bespectacled man with dirty blond hair, joined her. Other than the groundskeeper nearby, they were now the only two people left standing by Avery's grave. She shook her head violently when he put his hand on her shoulder and then fell to her knees as she clutched her stomach and let out a piteous cry. He knelt down beside her, giving what little comfort he could to his inconsolable daughter. Eventually, he helped Alexis get back on her feet and gently guided her toward their car.

As the Neils walked away, the old man spied a gentleman in a white suit standing underneath a jacaranda tree not far from the gravesite. He recognized him instantly and thought that he looked positively angelic. At one time they had been colleagues, until an irreparable rift had forever set them on divergent paths. He smiled and waved at the gentleman, who was focusing on Alexis. After a moment of deliberation, he decided that it was time to have a chat.

"It's been too long, my friend," the old man said when he finally reached the jacaranda tree. The gentleman said nothing. He moved closer and noted that not even one bead of sweat appeared on the man's brow, even though the scorching sun was now bearing down on both of them. He paused to carefully consider what he was going to say next.

"The believers are old and dying. The young ones don't care." He looked at the gentlemen to see what, if any, impact his words had made on him. "It's only a matter of time before the churches are completely empty. God will be nothing more to them than a footnote in the history books."

"You misjudge them," the gentleman replied as he coolly stuck his hands in his pockets. "There will always be those who believe."

The old man clapped his hands in delight. "Ah, so you do have a voice." Sensing that the gentleman had no interest in engaging him in a conversation on the general state of the Roman Catholic Church, he decided to get right to the heart of the matter. He was ready to make a deal.

He looked at Alexis, who was getting in the back seat of her parents' car, and said with mock sympathy, "So much grief at such a young age."

"Her family and friends will help her through this."

"That girl has been blessed with beauty, intelligence, and health. She also has friends and family that love her. It's easy to have faith when you've been given so much," the old man said. "But if you take those things away, what would become of her?"

"Of what significance is she to you?"

"Isn't the question really what significance is this girl to *you*…and Him?" the old man asked with an inquiring look. "She must be of great importance if He sent you here to watch over her."

"As usual, you are reading far too much into things."

"Am I? Then I presume He won't mind if I decide to play with her a bit?"

"What exactly are you proposing?" the gentleman asked, as he arched his eyebrows and, for the first time, looked his adversary in the eye.

"I propose to put the girl to the test," the old man said. "He's allowed me to do that before."

"I'm surprised that you even bothered to ask, considering the damage you've already done."

The old man feigned shock at the suggestion. "I would never do anything without His permission. Besides, Alexis' relationship with Avery was already falling apart by the time I started taking an active interest in their lives. So, do we have a bargain or not?"

"Her soul belongs to God, Satan."

"It belongs to whomever she pledges it to, Michael. Alexis will come to me willingly. You will see."

Over six thousand miles away, the Grand Master of the Order of the Brethren of the Cross, Hugo Molina, awoke with a start. He hadn't had a restful night's sleep in weeks. Tonight was no exception. He turned to look at the digital clock by his bedside; it was midnight. He turned on the lamp, reached for his glasses, and opened the top drawer of the nightstand to retrieve a well-worn copy of the Bible. He opened it carefully and proceeded to read portions of Psalm 144:

> *Blessed be the Lord, my rock,*
> *who trains my hands for battle,*
> *my fingers for war;*
>
> *My safeguard and my fortress,*
> *my stronghold, my deliverer,*
> *my shield, in whom I take refuge…*

The Grand Master closed the book and placed it back on the nightstand. He closed his eyes and tried to clear his mind, but the importance of the task entrusted to his care weighed heavily on his mind. The kind of war that he and The

Brethren were physically and spiritually trained to fight hadn't been waged in the scale he now envisioned for centuries. Yet here he was, preparing for a private audience with the Holy Father at the Apostolic Palace in the morning to obtain his consent to wage such a war. He had arrived in Rome just two days ago to meet first with the prefect of the Congregation for Institutes of Consecrated Life and Societies of Apostolic Life, Cardinal Giuseppe Bellini, and then with the Holy Father himself.

His train of thought was interrupted by a knock on the door. A moment later, a zealous young chaplain of The Brethren, Ignacio Escriva, who had accompanied him on this trip to Rome, slowly opened the door and said, "I saw that your light was on, Brother Molina. Is everything all right?"

He shook his head and gave Father Escriva a wry smile. "If only it were." He motioned for the priest to come in and invited him to sit in a chair by the window. He dutifully complied and sat with his hands folded in his lap.

"I trust your meeting with Cardinal Bellini went well."

"As well as can be expected."

The Grand Master saw a slight frown form on Father Escriva's face. "I don't mean to dispute the issue, but the signs are clear. The evidence is incontrovertible, and now we have the girl's name and location."

The Grand Master raised his hand in an attempt to interrupt the young priest's train of thought. He said, "Cardinal Bellini stressed the importance of taking a measured approach."

"What does that mean?"

"It means that we will likely be given the authority to send observers to monitor the situation."

"How many?"

"A handful, I suspect."

"Why so few?" the priest replied. "The last time this happened, the Holy Father sent an entire army…"

"That was centuries ago. We can hardly do that now, especially in this day and age." He shook his head and threw his hands up in the air as he said, "Can you imagine what kind of coverage we would receive from the cable news networks if we did that? The last thing we want to do is draw any kind of unwanted attention to us or our mission. I agree with Cardinal Bellini that less is more."

"What if the situation…escalates?" Father Escriva asked.

"Then we must report the situation to the relevant authorities and wait for permission to adjust our plan," he replied.

The Grand Master stood and walked over to the window. From that vantage point, he could see the dome of St. Peter's Basilica. At that moment, he felt as though the weight of the world were on his shoulders. "In all the years that I have spent in service to the Church and the Order, I never thought that I would live to see this day."

"Do you know who will be sent?"

"Arrangements are being made as we speak. Our Head Chaplain has already volunteered to go."

"Who else?"

"*El Arquero*." The Archer. The Grand Master saw Father Escriva's eyes widen. "Why do you look surprised? If the girl is in real danger, who else would we send?"

"But The Trials only took place a month ago. Don't we need more time to train him?"

"There is no time."

Father Escriva nodded and then asked, "Do you think he is up to the task?"

The Grand Master replied, "For her sake, he must be."

CHAPTER 2—BROKEN

"Alexis, you're going to be late for your appointment." It was the third time Lisa had called out to her in the last fifteen minutes. She could hear the impatience growing in her mother's voice with each admonition. Still, she couldn't seem to find the will to get out of bed. It had been a month since Avery's funeral. Her eyes alternated between the ceiling and the bare walls that made up the four corners of her room. She had taken everything down, especially the pictures; she couldn't bear to look at them. She also made sure that the blinds were shut tight, making it nearly impossible for any light to creep into the dark place she had created for herself.

Despite Alexis' protests, Lisa had insisted on getting her psychiatric help. She, on the other hand, just didn't see the point in going. Nothing the psychiatrist could say would bring her best friend back from the dead. Avery was gone…and it was her fault. Period.

Minutes later, the roar of the car engine and the sound of the garage door opening alerted Alexis to the fact that Lisa meant business and was going to make sure that she went to this appointment, whether she liked it or not. After dragging herself out of bed and rummaging through her closet for something clean and unwrinkled to wear, she put on a pair of jeans, a T-shirt and sneakers. Before heading out of her bedroom, she glanced at herself in the full-length mirror hanging from the door. What she saw was a solemn girl with dark circles under her eyes and greasy brown hair. She frowned, but decided that she had neither the will nor the time to do anything about it, and so she grabbed her purse off the doorknob and ran downstairs.

When Alexis opened the door to the garage, she saw Lisa sitting in the driver's seat with an exasperated look on her face as she tapped her fingers on the steering wheel. Alexis opened the passenger side door and slid into her seat. She avoided looking her mother directly in the eye as she braced for the lecture she knew she was about to receive.

As Lisa backed the car out of the garage, she looked at Alexis and said, "Anak ko, I'm not the enemy."

Not now. The last thing Alexis wanted to hear was another sermon about how screwed up her life was and what she needed to do to turn things around.

"You need help. Everyone's worried about you." Holding up her thumb and index finger an inch apart, Lisa said, "Your *kuya* Jeremy was this close to ending his missionary assignment to come back here because of the way you've been acting."

"I know, I know," Alexis said, annoyed by the fact that her mother had brought her older brother into the conversation. She turned her head toward the window, hoping that her mother would take the hint and say nothing more.

Undeterred, Lisa continued, "I don't think you do. The way you've been acting lately is not… normal. You're not eating or sleeping. You won't go out or see anyone, and when Dad or I try to talk to you, you just shut down…"

"Just stop, okay," Alexis said irritably. "I've heard this speech already."

The sound of Lisa's voice was grating on her nerves like a shrieking baby. She rubbed her temples and closed her eyes in an effort to ward off a headache and stay calm.

"You can't keep what you're feeling bottled up inside you," Lisa went on. "And it's not like we haven't been through this kind of therapy before. Even you can't deny that it helped you when you were first diagnosed with attention deficit disorder." She shook her head, adding, "I just don't understand why you're so resistant to any kind of therapy or counseling this time around."

Alexis snapped. "Why do you always feel like you need to fix me? Jeez, Mom, I just lost my best friend. Why can't you let me work things out for myself and grieve in my own way and in my own time?"

"Is that what you think I'm doing?"

"I'm so sorry that I haven't gotten over her death as fast as you would've liked me to," she said sarcastically. "You might as well face the fact that I'm never going to be as perfect as Jeremy. Who knows? Maybe my psychiatrist will prescribe me a 'perfect pill' that will make things all better."

Alexis knew that she had gone too far. The look on Lisa's face confirmed it. Then again, what choice did she have? If she hadn't said it, she was sure that her mother would have just gone on and on, lecturing and sermonizing, until she blew up at her. Maybe she would apologize later. But right now, what she desperately needed most was for her mother to back off and give her space.

However, it wasn't long before the silence between Alexis and Lisa felt just as oppressive. The wounded look on her mother's face as she cast sideways glances in her direction made her feel like she had committed a capital offense. She rolled down the window in order to get some fresh air.

Alexis breathed a sigh of relief when Lisa turned the car into the medical plaza's parking lot. She bolted out of the car as soon as her mother parked it and headed to the glass doors of the three-story building, determined to get as much distance between the two of them as she possibly could.

She walked up to the building directory sign on the first floor and then took the elevator up to the third floor. She didn't bother to look back or wait to see if Lisa was coming. After checking in with the receptionist, she strolled over to an end table with an eclectic selection of magazines strewn haphazardly on top of it. She picked up one of them at random and sat down. Her mother came in a few minutes later and took a seat next to her. Alexis buried her face in the magazine and acted like she was thoroughly engrossed in an article entitled *The Perils of Wearing Pink*. Thankfully, it wasn't long before she heard her name being called. She looked up and saw a petite brunette with horn-rimmed glasses standing by an open door, waiting for her.

Alexis walked up to the woman, who held her hand out and said, "Hello, Alexis. My name is Carrie Wilson. I'm going to be your psychiatrist. Please follow me."

Nondescript art hung on either side of Alexis as she followed Carrie down the hunter green hallway and into her office. The natural light coming from a large window behind the desk gave the room a warm glow. The walls were painted in earthtones and the furniture was plush with rounded corners. Two upholstered chairs were situated in front of the desk, while a large, comfortable leather sofa with dark green throw pillows was positioned just behind them. Above the sofa hung a painting of young children building a sandcastle on the beach. That, along with the family pictures on her desk, completed the cozy, lived-in feel of the room.

Alexis' eyes wandered over to the bookshelves, which were filled with books and magazines, and caught sight of a wind-up clock. It was 4:02 P.M. *Two minutes down, fifty-eight more minutes to go*, she thought dejectedly. She sank into one of the upholstered chairs and folded her hands in her lap.

"How are you doing today?" Carrie asked cheerfully as she sat down behind her desk and opened what Alexis assumed was her medical file.

"Fine," Alexis replied.

Carrie opened a notepad and took a pen out of her desk drawer. "I've met with your parents and read through your records, so I have a pretty good idea of your medical and psychiatric history. I understand that you experienced a very traumatic event recently." Alexis nodded slowly. "It's always hard to lose someone that you love, especially when that loss is sudden and unexpected."

I never got the chance to tell her I'm sorry. Alexis took a deep breath as she began to tear up.

"I thought it would be a good idea if we started off by you telling me about what your concerns are and what you hope to achieve in these sessions with me."

How many hours do you have to listen to my poor excuse for a life? Alexis thought bitterly, but having decided that she had no intention of telling Carrie what she was actually thinking, she said nothing at all.

At first, Carrie sat with her hands folded in front of her on the desk and watched Alexis squirm in her seat. A minute later, she picked up her pen and scribbled a quick note before clearing her throat and saying in a gentle tone, "Okay, why don't I just start with a few questions for you then. According to your medical records, you were diagnosed with attention deficit disorder when you were in second grade."

"I daydream a lot," Alexis said almost to herself. "My teacher noticed that I had a hard time focusing on things and kept having to remind me to pay attention. She told me once that I always looked like I was lost in my own world."

"How has your condition interfered with your day-to-day living?"

"I get distracted easily and have always felt awkward around people, especially when I don't know them." As Carrie scribbled more notes on her notepad, Alexis added, "I guess I've always felt slightly off. It's like I don't know what to say or do... and umm...I've also been told that I can be impulsive and emotional."

"Have you ever suffered from depression?"

She nodded slowly. "My mom would probably tell you that I've been depressed for a while now."

"Do you think she's wrong?"

"No," she replied honestly. "The last month has been the worst but I'd been feeling bad long before that." She looked down at her fingers and caught herself picking at the skin around her nails. *Damn. Not good.*

"What do you think triggered it?"

"My best friend, Avery, and I weren't getting along...and then she died." The urge to stick her fingers in her mouth and bite down on her nails suddenly overcame her as she added, "Avery was the outgoing, confident one. I just kind of tagged along. She watched out for me, made sure no one pushed me around. She was always there for me. I miss that."

"Can you tell me what happened between the two of you?"

Two words. Bobby Lane. "She started dating this guy we'd seen in church last summer. At first, I was really happy for her, but then I got worried when she started skipping school and getting in trouble in class. She admitted to me that they drank and smoked at his house when his parents weren't around."

"Did you tell her about your concerns?"

"She got mad at me when I told her that he wasn't good for her and that she needed to stop seeing him. She wouldn't listen. We argued a lot. At one point, it got so bad that I said I wasn't going to stand around and watch her destroy her life. I told her that she had to choose between me and him."

"What did she do?"

"She chose him," Alexis replied as a single tear ran down her cheek. She wiped it away. "I never gave up. I kept hoping she'd see through him eventually." More tears fell. "I'm sorry. Do you mind if we talk about something else?"

Carrie nodded and looked down at her notes. "You took stimulants until the age of thirteen. How well have you been able to manage without them?"

"I have my good days and my bad days," Alexis said. "The Adderall helped me focus, but I never felt quite like myself. I started picking at the skin around my fingers and biting my fingernails when I was on the medication. They felt itchy." Alexis looked down at her hands and sighed. "I still do that, especially when I'm nervous or anxious."

"Are you nervous or anxious now?"

"Just anxious to get out of here," she replied truthfully.

A slight smile spread across Carrie's face. "Well, I'll try very hard not to keep you any longer than is absolutely necessary. So, what can you tell me about your family?"

"What would you like to know?"

"Why don't you tell me some things about your family that you believe have shaped the person you are today."

Alexis thought a moment and said, "I come from a mixed race family. My father's people came from Ireland. They immigrated to the United States during the Famine and settled in Boston. That's where my dad grew up. My mother was born and raised in the Philippines."

"Have you had any issues growing up in a household like that?"

Alexis shook her head. "No, not really. I think it helps that we live in such a multiracial county like San Diego. There are a lot of kids I know who are like me. My mom and dad always told me that I should be proud of who I am and where I come from."

"Have you visited Ireland or the Philippines?"

"Yes, I visited Ireland twice," Alexis replied. "We used to go to the Philippines every summer and stay in Manila. Most of my mom's family still lives there. The rest live out in the province of Batangas."

"Do you speak the Filipino language?"

"You mean Tagalog? Yes, my brother Jeremy and I speak the language fluently. My mom made sure that we learned how to read and write it, too."

"Is there anything else about your family that has had a significant impact on your life?"

After a brief pause, Alexis said, "Both sides of my family are *very* Catholic. Many have served the Church as lay ministers, deacons, nuns, and priests. I'm actually related to the current Archbishop of Manila, Florencio de la Cruz. We've also had two bishops and one cardinal on my father's side of the family."

"What about your immediate family?"

"My father is a theology professor at the University of San Diego, and my mother is the Principal at Mater Dei Catholic High School. My older brother, Jeremy, is in the Philippines doing missionary work. He took a year off from the University of Notre Dame to do that. He left just a few days before Avery died."

Carrie jotted a few more notes on her notepad. "That's quite a resume. How do *you* fit in to all of that?"

"I'm going to be a junior at Mater Dei and go to church at Corpus Christi. I received the sacraments of Baptism, Reconciliation, First Communion and Confirmation there, and I used to be an altar server when I was younger. I also sing with the youth choir…but I'm taking a break from that right now."

"Did Avery sing with you in that choir?"

"Yeah," Alexis admitted and then shrugged her shoulders, adding, "I guess I just didn't feel much like singing after she died."

"So far, you've only told me what you've done as a Catholic, but you haven't shared with me what *being* a Catholic means to you."

Alexis thought about how best to answer. "I live in a house where one of the first things you see when you walk through the door is an altar with candles and statues of Mary, Joseph, and Infant Jesus on it. We have a tapestry of Leonardo da Vinci's *Last Supper* hanging on our dining room wall and crosses above every bed. Each room in the house was blessed on the day we moved in. When I was a child, my parents read Bible passages to me and my brother at bedtime and made sure we said grace before we ate dinner. I knew how to pray the rosary before I was five."

Carrie took her glasses off and rubbed the bridge of her nose. After she put them back on, she leaned forward in her seat and said, "What you've told me so far has been very illuminating. It's given me a much clearer picture about what you and your family do. What would, however, be even more helpful for me would be to know what you believe."

She lied and said, "I believe everything that I've been taught."

"You have absolutely no doubts about your faith?"

"None," Alexis said in as definitive a tone as she could muster.

Carrie looked at Alexis as though she were trying to assess her true state of mind. Alexis squirmed and looked away. What she thought about her faith and how it affected her life was none of her psychiatrist's business. As far as she was concerned, she had said all that she was going to say on the subject.

"Okay. So can you tell me a little bit more about your relationship with your immediate family members?"

"My parents are strict, but fair," Alexis replied. "To be honest, I've always been closer to my dad than my mom. That's just the way things are."

"And what about your brother?"

Alexis let out another sigh as she said, "Jeremy's a saint. He was an Eagle Scout, captain of the soccer team, and the valedictorian of his class. He was always busy doing something when we were growing up, but he always made time for me. He also stuck up for me, no matter what."

"Then it must have been doubly hard on you to lose your best friend while he was away," Carrie said sympathetically.

Alexis nodded. "I don't have many friends. Avery and Jeremy were the only people I could always count on to be there for me."

"Can you tell me what happened on the day she died?"

"It's in the police report. Have you read it?" When Carrie nodded, Alexis added curtly, "Then I'd rather not talk about it, if you don't mind."

"Are there any other issues that you'd like to discuss with me right now?"

Alexis shook her head as she gazed at the floor, wishing she could sprout wings and fly away.

Carrie put the notepad and pen down and placed her elbows on the desk as she said, "Alexis, I know you think that these sessions are going to be of little use to you, but I really think that they could help you cope and figure some things out, if you would just give them a chance."

Feeling slightly guilty about her behavior so far, Alexis offered, "Well, I have been having this weird dream lately."

"Go on," Carrie replied as she picked up her pen and placed it over the notepad.

"It always starts the same way. I'm standing on a pedestrian bridge. It's foggy and I can hardly see anything in front of me. It's so cold that I can see my breath. And then I hear…" Alexis said as her voice trailed off.

"What do you hear?"

"A girl's voice. She's telling me that *he's* here."

"Who is he?"

"I'm not sure." At that point, Carrie gave her a curious look. *She must think I'm crazy or making this up,* Alexis thought dejectedly.

"Is he someone you know?"

"No. The only part of his face that I can see clearly is his eyes. They're so blue. He's holding out his hand to me, like he wants me to come with him."

"Does he frighten you?"

Alexis gave a slight shake of her head. "I don't know what to think. The voice in my head keeps telling me that I shouldn't trust him."

"Does he say anything to you?"

"I see his lips moving, but all I can hear is the voice in my head. The closer he gets, the louder it screams. I try to cover my ears, but I can't block out the sound."

"What happens next?"

Alexis shrugged her shoulders and said, "I wake up. My mom or dad is usually by my bed asking me if I'm okay."

"What do you tell them?"

"There's nothing to say. It's a stupid dream." Alexis wanted to drop the subject. Carrie, however, had other ideas.

"How often have you been having this dream?"

"At first, only once every couple of days," Alexis replied. "Now I have it almost every night. The funny thing is that it seems like it's becoming…clearer."

"How so?"

"It seems more real each time I have the dream. The details are getting more vivid, less fuzzy. Does that make sense?" After Carrie nodded in response, Alexis asked her, "So what does it mean?"

Alexis could almost see the wheels turning in Carrie's head as she considered how to best respond. "To be honest, there is no definitive answer to your question. The mind is a complicated instrument. Sometimes dreams help us resolve an issue that we can't answer consciously. Other times, the things we see in dreams are metaphors or symbols for other things. Some say that dreams can be omens of what may happen in the future."

Alexis listened to Carrie's explanations and decided that all Carrie was telling her was a bunch of psychiatric mumbo jumbo. This confirmed in her mind what she had thought all along—that these sessions were going to be a monumental waste of time.

At the end of the appointment, Carrie told Alexis that she believed that they had made good progress and that she was looking forward to seeing her on a weekly basis. Although Alexis couldn't have disagreed more, she just nodded and shook Carrie's hand as she rushed toward the door.

The minute Alexis stepped into the reception area, her mother came up to her and asked, "So how was it?"

"I want to go home," she answered as she sulked past Lisa out the door.

CHAPTER 3—SIGHTINGS

Mass on Sunday was non-negotiable in the Neil household. For as long as Alexis could remember, she was told that a Neil was expected to attend every Sunday and on Holy Days of Obligation, barring death or some natural or man-made disaster. The few times she was brave enough to challenge the status quo, one or both of her parents, Eric and Lisa, would inevitably say, "You're a Neil," with an air of finality that ended any attempt to discuss the matter further.

It was 8:30 in the morning when Alexis dutifully got into the car with her parents in order to fulfill her Sunday obligation. She stared out the window and sighed while driving past wide streets lined with trees and cookie-cutter housing developments as Mozart's *Requiem* played on the car radio. The music sounded as gloomy as her mood.

Eric peered at her from the rear-view mirror and said, "Don't smile or your face will crack."

Alexis leaned slightly forward in her seat and furnished him with a big toothy grin. He shuddered and made a face while Lisa rolled her eyes and shook her head at both of them.

Lines of cars were coming in and out of Corpus Christi's long rectangular-shaped parking lot. Eric turned left into the sloped entrance between the church, an octagonally-shaped white building with a brown roof topped with a golden cross on its steeple, and St. Thomas Aquinas Parish Hall, a white, two-story multipurpose building with a gray roof. He parked in the first open spot in the middle of three aisles in the lot.

Alexis felt the heat from the sun bearing down on her as soon as she got out of the car. She was glad that she had opted to wear a short-sleeved white blouse with a printed flowy skirt and open-toed sandals. She squinted as she put her hands to her forehead to shield her eyes from the glare of the sun and then fished in her purse for her sunglasses. *Where are they?* she thought, frowning. She hated it when she forgot or misplaced things. Although she had been told otherwise, she still thought of her forgetfulness as more of a character flaw than a symptom of her condition.

While waiting for her parents by the car, Alexis saw a pair of parishioners steal a passing glance in her direction. Right after Avery's death, she often felt like a million pairs of eyes were boring into her as she sat in the pew during mass. To make matters worse, she caught sight of Anita Morales, a pretty brunette and the popular incoming president of her junior class, standing with her friends, Lea and Cecilia, in front of the parish hall. She groaned at the idea of having to deal with that unholy trinity and usually made a point of trying to avoid these attractive but vain girls at all costs. In fact, she was about to suggest to her parents that they all go into the church through a side door, when her mother and father were whisked away by a frazzled looking deacon, who wanted to have a quick word with them about the upcoming annual parish picnic.

Now alone, Alexis was making her way toward the church when a handsome young man with light skin and jet black hair caught her eye. She spotted him as he stood on the sidewalk in front of the church talking to a priest she didn't recognize. Her pulse quickened as her eyes tried to take in every detail. He was slim but muscular, with a crew cut, and was wearing sunglasses, a white button-front shirt, and jeans. She liked the way he carried himself, with his shoulders back and his hands at his sides. As she got closer, she got the feeling that there was something about him that seemed vaguely familiar to her, even though she was sure that they had never met before.

He had piqued her curiosity and Alexis found herself wanting to know more about him. In fact, it wasn't until she tripped over the edge of the sidewalk and nearly knocked over an elderly woman with a cane that she realized just how unaware of her immediate surroundings she had become since the moment she first laid eyes on him.

After apologizing to the woman, Alexis felt a tap on her shoulder. She turned and saw her cousin, Theresa "Tessa" Perez, a skinny Filipino-American girl with long, black hair and tan skin, smiling broadly at her. She was wearing a flower-printed summer dress and open-toed shoes.

"Didn't your mom teach you that it's not polite to stare?" Tessa said as she gave Alexis a hug.

"I wasn't," Alexis replied.

Tessa clearly didn't look convinced. In fact, Alexis could almost see the wheels in her cousin's head turning. *Another matchmaking scheme?* she thought glumly. *Hopefully not.*

"I can find out who he is if you'd like," Tessa said brightly.

Alexis' face began to flush as she vigorously shook her head. While trying to think of a way out, it suddenly dawned on her to ask Tessa why she had come to this mass.

"By the way, what are you doing here? You always go to the five o'clock mass."

"I came to see you," Tessa said. "You've been hiding out on me."

"I'm sorry. It's just…"

"You don't need to explain," Tessa replied. "I'm just glad to see you…Avery wasn't your only friend, you know." Alexis felt a slight pang of guilt as she recognized the truth of her cousin's words. "The youth choir hasn't been the same without you. Some people at the five o'clock mass have told us that they really miss hearing your voice. You're a really gifted singer. Any chance you'll be coming back soon?"

Alexis reflected a moment before answering. "To be honest, I haven't really thought about it. Besides, there are a lot of great singers in the choir. I'm sure you've had no problem finding people to fill in while I've been gone."

"No one sings like you and you know it. At least tell me that you'll think about coming back when school starts."

"I'll think about it. No promises though."

"Great," Tessa replied cheerfully. "Glad to hear you'll be back. I'll be sure to tell our fearless choir director, Tony, the good news."

At that point, Alexis decided that it was pointless to argue further and resigned herself to the fact that Tessa was most likely suffering from a serious case of selective hearing. Looking down at her watch, she saw that it was 8:55 and said to Tessa, "The mass is going to start soon. We'd better get inside."

When Alexis and Tessa walked through the front doors of the church, the vestibule was still filled with parishioners trying to get in and find a seat. The altar servers were lining up at the back of the church while Father Jim stood nearby in green vestments, talking to an usher. At that moment, the same priest who had been talking to the young man outside the church just minutes before, walked up to Father Jim, wearing a white tunic and a scarf-like vestment called an alb and stole.

"Who is that?" Alexis overheard a female parishioner ask one of the deacons. Alexis' ears perked up as she waited for his response.

The deacon replied, "Oh, that's Father Bernal. He's a visiting chaplain from Spain. Father Jim told me that he's going to be helping out with the masses here for at least the next couple of months."

Alexis would have stayed and listened further if she hadn't seen Father Jim signal to the cantor that the mass was about to start. She and Tessa quickly stepped into the main body of the church, with its tiled floors and wooden pews, and saw her parents sitting just two rows from the sanctuary. They sat down next to her parents just as the organ began to bellow out the first notes of the opening hymn. Alexis grabbed a missalette from the pew rack and opened it to sing with the rest of the congregation.

She watched the lector, priests, and altar servers process down the aisle and then scanned the pews for the young man, who seemed to be nowhere in sight.

During the first reading, Alexis glanced up at Father Bernal and suddenly felt the urge to shudder. Her reaction puzzled her since she didn't even know the man. And yet, his presence had provoked a sense of unease in her that only grew in intensity as the mass went on.

After receiving communion, she walked back to her pew and knelt down to pray. Looking up at the tiled wall behind the altar, she focused on the large cross upon which Jesus hung with a crown of thorns on his head. Next to her, her parents and Tessa were kneeling with their heads bowed and their hands folded in prayer. She wanted to be like them and feel God's presence, as she assumed they did. But instead, her efforts, as of late, usually left her feeling empty and alone. As Alexis glanced at the people processing up to the altar, she wondered if any of them felt as isolated as she did.

As Alexis sat there lamenting the dismal state of her prayer life, she once again caught sight of the young man as he moved up the main aisle to receive communion. His hands were folded in front of him while his eyes were fixed on the large cross behind the altar. She watched with rapt attention as he bowed before reverently extending his hands to Father Jim to receive the consecrated host. *Here,* she thought in awe, *was someone who believed.*

Alexis' eyes remained glued on him as he waited to receive the consecrated wine from a Eucharistic minister stationed at the other end of the front pew. He was only standing a few feet away when he suddenly turned and glanced in her direction. She felt a jolt of energy shoot through her entire body as she gazed into what she thought were the most piercing blue eyes she'd ever seen. Or had she seen him before? All at once, visions of the young man in her dreams flashed through her mind. Was the person standing in front of her one and the same? The idea confused and unsettled her.

Even so, Alexis couldn't find the will to look away from him. After he'd received the Blood of Christ, she found herself rising from her seat and turning her head toward the back of the church as he headed down a side aisle. It wasn't until she heard Lisa call her name that she became aware of what she was doing. The reproachful look on her mother's face made her shrink in her seat as she sat back down.

Tessa, in turn, patted her cousin's knee and playfully whispered, "Don't worry, Cuz. I'll definitely find out who that guy is for you."

Alexis' cheeks burned crimson; she wanted to sink into the pew and disappear. Still, it was only with great effort that she was able to keep herself from turning her head toward the back of the church.

Just before the final blessing, Father Jim stood, made a few general announcements, and then said to the congregation, "I'm very pleased to introduce Father Juan Pablo Bernal to you all. He comes to us from Spain and is here on a special assignment. He has kindly offered to assist me with the Sunday masses for the duration of his stay in the United States. I invite you all to introduce yourselves to him and give him a warm welcome."

As the congregation applauded, Alexis saw Father Bernal's eyes scan the room. She could have sworn that she saw a smile spread across his face as soon as his eyes fell upon her. She looked away, burying her face in the missalette just as the cantor announced the closing hymn.

Once the organ belted out the song's last chord, Alexis popped up from her seat and made a beeline for the back of the church, leaving Tessa and her parents far behind. She searched through the crowd of people exiting; she was determined to find that young man.

The vestibule was once again jam-packed as she made her way to the front doors. She realized with mounting frustration that it was going to be nearly impossible for her to locate him within this teeming mass of humanity.

Alexis did, however, spot someone she had neither expected nor wanted to see: Avery's boyfriend, Bobby Lane. He looked like he had just rolled out of bed. His black polo shirt and khaki pants were wrinkled, and his brown hair was greasy and unkempt. His shoulders were slouched as he shuffled behind his parents with his hands stuffed into his pockets.

Alexis caught up to him in a few quick strides and tapped him on the shoulder. Bobby turned around and groaned audibly when he saw her.

"Why are you here?" Alexis asked with barely suppressed rage.

"Don't make a scene, Alexis," Bobby pleaded as he nervously ran his fingers through his hair. His fingernails were dirty and jagged, and his eyes were darting back and forth like he was searching for some way to escape. "Coming here wasn't exactly my idea, you know."

"You look shaky. Is your conscience getting to you or are you just coming off another high?"

"I didn't do anything wrong," Bobby hissed. "Avery was no angel."

"You had a lot to do with that," Alexis replied as memories of Avery's last moments on this Earth coursed through her brain. She thought of Avery crying hysterically and rambling about something that Bobby had done just before she sped off in her car. She recalled the sound of screeching tires and crunching steel as cars crashed all around her. Finally, she remembered Avery's car lying at the bottom of the canyon with her lifeless body slumped over the steering wheel.

Although Bobby had been nowhere near the scene of the accident, she was convinced that he was just as responsible for Avery's death as she was. As she glared at him from where she stood, she became more determined than ever to find out exactly what had happened between him and Avery on the day she died.

"What did you do to her?"

"Just back off, okay," he replied nervously.

Just then, Tessa came up beside Alexis and placed a reassuring hand on her shoulder before turning her attention to Bobby.

"What are *you* doing here?" Tessa asked, eyeing him warily.

"I have just as much right to be here as you do. I guess you guys missed the part where the priest talked about how God's house is open to everyone." He pointed at Alexis and said, "She's had it in for me from the moment I started dating Avery. She did everything she could to break us up."

"That's not true," Alexis protested.

He took a step back and said to Tessa, "Do me a favor and keep that head case away from me."

"I wouldn't talk if I were you," Tessa said with a slight edge in her voice. "You better get out of here before things start to get ugly. Besides, I think your mommy and daddy are waiting for you."

Bobby turned toward his parents, who were eyeing them curiously, and walked away.

"What a piece of work," Tessa said under her breath. "He's so not worth getting upset over. Just let it go."

Alexis sighed. She knew, of course, that Tessa was right and that nothing good could ever come from any interaction with Bobby. Still, she got the feeling that their paths would soon cross again.

Tessa intertwined her arm with her cousin's and led Alexis toward the parking lot. When they got to the crosswalk between the church and the parish hall, Alexis heard her name being called. She looked around and saw that her father was waving at her as he stood by the bike rack next to Father Bernal. He motioned for her to come over. As she got closer, she noticed that her father looked troubled. She immediately suspected that the priest may have had something to do with that.

"Father Bernal, this is my daughter, Alexis," Eric said evenly. "This is her cousin, Tessa."

Father Bernal, a solidly built man with black hair and tan skin, smiled as he extended his hand to Alexis and gave her a firm handshake. He seemed very charming...and formidable.

The priest spoke with a noticeable Spanish accent as he looked at Eric and said, "She has grown into a beautiful young lady." After shaking Tessa's hand, he turned to Alexis and said, "You were just a toddler when I saw you last."

Taken aback by the realization that her father and the priest knew each other, Alexis gave her father a questioning look.

Eric said to Alexis, "Father Bernal and I are old friends."

"How did you meet?" Alexis asked.

"Our families have known each other for generations," Eric replied.

"We are both part of, what might you call it here, Eric, ah yes, a fraternity," Father Bernal interjected with a laugh.

Alexis looked from Father Bernal to her father for clarification. She thought it odd that her father had never mentioned the priest before or the "fraternity" that they both supposedly belonged to.

"Your father hasn't changed a bit," Father Bernal continued as he patted Eric on the back. The priest looked at Lisa, who was standing nearby and said, "Neither has your mother."

Father Bernal turned to Alexis and said, "You have your mother's eyes." That was something that Alexis had heard many times before.

"That's the only way people can tell I'm part Filipino," Alexis replied. "The rest of me is all Neil." Both Father Bernal and Eric smiled. "My brother looks more like my mom."

"Speaking of Jeremy, your father told me that he is in the Philippines."

"Yeah, he's doing missionary work," Alexis said. "He left in May."

"I am sorry that I missed him," the priest replied, sounding genuinely disappointed.

"How long will you be here?" Eric asked.

"That depends on how long it takes to complete my assignment."

Eric nodded gravely. "Did you come alone?"

Father Bernal shook his head and said, "No."

Alexis immediately thought of the young man that she had seen Father Bernal talking to before mass. Before she could stop herself, she blurted out, "Are the people you came with here today?"

"Why do you ask?" the priest asked as he cocked his head to the side.

"It's just that…" Alexis stopped mid-sentence when she saw the stern expression on her father's face. "I'm sorry. I didn't mean to pry."

"Not at all," Father Bernal responded and then reached out his hand to greet Lisa, who had walked over to join them.

Minutes later, an usher came up to Father Bernal and whispered something in his ear. After the usher had gone, he turned to everyone and said, "I am sorry but I must be going. Duty calls. It was wonderful to see you all."

"You should come over for dinner sometime soon," Lisa suggested.

"I would like that very much," he replied graciously.

"How about this Thursday? Could you come around seven o'clock?"

Father Bernal nodded and said to Lisa, "Yes, absolutely," and then turned to Eric and said, "There is much to be said and I look forward to filling you in on the details in person." Eric acknowledged his words with a slight nod as he shook the priest's hand.

When Alexis extended her right hand to him, he cupped it in both of his own and said, as he looked directly into her eyes, "I am so very glad to have met you. If there is *anything* I can do for you while I am here, please don't hesitate to ask."

Alexis sensed the sincerity in his words and suddenly felt a tinge of guilt for the initial impression of him that she had formed during the mass. Still, she thought the whole conversation between her, her father, and the priest had been odd.

As Alexis and her parents walked toward their car, she said good-bye to Tessa and then took one last look around the parking lot.

"Looking for someone?" Eric asked as he opened the car door.

Alexis shook her head and got in the car. As they inched their way toward the exit, she heard the sound of a motorcycle revving its engine and then heard her father say, "Very nice," as he looked at it longingly in the rear view mirror.

"Don't even think about it, Eric," Lisa replied. "Those things are death traps."

"I can dream, can't I?" Eric teased.

As their car moved up the exit ramp, she heard the motorcycle pull up just behind them. She felt her breath catch in her throat when she turned and saw its rider. Her father motioned for the motorcyclist to move up ahead of them. The young man gave her father a quick wave as he pulled forward. She watched him as he looked both ways before turning left onto the street. They turned right. As her father drove south, she looked out the rear window and watched the motorcyclist speed away. *Hopefully,* she thought, *I'll see you again soon.*

CHAPTER 4—SAINT MICHAEL THE ARCHANGEL

It was late summer and after a mind-numbing day of errands, which included an orientation meeting, doctor appointments, and last-minute shopping for school supplies, Alexis decided that she needed to go for a jog to unwind. She enjoyed the seclusion that the dirt trails, which wound through hills and canyons near her home, provided. Although she occasionally ran into a cyclist or fellow jogger, it wasn't unusual for her to go in and out of the trails without seeing a single soul.

Alexis had been jogging for about fifteen minutes when the sound of rustling in the bushes startled her as she raced down the side of a steep hill. She stopped to look around. Moments later, a little brown rabbit jumped out of the bushes. It sniffed the air and then quickly scrambled to the safety of the other side of the trail when it saw her. Alexis sighed and chided herself for being so skittish. Even so, she couldn't shake the feeling that she wasn't alone.

When she reached a fork in the trail, she had to decide whether to take a steep path leading to a main road close to home, or a circuitous path on a trail that snaked through a secluded canyon. She wiped the sweat from her brow with the back of her hand and looked at her sports watch; it was 6:50 in the evening. Even though her gut told her to take the shorter and steeper trail, she headed toward the more secluded one instead. For some unexplainable reason, she felt drawn to take the longer path.

Her right leg started cramping as she descended into areas with denser brush. She winced as the pain in her leg increased and then tripped on an exposed tree root. She braced herself with her hands just before falling to the ground face-first. When she rolled onto her side, she saw that her joints and limbs were badly scraped and bleeding. She stood up gradually and put some weight on her right leg to ease the pain from the cramp she was still feeling. Once the pain subsided, she took a few steps to make sure she hadn't suffered a major break or sprain. Satisfied that she was well enough to go on, she slowly moved toward the end of the trail.

As the sun descended from the sky, the trees began to cast long shadows on the ground. The bushes and other plant life also took on a sinister feel. Her eyes darted back and forth as she walked under trees which were so close together that it was hard to see the sky. She looked up at a nearby branch and saw a single crow staring at her. It cocked its head to the side and began to flap its wings wildly and screech. A cacophony of sound erupted as other animals responded in kind to the crow's cries. She put her hands over her ears to block out the sound.

Moments later, Alexis distinctly heard the sound of a coyote howling nearby. *Is the smell of my blood attracting its attention? Is it alone?* Recalling that coyotes tended to run in packs, she forced her aching body to move faster.

Another howl; much closer this time. Her pulse quickened as she broke into a run. She found it harder to see as darkness enveloped her. She stumbled into bushes that pricked her skin and drew fresh blood. She didn't bother to look back when she heard the patter of paws right behind her. She wanted to scream but knew that no one would hear her. So instead, she scrambled forward until the end of the trail appeared before her like a beacon of light in a dark tunnel. She breathed a sigh of relief when she saw two pedestrians in workout clothes walking alongside the paved road up ahead. However, her temporary respite was quickly shattered when she felt something nip at her heel. She shrieked and sprinted faster than she thought possible to the end of the trail. When she reached the road, she bent over to catch her breath. Once it had steadied, she straightened and drew up the courage to turn and look down the path from which she had just come. At the bottom of the canyon sat a large black dog with blood red eyes. A chill ran down her spine as it bared its razor-sharp teeth and contorted its face into what looked like a grotesque smile.

The sun had nearly set by the time Alexis turned onto her street. She saw an unfamiliar black Toyota Camry parked in the driveway and remembered that this was the night that Father Bernal was supposed to come over for dinner. When she walked onto the porch, she heard the sound of Lisa's agitated voice coming from inside the house. She peered through the front window next to the door and saw her parents standing in front of the fireplace in the living room with Father Bernal. Her mother was gesturing wildly and pointing her finger at the priest while Eric, her father, stood next to her, trying to calm her down. She thought about going in through the side door but decided against it since it would require that she climb over the fence. Looking down at the dried blood and scraped skin on her arms and legs and acutely feeling every aching muscle in her body, she decided that she was in no condition to do that at the moment.

Alexis took a deep breath before unlocking the front door and walking in. Eric was the first one to see her. Given the look on his face, Alexis assumed that she must have been a sight to behold. Lisa, whose back had been turned, looked at her father and then turned to face her. Her mother's eyes widened in shock as she put her hand to her mouth and gasped. Within seconds, she was at Alexis' side, inspecting her injuries.

"What happened to you, anak?" Lisa asked in a clearly agitated tone.

"I'm fine. It's no big deal."

"It's not okay. Look at you," Lisa replied.

"Your mother's right," Eric chimed in. "You need to tell us what happened."

"I was just jogging in the trails…"

"Were you alone?" Father Bernal interjected.

Alexis nodded and then turned to her parents and said, "Why are you making such a big deal out of this?" She felt like she was being interrogated.

"Anak," Lisa said irritably, "how many times have I told you not to go on those trails by yourself. It's not…safe." Alexis suspected that her mother was going to say something else but then reconsidered. Instead, she put a hand on Alexis' arm and said, "Let's go and get you cleaned up."

While being led to the kitchen, Alexis overheard her father invite Father Bernal to his study. Lisa steered her to a barstool next to the kitchen island. She sat down while her mother walked over to a kitchen drawer and pulled out a first aid kit.

When Lisa started to clean off the blood and dirt on Alexis' knees, she said to her mother, "I can do this myself."

Lisa, however, continued on as if she hadn't heard her daughter. When Alexis again offered to do it herself, her mother looked up at her and said, "Just let me do it. I can get this done in half the time you can."

At that point, Alexis knew that any further attempt to protest would be futile. As usual, her mother saw her as a helpless child and was treating her accordingly.

Alexis fumed silently while Lisa tended to the rest of the scrapes and cuts on her body. She resented the fact that her mother still felt the need to fix things for her. Sooner rather than later, that was going to have to change. She was, after all, going to be seventeen in November.

After Lisa finished patching Alexis up, she grabbed a plate from a kitchen cabinet, opened the refrigerator door, and pulled out some leftovers. She had just placed some rice on the plate when Alexis touched her arm and said, "Mom, I'm not helpless. I can get my own dinner just fine."

Lisa handed the plate over to Alexis and said, "Of course you can," and then picked up a sponge and began to wipe down the kitchen counter. "The food should still be warm. I just put it in the fridge, but go ahead and warm it up in the microwave if you'd like."

Her mother looked distracted. Alexis thought about asking her what was wrong, but knew that she would just give her some excuse for the way she was acting, which probably had nothing to do with what was really upsetting her. So instead, she decided not to say anything at all.

While Alexis waited for her food to warm up in the microwave, she said to her mother, "I'm sorry I'm late. I guess I lost track of the time."

"You're not that late…Father Bernal came early," Lisa replied as Alexis sat down on a bar stool and began to eat. "We didn't want to keep him waiting, so we decided to go ahead and eat without you."

Lisa tapped her fingers on the kitchen counter and then turned and walked toward the water cooler to get a glass of water. She filled her glass to the brim and then took a long, slow drink.

As Alexis raised a fork to her mouth, Lisa turned to her and said, "You should probably go and say a proper hello to Father Bernal after you eat."

Alexis promised that she would before taking another bite.

"Are you going to be okay?" Lisa asked as she put a hand on Alexis' shoulder.

"I'm good," she replied.

Lisa nodded and then drifted silently out of the kitchen.

After quickly downing her meal, Alexis put her dirty dishes in the sink and headed toward her father's study. When she walked into the hallway, she saw Lisa standing alone by the window in the living room with her arms folded in front of her. To Alexis, her mother looked like she was staring off into space. Alexis came up to her and asked, "Is everything okay?"

Lisa waved her off and said, "They're waiting for you."

Alexis dutifully headed toward her father's study. She noticed that the door was slightly ajar. She could tell from the sound of their voices that her father and the priest were having a tense conversation. Just as she put her hand on the doorknob, she heard Eric ask the priest, "How long have you known about this? Did Brother Molina know who the specific target was during The Trials?"

"No. We learned of it afterward."

"Why wasn't I informed sooner?"

"I thought it best to tell you and Lisa in person. Brother Molina agreed with me. As you know, this is not the kind of thing we would want intercepted. Only those that need to know have all the information. This is a very delicate situation."

"Do you realize what this means if the signs brought you here?"

Father Bernal replied, "I know this is hard to accept, but the facts are what they are. Brother Molina would never have sent me here otherwise."

Alexis heard her father's fist slam on the desk as he said, "Dammit, I know the protocol just as well as you do."

"Lisa must be made to see reason," Father Bernal said. "Your cooperation is vital to the success of this mission."

"You know that I will do what I can," Alexis heard her father say in a resigned tone. After a brief pause, Eric added, "So what happens next?"

"I must speak with her. If we are wrong, then we will find out soon enough. But if we are not…"

"Then her soul is in danger of being damned to Hell."

"The Brethren will do everything possible to keep that from happening," Father Bernal replied firmly.

"Is The Archer ready?"

"He has been given full authority to do whatever is required to fulfill his mission. He will be watching and will strike when necessary. All obstacles will be eliminated."

Alexis was both confused and fascinated by their conversation; she wanted to hear more. She knew, however, that she couldn't stand there much longer without being seen or heard. She also felt a slight tickle in her throat and decided to knock on the door before a fit of coughing gave her away.

Eric and Father Bernal's conversation abruptly ended as soon as she rapped her knuckles on the door. She walked in and saw her father standing in front of the window behind his large wooden desk. One of his hands was resting on his chair while the other held a letter with an elaborate letterhead on it. Father Bernal was standing on the other side of the desk with his hands folded behind his back. Both of them turned to greet her.

"How are you feeling?" Eric asked her. "Since you seem to be mobile and coherent, I'm assuming you haven't suffered a mortal wound."

Alexis smiled and said, "Afraid not. I guess you're just going to have to deal with me for a little while longer."

Eric folded the letter, stepped around the desk, and put a hand on her shoulder as he said, "You really should steer clear of those trails, at least for the time being. You never know what or who could be out there lurking in the bushes."

"The world can be a dangerous place," Father Bernal added. "It is important for you to be mindful of your surroundings, and you would be well advised not to put yourself in situations that may put you in danger."

Alexis nodded as she looked at their grim faces.

Eric walked back to the front of the desk, put the letter in a drawer, and locked it with a key. He then said to Alexis, "There's something that I wanted to show Father Bernal that's up in the attic. Could you do me a favor and keep him company while I go upstairs to try to find it?"

"Sure," she said as she gave him a questioning look. Eric winked at her in response as he walked out the door.

As soon as Eric left, Alexis turned to Father Bernal, who had walked over to a bookshelf to the right of the window. He pulled out a theology book written by her grandfather, Frederick Neil, and started to leaf through its pages.

"Your father is quite the collector when it comes to religion and art," Father Bernal said in an admiring tone as he looked up and scanned the room. Eric's book-shelves were bursting with theology books of varying ages and topics; on the walls hung paintings depicting various scenes from the Bible. The most prominent of them was an original painting that had been in the Neil family for generations, depicting St. Michael the Archangel slaying the dragon.

Alexis replied, "That's his job. He's very respected in his field of study. He's a great proponent of ecumenism; so was my grandfather. His classes are the most popular theology classes on the USD campus."

Father Bernal said, "Your father has always been a gifted orator. He also has a very keen mind. The Church is blessed to have a man like your father in the fold." He paused briefly, and then added, "Your parents tell me that you are doing very well in school. Do you have any idea what you would like to do or where you would like to go after you graduate from high school?"

"Not really," she said. "I'm still trying to figure things out. My brother's at the University of Notre Dame, so I'd most likely go there too, but I don't have to worry about applying to college for another year."

Father Bernal nodded, closed the book in his hand, and put it back on the shelf. He turned to Alexis and said, "These are very important years. There are many decisions that you will make that will determine the course your life will take. It is vital that you make the right choices."

"But how would I know that I'm doing that?"

Father Bernal said, "You surround yourself with people that show, through their actions, that they have your best interests at heart; and be open to the will of God. You will never be led astray if you put your trust in Him."

This sounded like platitudes that Alexis had heard many times before. "I understand the theology, Father, but what do I do when I can't hear God or don't feel His presence in my life?"

Father Bernal furrowed his brow. "Have you considered the possibility that you might be looking for God in the wrong places? Contrary to popular belief, He is not just an old man that makes pronouncements with a booming voice from the sky."

"Then where can I find Him?"

Father Bernal moved toward her and pointed his finger at her heart. "God lives here. I am sure you have heard the phrase, 'Wherever two or three people gather in My name, there am I in their midst.'" After Alexis nodded, he added, "He lives and works through us. Sometimes, the noise we hear in the world can make it hard to discern His will. But you must try. Believe me; it is well worth the effort."

As Alexis thought about what Father Bernal had just said, he turned his attention to an old and worn out prayer booklet containing a novena to St. Michael the Archangel, which was displayed in a glass case on the bookshelf.

"That belonged to Grandpa Neil," Alexis said. "It was his favorite prayer book."

"Do you believe that the Devil is real?" Father Bernal asked.

Although Alexis found the question both surprising and odd, she did her best to answer it as thoughtfully and thoroughly as possible. "I was taught that he's a being that exists in this world."

"Have you ever felt like you were in the presence of evil?"

Her recent experience on the trail immediately came to mind...and her recurring dream. However, a small but vocal part of her recoiled at the idea of making him privy to that information. *Besides,* she thought, *he'd probably think I'm crazy.* After another moment of deliberation, she just shook her head.

However, she did have a question of her own that she was eager for him to answer. "Father, before mass last Sunday I saw you talking..."

At that moment, Eric knocked and opened the door to the study. "I hope I'm not interrupting," he said, looking at Father Bernal.

"Not at all," Father Bernal quickly replied. "We were just finishing up." He turned to Alexis and asked, "I am sorry. Could you repeat your question?"

Alexis, who was not about to ask Father Bernal about the young man in front of her father, said, "Nothing. It wasn't important." Disappointed, she politely excused herself and walked out of the room.

After Father Bernal had left and Alexis had gone to bed, Lisa went back to the kitchen to clean up before turning in for the night. Her head hurt. She rubbed her temples as she stood in front of the kitchen sink, rinsing dishes and putting them into the dishwasher. Eric came up from behind and put his arms around her waist. Lisa closed her eyes and leaned against him as she tried to make sense of everything that she'd seen and heard tonight.

Eric whispered in her ear, "Have I told you how much I love you today?"

"Stop trying to butter me up, Eric. It's not going to work," she replied curtly.

"Lisa, they're just here to observe…"

"Observe what?" Lisa snapped back.

"The visions were very specific," he said patiently. "Juan Pablo wouldn't have been sent here without any cause. Brother Molina consulted with and got the approval from the Holy Father himself for this mission."

Lisa slammed the door to the dishwasher and bowed her head as she grabbed hold of the kitchen counter with both hands. "Who else knows about this?"

"Only those people that need to know at this point," Eric replied. Lisa frowned. "What's wrong?"

"Isn't there a part of you that thinks that what Juan Pablo told us is insane? Come on, Eric, what he's telling us sounds positively medieval."

"If he hadn't been the one who told us, then I might agree with you, but The Brethren…"

"Could be wrong," she interrupted. "For goodness' sake, Alexis' best friend just died practically in front of her eyes and the only other person she knew she could always count on is thousands of miles away. It's perfectly normal for her to be feeling sad, even depressed, under those circumstances."

"Which makes her the perfect target. All Juan Pablo's asking for right now is the chance to observe her and gather information."

Lisa replied, "I don't like the idea of people spying on Alexis, especially in her present state of mind. And didn't he say that the person who is going to be doing most of the observing is no older than she is?"

"Yes, but…"

"Have you met him?"

"Not personally, but I was there when he was chosen...and I knew the boy's father. He was a good man."

Lisa was about to push the button to start the dishwasher when Eric grabbed her hand, shook his head, and handed her the dishwashing soap. She grabbed it out of his hand, opened the dishwasher, and put the soap in the dispenser.

As Lisa turned the dishwasher on, Eric asked, "Should we tell her?"

"Absolutely not." After Eric nodded in assent, Lisa added, "And you need to make it clear to Juan Pablo that neither he nor anyone else that came with him should say anything to her either."

Lisa walked over to the kitchen island and sat down on a stool. Eric sat down next to her, took her hand in his, and said, "It's going to be okay."

"I hope you're right."

CHAPTER 5—SCHOOL DAYS

Just five more minutes, Alexis thought as she hit the snooze button and pulled the covers over her head to block out the sunlight pouring in through her bedroom window. She liked the feeling of being cocooned underneath her sheets. When her alarm clock once again blared music from her favorite radio station, she pushed the sheets away from her face and gazed up at the ceiling. It was Monday morning in the third week in August, which meant that it was the first day of the new school year...and she couldn't wait for it to be over.

It wasn't long before Alexis heard a knock on her bedroom door. It creaked open as her mother poked her head in and said, "Wake up, sleepy head. You're going to be late if you don't get up soon."

Alexis rubbed her eyes and yawned. She flung her feet over the side of the bed and reluctantly trudged to the bathroom. After a hot shower, she wrapped a towel around herself and moved toward the sink to brush her teeth. She rubbed her hands on the fogged up mirror and gazed intently at her reflection.

Just keep your head down and get through the day, Alexis told herself as she reached for her blow dryer and make-up bag under the sink. After drying and combing out the tangles in her wet hair and applying some powder and lip gloss, she headed back to her room and put on her school uniform: a logoed white polo shirt, pleated navy skirt, and black flats with white socks. Once she was sure that she had everything she needed for school in her backpack, she went downstairs to eat some breakfast.

Alexis walked into the kitchen and saw her father sitting on a bar stool at the kitchen island, reading a newspaper and drinking coffee while classical music played on the radio perched on the windowsill. Her mother was staring out the window as she stood in front of the sink with a mug in hand.

Eric looked up from his newspaper and said, "So how's my scholar this morning? Feeling better?"

"Could be worse," Alexis said flatly as she slid onto a stool next to him.

He put the newspaper down and furrowed his brow. "Come on, Alexis. You can do better than that."

She shrugged her shoulders and looked away.

Eric reached out and gave her hand a squeeze. "Just take things slowly. It's going to get better in time. You'll see."

Lisa came up behind Alexis and patted her on the shoulders as she turned to Eric and said, "She's going to be just fine."

Alexis gave Lisa a half smile before reaching for the box of Cheerios and pitcher of milk sitting on the island. Although she wasn't nearly as optimistic as her mother about her prospects for the day, she knew better than to argue with her. So instead, she kept her head down and quietly ate her breakfast.

As she mindlessly shoveled spoonfuls of cereal into her mouth, she heard the classical music station start to play Chopin's *Funeral March*. *How appropriate*, she thought; it matched her mood perfectly. Just after she swallowed the last of her cereal, her mother told her that it was time to go. She gave her father a quick peck on the cheek and then picked up her backpack and headed for the car.

A blast of hot air greeted Alexis as she stepped into the garage. Fortunately, the air conditioner was already on as Alexis got into her mother's vehicle. She had just set her backpack at her feet when Eric tapped on the car window and gave her a thumbs-up. She cringed as she watched him fumble for car keys in his coat pocket while holding a well-worn, over-stuffed briefcase in one hand and a thermos full of coffee in the other. To make matters worse, his glasses were askew and the space between the cars gave him little room to maneuver. Miraculously, he successfully retrieved his keys without a hitch and gave her one final wave before getting into his old beater of a car. *He's just like the absent-minded professor,* she thought to herself as her father's car sputtered out of the garage.

Alexis turned on the radio while Lisa backed the car out of the driveway. She closed her eyes, hoping her mother would take the hint. To her great relief, the car ride to school was blessedly silent.

She tensed up when they turned off of Magdalena Avenue and headed up the curved road that led to the school. As soon as Lisa parked the car in the faculty parking area, Alexis grabbed her backpack and followed her mother into the DePaul Center, the administrative office for the school. They had just walked through the glass doors when a harried secretary approached them.

Lisa gave her daughter's hand a gentle squeeze before heading toward her corner office, with the secretary nipping at her heels. Once she disappeared from view, Alexis took a deep breath before walking through a set of glass doors leading to the school campus.

Alexis' shirt stuck to her skin as she watched her peers in dark blue and white uniforms blanket the student parking lot and entrance to campus. She felt a tinge of sadness as she walked along the promenade, which ran from the DePaul Center to the school library, known as the Aquinas Center, and watched students greet one another with a hand shake, hug, or a high five. She remembered how Avery had bubbled with enthusiasm on their first day of school on this campus and all the big plans she had in store for them. Now all those dreams, like Avery, were gone.

Alexis kept her head down as she passed by the uniform, white cement buildings with brick siding and immaculately kept grounds. She made the split-second decision to turn left off the promenade and walk between the Guadalupe Center and the library in order to avoid walking past Anita and her friends. Although she recognized some other students, there weren't many that she felt she could approach. Avery had always been the trailblazer, her personal pied piper. Without her best friend, she felt insecure and rudderless.

She turned right onto the academic courtyard and headed down an arched walkway lined with more buildings named after saints. She had just passed the large brown doors of the Marian Chapel when she heard Tessa call out her name. She turned and saw her cousin standing and waving to her by a gray cement bench in front of the library. Tessa's boyfriend, Jake Lewis, a good-natured and tech-savvy student of African-American and Asian descent, was sitting next to her talking to two other students, Manuel Gonzalez, a short boy with black hair and Tobey Finchley, a tall, lanky boy with coke-bottle glasses.

Tessa greeted Alexis with a hug and then motioned for her to sit down between Jake and Tobey, who smiled and said hello to her.

"Doing okay?" Tessa asked with a concerned look.

Alexis nodded as she sat down and placed her backpack at her feet. "I'm fine. You worry way too much."

"I'm your cousin. I'm supposed to worry about you," Tessa replied as her eyes scanned the corridor. "Listen, I've got some great news."

Alarm bells immediately began to ring in Alexis' head as she pursed her lips and crossed her arms in front of her.

Tessa frowned. "Don't look at me like that. There's no need to get defensive."

"It's just that…"

"What?"

"Never mind." It was too early in the morning to get into a debate with Tessa, and Alexis had neither the will nor the energy at the moment to do it.

"Did you know that Tobey has a peer buddy?" Tessa asked with great excitement.

Tobey pushed his glasses up the bridge of his nose as he turned to Alexis and said, "He's one of the exchange students our campus is hosting this year. He's pretty cool. I think you'd like him."

"He might even be in some of your classes," Tessa added enthusiastically. "I was going to introduce you to him, but he walked off just before you got here."

"Oh, that's too bad," Alexis replied, breathing a sigh of relief.

She stood up as soon as the five-minute warning bell rang and started to walk away when Tessa grabbed her arm and said, "You'll thank me when you meet him."

Alexis wasn't so sure she agreed, but thought that now was probably not the time to burst Tessa's bubble, so she just smiled and played along as best as she could in order to placate her cousin and get to class on time.

Alexis walked into her first class of the day, theology, in Loyola Hall and saw her teacher, Antonio Marquez, writing an outline on the dry erase board. Mr. Marquez was a bubbly and energetic man whose classes were among the most popular on campus.

She took a seat near the front of the room and carefully placed her textbook, notebook, and pen on the desk. Although she heard other students come into the classroom, she didn't bother to look back. She figured that many of them were probably the same people that had been in her theology classes for the last two years.

After the last warning bell rang, Mr. Marquez turned toward his students and said, "Welcome, welcome. My name is Antonio Marquez. I will be your sacraments teacher this semester." He walked around his desk and then leaned against it as he looked around the classroom and asked, "So, can someone tell me what the seven sacraments are?"

Nearly everyone in the classroom raised a hand. Mr. Marquez smiled and picked someone who was sitting behind Alexis.

"The seven sacraments are Baptism, Reconciliation, Eucharist, Confirmation, Anointing of the Sick, Matrimony, and Holy Orders," said a male student, who spoke with a Spanish accent.

The sound of his voice was both soothing and seductive. It reminded her of the dashing masked figure that she had fallen head over heels in love with in one of her favorite childhood movies, *The Mask of Zorro*. She smiled to herself when she recalled how she had told her parents over and over again that Zorro was going to carry her off into the sunset and marry her someday.

However, her teacher's booming voice quickly brought her back down to Earth. "Very good," replied Mr. Marquez. "And your name is…"

"Rafael Cordero, sir."

"Ah…Mr. Cordero, aren't you one of the exchange students that we have the pleasure of hosting this year?"

"Yes, I am, sir."

When the students seated around her turned to look at this newcomer, she followed suit. She nearly went into shock when she saw that the young man with piercing blue eyes, who had so captivated her attention at church, was sitting just two seats behind and to the left of her. She looked away as soon as his eyes met hers.

The rest of the class was a blur. Although Alexis saw Mr. Marquez's mouth moving, her mind failed to register a single thing he said. When the bell rang, she looked down at her notebook and saw that she hadn't written anything down. She slowly packed up her things with trembling hands as she screwed up the courage to take a second look behind her. When she finally stood up and turned to leave, Rafael was already gone.

When she walked into her next class, English, at Sienna Hall, she spotted Rafael sitting near the back of the classroom talking to Anita. She could tell by the way Anita sat, with her legs crossed and her skirt slightly hiked up, that she was already trying to sink her claws into him. It irked her to see the way Anita smiled and tossed her head as she spoke to him; she suddenly felt the overwhelming urge to throw something at her.

While Alexis stood rooted to the doorway, seething with anger, Manuel tapped her on the shoulder and said, "Move it, Neil."

She rolled her eyes at Manuel and then sat down in the first available seat near the door. She opened her backpack and was taking out her textbook when she saw Anita whisper something into Rafael's ear. She looked away and slammed her textbook on the desk. Manuel turned to her and said, "What's up with you?"

"None of your business," she shot back as she took out her notebook and slammed that on the desk, too. Although she was certainly mad at Anita, she was more upset with herself for even being upset at all. She had no right to be angry. They hadn't even been introduced. Yet the thought of Anita flirting with Rafael, while she sat only a few seats away, was almost too much to take.

Alexis decided that the best thing for her to do under the circumstances was to ignore them. Although she managed to avoid looking in their direction, she soon realized that any effort to focus on anything her English teacher was saying was going to be an exercise in futility. When the bell rang at the end of class, she again found her notebook devoid of a single entry. Angry and frustrated beyond words, she shoved her things in her backpack and fled out the door.

Alexis knew that she needed to calm down. She saw that a yellow *wet floor* sign was blocking the entrance to the nearest girl's bathroom. When she was sure no one was looking, she stepped to the side of the sign and went inside. It was empty and eerily quiet. Only one light was flickering in the far corner of the bathroom. She leaned against the wall and closed her eyes. It felt good to be in the dark…and alone.

Her eyes, however, flew open the instant she heard something stir in the bathroom stall furthest from the door. She saw puffs of smoke wafting through the air above the stall. She walked toward it and knocked. A moment later, Lizzie, a green-eyed, red-headed girl dressed in a navy blue pleated skirt and polo shirt opened the stall door. She walked past Alexis without saying a word and headed toward the mirror. Lizzie stopped in front of it and gazed at herself as she took a long, slow drag from the cigarette in her hand.

Lizzie looked at Alexis' reflection in the mirror and said, "What are you looking at?"

Alexis noticed that the hand that held the cigarette shook slightly.

"That stuff can kill you, you know."

Lizzie turned toward Alexis, puffed on her cigarette and then exhaled the smoke within inches of Alexis' face.

"Really?" Lizzie replied. "Want one?"

Alexis shook her head.

"What's it to you anyway, Miss Goody Goody? Why don't you just run on back to your mommy and daddy and leave people like me who live in the real world alone?"

"Then go ahead and kill yourself," Alexis blurted out. She hated the fact that Lizzie always seemed to know what buttons to push.

Lizzie smirked as she said, "Oh, Mac. What am I going to do with you?" She had called Alexis by that name since they were kids. "Besides, I've heard you have more important things to worry about right now than me."

Alexis felt bad about losing her temper, especially with Lizzie. Despite her faults, Lizzie was one of the few people at school that Alexis could genuinely call a friend. Since she had so few of them, she felt the need to do everything she could to keep the ones she had.

"I have no idea what…"

"Oh please," Lizzie interrupted. "Do you think I'm blind? Come on, Mac. Admit it. You think I don't know all about what's his name?"

"His name is Rafael," Alexis replied as blood rushed to her face.

"Don't worry, your secret is safe with me."

"There's nothing to tell," Alexis replied, defensively. "Besides, I saw him talking to Anita."

"I wouldn't worry about her," Lizzie said. "From what I've seen, that boy only has eyes for you."

"Why do you say that?" Alexis asked, surprised.

"I saw him watching you while you were sitting with your friends by the library before school started this morning."

Alexis shook her head in disbelief. She couldn't fathom how that could be even remotely possible.

"He's new," she offered. "He was probably looking at a lot of other people, too."

Lizzie shrugged her shoulders, put the cigarette out on the sink, and then flicked it in the trashcan. As she headed toward the bathroom door, she said, "Could be, but don't say I didn't warn you."

"What are you talking about? You're not making any sense."

"Trust me. I would stay away from that guy if I were you," Lizzie said and then walked out, leaving Alexis standing alone and feeling utterly confused.

At lunchtime, Alexis headed toward the Tekakwitha Café. The smell of tacos, hamburgers, and pizza wafted through the area as she stood in line to buy lunch. She groaned when she saw Anita, Cecilia, and Lea get in line behind her. Although she tried to ignore them, she could still hear them cackling away above the din of the lunchtime crowd.

She overheard Cecilia ask Anita, "So how are things going? Do you think he's interested?"

"What do you think?" Anita replied in a condescending tone. "Don't I always get what I want?"

"So, when are you going to see him again?" Lea asked.

"I'm going to invite him to go with us to Starbucks after school," Anita replied. "It's the least I can do to make sure he feels welcome."

The sound of their simultaneous giggling made Alexis' ears hurt. Luckily, she had reached the front of the line and had no choice but to tune out their conversation as she placed her order.

Alexis juggled a sandwich, a bag of chips, and bottled water in her hands as she went in search of her cousin. She quickly found Tessa and Jake sitting at one of the white cafeteria tables next to the Cafe. Manuel and Danny Phelps, a freckle-faced boy with red hair, were also sitting at the table with them.

Alexis sat down next to Tessa, who said to her, "Hey, Cuz. How's your first day going so far?"

"Other than running into Anita and her gaggle of goons in nearly every class, it's been okay I guess."

Tessa offered her some chips and said, "Don't let them bother you." She pointed at Alexis' forehead, adding, "It would be a total waste of your mental energy. You've got better things to do with your time."

Danny took a bite of his sandwich and said to Alexis, "So, is it true that Tessa is trying to hook you up?"

Tessa shot Danny a murderous glance. He made a face as he shrank back in his seat.

Manuel leaned toward Alexis and said, "Hey, if you need any tips, you know I'm always here to help."

"You're probably the last person she would or should ask," Tessa said dismissively.

Ignoring Tessa's comment, Manuel said, "We're buds, right? You know I'd never steer you wrong." He took a sip out of his water bottle and then added, "You gotta let a guy know that you like him. Look at me. When I go up to a girl, I stand there and let her take it all in, and then…"

"She goes 'Ahh' and runs away," Tobey chimed in as he put his food on the table and sat down next to Tessa.

Manuel sneered at Tobey, who shrugged his shoulders, and then turned his attention back to Alexis. "Like I said, you gotta give a guy some love." He gazed at Tessa longingly and said, "You need to look into his eyes and say something like, 'You are the guacamole on my carnitas.'" Danny and Tobey snickered. He then picked up a chip and gave Alexis a smoldering look as he said, "You are the salsa on my chips."

"Have you tried the salsa? It's really awful."

Alexis looked up and saw Rafael standing right in front of her. He shook Jake's hand as he sat down and then smiled as he waved to her other friends at the table.

Tessa nudged Alexis in the ribs and whispered, "He's Tobey's peer buddy."

Rafael stood up slightly as he extended his right hand toward Alexis and said, "Hello. My name is Rafael."

At first, Alexis just stared at his outstretched hand. She couldn't believe her luck. After some prompting from Tessa, she stood up and knocked over her water bottle as she reached out to shake his hand, spilling its contents all over Rafael's food and clothes. She followed that up by stepping on Rafael's hand when he tried to retrieve her water bottle, which had rolled onto the floor, and then knocked her head into his when she leaned over to apologize to him. To make matters worse, she clearly heard her friends gasp with each misstep.

Could she have made a worse first impression? She didn't think so. If there were a rock she could have crawled under, she would have done it gladly.

Alexis watched helplessly as Rafael rubbed his hand and then the side of his head before excusing himself to go and get some napkins to clean up the mess she had made.

As soon as Rafael was out of earshot, Manuel leaned toward her and said, "Way to go, Alexis."

Under his breath, Danny said to Tobey, "Maybe he likes klutzy girls."

"Shut it," Tessa commanded in an icy tone. She turned to Alexis and patted her shoulder reassuringly as she said, "It'll be okay."

Alexis shook her head and then buried her face in her hands.

When Rafael came back with a handful of napkins, Alexis offered to help him clean up the mess. He politely declined her offer, insisting that she remain seated as he wiped down his side of the table. After throwing the soggy napkins away, he surveyed his water-soaked meal; she cringed when the mushy bread from his sandwich slid off as he tried to pick it up.

"Dude, that's gross," Danny said.

Rafael put his soggy sandwich down and shrugged his shoulders as he said, "I really wasn't that hungry anyway."

Tobey motioned for Rafael to come over and sit by him after Jake pointed out that the cafeteria bench was still wet. After Rafael took a seat between Tobey and Tessa, Tobey handed Rafael half his sandwich while Jake gave him an unopened bottle of water. Even Manuel threw him a bag of chips. Rafael graciously accepted everything he was offered.

All Alexis wanted to do was to get as far away from Rafael as possible. Unfortunately, her cousin, who was still determined to salvage her matchmaking efforts, kept Alexis from fleeing by holding her arm in a vice-like grip. She squirmed in her seat as Tessa provided Rafael with a glowing account of her life since birth. Rafael nodded politely and listened as he ate her friends' donated food. Tessa pounced when he mentioned that he played the guitar.

"Do you sing, too?"

"Yes, I do, but…"

"Jake, Alexis, and I sing with the youth choir at Corpus Christi for the five o'clock Sunday mass. We rehearse on Monday nights at seven in the parish hall. You should totally come and join us tonight."

The warning bell rang before Rafael could answer. Alexis shot up from her seat, picked up the remains of her lunch, threw her backpack over her shoulder, and made a beeline for the trashcan. She knew that she probably should have said goodbye to her friends, but, at the moment, the need to get away overpowered her sense of propriety. She told herself that she would make amends and explain herself to Tessa later.

Before heading to her next class, Alexis went to her locker to switch out her textbooks. She was just about to close her locker door when she saw Rafael standing a few feet away in front of his open locker talking to Anita. Resigned to the fact that he probably thought she was a bumbling idiot, she prayed that he would pretend not to notice her as she walked by.

As Alexis secured her backpack onto her shoulders, she overheard Rafael say to Anita, "It was very kind of you to offer, but unfortunately I already have other plans."

She glanced at Anita's face and saw that she didn't look at all pleased. She smiled to herself and thought, *So much for Anita getting everything that she wants.*

Alexis tried to slink past Rafael as Anita walked away. She was nearly past him when she heard him say, "Alexis, wait!" She came to an abrupt halt. *Did he really call my name?* She felt her heart hammering in her chest as she slowly turned to face him.

"Are you headed over to Seton Hall?" Rafael asked as he slung his backpack over his shoulder.

"Yeah. I've got chemistry."

"Me, too," he replied. He closed his locker door and said, "May I walk with you?"

Alexis was stunned. She had spilled water on his clothes, stepped on his hand, nearly given him a concussion, and ruined his lunch and yet, here he was, asking her if it was okay for him to walk with her to class.

"Aren't you afraid I'm going to hurt you or something?"

Rafael smiled and said, "Well, are you?"

An embarrassed smile spread across her face as she shook her head.

"Good. Let's go," he replied.

They walked into class and took a pair of open seats at a rectangular table with beakers, flasks, stirring rods, and test tubes in a rack. Manuel looked surprised as he took a seat across from hers at the table. When Rafael looked down to read his notes, Manuel pointed his finger from Alexis to Rafael and then leaned toward her side of the table and asked, "How did you manage that?"

Alexis responded with a sheepish grin and a shrug of her shoulders.

After taking her textbook out and laying it on the table, she looked across the room and saw Anita at another table glaring at her. It took all her self-control to resist the urge to smile and wave. When she turned her head to face Manuel, he motioned for her to come to his side of the table.

When she did so, Manuel opened his textbook and pretended to show Alexis something on the page as he said under his breath, "You better watch your back. I think you just got on the ice queen's bad side."

She was about to respond when their chemistry teacher started her lecture. After sliding back to her seat, she took out her notebook and settled in. At the end of class, she looked down and smiled. She had stayed focused and had a page full of copious notes to show for it. And for the first time in months, she actually felt happy. However, she also felt a slight pang of guilt for feeling this way, and wished that Avery had been there to share this moment with her.

During her next class, Alexis found herself daydreaming about Rafael. She pictured them walking hand in hand on a moonlit beach, or resting her head on his shoulder as they sat in a darkened movie theater. In her imagination, the possibilities were endless. She found that the harder she tried to push these thoughts aside and focus on the lecture, the more entrenched they became in her mind. She had felt an intense connection to him from the first moment she'd seen him. Still, she reminded herself that she had almost no experience when it came to love and romance and couldn't think of what she could offer him that would make her stand out from all the other girls who were also interested in getting to know him.

Alexis went straight to her locker at the end of the school day. She kept her eyes peeled for any sign of Rafael as she put everything she would need to take home with her in her backpack. She felt her heart flutter when he smiled and waved at her as he came up to his locker. That was all the invitation she needed to walk over to him. As she stood there, she watched him put on a pair of gloves and pull out a motorcycle helmet. She also noticed that he had a wooden cross on a leather strap hanging inside his locker door.

When Rafael saw Alexis eyeing the cross, he said, "It's been in my family for generations. It was handed down to me when I was ten years old."

"Is it passed down from father to son?"

"Not exactly. It is a tradition in my family for the eldest son to give this cross to the woman he intends to marry. It is then passed on to their eldest son to give to his future bride." He reached out and touched it briefly, and then looked over at Alexis and said, "It is one of my most prized possessions."

Future bride, she thought. *Whoever she is, she's going to be one lucky girl.*

Alexis was still staring at the cross when Rafael closed his locker and asked, "May I walk you to your car?"

"Uh…sure," she replied, feeling flustered. "You're actually going to be walking me to my cousin's car. We carpool in the afternoons."

When they got to the circular drop off area, she noticed that there was a long line of cars snaking out of the quickly emptying parking lot. Alexis spotted Tessa's yellow Volkswagen Beetle, but her cousin was nowhere in sight. Her eyes then fell upon a black motorcycle parked nearby. It looked like the same one that she had seen him riding out of the church parking lot. He motioned for her to follow him when he saw her staring at it.

Rafael said as he placed the helmet on his head and secured the strap, "It's a Harley-Davidson Sportster. My host family owns three Harleys. They said that I could use this one whenever I wanted to." He patted the handlebars, adding, "In Spain, I ride a motorcycle just like this one."

Alexis watched with rapt attention as he mounted the bike, pulled out the choke and then the clutch with his left hand, turned the key, pushed the start button, and then twisted the throttle with his right hand. The sound of the engine reverberated throughout the parking lot. She saw more than a few of the students turn their heads in their direction.

"It has to warm up a little before you put it in gear."

Alexis nodded. She wanted to say something clever, but her mind went completely blank.

"Let me know if you ever need a ride to or from school."

"Oh, that's really nice of you," she replied as visions of riding as a passenger on his motorcycle flashed through her mind. She could almost feel the wind in her hair as she pictured them zooming down the street with her arms wrapped tightly around his waist.

"Don't worry. I will be driving a car most of the time." She sighed. *So much for that daydream.*

When they saw Tessa coming toward them, he said, "I guess I should get going." She nodded. He added, "So, I will see you tonight then."

"Tonight?" Alexis couldn't think of why she would be seeing him that evening.

"Aren't you going to choir practice?" he asked. "It starts at seven o'clock, right?"

"Oh, yeah. I almost forgot. Thanks for reminding me."

Rafael gave her a thumbs up and then slowly pulled away on his motorcycle. Tessa waved at him as they crossed paths and then walked over to Alexis. They stood next to each other in silence as they watched him ride away.

As soon as he had turned onto Birch Road from the main campus entry, Tessa grabbed hold of both of Alexis' arms and said, "I need details."

Alexis gave Tessa a sly smile as she said, "He asked me if he could walk me to class after lunch and sat next to me in chemistry." Tessa's eyes widened in surprise as a grin spread across her face. "He also offered to give me a ride home from school whenever I need one."

"You should totally take him up on that. Did he say anything else?"

"He told me that he was going to choir rehearsal tonight."

Tessa squealed as she said, "So I guess that means that you'll be singing with the youth choir again on Sunday evenings from now on, right?"

"I guess so."

Her cousin put her hand on Alexis' shoulder and gave it a squeeze. "I'm so happy for you, Cuz. It sounds like he's really interested in getting to know you. That's so awesome."

Tessa's enthusiasm was infectious. After her cousin unlocked the car, Alexis opened the passenger door and realized that she was feeling a little euphoric herself. Still, she didn't want to let herself get too carried away at this point. She said to Tessa, "It's early yet. Anything could happen."

"I saw the way you looked at him at church and, from what you told me, it sounds like he's into you, too," Tessa replied as she started the engine.

"I think you might be reading too much into things," Alexis said as she fastened her seatbelt.

"I don't think so. With all the stuff you did to him at lunchtime, honestly, I was surprised to see him talking to you at all," Tessa teased.

"I guess you're right." Although the memory of what had happened made her shudder, she was relieved that it had not irreparably harmed her chances with Rafael. When she pulled down the car visor to take a look at herself in the mirror, she saw that her reflection looked hopeful and happy.

"I told you that you'd thank me when you met him." Both of them laughed. "By the way, you're welcome."

"Thank you," Alexis replied with a grin.

CHAPTER 6—CHOIR PRACTICE

It was 6:55 in the evening by the time Alexis rode her bicycle into the church parking lot. *That's strange,* she thought as she looked around the empty lot. *Didn't Tessa say that rehearsal was at seven o'clock?*

She had just taken off her helmet and secured her bicycle to the rack when strong gusts of cold wind began to sweep past her, making her feel like she was in the middle of a wind tunnel. She shivered and hugged herself to keep warm. Strangely enough, she noticed that no tree branches or plants were swaying in the canyon next to the parking lot. Although she thought that was strange, she shrugged it off and headed toward the parish hall.

A disheveled-looking woman who was talking to herself caught Alexis' eye as she stood by the crosswalk between the church and the parish hall. The woman was wearing a thick, but visibly worn gray coat over a tattered dress and had a scarf on her head. Her skin was weathered and deeply lined while her fingers looked gnarled and claw-like. Alexis wrapped her arms even more tightly around herself when she saw that the woman was leering at her.

What could that woman be doing here at this time of night? The parish office had closed hours ago and Alexis knew of no other church group that had meetings this late on Monday nights. In fact, she couldn't think of a single reason why the woman would be here. Although her curiosity was piqued, she decided to just step up her pace and avoid any further eye contact with her.

Alexis breathed a sigh of relief when she entered the large, cavernous main hall with brown-paneled high ceilings and large saucer-shaped lights. Her eyes scanned the room and then lingered on the cross hanging above the stage. She crossed herself as her gaze wandered toward the colorful banners decorating the walls opposite the glass doors. Three rows of padded chairs had been set up in the middle of the hall. She walked up to one, sat down and put her backpack down beside her.

Alexis had just taken out her music binder when she heard her phone beep. She took her phone out of her backpack and she saw that Tessa had just sent her a text message. It read, "Practice is @ 7:30. Sorry 4 late notice ☺ See u soon!" She looked at the clock just above the glass doors. It was exactly seven o'clock.

Great. What now? Just then, she saw a car pull into the parking lot. Although she couldn't see who it was from where she was sitting, she was certain that it was Rafael. She frowned slightly when she realized that she had been set up by her cousin. *Jeez, Tessa,* she thought, *what have you gotten me into now?*

Rafael, who was wearing jeans and a t-shirt, looked puzzled as he checked his watch after stepping into the hall.

"We're early," Alexis said in response to his unasked question. "I just got a text from Tessa saying that rehearsal is at 7:30."

Rafael nodded and then sat down in a chair next to her. "So, what do we do now?"

"We wait," she replied as she shrugged her shoulders and looked down at her hands. After a minute or two of awkward silence, she stood up, walked over to the grand piano on the stage, and started going through the folders of music sitting on top of it. She glanced at Rafael, who was still sitting, and asked, "Are you a tenor or a bass?"

"I am a baritone," Rafael replied, "but I think that I am a better musician than a singer."

"What kind of instrument do you play?" she asked. She felt relieved that she had stumbled upon something they could talk about.

"I was trained to play classical guitar, but I also play other types of music as well."

Rafael walked up to the stage and stood next to her. His proximity made her feel weak-kneed. She bit her lip and tried to look like she was engrossed in the piece of music she was holding. He picked up one of the folders and opened it up. "What kind of music does this choir sing?"

"Contemporary mainly," Alexis said as she sat down on the piano bench. "We usually sing with a guitar player and pianist. Our director, Tony Alonso, picks out the music for us. Jake's our pianist. We don't have a guitar player right now. The last one we had just graduated and went off to college. Do you think you might want to do it?"

Rafael laughed as he said, "You are very trusting. You haven't even heard me play yet."

"Well, I assume that a classically trained guitar player would be more than qualified to play the kind of music we sing."

He said, "There is just one problem. I left my guitar in Spain."

"I'm sure Tony will let you borrow one of his."

"Do you play any instruments?" Rafael asked as he sat down next to her.

Alexis' pulse began to race as she slid her hand over the piano keys and said, "I've studied piano, but I'm more of a singer than a musician."

Rafael nodded. "I am very much looking forward to hearing you sing. Tessa told me that you have a very beautiful voice."

"She exaggerates," she said as she turned to look at him. He was so close now, and they were completely alone. Although she did her best to stay calm on the outside, inside, she felt like a bundle of nerves.

"I doubt that very much," he said with a smile. "Even my host family tells me that they really enjoy hearing you when you cantor the mass."

The realization that Rafael had talked to someone about her both puzzled and intrigued her. "How can that be? I didn't meet you until today."

At first, Rafael looked like he had been caught off guard but then quickly recovered, saying, "I saw you talking to Father Bernal after mass last weekend, so I asked him who you were. Later on, I mentioned your name to Mr. and Mrs. Daniels while we were eating dinner. They knew who you were right away." As he looked down at his watch and then toward the glass doors, she got the impression that this was not a line of conversation that he wished to pursue. She decided to oblige him and change the subject.

"What made you decide to come here?" The look on his face made her think that she had just asked another question that he was either unprepared or unwilling to answer. She quickly added, "You don't have to tell me if you don't want to."

"I am sorry. I do not mean to be so hesitant in answering your questions…it is sometimes difficult for me to find the right words to say in English."

"I think you speak English very well," she replied. "Besides, we've got the time. No worries."

"Thank you. That was a very nice thing for you to say. I have always wanted to visit the United States. I was very happy when I was told that I was the one who had been chosen to come here."

Although Alexis thought that his use of the word *chosen* was strange, she chalked it up to the fact that he wasn't a native English speaker. "How do you like being here so far?"

"People have been very kind, very welcoming, and I could not have asked to stay with a nicer host family."

"Do you ever feel homesick?"

"Of course. I miss my family and friends very much and I hope to see them again someday."

Someday? She thought that was another interesting choice of words.

"Do you have any siblings?"

"Yes, a twin brother." Her eyes widened in surprise at the news. "Many people have said that we look almost exactly alike. The only real difference is that I have darker hair than he does."

"Is he anything like you?"

Rafael smiled as he said, "Alejo is much more outgoing than I am. He loves to tell jokes and does very good impersonations. When we were young, he would often fool people who did not know us well into thinking he was me."

"Why would he do that?"

"To get out of trouble," Rafael replied with a slight laugh. "In my family, Alejo was the mischief-maker while I was known as the good son."

"So, were you the good son?"

"Not always, but I managed to get into a lot less trouble than my brother. Still, I think that you would like him," he said hopefully. "Alejo is a very important part of my life. You can't really know who I am without him."

"I'll try to keep an open mind. So, what are your parents like?"

Rafael hesitated briefly and then said, "They were wonderful people. They died when I was ten years old. I was raised by my aunt and uncle."

"I'm so sorry," Alexis said in the belief that she had just overstepped her bounds.

"Don't be," he said with a shake of his head. "I have been very fortunate. My aunt and uncle are very loving, very spiritual people. I would not be the person I am today if it had not been for them."

"My brother, Jeremy, is like that," Alexis replied. "He's practically a living saint. He always does the right thing…Sometimes it's hard to live up to someone like that."

"You should not compare yourself to him," he said gently. "You are not your brother. God endows each one of us with unique gifts. Our job is to discern what those gifts are and then use them in accordance with His will."

Just then, Alexis saw Tessa and Jake walk in wearing shorts and t-shirts. She stepped away from Rafael and pulled her cousin aside.

When she was certain that they were out of earshot of everyone else in the room, she said to Tessa, "Seven o'clock rehearsal, huh? Seriously?"

Tessa smiled and said, "Chillax. It was an honest mistake, Cuz. Won't happen again."

"It better not. By the way, weren't you cold out there? The wind nearly knocked me down when I first got here."

Tessa looked at her like she had grown a pair of antlers on her head and said, "You're kidding right? It's hot as heck out there. I wish there had been a breeze when I came in. Look at Jake. He's still sweating up a storm over there."

Alexis glanced at Jake, who was standing by the piano with beads of sweat on his forehead as he fanned himself with a piece of sheet music. As the other members of the choir trickled in, she noticed that he wasn't the only one who looked hot and sweaty. Rather than raise any alarm bells in her cousin's mind about her sanity, she decided to just let the matter drop.

When Tony, the youth choir director, arrived, the first thing he did was walk over to Alexis and welcome her back. She, in turn, introduced Rafael to him and promptly mentioned the fact that he played the guitar. Tony, who was overjoyed at the news, immediately went back out to his car to get his extra guitar. When he returned, he handed it to Rafael and asked him to play something. Rafael readily agreed.

The minute Rafael touched the strings of the guitar to play *Malaguena*, she and everyone else in the room knew that the instrument was in the hands of a well-trained and gifted musician. After much applause, he was unanimously given the position of youth choir guitarist.

The rehearsal itself went off without a hitch. Afterward, Tessa walked over to Alexis and asked, "Instead of a closing prayer, would you mind leading us in singing *God Almighty?*"

Alexis nodded and walked to the middle of the room while Tessa handed the sheet music to Jake, who was still seated at the piano. She felt the eyes of the entire choir fall upon her as they joined hands and formed a circle. She closed her eyes and thought, *For Your glory, not mine,* as she took a deep breath while Jake played the opening chords of the song.

While singing the first verse, Alexis marveled at how this simple act always seemed to lift her spirits. She felt Tessa and Rafael's grip on her hands tighten as she moved on to the refrain. She blushed when she caught Rafael smiling at her and then felt a chill run down her spine as the sound of their combined voices reverberated throughout the main hall. Standing next to her peers with their hands intertwined and their blended voices rising up into the ceiling, she thought she almost felt the presence of God.

Afterward, Alexis and Rafael volunteered to stay behind to help Tony put the chairs and music away. While Tony carried music and hymnals to the music room in the church and Rafael put away chairs, Alexis took a break and walked toward the nearest restroom. When she moved past the glass doors of an alternate exit on the north side of the building, she again saw the woman, who now seemed to be slowly making her way toward the back of the church. As she stepped out of the parish hall, she noticed that it had gotten foggy outside and that the outdoor lights in that part of the churchyard weren't on. Fearing that the woman might trip and fall into one of the numerous rose bushes in the area or hurt herself in some other way, she called out to her. At that point, she only saw the woman's faint outline in the increasingly dense fog. She noticed, regardless of what Tessa had said, that it now felt even colder than it had been when she arrived; she could actually see every breath as she exhaled. She picked up her pace. She didn't want to be out here alone any longer than she had to. When she heard a faint cry, she again called out to the woman and then felt something brush past her. Her instincts told her to run, but her feet felt like they were rooted to the spot.

Without warning, a pair of gnarled hands grabbed her arms from behind and held them in an iron-like grip. She could smell the woman's putrid breath bearing down on her as she put her mouth next to Alexis' ear and said, "The Master will have his prize. You belong to him."

The woman cackled as Alexis let out a muffled cry. She tried to break free from the woman's grasp, but soon realized that the more she struggled, the tighter her grip became. She felt trapped and had no idea how she was going to escape.

She was starting to lose hope when she heard a voice in the distance calling her name.

"Archer," the woman said with a snarl. Miraculously, she immediately loosened her grip on Alexis and then spun her around. Alexis gasped and shook with fear as she looked into her hideous face and red eyes.

"This is only the beginning," the woman warned her. "No one will be able to save you." With that, the woman stepped back and then vanished into thin air.

Blind with fear, Alexis ran toward the voice that was calling her name. It wasn't long before she felt another pair of strong hands grab hold of her. She screamed and flailed her arms until she realized that it was Rafael. She had never felt so happy and relieved to see anyone in her life. She flung herself into his arms and buried her face in his chest.

"Alexis, are you all right?" Rafael asked, as she shook uncontrollably in his arms. "My God, you are so cold."

"I s-saw a w-woman w-walking and I j-just…" she stammered. She knew that she was acting crazy, but, at the moment, she was too distraught to care.

"Why don't you stay here while I take a look," he replied.

"No! Don't go. Please don't leave me here alone," she begged as a new wave of hysterics overcame her.

"What happened? What did you see?"

Alexis shook her head and frantically tried to pull both of them as far away from the back of the church as she could. Her body continued to tremble as she fought the urge to cry.

"Don't leave me," she repeated over and over.

Rafael gently placed his hands on either side of her face and said, "There is nothing to fear. I am here now."

Alexis nodded and tried to take a few deep breaths to calm down. It didn't work. As hard as she tried, she couldn't block out the woman's face, the sound of her voice, or how it felt for her arms to be bound by those gnarled hands. Her muffled cries turned into loud sobs as the tears she had fought to keep at bay started flowing down her cheeks.

Rafael put his arms around her when she continued to cry and whispered softly, "You are safe. No one is going to hurt you now."

A few more minutes passed before Alexis was finally able to regain her composure. Luckily for her, Rafael appeared to be more than happy to stay with her until she calmed down enough to tell him that she had left her backpack in the parish hall. They caught up with Tony just as he was about to lock up the building. She ran in and retrieved her backpack while Tony and Rafael stood by the door.

After saying goodbye to Tony, Rafael insisted on walking her to her bicycle. Her hands shook as she tried to find the key in her backpack to unlock it from the rack. He put his hands over hers to steady them and offered to drive her home. She happily took him up on his offer. After securing her bicycle to the trunk rack on his car, he opened the car door for her and asked for directions to her house.

Rafael drove into her driveway ten minutes later. He took her bicycle off of the rack and put it on the porch while Alexis waited, immobile, in the car. Although she felt numb inside, she found his presence heartening. Not wanting to appear ungrateful, she forced herself to smile at him as he opened the door and offered her his hand. It felt warm and reassuring as he walked her to the front door.

Alexis fumbled for her keys in her backpack and then dropped them on the ground. He picked them up and offered to open the door for her. She looked down at her unsteady hands and reluctantly agreed.

After Rafael unlocked the door, he turned to her and said, "Would it be okay with you if I send you a text later? I just want to make sure you are okay." He reached for his back pocket and said, "I have my cell phone right here. I can input your number before I leave."

At first, Alexis just stood there, thunderstruck. She couldn't believe that he would actually ask her for her phone number.

Alexis was about to say yes when he interjected, "I am so sorry. I did not mean to be so forward with you. You barely know me. I completely understand if…"

"Oh, no!" she exclaimed. "It was totally fine for you to ask. Actually, I think it's really sweet of you to want to check up on me."

Alexis watched him type as she relayed the numbers to him. Afterward, Rafael said, "You are going to be okay. I will be here for you if you need me."

Her heart told her that he meant every word that he said.

As they stood facing each other in front of the door, Alexis had no idea what to say next. So she did the first thing that came to mind: she kissed his cheek and then quickly said good night.

After she took a step back, she glanced at him and saw that he was smiling at her. She blushed as he said, "Good night to you too, Alexis."

CHAPTER 7—FRIENDSHIP AND RIVALRIES

Alexis woke, groggy and tired, to the sound of her cell phone beeping after a night of fitful sleep. She had slept with the lights on and the bed covers pulled tightly around her. Only the memory of Rafael's reassuring presence tempered her recollection of the nightmarish experience that kept replaying in her mind like a tape stuck on a loop.

She reached over and picked up her phone. Rafael had left her a text message. It read, "howru? tc." How are you? Take care.

Alexis quickly replied with a text that read, "Fine. Thx. Sys." Fine. Thanks. See you soon.

Her spirits buoyed, Alexis got ready for school and headed out the door as soon as Tessa's car pulled up to the driveway.

Tessa was looking at herself in the visor mirror when Alexis got in and said, "Thanks for picking me up."

"No problem, Cuz. Anytime." As Tessa backed out of the driveway, she asked, "Have you driven at all since Avery died?"

Alexis shook her head. She had totaled the car she was driving on that day and was in no hurry to get behind the wheel again.

"Don't get me wrong. I don't mind giving you a ride whenever you need one. I just think that the longer you wait, the harder it's going to be for you to get back into the swing of things."

"I know," Alexis replied. "I'm just not ready yet."

Alexis knew that Tessa meant well and had her best interests at heart. She also knew how protective her cousin could be of her. Not wanting to worry her needlessly or risk the possibility that her parents would find out about what happened through Tessa, she decided not to tell her cousin anything about last night's incident with the old woman.

Once they got to school, Tessa dropped Alexis off in front of the DePaul Center before parking her car. She looked for Rafael in the academic courtyard but couldn't find him. She did, however, spot Tobey fumbling, as usual, with his things. She watched as he dropped his pencil box on the ground just as Mateo Robles, a brutish and quick-tempered student, walked by. Mateo nearly slipped and fell after stepping on one of the many pens that had fallen out. Only Tobey's profuse apologies, coupled with the presence of an administrator nearby, kept him from being pummeled by Mateo on the spot. As Mateo stormed off, she walked over to Tobey in order to help him collect his things.

"Hey, Alexis," Tobey said as he picked up his pens.

"Hi, Tobey. Have you seen Rafael?"

Tobey wrinkled his nose and scratched his head as he said, "I think I saw him go into the chapel a minute ago."

"Thanks...and try to be more careful next time, okay? Mateo's bad news. You don't want to give him an excuse to beat you up."

Tobey waved her off, insisting that he was fine.

When Alexis reached the large wooden doors of the Marian Chapel, one of the chaplains just happened to be heading out and kindly held one of them open for her.

It took a moment for Alexis' eyes to adjust to the darkness of the room after having been in bright sunlight just seconds earlier. Only natural light coming through windows set high along the sides of the chapel illuminated the room. The lack of noise within the structure also sharply contrasted with the raucous sound of students outside. She was glad that her black flats made no sound as she stepped onto the white and black tiled floor.

As Alexis stood at the entrance, she looked up at the rose window above the altar, which contained a stained glass depiction of the Holy Family, and then scanned the rows of wooden chairs with kneelers. She quickly spotted Rafael leaning forward in a seat near the altar with his head bowed in prayer. He was holding a rosary in one hand and a prayer book in the other. From where she stood, she could almost feel the intensity and devotion with which he prayed and suddenly felt like an intruder who was eavesdropping on a private conversation. She wondered how he had been able to maintain such a strong relationship with God after having suffered what must have been the most devastating loss a child could ever experience. In her case, Avery's death had shaken her to the core and made her question everything about her faith. As she watched him pray, she thought that maybe he, of all people, would understand what she was going through and be the one to help her move on from the shattering loss of her best friend. In the end, she decided to let

Rafael have his moment with God without interference and quietly exited the chapel without being seen.

Minutes later, Rafael greeted Alexis with a kiss on each cheek and asked her how she was doing as they stood just outside the door of their theology class. His gesture caused her face to turn a bright crimson as she struggled to pull herself together enough to answer his question without stumbling over her words. Although she felt flustered, she reminded herself that it was customary for Spaniards to greet their friends that way. Still, she had a feeling that the type of attention he was giving her would not go unnoticed by her classmates.

It wasn't long before her suspicions were confirmed. After theology, she spotted Anita's friends, Cecilia and Lea, staring at them as she and Rafael walked side-by-side to their next class. When they got there, she caught Anita sulking in her seat as she pretended not to notice them. It took everything in her not to laugh. In fact, she had to admit that she rather enjoyed having the tables turned until Manuel, who was sitting directly behind her, tapped her on the shoulder and whispered in her ear, "You're so dead." His snarky comment starkly reminded her of the perils of crossing Anita.

By lunchtime, she felt numb from all the snide and underhanded remarks that Cecilia and Lea hurled in her direction during gym class. Tessa told her to just brush it off and to ignore them. Her other friends agreed and theorized that they probably were acting on Anita's orders. Although they meant well, she knew that following their advice was far easier said than done.

When Rafael joined them at the cafeteria table, they broke into subgroups of conversation until the topic of homework came up.

"I could build a fort with all my textbooks," Danny lamented as he took a bite out of his sandwich. "I feel like I'm carrying a ton of bricks on my back."

"I'm probably going to go blind from all the reading I have to do," Tobey interjected.

"Aren't you already blind?" Manuel quipped as he pointed to Tobey's glasses, which were precariously close to falling off the edge of his nose. Tobey repositioned his glasses, wadded up a granola bar wrapper and threw it at Manuel.

Manuel ducked and then took the reading list for his English class out of his backpack as he exclaimed, "Can you believe that our first assignment is to do a book report on William Faulkner's *As I Lay Dying*? After I read the first page, I felt like dying."

Alexis nearly choked on her pizza while the others laughed.

"That's classic literature, I'll have you know," Tessa informed Manuel with a slight air of superiority.

"Oh yeah? Well then, you read it," Manuel replied.

"I did, you dork, last year. Jake and I are seniors, remember?"

"Keep it down, guys," Jake said as he looked over at a nearby administrator. "The last thing we need is to attract any unwanted attention." He then turned to Rafael and said, "What about you? Do you think you're getting more homework here than you do back home?"

Rafael thought a moment and said, "I don't think that there is much of a difference. The thing that makes it harder for me here is that I often have to translate my thoughts from Spanish to English when I write. I find that it slows things down. In the past, I have found study groups to be very helpful."

"Me, too," Alexis chimed in. "Avery and I used to study together all the time."

The table suddenly went silent as her friends exchanged uncomfortable glances. It dawned on her that this was the first time that she had mentioned Avery in conversation since the accident. Although Rafael couldn't have understood what was going on, she could tell that he sensed that she had just said something significant.

"Would you like to study with me?" Rafael offered. "We have quite a few classes together. It would make sense for us to do that."

Suddenly, every eye seemed to be on her as they waited for her response. She was literally too stunned to speak. Danny, who was sitting next to her, leaned in and whispered, "I think he was talking to you."

Alexis gulped and then asked Rafael in a high-pitched and shaky voice, "What did you have in mind?"

"We could, maybe, study in the library after school."

Everyone's eyes seemed to be ping-ponging back and forth between the two of them like a tennis match. The ball was now in her court.

"That sounds…great," she replied. "The only problem is that I carpool home with Tessa every day right after school."

"I could take you home," he offered. "That would not be a problem."

Tessa quickly interjected, "I was about to tell you that the carpooling thing isn't… uh…I've got plans, yeah. It's, I mean, that's just not going to work for me, Cuz. Sorry."

Alexis was speechless. Tessa had to be the worst liar ever. Alexis looked over at Jake, who had buried his face in his hands while the others stared at her cousin in disbelief.

Despite Alexis' nervousness and embarrassment, she knew that she had to act fast. Rafael was offering to spend time with her and, in doing so, was handing her the perfect opportunity to get to know him on a one-on-one basis. Summoning up her courage, she looked him directly in the eye and said, "Sure. When would you like to start?"

At the end of the school day, Alexis packed up her things and headed straight to the library. Her feet felt like they were gliding on air. As she stopped to look at her reflection in the glass doors, she heard someone behind her say, "Meeting someone?"

Alexis turned and saw Anita standing a few feet behind her. From long experience, she knew that Anita only spoke to people she deemed worthy of her time. Knowing that she wasn't one of those people, Alexis deduced that the only reason Anita was striking up a conversation with her now was because of Rafael. Anita's lips were contorted into a smile that didn't reach her eyes. In fact, she reminded Alexis of a predator on the verge of striking its prey. She tightened her grip on the straps of her backpack and steeled herself for what she knew was going to be a very unpleasant conversation.

"Alexis. You're just the person I was looking for." Anita's voice sounded cold and calculating.

Alexis eyed her suspiciously. "Get to the point, Anita."

She knew that the pout and offended look on Anita's face was contrived and thought that Anita could definitely have won a Razzie Award for her performance.

"Don't be so crabby, Alexis. It doesn't become you."

"What does it matter to you?"

"You can at least be civil," Anita replied. "Honestly, sometimes you act like I killed your cat."

"I'm allergic to cats...and to you."

Anita flashed Alexis with a toothy grin as she moved a few steps closer. She cocked her head slightly to the side and said, "You may not like me, but a lot of other people do, and if it comes down to having to choose between us, you'd lose."

"Like I care what you or anybody else thinks about me," Alexis said defiantly.

"Are you sure about that? I think you care very much about what Rafael thinks. It would be a shame if he got the wrong impression about you."

Alexis's grip on the straps of her backpack tightened further as she tried to maintain her composure. She wanted so badly to find the right words to say to show Anita that she was not someone that could be bullied. But, to her great frustration, the words she sought failed to materialize.

"What exactly have you told him about yourself? How much have you told him about Avery?" Alexis had barely said a word to him about her. She assumed that the look on her face betrayed her thoughts when Anita added, "I guess if I were you, I probably wouldn't want to let him know that my dearly departed best friend was a hot mess...or that I was the one who drove her off the road."

"It wasn't like that," Alexis protested. "Another car rammed into mine. I lost control and hit Avery's car by accident."

"Admit it. You're the reason that Avery's dead."

Tears began to well in Alexis' eyes as she fought to rein in her emotions. She didn't want to give Anita the satisfaction of knowing that she had gotten to her, or provide her with any ammunition that she could use to put a wedge between her and Rafael. With her nerves nearly at the breaking point, she turned on her heel and said, "This conversation is so over."

Anita grabbed her right arm and hissed into her ear, "This conversation is over when *I* say it is. No one, especially you, walks away from me."

"Let go of my arm," Alexis said as she tried to pull away. She could feel Anita's manicured nails digging into her skin and cutting off her circulation.

"Stay out of my way or you'll be sorry," Anita said as a final parting shot before letting go of Alexis' arm and leaving her there.

Alexis stood there, shocked and dumbfounded, but resolute. *So you want Rafael,* she thought. *You'll have him over my dead body.*

Alexis tried to push the incident out of her mind. She took a deep breath to calm her frayed nerves as she entered the library. She quickly found an open table and sat down. She took out the textbooks for the three classes that she and Rafael shared: theology, English, and chemistry, and stacked them on top of one another. She also took out her notebook and pen, methodically placing them next to her books. When she finished setting up her things on the table, she looked at the clock on the wall and saw that it was already 3:10. Rafael was ten minutes late. She looked toward the glass doors, wondering where he could be. *Did he forget or change his mind?* She tried to distract herself by reading, but soon discovered that she was too preoccupied to focus on the words that were written on the page. She spent the next few minutes tapping a pen on her notebook and fidgeting with her hair. As she looked around the library, she saw other students huddled in groups; she was the only one who was alone. She began to feel like a bride who had been jilted at the altar. She couldn't decide whether to stay or go. After a minute of agonizing indecisiveness, she opted to give him a few more minutes to show up.

Alexis noticed a discarded newspaper lying on the table and picked it up. The front page had articles about war in the Middle East, natural disasters in China, and corruption by corporate and government officials at home and abroad. By the time she started skimming the editorials, she was feeling thoroughly depressed.

The headline of one of the editorials read, "The Catholic Church: Help or Hindrance?" Alexis decided to read it. She had just finished reading the last line of the editorial when Rafael walked into the library.

Rafael stopped and stood across from where she was sitting. She smiled at him and said in as cheerful a voice as she could muster, "Oh, there you are. Glad you could make it."

He laid his backpack on the table and said, "I am sorry for being late. I hope that I did not keep you waiting too long."

Alexis shook her head. Rafael looked relieved.

"I made the mistake of telling my statistics teacher, Mr. Bradley, where I was from. He stopped me after class to tell me all about his trip to Spain last year and tried to engage me in a conversation in Spanish."

"I didn't know Mr. Bradley spoke Spanish."

"He doesn't," Rafael replied with a conspiratorial smile.

"I'm sorry," Alexis said as she cupped her hands to her mouth, trying to suppress the urge to laugh.

"So was I." Rafael then glanced at the newspaper in her hand and asked, "Anything interesting?"

"Only if you like hearing about death, destruction, and the imminent collapse of the Catholic Church," she replied as she slid the newspaper toward him.

Rafael took the newspaper and spent the next few minutes skimming through the editorial she had just read. When he finished, he put the newspaper down on the table and asked her, "Did you get a chance to read this?"

Alexis nodded, praying that he wouldn't pursue that line of conversation any further. Given her current state of mind about her faith, she wasn't particularly comfortable with getting into a philosophical discussion with him about the Church.

"Do you agree with the editorial writer's opinion?"

Oh boy. I was afraid he was going to ask me that. Rafael slid the newspaper back toward her; she reread the opinion. She felt like she was being tested and wondered if there was a particular answer he was looking for. She struggled to find the right words to say; she didn't want to offend him but didn't think that it would be right to give him anything less than her honest opinion.

"I agree to the extent that there have been moments in the Church's history where its actions haven't lived up to its teachings," Alexis began.

"What do you mean? Can you be more specific?"

"Well…there's the Inquisition, the priest abuse scandal…"

Rafael leaned forward in his seat and asked, "Do you think that the bad things that have been ascribed to the Church outweigh the good?"

"Not necessarily, but the bad stuff can make it hard for people to see the good. What do you think?"

Rafael contemplated her answer, and then said, "I think that most practicing Catholics are good people who are trying to do God's work. I also believe that the mistakes of a few people should not undermine the validity of the institution itself."

"I agree. But what do you tell people who say that the Church is broken and dysfunctional?"

"Alexis, I think we are all sinners," Rafael said. "I believe we were created in the likeness of God, but that doesn't mean that the people within the Church are infallible. That is why reconciliation is one of the Church's sacraments. If the people in the Church were perfect, why would we need that sacrament?"

"Do you ever doubt your faith?"

"Of course I do," he replied. "I am sure that everyone does at some point in their life."

At that moment, Alexis remembered a question that Father Bernal had asked her weeks before and decided to pose it to Rafael. "Do you believe that the Devil exists?"

"Absolutely," he replied without any equivocation. "He constantly preys on our weaknesses in order to separate us from God's light. Unfortunately, our sinful natures make it easy for him to enter into our lives and lead us astray."

"What is the Church's role in all of this?"

Rafael replied, "I believe that the Church exists to give us the tools to be a beacon of light in the darkness and its teachings provide us with a blueprint for achieving eternal life with God."

Alexis considered his words carefully and then asked, "What can someone like me do to protect myself from the Devil and his influence?"

He said, "Pray and do your best to align your thoughts and actions with God's will. I would also stay away from occult practices and divination. Dabbling in such things can open you up to diabolical attachments. It is very important that you remain vigilant at all times. You can never let your guard down…ever."

The intensity with which Rafael said the words caught Alexis off guard. She said, "You make it sound like the Devil wants *my* soul."

Rafael looked slightly embarrassed and averted his eyes from her gaze. "I must apologize. I have a tendency to get carried away when I engage in these types of discussions. I hope I did not frighten or offend you. That was not my intent."

Alexis shook her head and said, "Lately, I haven't felt anything when I've tried to pray. Sometimes I think that maybe God's written me off and doesn't think I'm worth bothering with. If that's the case, then I don't see why the Devil would want to bother with me either."

"Don't ever think that you don't matter," he said earnestly. "Every person who is a member of the Body of Christ has a role to play. The Church could not possibly fulfill its mission without every one of its members serving as its ambassadors to the world."

"What could I possibly do to make a difference?"

Rafael smiled at her and said, "We show others that we are people of faith by the way we act and in the way we live our lives. God endowed you with certain gifts; your voice, for instance. I literally felt his presence in the room when you sang *God Almighty* at the end of rehearsal. I am sure that I was not the only one who felt that way."

"I'm no one special…"

Rafael adamantly shook his head as he reached out and touched her hand. The sensation of his hand on hers reverberated throughout her body as if she had been hit by a bolt of lightning. He said, "Yes, you are. I pray that I will be there to see you develop into the person God meant for you to be." He gave her hand a gentle squeeze and said, "But for now, I think that getting our homework done should be our top priority if we want to get passing grades this semester."

Alexis agreed and asked, "So what will it be? Theology, English, or chemistry?"

Alexis immediately sensed that something was amiss when she arrived at home and saw that there were no cars parked in the driveway. Eric had told her that he was going to be home early on Tuesdays and Thursdays this semester and hadn't indicated to her at breakfast this morning that he was going to be late. *Did his beater car finally conk out on him?* Given that distinct possibility, she called out to her father and looked in every room downstairs before ending up in front of his study. She knocked on the door several times. When he didn't answer, she decided to walk in anyway.

Natural sunlight coming through the window illuminated the room as she walked over to Eric's desk. She found a barely legible handwritten note lying on top of it. She picked it up and saw that it had the current day's date written on it along with a flight itinerary to the Philippines. She was about to look around for more clues when she heard the front door open. She put the piece of paper back down on the desk and silently made her way to the door. When she peeked out, she saw her mother heading toward the kitchen. She stepped back so as not to be seen and waited a few minutes before opening the door and creeping out of the study.

Lisa was standing by the sink with a cup of coffee in her hand when Alexis walked into the kitchen. She didn't seem to notice that her daughter was there as she took a sip and stared out the window. She thought that her mother looked upset and distracted. She also noted that her mother was home earlier than usual.

Thinking that her mother probably wanted to be alone, Alexis tried to slowly and quietly back out of the room. However, her effort to remain unnoticed failed the moment she banged her elbow against the doorframe.

Lisa glanced in her direction and said, "Oh Alexis, you're home."

"Yeah…Is everything okay?"

Although a smile briefly crossed Lisa's face, she shook her head and motioned for Alexis to come and sit down with her at the island.

"Where's Dad?" Alexis asked as she sat down.

"He's gone," Lisa said as she took another sip of her coffee. "He left for the Philippines this afternoon."

"Did something happen to kuya?" She could tell from the look on Lisa's face that she was on the right track. "Mom, please tell me."

"Your father got a call from Sister Nora Dunn this morning. She told him that your brother contracted malaria and is very sick. He collapsed in a field while handing out supplies to some villagers in Mindanao. Your father's flying over there to see him."

"Where is Jeremy now?"

"For now, they're keeping him in the village where he collapsed," Lisa replied. "They've been giving him medication, but the supplies are starting to run low."

"Why isn't he in a hospital?" Alexis demanded.

"He was doing field work in a very remote area," Lisa replied. "The nearest big city is miles away."

"They have cars there, and planes! There must be a way to get him to a place where he can be properly cared for."

Lisa put her elbows on the island and placed her right hand against her forehead as she said, "All the airplanes in the area have been grounded because of the typhoon and the roads are flooded."

"Then how is Dad going to get to him?"

"We have lots of family there. They know people who will be able to help him get to your brother as quickly as possible."

"Mom, if the conditions there are as bad as you say, isn't Dad going to be putting himself at risk, too?"

Lisa sighed. "You know your father. You and your brother mean the world to him. It would have driven him crazy to have stayed here and waited, especially knowing how sick your kuya was. He had to go. There's no way I could have stopped him."

For the second time in months, Alexis felt like the world as she knew it was collapsing around her. "Do you think they're going to be okay?" she asked as her voice quivered.

"I don't know," Lisa replied.

Alexis reached out and placed her hands over her mother's. For a moment, they sat there in silence with their eyes cast down, each one lost in their own thoughts.

After dinner, Alexis beat a hasty retreat to her room. As she lay in bed, tossing and turning, thoughts of her brother, sick with a fever in some remote village, preyed upon her mind. Finally, she drifted off to sleep...

Once again, Alexis found herself standing on the pedestrian bridge surrounded by darkness and fog. Gusts of cold wind were sweeping past her as she tried to adjust her eyes to the blackness that surrounded her. She sensed that she wasn't alone. She felt something brush past her and then heard a disembodied voice tell her, *The Archer will kill you where you stand.* In the distance, she saw a figure slowly approach her. Suddenly, malevolent laughter filled the air. She fell to her knees and looked down on the ground as she covered her ears to block out the sound. When she finally looked up, she saw a pair of pitiless blue eyes staring down at her. She froze when she saw Rafael raise the bow and arrow in his hands and aim it directly at her heart as the voice said, *Time to die, Alexis.*

Alexis awoke, screaming and crying hysterically with Lisa desperately trying to calm her down.

Alexis walked into theology class the next morning and saw Rafael sitting in the middle of the classroom looking through his notes. The sight of his backpack on top of an empty desk right next to his cheered her up considerably. Was he saving it for her? She hoped so.

Rafael stood up as soon as he saw her, picked up his backpack, and motioned for her to take the empty seat.

"Good morning, Alexis," he said cheerfully. However, his demeanor quickly became more subdued when he saw her face. Alexis' eyes were red and puffy from crying and lack of sleep. "Are you okay?"

Mr. Marquez started his lecture before she was able to respond. So instead, she handed him a slip of paper saying, "I'll tell you later" on it and then tried to focus on what the teacher was saying in order to get her mind off her troubles.

Since there was so little time between classes, Alexis waited until lunch to tell Rafael about her brother. When she met him in the library after school, she found that the words on the page of the textbook she was trying to read weren't registering in her brain. She pushed it away in frustration and sighed.

Rafael, who was reviewing his notes on his laptop, looked up and said, "Would you like to go for a walk instead? You don't look like you are in the mood to study right now."

Alexis nodded and quickly packed up all her things while Rafael put his laptop in his bag. When he asked her where she wanted to go, she suggested Mountain Hawk Park, which had a walking trail with scenic views of the mountains and a shimmering blue lake.

The sun was still high by the time they drove into Mountain Hawk's circular parking lot. They walked around the splash pad and playgrounds until they reached an earth-toned cement bench that faced the lake and the mountains beyond it. She could hear the sound of dogs barking and children behind them on the playground as she sat down next to Rafael.

"This is a very pretty place," Rafael said as he took in the panoramic view. "Do you come here often?"

Alexis kept her eyes focused on the lake as she said, "I like to come here when I need to be alone and think."

"This seems like a good place to do that," he replied. He leaned forward, resting his elbows on his legs and his chin on his hands, and looked straight ahead.

Alexis looked down at her hands and saw that the tips of her fingers looked raw from being picked at and bitten. Embarrassed, she hid them under her legs and then glanced at Rafael, who had a faraway look in his eyes. She wondered what he might be thinking of.

As the minutes passed, she found herself feeling more and more restless. *He must be bored out of his mind.* Unable to stand the silence any longer, Alexis said, "We can leave if you have something else you need to do. I'm probably not the best company right now anyway."

"Don't worry about me," he replied as he turned toward her, concern etched on his face. "I am fine. I just want to make sure that you are okay."

She nodded then looked away as she suddenly felt the urge to cry. Probably sensing that she was on the verge of tears, he reached into the front pocket of his khakis, pulled out a handkerchief, and handed it to her.

"Thanks," she said, taking it from him. She looked down at the handkerchief, which was embroidered with the initials "JC" on it, and said, "You don't see these very often anymore."

As Alexis ran her fingers over the embroidered letters, he said, "It belonged to my father. Those are his initials. J.C. Javier Cordero."

"What was your mother's name?"

"Her name was Sofia," he said quietly. "She was beautiful in every way. When my brother and I were small, she would sing us to sleep. Sometimes at night when I close my eyes and think of her, I can still hear her voice. She was a very devout Catholic and instilled that love for the Church in my brother and I."

Alexis was touched by the fact that Rafael kept mementos of his father with him. First, the wooden cross. Now, the handkerchief.

"Do you miss him?"

"Every day. He was a great man and a wonderful father...I loved him very much."

"If you don't mind my asking, how did they die?"

"They lost their lives in a car accident," he said slowly. "They were hit by a drunk driver who was driving on the wrong side of the road. They died instantly. My brother was in the back seat of the car and was very badly injured."

"Where were you?"

"I was sick at home with my aunt. Father Bernal was the one who came to my house to tell me that my parents had passed away. It was the worst day of my life."

"What's the connection between you and Father Bernal?"

"He and my father were childhood friends," he replied.

Alexis again looked down at the handkerchief. She started to give it back to him as she said, "This means a lot to you. I don't feel right using..."

"Please keep it," he cut in. "Items like these are meant to be used."

"Can I ask you something else?" He nodded. "How were you able to move on after they died? Sometimes, I still have a really hard time accepting the fact that my best friend, Avery, is dead. And now, with my brother..."

Alexis' lip quivered as the words got caught in her throat. She took a deep breath and told herself to hold it together, but the harder she tried to keep what she was feeling hidden inside, the stronger the need to express it became. She felt like a dam that was on the verge of bursting. It wasn't long before she reached the point where she knew that she couldn't hold it in any more. She bowed her head and let the tears flow.

"I'm so sorry. I don't know what's wrong with me," she said as she dabbed at her eyes with the handkerchief.

Rafael knelt down beside her and gently placed his hands over hers as he said, "There is no need for you to apologize. You have every right to be upset."

"We...should...just...go," she said, choking back tears.

He shook his head as he continued to hold her hands. "I am happy to sit with you as long as you need me to."

Alexis nodded and then cried even harder. He put his arms around her as she buried her face in his shoulder. He patted her back and gently rocked her as he quietly said, "Shh," in her ear. As soon as her tears began to subside, he let go of her and sat back down on the bench. She leaned against him as he took hold of her hand and intertwined his fingers with hers.

She looked over at him and said, "You're all kinds of awesome. Did you know that?"

Rafael shrugged his shoulders and said with a laugh, "Not really. I am certain that there will be many days when you will look at me and think that I am not so wonderful."

Alexis shook her head. "I doubt that, and thanks for being here for me."

"I am your friend. That is why I am here."

"Absolutely," she replied. *Friends.* She told herself that was probably all she should expect from Rafael, especially knowing that more popular girls like Anita had him in their sights.

CHAPTER 8—INTERVENTION

Alexis didn't quite know what to make of her relationship with Rafael. He had gone from being a complete stranger to her nearly constant companion within a matter of days. He sat next to her at lunch and in every class they shared, studied with her in the library after school and drove her home every day. On the weekends, they often met up with their friends to see a movie or eat at a local restaurant on Saturday nights, and they sang together at mass on Sunday evenings with the youth choir. He had filled the gaping hole that Avery left behind when she died and gave her what nobody else could: a reason to go on.

Thanks to Anita and her gossiping friends, Alexis knew that they had become a frequent topic of conversation at school. Although she could see how his attentiveness could be mistaken for attraction by her classmates, the reality was that he had neither said nor done anything to show her that he wanted to be anything more than her friend. She tried not to dwell on that fact even though her feelings of disappointment gnawed at her and, instead, focused on how much better her life had become now that he was a part of it.

Rafael was patient and kind. He listened without judgment and his friendship came without strings. He was also very protective of her. At times, she thought she saw an alertness in his eyes that made her think that he was waiting to fight off an unseen enemy lurking in the shadows.

One day, as Rafael was about to drop off Alexis in front of her house, he looked over at the empty driveway and asked, "What time does your mother come home?"

"It depends," she replied with a shrug. "Usually by six o'clock at the latest."

"Are you normally alone until she gets home?" he asked, looking concerned.

She gave him a quizzical look as she laughed and said, "I'm sixteen, Rafael, and perfectly capable of being on my own until my mother gets home."

"I am sure that you are," he said, with a slightly embarrassed look. "Would you mind if I came in anyway?"

"So you think that there might be monsters hiding in the attic waiting to attack me?"

"No, just demons maybe," he said half-jokingly.

Although Alexis knew that her mother would disapprove of her having a boy in the house while no one else was home, she motioned for him to follow her inside anyway. She gave him a quick tour and then led him to the kitchen. As he sat down on one of the bar stools, she handed him a soda and asked him if he wanted a snack. He said yes to the former and no to the latter.

Alexis pulled some Filipino sweet bread, Ensaymada, out of the refrigerator, warmed it up in the microwave, and then set it down in front of her as she took a seat next to Rafael. As the smell of the warm bread wafted through the air, she felt her stomach rumble in anticipation. When she noticed that Rafael was eyeing her snack, she asked, "Would you like to have some?"

"No thank you," he said half-heartedly. "I don't want to impose."

"Rafael, you're practically salivating. There's more in the fridge. It's fine."

Alexis got another piece, warmed it up for him, and then watched in amazement as he proceeded to devour it in two seconds flat. After he had taken his last bite, he put his fork down and gave her a sheepish look as he said, "I guess that I was hungrier than I thought."

"Doesn't your host family feed you enough?" she teased.

Rafael replied, "Actually, Mrs. Daniels is a very good cook and always keeps the refrigerator very well stocked for me."

As Alexis gazed at Rafael's smiling face, she thought about how nice it felt just to be here with him. Although she'd only known him for a short time, it was hard for her to imagine life without the boy who was sitting in front of her. She had often thought of telling him about her recurring dream and all the other strange things that had happened to her, but the possibility of alienating him with that information always seemed to stop her in her tracks. But this time the need to confide in him pressed on her mind, urging her to speak.

Throwing caution to the wind, she asked "Do you believe in fate?"

"I believe that God has a plan for each one of us, but that He gave us the ability to choose whether or not to follow it," he replied. "Why do you ask?"

"It's just that…never mind," she replied, biting her lip.

"No, tell me," he insisted as he picked up his soda to take a drink.

She took a deep breath and said, "I know that this is probably going to sound strange, crazy even, but I think I saw you before we met."

Rafael cocked his head slightly to the side as he put his soda down and asked, "What makes you say that?"

"I've seen you before…in dreams," she said as images of him standing on the bridge flashed through her mind. She suddenly felt cold and shuddered as she remembered the voice in her dream warning her that Rafael meant to do her harm.

Alexis was brought back to the present moment when she felt his hands grasp hers. "Are you okay?" When she nodded, he said, "Please tell me more."

"I started having these dreams not long after Avery died. At first, they only happened once every couple of days, but they're becoming more frequent now."

"How often?" he asked as his grip on her hands tightened.

"Almost every night," Alexis replied nervously. "I'm always standing on a bridge. I can hear someone talking to me but I can't see a face and then you arrive. In the beginning, the only part of your face that was clear to me was your eyes. But when I saw you in church, there was a part of me that thought that you might be the boy that I'd been dreaming about."

Alexis was unable to gauge Rafael's reaction from his expression or demeanor. His face was inscrutable. Although she felt her nerve begin to falter, she knew that, at this point, there was no going back. She went on, "In my dreams, I see that your mouth is moving, but I can't hear the words. And lately, you've had a bow and arrow in your hand."

She saw his eyes widen and instantly felt foolish for letting him in on her secret. She pulled her hands away from his grasp and said, "I'm so sorry. You probably think I'm nuts."

"No, not at all," Rafael replied. "I am glad that you felt you could tell me this. I don't want you to ever think that you have to censor your thoughts and feelings with me."

Alexis looked at him with wonderment and said, "Are you for real?"

"The last time I checked, yes," he replied as a smile formed on his face. "And I am happy to be at your service whenever you need me."

"Even though you probably think that I have a few screws loose…"

"I think that you are as sane as I am and have been handling the trauma in your life as well as can be expected. Don't forget, I also have known the tragedy of losing someone I loved."

"And I think that you're handling the crazy thing that I just told you amazingly well," Alexis replied. "I half expected you to run out the door, especially when I mentioned the bit about the bow and arrow. I might as well have told you that I saw Legolas from *Lord of the Rings* on that bridge."

"I am flattered that you would even compare me to someone like Legolas," Rafael said with a grin. "His character was a man of principle in addition to being a fearsome warrior, but I am afraid that you would find me lacking in comparison."

For a moment, an awkward pause descended upon their conversation as Alexis struggled to think of what to say next. She was saved from reinitiating the conversation when Rafael asked, "Besides the dreams, have you had any other strange experiences in the last few months?"

Although Alexis loathed to divulge anything else to Rafael, she figured that whatever she told him at this point probably wasn't going to make much of a difference in the way he thought about her. She took a deep breath and said, "Remember the night you ran into me after rehearsal?"

"Yes…"

"Well, I saw…or at least I thought I saw a woman walk to the back of the church. Even though she gave me the creeps, I followed her. She grabbed my arm and wouldn't let go. I felt like I couldn't breathe. I was so scared."

"What did she look like?"

"All I can remember were her red eyes…I'd seen eyes like those before. She told me something about her master getting his prize and said the word 'Archer' just before she let me go. Luckily, you showed up a few minutes later."

Rafael shook his head and said, "I am so sorry. I should have gotten to you sooner. Tony told me that you had just gone to the restroom. I started looking for you as soon as I realized that you had left the building."

"It's okay…"

"No, it is not," he said adamantly. "I should never have left you alone that long."

Rafael's comments puzzled her. It sounded like he believed that what had happened to her that night was at least partially his fault and that he had failed her in some way, which made no sense.

"Don't be too hard on yourself. I was the idiot who decided to follow that creepy woman and run in those trails by myself."

"What happened to you in the trails?"

"I hurt myself while jogging and was limping home when I got the feeling that something was following me. I started running as fast as I could when I heard dogs howling around me. When I got to the end of the trail and looked back, I saw a large black dog with red eyes staring at me."

"Is there anything else you would like to tell me?"

There was one more thing, but she couldn't bring herself to tell him about *her*. And so she lied and responded by slowly shaking her head.

"Does anyone else know about what you have just told me?"

"I did tell my psychiatrist about the dreams but not about the woman or the dog," she replied.

"Have you thought about talking to a priest about your experiences? Someone like Father Bernal might be able to give you greater insight into what you might be experiencing. I am certain that anything that you say to him would be kept in the strictest of confidence."

"I don't really know him…and honestly, he's kind of…"

"Intimidating," Rafael said, finishing her sentence. "He can also be very compassionate and caring…a great ally in times of strife. Believe me, I know that from personal experience."

Alexis was about to respond when they both heard the sound of the garage door opening. Lisa was home. Her mother walked into the kitchen a few minutes later and froze where she stood the moment she saw Rafael sitting beside her daughter.

Rafael immediately stood up and said, "Good evening, Mrs. Neil."

Lisa looked grim. She acknowledged his greeting with a curt nod as she pursed her lips and flung the mail in her hand onto the kitchen counter. Alexis sensed anger and fear lurking behind her mother's stony expression and wondered why her mother was having such a visceral reaction to Rafael. Although seeing her alone with Rafael in the house probably caught her mother off guard, she didn't think the situation warranted the chilly reception her mother was giving him.

Alexis felt the tension in the room rising with each passing second. Knowing that asking her mother what was wrong in front of Rafael would probably set her off, she decided that the best thing for her to do was to act like everything was fine. She smiled and said in as cheerful voice as she could muster, "Mom, this is Rafael Cordero."

Unfortunately, Lisa seemed to be in no mood for compromise. She walked up to Rafael and said, "I *know* who you are," as her eyes bored into him. "Father Bernal told me about you. You're the exchange student from Spain, right?"

"Yes, Mrs. Neil," Rafael replied in a deferential tone. "We met briefly at the orientation meeting. It is a pleasure to see you again."

Lisa glanced over at Alexis and then back at Rafael. "So tell me, have you learned anything of interest since you've been here? I'm very curious to know what you've observed so far."

After a brief pause, Rafael said, "I am doing my best to document everything that I have seen and heard. There has been a lot to take in. I am learning a lot."

It almost sounded to Alexis as if they were talking in some kind of code, but she let it pass.

Lisa nodded. "Alexis tells me that you've become quite a good friend of hers."

"I have really enjoyed getting to know your daughter," he replied. "She has been very welcoming and kind."

"He's a great study partner," Alexis chimed in. "It's worked out really well, especially since we have so many classes together. I thought you wouldn't mind if he came in for a little bit. We've been in the kitchen the whole time. Honest."

"Well…that's something," Lisa said as she opened a drawer and retrieved a wooden letter opener with a gold embellished handle. She picked up a large envelope and placed the pointed end of the opener at one corner and sliced it open as she said, "Alexis deserves to be around people who have her best interests at heart, especially after what she's been through. It's very important that she gets the right kind of support. The last thing she needs is to have her head filled with misguided notions."

Rafael's body stiffened, but his voice remained calm as he asked, "Mrs. Neil, is it wise to rule out possibilities just because it cannot be scientifically proven? Would it not be better to look at all available options?"

There it is again. What are they talking about?

Alexis noticed that her mother's knuckles were turning white as she gripped the letter opener and pointed it at Rafael. "I appreciate your concern, Mr. Cordero, but I think that I'm in a much better position than you to decide what's best for Alexis."

"Mrs. Neil, I am very sorry. I have offended you. I did not mean to overstep my bounds."

"Not at all," Lisa said coolly and then looked down at her watch and said, "It's getting late and Alexis and I still haven't eaten dinner. Anyway, I'm sure your host family is probably beginning to wonder where you are."

Alexis stared at her mother, wide-eyed and open-mouthed. She felt sorry for Rafael and embarrassed for herself. Most of all, she was angry at her mother.

Rafael, on the other hand, seemed as unflappable and gracious as ever. He said to Alexis, "Your mother is right. It is getting late. I should be going."

Alexis nodded slowly and then frowned at Lisa as Rafael picked up his backpack and said good night. She followed him out of the kitchen, leaving her mother staring after them.

Rafael was about to open his car door when Alexis put her hand on his shoulder and said, "I'm so sorry. I have no idea what just happened back there. She's usually not like that with my friends."

"There is no need to apologize," he replied evenly. "She is probably under a great deal of stress, especially with what has happened to your brother. You are very lucky to have a mother like her. I can see that she loves you very much."

"And she's also way too overprotective, overbearing, and…"

Rafael patted the hand that was resting on his shoulder and said, "I would not be too hard on her if I were you. I am sure she is only doing what she thinks is best."

"I suppose," Alexis conceded as she silently reveled in the sensation of his touch and the feelings it ignited in her.

After Rafael got into his car, he rolled down the window and looked up at her. She took a step forward and leaned against the door. She felt her pulse quicken at the realization that his face was merely inches away. He gently placed his hands on top of hers and gave them a squeeze. He said, "Good night, Alexis. I will see you tomorrow."

Alexis nodded and then stepped back as he backed out of her driveway. Once his car was out of sight, she spun around, slammed the front door, and stormed into the dining room where Lisa was going through the day's mail. She pulled the chair closest to her mother's out roughly, sat down, and glared at her with her arms folded in front of her.

Lisa sat back in her chair, looked her daughter directly in the eye, and asked, "What is it, Alexis?"

Alexis answered her mother's question with a question of her own. "What the heck was that all about?"

"I could ask you the same thing. What am I supposed to think when I come home and see him here with you?" Lisa retorted.

"We're just friends, Mom," Alexis replied, defensively. "You saw us when you walked in the kitchen. We were just talking."

"I'm not blind," Lisa said. "You think I haven't noticed how much time you've been spending with him lately. I always see you with him on campus. Even the staff's noticed and more than one person has come up to me and asked about the two of you."

"Mom, you're reading too much into things and being way too judgmental."

"How much do you really know about him?" Lisa asked. "What has he told you about himself? What a person is like on the outside and who they really are on the inside can be two completely different things."

"Jeez, Mom," Alexis replied, "you make it sound like he might be some kind of criminal. We study together after school and sing in the church choir on Sundays, and when we go out, it's always as part of a group. We've never, not once, gone out together alone."

Lisa shook her head and looked unconvinced as she said, "You're still in a very vulnerable state and frankly, it seems like you're clinging to this boy for dear life. Your attachment to him concerns me, especially when you don't know all the facts. I've been around a few more corners than you have. You have to trust me on this."

"I'm not a child and I'd appreciate it if you'd stop treating me like one," Alexis snapped as she leaned forward and slammed her fist on the dining room table. "You're not going to dictate who I can and cannot see."

"Don't raise your voice to me, young lady," Lisa replied. "You're twisting my words and completely missing my point."

Her mother's apparent animosity toward Rafael baffled her. As far as she knew, there was absolutely nothing objectionable about him. He was a devout Catholic and an intelligent, thoughtful, polite, and considerate young man. In short, she thought that he was everything her mother could ask for in a boy who might be dating her daughter.

"You don't even know him. How can you possibly dislike him already? He's one of the nicest people I've ever met. You don't have anything to worry about with him."

Lisa sighed. "Alexis, I don't want to fight with you."

"Then stop trying to ruin the best thing that's happened to me since Avery died," she said with an earnestness that surprised even her.

Lisa took a long, hard look at Alexis as she sat back and picked up the mail once again. Alexis could almost see the wheels in her mother's head turning as she considered her options. Finally, her mother said, "Okay, anak, here are my terms. I'll allow you to bring him here provided that you respect the rules of this household at all times." She recalled the lecture her parents had given to Jeremy when he was in high school as she slowly nodded her assent. *Members of the opposite sex stay downstairs at all times. No open displays of affection and absolutely, positively no significant other in the bedroom with the doors closed. Ever.* "Just promise me that you'll take things slowly with him. Don't rush into anything and keep your eyes and your options open. Are we clear?"

"Fine," Alexis said, feeling triumphant, and then stood up and walked out of the dining room without a backward glance.

CHAPTER 9—CONFRONTATIONS

Alexis was waiting by her locker for Rafael on a Friday afternoon when she heard the sound of raised voices and footsteps heading in her direction at a rapid pace. Seconds later, she saw Tobey turn the corner and sprint toward her. He was clutching a few books in one hand and a notebook in the other. His glasses were askew and his face looked flushed with the effort of trying to make a quick getaway. Her heart sank when she saw Mateo round the corner with two of his friends close behind. His hands were balled into fists and his face looked purple with anger. It was readily apparent to her that Tobey was his intended target.

Tobey stopped right in front of Alexis. He looked panic-stricken and was close to tears. She asked him, "What's going on? Why is Mateo after you?"

Before Tobey could answer her questions, Mateo grabbed the back of his shirt and spun him around. Mateo's two henchmen now stood on either side of him and snickered. Alexis' eyes scanned the empty hallway in vain for a teacher or administrator. With increasing desperation, she also wondered where Rafael could be.

"I said I was sorry. I swear I didn't mean to bump into you," Tobey pleaded as Mateo shoved him against the lockers.

"I told you the last time you messed with me that you'd be sorry. Now it's time for you to pay, you little punk." Alexis thought that Mateo was playing the part of a thug to the hilt. He said, "Tell you what. Since I'm such a nice guy, I'll give you a five second head start to try and get out of here before I beat the crap out of you."

Tobey nodded and then tried to run, but his attempt to get away was foiled from the start by one of Mateo's friends who deliberately tripped him. He fell to the ground with a thud while the other two boys roared with laughter. Alexis felt heartsick as she watched Tobey's glasses slide off his face and land a few feet from where he fell. The books that were in his hand were now strewn on the ground while the loose papers in his notebook scattered in every direction. She was almost too horrified to watch as Mateo closed in on Tobey, who was struggling to find his glasses. She thought of running for help, but didn't want to leave Tobey alone, just as Mateo was about to pounce on him.

Out of ideas and desperate to stop her friend from being hurt, Alexis got in between Mateo and Tobey and said with all the courage she could muster, "Leave him alone!"

Mateo stopped and looked at Alexis with a malevolent sneer and said, "Get out of the way."

Alexis stood her ground and pleaded, "Can't you just walk away? He didn't mean any harm."

Mateo looked at Tobey, who had managed to retrieve his glasses, and said, "So you've got girls protecting you now?" and then said to Alexis in a menacing voice, "I said, get out of the way."

"What are you going to do if I don't?"

Mateo moved his face to within inches of Alexis' and stared her down with a disdainful smirk on his face. "Then, I guess I'll just have to make you."

"Don't hurt her," Tobey pleaded as he stood up and faced Mateo. "Your beef's with me."

Mateo nodded and then pushed Alexis aside as he took a step toward Tobey. Although Tobey looked like he was about to faint, he just stood there, awaiting his fate. Alexis felt a mixture of frustration and helplessness as she watched the nightmarish scene unfolding before her very eyes. She wanted to lash out at Mateo but knew that she was no match for him. *Where is Rafael?* When she saw Mateo cock his right arm back to strike Tobey, she grabbed it and screamed, "Stop it!"

Mateo turned and slammed Alexis into the lockers with his left hand. She let out a painful cry as she felt her back and head hit the locker doors. She then slid down to the ground and curled up in a ball.

The situation seemed hopeless until the moment Alexis saw Rafael racing towards them like an avenging angel. His jaw was set and his hands were clenched into fists as he fixed his steely blue eyes upon Mateo.

One of Mateo's henchmen tried to warn him, but Rafael swooped down on him before he had the chance to turn his head. Rafael grabbed his upper left arm, whipped him around, and pinned him against the lockers. He moved like someone who was very well-trained in hand-to-hand combat. Mateo cried out in pain as Rafael jammed his thumb into Mateo's armpit and used the other fingers to pinch the nerves in this bully's upper arm. He pressed his other arm across Mateo's back to keep him from wriggling out of his grasp.

Rafael shot Mateo's friends a menacing look and said, "Take one step closer and I promise you that I will break him." Mateo continued to cry out in pain. By his words, Rafael was both daring them to come to Mateo's aid and warning them that they would suffer the same fate if they tried.

He leaned his head toward Mateo's ear and said, "If you ever lay a hand on Alexis again you will answer to me." Mateo nodded as his face contorted in pain.

Apparently satisfied with Mateo's answer, Rafael shoved him toward his dumbstruck friends and said, "Walk away...now." The two other boys caught him as he stumbled forward, casting terrified glances toward Rafael as they scurried away like rats.

Alexis looked at Tobey, who had buried his face in his hands as he wept, and then to Rafael, who was watching Mateo and his friends beat a hasty retreat. She wondered what might be going through his mind and was also worried that he might be upset with her for putting herself in such a dangerous situation.

As soon as Mateo and his friends were out of sight, Alexis noticed a sudden change in Rafael's demeanor. When he turned toward her, he looked ashen-faced and shaken by what had just happened. He slowly bent down, knelt in front of her, took one of her hands into his, and said, "I am so sorry that I did not get here sooner. Please forgive me." He reached out and touched her face with his other hand and then leaned forward and gently kissed her forehead.

Alexis looked up and saw Tobey staring down at them. His voice was shaking slightly as he said to Rafael, "Thanks so much. I thought I was a goner there for a second."

Rafael stood up and patted him on the shoulder. "You are very welcome," he replied. "You need to watch out for that boy. Let me know if he ever tries to bother you again."

Tobey nodded, picked up his books and went about retrieving as many of the loose papers as he could. Rafael held his hand out to Alexis and helped her up. When he suggested that she go and see if the school nurse was still on campus, she politely declined, insisting that she was fine.

Once Tobey had gathered all his things together, he gave Alexis a hug and said, "Thanks for trying to stand up for me...but please don't ever do that again. I would have never forgiven myself if something had happened to you. I owe you one."

As Alexis watched Tobey walk away, she wondered what she and Rafael were going to say to each other once they were completely alone. Once Tobey was out of sight, she turned to Rafael and said, "I couldn't just stand by and watch him get beaten up without trying to do something."

Alexis braced herself for a reprimand. Instead, Rafael merely said, "I think what you tried to do was very noble," and then averted his eyes from hers. He looked like he was replaying the scene in his head. "When I saw you slump to the ground after Mateo had shoved you I—I…," he stammered.

She put the tips of her fingers to his lips and said, "You came, and you're here now. That's all that matters."

For a minute, they just stood there, staring at each other. Although no words passed between them, she felt that his eyes spoke volumes about the way he was feeling. At that moment, she sensed their relationship had crossed an invisible line and that there would be no going back. Thus, it came as no surprise when he reached out and pulled her into his arms. She could feel her heart hammering in her chest as he stroked her hair and held her tight. She closed her eyes and savored the moment. She couldn't have cared less if anybody had seen them. She was utterly and hopelessly in love with him and, for the first time, felt that he might feel the same way about her, too.

On Monday, rumors of the altercation had spread throughout the campus. Alexis did her best to ignore the gossip and tried to act as if nothing had happened. Rafael and Tobey did the same. The only thing that was noticeably different was the terrified look that Mateo gave them whenever he saw them.

As usual, Alexis walked into the school library after school and sat down at the same table where she and Rafael would normally study. Out of the corner of her eye, she saw Lizzie walk by the bookshelves and head toward one of the private study rooms in the back. Since Rafael had not yet arrived, she decided to follow her friend and have a little chat with her. When she peeked through the window of the room Lizzie had entered, she saw that it was dark and appeared to be empty. She turned the doorknob and went in.

Alexis was immediately struck by how cold the room felt. She thought that the thermostat must be malfunctioning as goose bumps formed on her arms and legs. A moment later, she saw a solitary figure sitting in the far corner of the room.

Alexis approached Lizzie cautiously and said, "Why don't I turn on a light?"

"No, I like being in the dark," Lizzie replied.

Alexis shrugged her shoulders and sat down next to her. Lizzie leaned forward in her seat and said with a slight hint of sarcasm, "So how's it going with Mr. Wonderful?"

"We're fine," Alexis replied defensively.

"Are you sure about that?"

Alexis was irritated by the question and the tone Lizzie had set for their conversation. She immediately made up her mind to get up and walk out if all Lizzie was going to do was tear him down.

"You don't know him like I do," Alexis said. "He's been really good to me, a great friend."

"Isn't that the problem? It's been a couple of weeks now, hasn't it? Has he said anything to you about wanting to be more than just your friend?" Alexis shook her head. "He's just toying with you Alexis, and you're playing right into his hands."

Although Alexis didn't want to admit it, she couldn't dismiss the possibility that Lizzie could be right.

"How can you be so sure?" Alexis asked as she remembered how Rafael had held her after Tobey's run in with Mateo.

Lizzie gave Alexis an exasperated look. "Okay. Let's be specific. Has he ever asked you on a date? Or tried to kiss you? Or does he usually try to keep a respectable distance between the two of you?"

The answers to the questions were *no*, *no*, and *yes*. Even so, a small but insistent part of her brain told her that Lizzie had to be wrong. If she were right, then why did he sometimes look at her the way he did when he thought she wasn't looking or hold her the way he did during those times when she had felt most vulnerable and scared? After all, Rafael was from a different culture and had a very formal upbringing.

As Alexis racked her brain for answers, she noticed that Lizzie was tapping her fingers on the table as she waited for Alexis to respond. Finally, Lizzie threw her hands up in the air and said, "If you're just going to sit there and try to think of ways to defend him, I'm not going to waste my breath."

"Hold on. Just because he hasn't said anything yet doesn't mean that he doesn't care," Alexis argued.

A mischievous grin spread over Lizzie's face as she said, "Okay. Then let's go and test my theory. You're going to be studying with him in the library, right?" Alexis nodded. "Why don't you try and flirt with him? Put your arm on the back of his chair and then lean in and whisper something naughty in his ear. Be creative."

"I couldn't do that," Alexis replied. The mere thought of trying to seduce Rafael in the middle of the school library horrified her. Besides, she was a novice at such things. Still...

"If he's interested, you'll know pretty quickly. If he's not, you'll thank me for saving you from wasting your time on someone that doesn't really care about you."

"Do you think he knows how I feel about him?" Alexis asked in an anxious tone.

Lizzie put her right hand underneath Alexis' chin and pointed to Alexis' eyes with her left hand as she said, "Your eyes are giving you away. Anyone within a ten-mile radius can see that you're in love with him. Look, Mac, I don't want you to get hurt, but I think it's time for you to see this guy for who he really is."

"Have you spoken to my mother lately? You sound exactly like her."

"Then maybe you should listen to her," Lizzie replied.

Alexis rolled her eyes. "Go ahead and just say whatever you're going to say. I know that you're dying to tell me anyway."

"He's a zealot; a true believer. Someone who is so devoted to his faith that he'll do anything and everything to protect it."

"I already know that he's a devout Catholic. That's no secret. There are a lot of people here that are like him. Why should I be worried about that?"

"His friendship with you is no accident," Lizzie replied. "I know for a fact that he's part of a religious cult, and you know what else? He was sent here to watch you."

Alexis' eyes widened in surprise as she said, "What are you talking about? Do you realize how crazy that sounds? Besides, how would you know that?"

Lizzie replied, "I overheard him talking about you with a priest the other day at church."

"Father Bernal?"

"Yeah, I think so. He's the one with dark hair and brooding looks, right? After I overheard their conversation, I did a little research and asked around. I found out that Father Bernal is the head chaplain of a military religious order in the Church called the Order of the Brethren of the Cross. Have you heard of it?"

Alexis vaguely remembered hearing about The Brethren before but couldn't place where or when. She shrugged her shoulders and said, "So what? A lot of priests are tied to religious orders."

Lizzie shook her head and said, "You're so naive, Alexis. That's why he probably laughs his head off about you when you're not around. You saw how Rafael handled Mateo. Mateo was like a rag doll in his hands. You really need to get your head out of the sand and open your eyes."

"What exactly would I see?"

"That Rafael is no ordinary boy. The sooner you realize that, the better off you'll be."

As far as Rafael was concerned, Alexis felt like Lizzie was doing everything she could to pull the rug out from underneath her.

Alexis asked, "So how do I know that what you're telling me is true?"

"Why don't you find out for yourself?"

"How do you propose that I do that?"

"You could always hack into his computer or phone."

Alexis' jaw dropped. "Are you crazy? Aside from the fact that doing that could send me to jail, I wouldn't know the first thing about how to do it."

"Then go and find someone that does."

Alexis' mind was reeling. Not only was she supposed to come onto Rafael, now Lizzie was suggesting that she hack into his phone or computer. Even so, she suddenly realized that she did, in fact, know someone who would know exactly how to help her do it, if necessary.

Just then, Alexis looked out the window and saw Rafael sitting at the table waiting for her. She turned to Lizzie and told her that she had to go. As she stood up, Lizzie grabbed her by the arm and said, "Don't let that pious schoolboy exterior fool you. Underneath, he's absolutely lethal."

Lizzie's last words rang in Alexis' ears as she walked toward Rafael. He looked up and smiled at her when he saw her approaching. He said, "I was beginning to wonder where you were."

Alexis noticed Rafael was sitting, as usual, just across from where she had put her backpack. She decided to test Lizzie's theory about him right then and there. She walked around the table, moved the empty chair closer to him and sat down. The words *be creative* rang in her ears like a dare as she crossed her legs, put a hand on the back of his chair, and leaned toward him. She smiled flirtatiously as he slowly turned his head in her direction. Her resolve, however, crumbled as soon as his eyes locked onto hers. She froze in place and was about to move back when a small, but insistent voice goaded her on. She reached out for his hand, which was resting on his thigh, but grabbed hold of his thigh instead when he brought his hand up toward the table a split second before she made her move. She was mortified. That had not been her intent at all, but now she was stuck and didn't know what to do.

Rafael's body stiffened and his eyes widened in surprise. A second later, he looked at the librarian, who was busy staring at a computer screen, and then leaned his head toward her ear and whispered, "We could get a detention for doing that kind of thing in here."

Alexis immediately pulled her hand away from Rafael's thigh, stood up, and grabbed her backpack. *What was I thinking?* she thought angrily. Lizzie was right and she was just a stupid girl who was foolish enough to think that he would respond in kind.

Rafael reached out for her arm as she turned to leave. She yanked it away from his grasp and hissed, "I don't need a lecture on school policy, thank you very much. I know the rules just as well as you do. My mother's the principal, remember?" She turned on her heel and headed toward the door, leaving him looking shocked and confused.

Alexis heard the door to the library open just after she had walked out. Rafael called after her, but she refused to turn around and acknowledge him. She quickened her pace as the sound of his footsteps came closer.

Within seconds, Rafael had caught up and stepped in front of her. He looked her directly in the eye and said, "Will you please stop and tell me what is wrong?"

"This," she said as she pointed from him to her, "is not working for me."

"What is wrong with the way things are?"

Alexis gasped. "Are you really that clueless?" she asked a little too loudly. She sensed that her actions were drawing the attention of other students but she was too upset to care. "You think I don't know what's going on, that I don't see what you're doing. I'm not stupid, you know. Lizzie warned…"

"Who is Lizzie?"

"Never mind," Alexis hastily replied. She wasn't about to rat out her friend to him. "There's nothing more to say. Please get out of my way."

At first, Rafael was at a complete loss for words, but when she tried to step around him, he said, "Just let me get my things in the library. Maybe we could go somewhere and…"

"I'm not going anywhere with you right now," she cut in.

"We need to talk," he said with a hint of frustration in his voice. "I cannot make things better if you refuse tell me what is wrong."

Alexis was trying to think of a way to escape when she spotted Jake walking toward the student parking lot. She ran past Rafael before he could stop her and sprinted in Jake's direction as she shouted out his name. Jake stopped and turned with a bemused look on his face as he watched Alexis racing toward him with Rafael following close behind.

The minute Alexis caught up with Jake, she asked him, "Could you please tell Rafael that I'll be getting a ride home with you today?"

Before Jake could answer, she saw that Rafael was once again standing next to her. She ignored him as her eyes pleaded with Jake to deliver her from this mess.

Jake looked from Rafael to Alexis and then back again. He pressed his lips together and said, "I got her man. No worries."

Alexis turned to Rafael and said, "Please just go. I can't do this right now."

At first, Rafael just stood there and stared at her. He looked as though he couldn't believe what was happening and didn't know what to do next. After a few more tense moments, he lowered his head and walked away.

After Rafael had gone, Alexis turned to Jake and said, "Thanks."

"No problem," he said. "First big fight, eh? I guess it had to happen sometime."

"He's not my boyfriend," she said, feeling the need to make the clarification. "Why would you think that?"

"Uh…let me think. Maybe it's because you guys are always together and, oh, that he nearly ripped Mateo's head off over you."

"But you've never seen us…"

"I thought you guys were just keeping things on the down low. Students aren't exactly allowed to show PDA on campus and I don't think either of you are the type to make out in front of people."

"He acts the same way off campus, too."

"Maybe it's a cultural thing," Jake offered.

Alexis shook her head. She had already considered that possibility. "I doubt it. Our relationship is nothing like yours and Tessa's."

"Every relationship's different Alexis," he interrupted. "Besides, Tessa and I have known each other since kindergarten."

"At least you know she loves you. She probably tells you that every day."

"How do you know that Rafael doesn't feel the same way about you? Some people just aren't good at saying 'I love you.' But that doesn't mean that they don't. Then there are people who say 'I love you' to someone at the drop of a hat and don't really mean it." Jake scratched his head a moment, adding, "I would look at what he does more than what he says. From what I can see, I think he cares about you a lot."

Alexis sighed. "I really screwed things up, didn't I?"

Jake put his hand on her shoulder and said, "It'll be okay. You just gotta work it out with him, you know."

At that moment, Alexis remembered her conversation with Lizzie and decided that now was as good a time as any to ask for Jake's help with Lizzie's other suggestion. "Umm, Jake. You're good with computers right?"

"Yeah," Jake said. "Tessa doesn't call me a geek for nothing."

"Do you know much about…hacking?"

"I know that it's illegal and that you can get into a lot of trouble for it," he replied, eyeing her suspiciously. "Why are you asking?"

Based on Jake's initial response, Alexis decided to take a different approach. "Hypothetically, would you be able to show someone how to monitor somebody else's phone or computer?"

"Sure, there are all sorts of programs out there that do that kind of stuff."

"Do *you* have access to those kinds of programs?" Alexis asked hopefully.

"Sure I do. You know my dad's a cyber-security specialist. We talk about that stuff all the time."

"Would you be able to show *me* how to do it?"

"Who are you trying to snoop on? And why?"

From the look on Jake's face, Alexis knew that there was no way he would help her if she didn't level with him to some extent. Although it briefly crossed her mind to conceal her true intentions, she decided to tell him just as much of the truth as she needed to in order to secure his assistance.

"It's Rafael. I'm worried that he might not be what he seems."

"What? No way!"

"Jake, just listen…"

"Where in the heck did you get that idea?" For a moment, Jake looked like he had been caught totally off guard by her comment, but after a light bulb seemed go off in his head, his face suddenly looked grim. He asked her, "Has he been mistreating you?"

Alexis shook her head. "No, not at all. In fact, I have the opposite problem. He's too respectful of my personal space. It's just that I've heard things about him. Getting into his phone or computer might help me figure out if the things that I've heard are really true, but I can't do that without your help."

"Why don't you just talk to him? He doesn't seem like the kind of guy that has anything to hide."

"I can't do that. I just can't…So will you help me or not?"

"I don't know. I gotta think about it, but if I do, this little project is going to be something only you and I know about. Tessa would kill me if she found out."

CHAPTER 10—RETURN OF THE SON

Alexis' eyes widened with curiosity as soon as she saw her Aunt Cora Perez's car parked in the driveway. But it was the sight of her father's car parked alongside it that sent her heart racing. After thanking Jake for the ride home, she hurried toward the front door.

Her Filipino grandmother, who she called Nanang, greeted her warmly when she opened the door and walked in. Nanang cradled Alexis' face in her hands and said in Tagalog, "*Kumusta ka apo ko?*" How are you, my grandchild?

"*Mabuti na ako,*" Alexis replied. I'm fine. "*Na gagalak akong makita ka. Maganda ka parin katulad ng dati.*" It's good to see you. You look as beautiful as ever.

Nanang beamed. "You, apo ko, are the beautiful one."

Alexis smiled back at Nanang and then looked at Aunt Cora, who was standing nearby. She called out to her aunt and asked, "So, what's the occasion? I wasn't expecting to see you here today."

Her aunt gave her a sly smile and motioned for her to go toward the kitchen. She said, "Everyone's in there. Tessa is picking up Joey from soccer practice. They should be here soon."

The smell of food sizzling in frying pans filled the air as she walked toward the kitchen while the sound of her family members' animated voices filled her ears. She was just about to turn into the kitchen from the hallway when she ran into her father. She let out a startled squeal and leapt into his arms. When she stepped back to take a look at him, she thought that he seemed tired and worn-out, even though she knew he was doing his best to put up a cheerful front.

"Why didn't you tell us you were coming home today?" Alexis asked excitedly.

"I didn't want to get you and your mom's hopes up until *we* had actually arrived," Eric replied.

Alexis' eyes suddenly glistened with tears when she saw her older brother, Jeremy, sitting on a bar stool at the kitchen island. He was finally home.

"He's been waiting for you," Eric said, nudging her forward.

As Alexis approached Jeremy, she thought that he looked like a mere shadow of his former self. He was sitting with his shoulders slumped forward and appeared to be leaning on his elbows in order to steady himself. He looked tired and gaunt, like a toothpick that could be split in two with the slightest application of pressure, and his skin looked sallow.

Alexis willed herself not to break down as she put her arms around him and leaned her head against his shoulder. Jeremy gently patted her hands as he turned to her and smiled. Despite what he had been through, she was amazed to see the degree of warmth, love, and contentment that still radiated from every fiber of his being. She was relieved to see that that part of him hadn't been lost in the jungles of the Philippines.

Jeremy braced himself with one hand on the island and the other on the back of his bar stool as he tried to stand up and face her. She felt his bones as she put her arms around his waist to help him stay steady on his feet.

"I'm going to see the doctor tomorrow," Jeremy said in an obvious effort to allay the concern he must have seen in her eyes. "I'm just a little tired. It was a long flight."

Alexis was about to open her mouth to speak when their father walked up to them and said, "I hope you're hungry. I think Mom, Cora, and Nanang made enough food for a town fiesta."

Her eyes scanned the kitchen, which was filled with a wide assortment of traditional Filipino main dishes on countertops or cooking in frying pans while desserts on platters sat on top of the island. She smiled when she saw her uncle, Arturo "Turing" Perez, a short and stocky, round-faced man, licking his fingers while happily sampling bite-sized portions of rice cakes called Bibingka and Sapin-Sapin.

A minute later, Tessa walked in with her younger brother, Joey, a gregarious and animated boy of fourteen. While reaching for a piece of Sapin-Sapin, Joey used a word in Tagalog meaning older female cousin as he said to Alexis, "Hey, *Ate*, I heard that your boyfriend nearly beat the crap out of Mateo on Friday."

Before Alexis could respond, Jeremy said, "Whoa…What boyfriend?" Alexis gave Joey a sidelong glance. "And who is Mateo?"

Joey happily filled Jeremy in. "I think his name is Rafael, right?" he said as he turned to Tessa for confirmation. After his sister nodded, Joey added, "I've seen him at my dojo. He trains with Akira Shigata and two other guys."

Alexis' ears perked up. "Who's Akira Shigata?" she asked.

"He's just the world champion in karate for his age group. I almost peed in my pants when I saw him at school the other day. His uncle, Mr. Kawamura, owns the dojo I go to," Joey said as he opened a can of soda. "They usually come in at the end of the day when the rest of us are leaving. One time when I forgot my backpack at the dojo, I went back and got to see them fight each other. Rafael and Akira were standing just a few feet apart. I nearly flipped out when I saw that they had short swords in their hands. When one of the other guys gave the signal, they went after each other. I thought that Akira would take him down for sure."

"So what happened?" Jeremy asked.

"Rafael disarmed and pinned Akira down in no time flat. I couldn't believe it." Given the way he'd handled Mateo, she wasn't surprised to hear what he had done.

"How often do you see them there?" Alexis asked.

"I see him come in at least three or four times a week. Another thing I noticed was that the other three guys called Rafael 'Arquero' and acted like he was their leader." He asked Jeremy, "Doesn't that mean 'Archer' in Spanish?"

Jeremy nodded. "Let's get back to Rafael and Mateo…Who is Mateo? And what happened between the two of them?"

"Mateo's a bully," Joey said as he took another bite of his dessert. "I heard that he was all set to mess Tobey up when Alexis got in the way. Rafael got there just when the shit was going to hit the fan and scared the crap out of Mateo. I bet he could have ripped Mateo apart if he'd wanted to." He turned to Alexis and said, "Don't worry though. Nobody's going to rat him out. It's all on the down low."

Not anymore, Alexis thought. "Then how do you know about it?" she asked.

"Everyone in school knows what happened. It's become like an urban legend."

Oh, great! Alexis knew that once she and Jeremy were alone that she would have some serious explaining to do in order to set the record straight on Rafael.

"Hey," Joey asked Alexis, "do you think you could ask Rafael if he could show me some of his maneuvers sometime? I heard he disabled Mateo in like one move."

"He sounds an awful lot like Superman to me," Jeremy said with a wink and a smile at Alexis.

A moment later, Eric, who had been helping Lisa bring the main dishes into the dining room, again came up to them with two bowls filled with rice balls in coconut milk and said, "Does anyone want some Bilo-Bilo?"

Joey reached out for one of the bowls in Eric's hand and said, "I've always wondered why so many Filipino desserts repeat the same word twice." Tessa shrugged her shoulders as she took the other bowl and put a spoonful of Bilo-Bilo in her mouth. After she swallowed, she said, "You hear that with Filipino names too."

"It has something to do with the way the Filipino language was constructed," Eric chimed in from behind them as he reached for some glasses in the cabinet.

Jeremy added, "I remember one time when Uncle Turing asked my teacher, Mrs. Garcia, if she wanted some Puto at a party." Tessa nearly spit out her food while the others laughed.

"Hey, doesn't that mean whore in Spanish?" Joey asked.

Tessa nodded as Jeremy replied, "And it also just happens to be a tasty Filipino dessert too."

"Your Uncle Turing is an idiot," Nanang said as she eyed Uncle Turing, who was standing by the refrigerator next to his wife, Aunt Cora, and stuffing another piece of Bibingka in his mouth. Seconds later, Lisa walked up and scolded them all for eating dessert before dinner and then shooed them out of the kitchen.

Alexis' stomach began to growl as she sat down by Tessa at the dining room table, which was filled with platters full of Lumpia (egg rolls filled with vegetables and meat), fried rice, Pancit Palabok (a noodle dish), Pork Adobo (a vinegary stew), Pan de Sal (sweetbread), and salad. She smiled to herself when she saw her mother slap her father's hand away from the serving spoon for the Pancit as she walked by and said, "We need to say grace first." *Finally,* she thought, *we're all together and safe.*

Once her parents had taken their seats at either end of the table, Lisa asked Jeremy to lead them in prayer. After they had all made the sign of the cross, bowed their heads, and folded their hands together, her brother said, "Bless us O Lord, and these Thy gifts, which we are about to receive, from Thy bounty, through Christ, Our Lord. Amen."

Everyone dug in. Uncle Turing was already going for seconds when Aunt Cora scolded him for eating too much, too quickly. The mood at the table was upbeat until Uncle Turing insisted on hearing a blow-by-blow account of what had happened to Jeremy in the Philippines. Her family hung on every word as Jeremy told them about a small village near Mt. Apo, on the island of Mindanao, where he had been sent in order to help its inhabitants prepare for a typhoon that was set to devastate the area.

"I helped bring in supplies, set up shelters, and evacuated the old and the sick from the area. I was working with a nun, Sister Nora, who told me that there had been a recent outbreak of malaria among the local population."

"When did you suspect you were getting sick?" Aunt Cora asked.

"I remember waking up one day and feeling really cold. I had been working non-stop for days so I thought it was just fatigue and the weather. I was told that I passed out in a field while unloading first aid supplies. I don't remember much after that."

Uncle Turing looked at Eric and asked, "Did you have trouble getting to him?"

"Flooding made the roads to the village nearly impassable, but a local priest, Father Jorge Balio, offered to take me there. We used a car and took a boat as far as we could and then walked the rest of the way. By the time we got to the village, Jeremy was already on the mend, but we couldn't risk staying there since medical supplies were running low and the weather forecasters were predicting more rain."

Eric paused a moment to take a sip of water and then said, "We were getting close to Davao City when one of those small buses you call a *jeepney* nearly hit us. I lost control of the car and it skidded toward a river that ran parallel to the road. I got out first. Father Balio pushed Jeremy out of the car while I pulled from the outside. I had just laid Jeremy on the ground when the car started sinking into the river. I tried to reach for Father Balio before the car sank but the current was too strong. It swept him and the car away. There was nothing I could do…" His voice trailed off as tears filled his eyes.

Everyone sat in stunned silence as they tried to digest what they had heard. Eric cleared his throat and continued, "Not long after, I flagged down a young couple who were driving by and they gave us a ride to Davao City. We contacted the local authorities and told them about what had happened to Father Balio, but we never heard anything more. We caught the earliest flight we could get to Manila. The doctors at the University of Santo Tomas ran a series of tests to make sure that Jeremy was well enough to travel before I booked us a flight home."

Nanang, who was sitting next to Jeremy, patted his hand and said, "We must thank God that you and your father made it home safely." The others at the table nodded their heads in agreement.

Alexis, on the other hand, didn't think there was much to be thankful for, especially since her brother and father had barely escaped with their lives and still seemed to be suffering from the aftereffects of their ordeal.

Not wanting to dwell on what had happened to them, Alexis tried to change the subject by asking her brother, "So what do you think you'll do now?"

Jeremy paused to consider her question and then said, "I went to the Philippines because I needed to think things through. It's funny, but as bad as things got over there, I never felt more at peace with myself then when I was ministering to those villagers. It made me realize what my true vocation in this life needs to be."

"What are you saying?" Alexis asked, even though she was almost certain what his answer was going to be.

Jeremy looked at each of his parents and then said, "With your blessing, I've decided that I'd like to become a priest."

A roar of approval erupted from the table. Eric smiled and nodded yes while Lisa, who was sitting next to Jeremy, reached out, grabbed hold of his hand, and gave it a squeeze. Alexis, on the other hand, couldn't believe what she was hearing. Given all the things that had happened to her brother and father, Jeremy's announcement was almost more than she could bear.

After the initial shock had passed, Alexis blurted out, "You can't be serious. How can you even think about becoming a priest after what you've been through?"

A deathly silence filled the room as all eyes turned to her.

"Anak ko, why are you talking to your kuya like that?" Lisa asked.

Alexis replied angrily, "Somebody has to knock some sense into him. He's throwing his life away, and for what? He went to the Philippines to serve God and it nearly killed both him and Dad. Am I the only one who sees that?"

"Alexis," Eric said sternly, "now is neither the time nor the place to be having this conversation. Your brother has been through a lot. So have I. The last thing we need right now is for you to be criticizing him after he's just told us about the most important decision he's going to make in his life."

Alexis shook her head at Eric and said, "I'm not attacking him. I'm trying to save his life." She turned to Jeremy and said, "Kuya, please don't do it."

The look on Jeremy's face told Alexis that her words had hurt him deeply. As she looked around the table, she realized that no one else seemed to share her point of view. Knowing that the only thing that she had succeeded in doing was to alienate herself from everyone in the room, she stood up and asked her father if she could be excused. As soon as Eric nodded, she ran upstairs, slammed the door to her bedroom, and flung herself onto the bed.

A few minutes later, Alexis heard a knock on the door.

"Go away," Alexis said.

"Can I come in for a minute?" Jeremy asked from the other side of the door.

Alexis got up slowly, walked to the door, and let her brother in. Jeremy took a seat on the edge of the bed while she lay back down and buried her face in a pillow. She felt awful and knew that nothing she could say now would make up for the pain she'd caused him, but she also knew that he loved her unconditionally and would not hold it against her.

She spoke first. "I'm sorry. I didn't mean to hurt your feelings."

"I know you meant well. No offense taken," Jeremy replied as he patted her leg. Alexis sat up next to her brother.

"Is that why you broke up with Mia before you left for the Philippines? Were you thinking about it even then?"

Jeremy looked like his mind had drifted elsewhere as he leaned forward, placed his elbows on his knees and rested his chin in his hands. "It's not fair to keep someone hanging on when the relationship is not going to go anywhere…She deserved better than that." He stood up and walked over to her bedroom window, adding "I've felt the call for a while now. It just took going to the Philippines to get me to make a decision."

"I'm glad you're home, kuya. Things weren't the same around here when you were gone."

"You mean you don't enjoy being queen of the castle? No one here to fight with over the bathroom or the T.V.?"

Alexis shook her head. "For all the good *that* ever did. You always made sure I knew who was in charge. I've just missed having you to talk to. Nobody understands me like you and…"

"Avery," they said simultaneously.

"I was there when she died," Alexis said. In an instant, she was transported to the afternoon when she got a frantic call from Avery, who had asked her to come and meet her. "Avery was crying and looked really freaked out when I met up with her at Veterans Park. You know, the one off East Palomar? When I asked if Bobby had done something to her, she got hysterical and started saying crazy things."

"What kind of things did she say?"

"She was babbling mostly. Here and there, it sounded like she was trying to warn me about something. I grabbed the car keys out of her hand, but she took them right back and then ran to her car and drove off. I got into my car and tried to follow her, but she was driving too fast down Telegraph Canyon Road. I sped up to catch her. It all happened so fast…"

Jeremy sat back down beside her and called her by a pet name meaning little girl in Tagalog as he said, "Don't beat yourself up about it, *Neneng*. You did what you could."

"Did I? She's dead, kuya. It was my car that knocked hers off the road."

"Are your therapy sessions helping?" he asked.

Alexis shook her head. "It's been a huge waste of time and money. I told Mom and Dad that I want to stop, but they won't listen to me."

"What about Father Jim? Have you thought about going for some spiritual counseling, too?"

Alexis sighed. "God doesn't hear me. And when I pray, I feel…nothing."

"Everyone has those moments. It doesn't necessarily mean that God isn't there or that He doesn't care about you. He loves each one of us more than we can possibly imagine."

"Then where is He?" Alexis asked with mounting frustration. "How exactly do I find Him?"

"He is everywhere and works through the people in our lives. Your problem may be that you're trying to look for Him through too narrow a filter."

Alexis remembered that Father Bernal had said similar things to her when he had come over to the house for dinner a couple of weeks ago. "I've heard that before."

"Great minds think alike," Jeremy joked. "I also think that each one of us is called to bring the Gospel to life by the way we choose to live and the choices we make. If you're going to follow Jesus, it means that you're going to have to pick up His cross, but there are consequences for doing that, especially in this world."

As she listened to her brother speak, she couldn't help but think that he already sounded like a priest. To her, he was also like a confessor. She had always trusted him to keep their conversations in strictest confidence. She also valued his opinion. With that in mind, she decided to bend his ear about Rafael.

"Kuya, do you remember the guy that Joey mentioned earlier?"

Jeremy nodded and said, "How could I forget? It's not every day that you hear that your little sister is dating a superhero."

She frowned. "Rafael and I aren't dating," she said for the second time that day. "He's been a great friend, but I think I might have screwed things up with him."

Jeremy ruffled her hair and said, "Then you should do whatever it takes to make things right."

Alexis shook her head. "You've heard of the saying, 'It's easier said than done,' right? How do you begin to say sorry to someone after you've acted like a complete idiot in front of them for no reason?"

"What did you do exactly?" Jeremy asked. Alexis felt her face flush as she recalled her botched efforts to seduce Rafael. She buried her face in her hands. He looked at her and said, "It's that bad, huh?"

She took a deep breath. "It's just that I really like him. I wanted to see if he felt the same way about me. So when I met him in the library, I sat next to him rather than across from him like I usually do."

"That doesn't sound bad."

"It gets worse," Alexis said. "Then, when I was sure the librarian wasn't looking, I put my hand on his thigh...It *was* an accident! I was reaching for his hand and he moved it at the last minute, and before I knew it..." She put her face in her hands once again.

"You what?" Jeremy exclaimed. "What did he do?"

Alexis looked up at her brother and said, "He leaned toward me and whispered that we'd get detention for that, so I got embarrassed…and mad at myself, more than anything else…I just got up and ran away."

Jeremy shook his head and then started to…laugh. Alexis was surprised and slightly offended by his reaction.

"It's not funny."

"Neneng, did it ever occur to you that he might have been teasing you when he said that?" Alexis shook her head. "So what happened next?"

"He ran after me. He tried to get me to stop and talk to him, but I pushed him away. And now, I have no idea what to say to him the next time I see him."

"Why don't you just start with 'I'm sorry' and go from there. I bet you anything he'd be willing to forgive and forget."

Alexis nodded her head, hoping her brother was right. She put her hand on his shoulder and said, "You should get some rest. You look like hell."

Jeremy laughed and said, "I feel like hell." He gave his sister a hug, walked to the door, and then turned to her and said, "Love you, Neneng."

"Love you, too, kuya," Alexis replied with a smile.

CHAPTER 11—HOMECOMING

Alexis' palms were sweaty and her heart was pounding in her chest as she paced back and forth in the girls' bathroom, trying to think of what she was going to say to Rafael. When she finally ventured out, she was disappointed to find that he wasn't in any of the usual places. She swung by the chapel and their theology class before heading to the courtyard where she had the misfortune of running into Anita instead.

Anita approached her with a smirk and a glint in her eyes. She handed Alexis a flyer with a picture of intertwining masks on it, advertising the upcoming homecoming dance. The theme was *A Night at the Masquerade*. As Alexis looked at it, a vision of being twirled around on the dance floor by Rafael flashed through her mind and made her smile. However, the sound of Anita's sickly sweet voice brought her back down to Earth with a thud.

"I heard that you had a falling out with Rafael yesterday," Anita said.

Alexis wanted to roll the flyer into a wad and chuck it at her head but was determined not to give Anita the satisfaction of knowing that she'd gotten her goat.

"Really? Where did you hear that?" Alexis asked, feigning indifference. "Your sources must be faulty. We're actually doing just fine, thank you very much."

"That's not what I heard…Anyway, I guess this means that at least you won't be going to the dance with him, will you?" Alexis felt her blood pressure begin to rise while Anita grinned at her like a Cheshire cat. "I have to admit that even I thought you had him completely snagged, but I knew you wouldn't be able to fool him for long. Girls like you just don't belong with guys like him."

"And you do?" Alexis snapped.

"We'll see, won't we?" Anita replied with a girlish laugh. The sudden urge to slap that pretty little face of hers was nearly too much for Alexis to resist.

Anita winked and waved at Alexis before walking away and moving toward a group of students standing nearby. The sight of that girl smiling and turning on the phony charm as she handed out more flyers made Alexis feel sick.

Moments later, Tessa tapped her on the shoulder and said, "What did she want?"

"Rafael," Alexis said matter-of-factly. "What else? She actually thinks that he'll ask her to go to the homecoming dance."

Tessa replied, "You've got to be kidding me, right? That's never going to happen."

"And why is that?"

"Because Rafael's got taste and a functioning brain."

"I guess we'll just have to wait and see," Alexis replied.

"Don't be such a pessimist," Tessa said as she put her hand on her cousin's shoulder. "By the way, Jake told me what happened between you and Rafael yesterday. Is there anything I can do to help?"

Alexis shook her head. "Only if you can wave a magic wand and erase every stupid thing I did and said to him."

Despite Tessa's reassurances, there was a part of her that worried that her misstep had given Anita the opening that she was looking for to swoop in and steal Rafael away from her.

Alexis slid into an empty seat in the classroom just as the final warning bell rang. She was surprised to find that Rafael wasn't there. When Mr. Marquez turned his back to the class to write something on the board, she snatched her cell phone out of her backpack and checked for messages. She frowned when she saw that there were no messages or texts from him. He didn't show up for their next class either. To top it off, Anita and her friends once again made her life a living hell during gym class. By lunchtime, all she wanted to do was crawl under a rock and die.

Alexis found her friends, minus Rafael, sitting on a grassy area near the cafeteria benches. Manuel and Danny were happily devouring their sandwiches while chatting about the San Diego Chargers' chances of getting into the playoffs. Tobey and Jake, on the other hand, were engaging in an intense debate about the future of cyber technology. Tessa looked like she was tuning them all out as she focused her attention on the fashion magazine she was flipping through. She motioned for Alexis to sit down beside her as soon as she saw her cousin heading toward them.

Alexis took out a tuna sandwich, banana, and bottled water from her backpack and set them down in front of her. After she unwrapped her sandwich, it occurred to her that she had absolutely no desire to eat. Her stomach was in knots and her chaotic mind was refusing to settle down.

"Why so glum?" Manuel asked Alexis as he took another huge bite of his sandwich. "Trouble in paradise?"

"Leave her alone," Tessa replied curtly. "Can't you see that she's already upset?"

Alexis wrapped up her food and put it in her backpack and then picked up her bottled water and took a sip. She looked down at her fingers and realized that she had once again gnawed her nails down to the quick. *Not good.*

"Have you seen Rafael today?" Tessa asked Tobey, who was taking out an apple from his backpack.

Tobey shook his head. "No, not today."

Tessa turned to Alexis and said, "Why don't you give him a call?"

"You know I can't do that. Not after what I said to him yesterday."

Tessa frowned slightly and then held out her hand to Alexis as she said, "Give me your cell phone."

"Why?" Alexis asked.

"Just give it to me." Despite her misgivings, Alexis reluctantly handed it over to her cousin.

"What are you doing?" Alexis asked as Tessa accessed the keypad on her phone and started typing.

"What you should be doing," Tessa replied as she clicked the send button.

Alexis snatched the phone away from her cousin. "What did you say to him?"

"Calm down, Cuz. I just said 'How are you?' That's it," she replied.

"You shouldn't have done that."

"What else was I going to do, sit here and watch you have a pity party because you don't have the courage to face him? No thank you. You obviously have some stuff that you need to work out with him and the sooner you do it, the better."

Alexis looked nervously at her cell phone. It remained maddeningly silent in the minutes that followed. After she had checked her messages for what felt like the fiftieth time, she glanced at Tobey and immediately sensed that something was wrong. He had broken off his conversation with Jake and was staring with a troubled expression on his face at something behind her. Curious, she was about to turn her head in that same direction when Tobey cried out, "Alexis, don't."

At about the same moment she heard Danny exclaim, "Uh oh," while Manuel shook his head. Before anyone could stop her, she spun around and saw Rafael with Anita.

Tessa grabbed her arm and said, "There must be some perfectly logical explanation for why he's talking to her. You can't just assume the worst."

Alexis' mind had stopped working. Her body became rigid as the voices in her head screamed, "You screwed up. This is all your fault." Just then, Anita looked over at her and smiled. Alexis' shoulders started to heave up and down as she battled the urge to cry.

Only Tessa's firm grip on her arm kept her from jumping up and running away as she watched Anita shamelessly flirt with Rafael right in front of her eyes. She tried to jerk away, but Tessa refused to let go of her arm and begged her to wait and see what Rafael had to say.

Under his breath, Manuel said, "This could get ugly," when Rafael started toward them. Danny asked aloud, to no one in particular, "Should we go?"

Tobey, in turn, looked at Jake, who shrugged his shoulders.

Rafael stopped in front of Tobey, who looked up at him and asked, "Hey, man, where were you this morning?"

Rafael sat down and said, "There were a few things I needed to take care of."

"Are you sick?" Tobey asked.

Rafael shook his head and then looked directly Alexis. She quickly averted her eyes from his face.

Tobey offered Rafael an apple, which he politely refused. He then said to Rafael, "I saw you talking to Anita. What was that about?"

"Nothing," he replied. "She was just talking to me about the homecoming dance."

The tension amongst the group spiked immediately as every head turned in Rafael's direction. Tobey pressed on. "Did she ask you to go with her?"

Rafael looked slightly miffed by the question. "Not alone. She mentioned going with a group of people."

Tobey glanced at Alexis to see if she wanted him to go on. She gave her friend an almost imperceptible nod and noticed, out of the corner of her eye, that Rafael's eyes were trained on her face. She pretended to search for something in her backpack.

"What did you say?"

"I thanked her for offering…but I said no."

Alexis immediately looked up and saw the astonished looks on all her friends' faces. Manuel blurted out, "Why?"

"Because I want to go with someone else."

Tessa nudged Alexis in the arm as the slightest trace of a smile began to form on her face. When she finally drew up the courage to look at Rafael, his expression floored her. He was looking at her expectantly, as if awaiting some sign that things were okay between them. She also detected an undertone of longing and desire in his eyes that caused her face to turn a deep shade of crimson.

"That's it," Manuel cried out as he packed his lunch away and got up. He motioned to Danny and Tobey and said, "Let's get out of here."

"Where are we going?" Danny asked. "I haven't even finished my lunch yet."

"The chapel," Manuel replied as he grabbed Danny's arm and started pulling him up. "We need to pray and repent our sins."

"Right now?" Tobey asked. "I just went to confession."

"And when did you do that?" Manuel asked.

"What is this? The Inquisition?? Yesterday," Tobey replied irritably.

Manuel pointed to his temple and said, "Do you have any idea how many times you've probably sinned in your mind since then? Hey, Danny, how many seconds are in a minute?"

"Sixty," he replied.

"Exactly," Manuel said. "And you've probably had a sinful thought for every one of those sixty seconds."

"Speak for yourself," Tobey said.

"I think he's right, man," Danny chimed in.

"Just get up," Manuel ordered. Tobey and Danny reluctantly complied.

"You're going in the wrong direction," Tessa offered. "The chapel's that way."

"We knew that," Manuel replied. Without skipping a beat, he turned and started to walk in the other direction with Tobey and Danny following morosely behind.

Following suit, Tessa exclaimed, "Jeez, look at the time. Jake, we've gotta go to the library," as she motioned for Jake to get up and follow her.

"Why now?"

"We have that project to do, remember?" Tessa said impatiently.

Jake looked clueless. Tessa glared at him. He got up.

Alexis put her hand on Tessa's shoulder as they both stood up and whispered in her cousin's ear, "Don't you dare leave," as she pulled Tessa a few steps away from Jake and Rafael.

Alexis overheard Rafael ask Jake, "Are American girls always like this?"

"No, it's just those two."

Despite Alexis' last minute pleas, Tessa insisted that she and Jake had to go. Knowing that any further attempt to change her cousin's mind would be futile, she accepted the inevitable and watched helplessly as Tessa and Jake left her alone with Rafael.

Alexis was at a complete loss as to what to do next. When she turned to face Rafael, he smiled at her tentatively. At first, they just looked at each other, saying nothing. There was so much she wanted to tell him. If only she could find the right words. As the seconds passed, the need to say something…anything…built up inside her until she felt like she was going to burst if she kept silent any longer.

"I'm sorry," they said to each other simultaneously.

"Why are you sorry?" Alexis asked.

"Because I hurt your feelings," Rafael replied. "Why are you sorry?"

"Because I'm an idiot," she blurted out.

She saw Rafael try to hide a smile as he shook his head. "That's not true at all."

Alexis cleared her throat and rolled her shoulders back as she said, "Was there something you wanted to talk to me about?"

Rafael nodded and moved closer. Her pulse started to race as he held out his right hand to her. She offered him her left hand. The warmth of his palms pressing against hers was making her feel light-headed and giddy. His eyes remained firmly fixed on her face as he asked her, "Would you do me the great honor of going to the homecoming dance with me?"

"I'd love to go with you," she said, beaming.

Rafael nodded as he gave Alexis' hand a quick squeeze. When he let go of her hand, she noticed that his usually stoic face had broken into a broad smile. She felt like her heart was going to burst out of her chest at any moment. However, the idyllic moment was soon interrupted by the sound of his growling stomach. She started to laugh as his face reddened with embarrassment.

He took a step back and said, "Look, I haven't eaten all day. Could you wait for me here while I go and buy something to eat at the Café?"

"Sure. I haven't eaten yet either."

"Would you like me to get something for you?"

Alexis shook her head and told him that she had brought her lunch to school. When he stepped away, she found that her appetite had come back with a vengeance as she tried to wrap her mind around everything that had just happened. Rafael had actually turned Anita down and asked *her* to go to the homecoming dance instead. Maybe he really *was* her boyfriend. That, in itself, was cause for celebration. More importantly, he hadn't held the library incident against her in any way. All in all, she had a lot to be thankful for. And, try as she might, she couldn't help but secretly hope that Anita had seen the whole thing.

The days leading up to the homecoming dance were a blur thanks to Tessa's nonstop plans and preparations. Alexis did her best to suppress the urge to groan as her cousin constantly pushed fashion magazines in front of her during lunchtime as if the future depended upon the pearls of wisdom that could be found within those pages. Tessa's endless droning about the latest trends was also driving her crazy. At one point, she tried to enlist the help of Rafael and Jake in the hope that one or both of them might rescue her but soon discovered that they had no interest whatsoever in incurring Tessa's wrath. She was on her own.

To make matters worse, Tessa insisted that Alexis' after school study sessions with Rafael be put on hold so that they could go to the local malls and boutiques in search of the *perfect* dress. While looking at the racks in one store, she was at first drawn to a hot pink backless dress, but put it back when she realized just how revealing it was. She did the same thing with a light blue cocktail dress which would have barely covered her upper thighs.

She quipped to Tessa, "I bet you two-thirds of these dresses are going to be off-limits for our dance." The school had posted strict guidelines for proper attire and warned that students who did not dress appropriately would be sent home. She pulled out a black dress with a plunging neckline from the rack, turned to Tessa, and said, "They would so kick me out if I showed up in this one."

"You can be trendy *and* tasteful," Tessa replied. "Those two things are not mutually exclusive."

After what seemed like days of endless searching, Alexis finally got Tessa's seal of approval on a short-sleeved white cocktail dress with lace embroidery. When the cashier gave her the receipt, she breathed a sigh of relief and headed out the door. She was tired and wanted to go home. Tessa, however, had other plans.

As they walked to the car, Tessa said, "Now all we need to do is get you some shoes and accessories. I know just the place! And don't forget, we have appointments for manicures and pedicures on the day of…."

Alexis sighed and found herself tuning her cousin's voice out as they walked to Tessa's car.

On the evening of the homecoming dance, Alexis stood in front of a full length mirror, admiring the handiwork of her cousin and mother. She almost didn't recognize herself. Her face was fully made-up, her nails were done, and her hair was perfectly styled. But more importantly, she looked radiant and content.

"You're an absolute vision," Lisa said as she stood behind her daughter. If her mother had any misgivings about Rafael taking her to the dance, she didn't let on.

"Your dad and brother are downstairs," Lisa added. "They're waiting to see your complete transformation."

"Can you do me a favor and ask them to please go easy on Rafael?" Alexis implored her mother. "I don't want them to scare him away before we've even gotten to the dance."

Lisa put her hands on Alexis' shoulders and said, "Don't worry. I'll make sure they're on their best behavior tonight. You just worry about having a good time."

Alexis turned around and gave her mother a hug. "Thanks for everything."

"You're very welcome," Lisa replied. After her mother left the room, Alexis checked herself one last time in the mirror and took a deep breath as she anticipated the evening that lay ahead of her.

As Alexis walked down the stairs, she saw Jeremy looking up at her from the bottom of the staircase. He took her hand as she stepped off the last stair and twirled her around. She smiled from ear to ear as he showered her with compliments.

"I'm looking forward to finally meeting this guy," Jeremy said. "I think you've been purposely keeping him from coming inside when he drops you off from school."

Alexis looked at him in mock surprise; Jeremy responded with a knowing look. She knew that he wasn't at all fooled by her half-hearted attempt to feign ignorance.

When the doorbell rang, Jeremy raced ahead of her to the door. She heard Lisa say to her brother from the living room, "Be nice, Jeremy."

He motioned for Alexis to stand back a few feet as he put his hand on the door knob and said, "I'll handle this."

"That's what I'm afraid of," she replied anxiously.

When Jeremy opened the door, Alexis saw Rafael dressed in a white dinner jacket with a black bowtie, slacks, and perfectly polished shoes. He took her breath away. He smiled at Alexis and then extended his hand to Jeremy and introduced himself. Jeremy invited him in and then excused himself to give them a moment alone together.

Rafael took an all-white wrist corsage of roses, freesia, and sheer ribbon from its florist's box, turned to Alexis, and said, "May I?" Alexis extended her left arm as he deftly placed it on her wrist.

Alexis smiled as she admired it and said, "It's so pretty. Thank you so much."

She walked over to the foyer table and picked up his matching boutonniere, consisting of a single white rose. As she lifted it to the lapel of his jacket, she said, "I promise I won't poke you."

"Don't worry. I trust you," Rafael said with a laugh.

"You really shouldn't," Alexis replied. Her fingers shook as she tried to pin the boutonniere to his lapel. She said, "I'm sorry. I guess I'm just a little nervous."

Rafael gently placed his hands on her wrists and said, "So am I. Is there anything I can do to help?"

Alexis shook her head. "No, I can do this."

As she pinned the boutonniere on him, he leaned forward and whispered in her ear, "You look beautiful tonight."

Alexis blushed and said, "Thanks."

Just then, she heard Jeremy clearing his throat from behind her. When she turned to look at her brother, he said with a grin, "The parental units are ready for you in the living room, cameras in hand." Rafael offered Alexis his arm, which she gladly accepted. As they walked by Jeremy, he patted Rafael's shoulder and said, "Good luck," and then winked at his sister.

Lisa was standing by the lit fireplace as Eric approached Rafael. Alexis moved toward the couch while Jeremy walked over to their mother. As Eric shook Rafael's hand, she thought she overheard her father quietly say to Rafael, "*Deus Tecum.*" May God be with you.

Alexis cocked her head slightly to the side as she glanced at her father and thought, *that's an odd way to greet your daughter's date.*

Rafael's response was equally baffling. "*In Aeternam.*" For eternity.

Catchphrases? she wondered. They were acting like members of some fraternity or secret society. *Is there a connection between my dad and Rafael? And how does that fit in with Lizzie's theory about Rafael being part of a religious cult?*

Several snapshots later, Eric motioned for Rafael to sit on the couch next to Alexis as he took the armchair opposite them. He leaned back in his seat and folded his hands in his lap. "I hope you've been enjoying your stay in Chula Vista so far."

Rafael nodded. "The weather and the amenities are amazing. I can see why so many people like to live here."

"Appearances can be deceiving," Eric replied. "Actually, I've been told that we might be in for some rough weather in the near future. Is that what you've heard?"

Lisa and Jeremy turned and looked at Rafael as he paused to consider Eric's question. Her mother took a seat in a chair beside her husband while Jeremy stood behind Lisa with his hands resting on the top of the chair.

"I have heard varying reports from a number of sources, but I think you may be right, sir."

Alexis noticed Lisa's grip on the arms of her chair suddenly tighten while Jeremy clearly looked upset. Only Eric seemed to be unfazed by Rafael's answer.

"What is your information based upon?" Eric asked.

Rafael replied, "My personal research, as well as accounts from *trusted sources,* which are in line with the prediction."

Eric took his glasses off and leaned forward in his seat. He seemed troubled as he said, "That's unfortunate."

To Alexis, the whole conversation between Rafael and her father was beyond cryptic. In fact, it sounded like they were speaking in some sort of code that only she had not been given the key to. At that moment, she vaguely remembered the odd conversation between her mother and Rafael that day in the kitchen. *What is going on?*

Seemingly eager to change the subject, Rafael turned to Jeremy and said, "I heard that congratulations are in order. Alexis tells me that you've decided to become a priest." He glanced at Eric, adding, "I am sure that there are many people who would be very interested to hear this news."

"The people that need to know already do," Eric said. "We have nothing to hide."

"I apologize if I misspoke," Rafael replied. "Father Bernal has told me of your family's contributions to the Church, which are well known and appreciated."

"There's no need to apologize. I may sometimes be overprotective when it comes to my children." Eric gazed at Alexis and then said to Rafael, "I've always thought of my daughter as a precious gift from God. As a father, it's important for me to know that she is with people who will love and take care of her. These aren't easy times for young people to be growing up in. There are so many wrong turns they can take, so many things that can lead them astray… "

"There is no need to worry, sir," Rafael replied. "She is safe with me."

"We're counting on that," Eric said in a matter of fact tone. He stood up and said, "It's getting late. You should be going."

Rafael rose from his seat and extended his hand to Eric. He said, "It was a pleasure to make your acquaintance, sir."

Just after Rafael, Alexis, and her father had walked out the door, she realized that she had left her white shawl hanging in the coat closet; she went back inside to get it. After retrieving her shawl and with her clutch purse in hand, she headed back toward the front door. Just as she put her hand on the doorknob, she overheard her father say to Rafael, "Take good care of my daughter."

"Of course, Mr. Neil. That is why I am here."

When Rafael and Alexis arrived at the homecoming dance, the gym was already buzzing with activity. Student government officers were greeting people, taking tickets, and handing out masks. Meanwhile, the administrative staff and parent volunteers did their best to be as unobtrusive as possible. The sound of idle chatter and loud music bombarded her ears as they walked through an arch and into the masquerade ball. The gym had been magically transformed into a beautiful ballroom, complete with faux columns, candelabra, and chandeliers. The lights in the gymnasium were slightly dimmed, but she could still clearly see tables along the sides of the room and a large open space in the middle. A stage had been set up for the disc jockey, who was already playing songs from his playlist. There were also several stations where people could get appetizers and drinks.

Alexis spotted Tessa, who was wearing a lavender chiffon overlay sheath dress, and sat down next to her. Jake arrived soon afterward with a plate full of appetizers. He quickly enlisted Rafael to help him get drinks for everyone.

A few minutes later, Manuel walked up in a light blue, 1970s style tuxedo with a ruffled shirt that would have made John Travolta proud. His date was a short, round-faced girl with a dour expression on her face. Danny and Tobey, who were wearing dress shirts, slacks, and ties, followed closely behind with their dates from a sister school, Our Lady of Peace.

Tessa took one look at Manuel and said, "You are not sitting at this table looking like that. No way."

Manuel gave her an incredulous look and sat down anyway. The others took the rest of the empty seats at the table.

After everyone had had their fill of drinks and appetizers, they hit the dance floor. They laid claim to a corner spot near their table and danced to remixes of the latest pop and R&B hits from Taylor Swift to Beyoncé. Alexis laughed as she caught the mortified expression on the face of Manuel's date as he tried to impress her with his spin on the latest dance moves. It even caught the attention of one of the administrators, who walked up to Manuel and politely warned him to tone it down. Alexis couldn't remember the last time she'd had this much fun.

They had all been dancing for some time when the DJ asked the crowd how everyone was doing. After the roar of approval subsided, he announced that it was time to slow things down. Danny, Tobey, and Manuel walked off the dance floor with their dates, insisting that they needed a break.

When the DJ started playing Justin Timberlake's *Not A Bad Thing,* Alexis' felt her pulse quicken as she watched Jake wrap his arms around Tessa. A moment later, Rafael tapped her on the shoulder. She slowly turned around. He placed his hand on her chin and tilted her face upwards. She felt her breath catch in her throat as she looked into his eyes. He placed one hand on her waist and pulled her close as he clasped her other hand. She prayed that he didn't feel her heart pounding in her chest as she laid her head on his shoulder. She closed her eyes and told herself to relax and just enjoy the moment. In the middle of the song, she opened her eyes and saw him staring down at her. Almost instinctively, she tilted her head slightly to the side as his lips slowly edged closer to hers.

Alexis was closing her eyes in anticipation of what was about to happen when she felt someone bump her from the back. She turned and saw one of Anita's sidekicks, Lea, standing there with her date. She looked at Alexis and offhandedly said, "Oh, sorry." It took all her self-control not to lash out at Lea. She noticed that Cecilia and

Anita, who were standing just a few feet away, were giggling to themselves as they looked in her direction. She was about to walk over to them when she heard Rafael whisper in her ear, "Is everything all right?"

"I'm fine," Alexis said as she tried to rein in her anger. Then, she added, "If it's okay with you, I think I need a break." He nodded and followed her off the dance floor.

Rafael's cell phone beeped as soon as they got to their seats. After checking his phone, he said to Alexis, "I am sorry, but I need to make a phone call. I will be right back."

He walked toward the arch near the entrance to the gymnasium with his cell phone in hand. Alexis looked down at her watch. It was nearly eleven o'clock. *Only one hour left and then the princess will turn back into the chambermaid.* Moments later, Tessa and Jake joined her at the table. She spoke with them for a few minutes before picking up her things and going to the restroom to freshen up. After being forced to stand in a tortuously slow line, she quickly reapplied some powder and lipstick before heading back to the gym.

Alexis immediately sensed that something was off the moment she stepped out of the restroom. She felt disoriented as she scanned the room for Rafael. The music seemed three times as loud and the sound of people's voices hurt her ears. She stumbled back but was caught by a pair of familiar hands.

Lizzie guided her to a nearby wall and said, "You look as green as my grandma's throw rug. Maybe you should go outside and get some air."

Alexis shook her head and said, "I can't do that. They won't let you back in if you leave."

"Well, you don't look like you're in any condition to stay here. Besides, I saw your date walk out the door a couple of minutes ago."

Why would he do that? Alexis wondered as all the sights and sounds in the room continued to overwhelm her heightened senses. She had to get out of there. She didn't bother to tell her friends since they all seemed to be having a good time on the dance floor. Besides, she reasoned, Rafael was already outside and was not the kind of person that would just leave her there.

"Maybe you're right," she said and walked out the door.

Alexis shivered as the cold night air whipped her hair about. She wrapped her shawl tightly around her shoulders and looked around. It only took a minute for her to find Rafael. He was facing the darkened school stadium as he stood alone in the middle of a large, grassy lawn. She called out his name, but he acted like he didn't hear her. She stayed close by as he headed toward the stadium and climbed over the fence. After taking a look around to make sure no one was watching, she dashed to the fence, took off her shoes, and climbed over, too. When she reached the entrance, she saw him walk down the stairs and take a seat in one of the midfield bleachers. She followed suit. He turned and looked up at her as he took off his dinner jacket and loosened his bowtie.

"What are you doing here?" she asked.

"You should not be here." Rafael's voice sounded different, almost menacing.

"Neither should you," Alexis said defensively. "You know we won't be able to get back into the dance." It occurred to her to turn and walk back up the stairs, but she decided to follow things through, since she had already come this far. Besides, where would she go? She sat down next to him, set her purse down, and stared out into the darkness, waiting for him to make the next move.

Unable to stand the silence between them any longer, Alexis asked, "Why did you leave the dance without me?"

"That is none of your business." His response and his tone unnerved her. He'd never spoken to her like that before.

"Fine," she said. Alexis stood up and turned to walk away when she felt Rafael's hands, which were as cold as ice, grip her arms like a vise and pull her back down.

He looked into her eyes and said, "We both know why you are here, don't we?"

"I don't know what you're talking about," she replied, feeling confused.

"But I think you do," he said as he wrapped his arms around her and slowly and sensuously began to kiss her neck and face. His hands sought and found the zipper to her dress. He started pulling it down as he whispered in her ear, "What do you want to do now, Alexis?"

Before she could answer, he pushed her down onto the cement bleacher and moved on top of her as he whispered, "Isn't this what you wanted from me?"

Alexis' eyes widened in surprise as he plunged his tongue into her mouth and roughly kissed her lips. Her instincts told her that something was terribly wrong and that she needed to push him off and get away as fast as she could. She had imagined that his lips would feel warm and that she would feel safe and secure in his arms. Instead, she felt assaulted. There was no gentleness at all in his touch. He was cold and demanding as he kissed and groped her body without any thought as to what she was thinking or feeling.

Her doubts and fears only increased with each passing minute. Still, it was not until he unfastened her bra and started to move his head downward that she finally pushed him away and begged him to stop. His body stiffened as he moved back. He looked at her like she had just slapped him in the face and almost spat, "You should *never* start what you are not prepared to finish."

Alexis shook her head as she sat up and said in a shaky voice, "It's not that I don't want to be with you...It's just..."

He stood up and looked down at her as he said, "Go home, Alexis."

"Please don't be mad," she pleaded.

Rafael put his hand under Alexis' chin and then moved his face to within inches of her own as he said, "Go home to your mommy and daddy. I don't have time to play with little girls like you." With that, he left her sitting alone as he bounded up the stairs.

Alexis was in shock. What happened to the boy who, only a few hours earlier, had promised her father that he would take care of her?

She started to shake violently as she emitted a strangled cry. She bent over and buried her head in her hands and began to weep as her heart shattered into a million pieces.

CHAPTER 12—MISUNDERSTANDINGS

Alexis sat on the bleachers, dazed and alone, as she replayed what had happened between her and Rafael over and over again in her mind. Although the cold night air should have chilled her to the bone, she made no attempt to cover herself. Instead, she rocked back and forth with her legs curled up and rested her chin on her knees.

Eventually, she brushed the hair away from her face, refastened her bra, then zipped up and straightened her crumpled dress. She used the edges of her shawl to wipe away her smeared makeup, picked up her purse, and then climbed back over the fence to retrieve her shoes. It wasn't long before Jake and Tessa found her wandering aimlessly on the senior lawn with shoes and shawl in hand. Tessa immediately began to rub Alexis' ice cold hands while Jake put his dinner jacket over her shoulders.

When Tessa asked her what had happened, Alexis shook her head and told her that she didn't want to talk about it. The look on Alexis' face also warned her cousin that now was not the time to press the matter further. Tessa complied, albeit reluctantly, with her cousin's wishes and asked no more questions as they walked to Jake's car.

After Jake unlocked the doors, he mentioned that Rafael had asked him to take her home. An emergency had come up that apparently required his immediate attention. Alexis nodded her head and stared blankly out the window. Although Jake and Tessa occasionally glanced in her direction as they drove, neither of them said anything more to her.

When they got to her house, Tessa told Alexis that she would call her in the morning to make sure that she was all right. They waited in the driveway until she walked inside and closed the door behind her. Alexis was relieved to find that everyone had already gone to bed. She took off her shoes and quietly headed upstairs. She didn't bother to turn on the light or change when she got to her room. Instead, she just pulled the covers over her head and let the darkness envelope her.

The next morning, Alexis lay in bed and stared up at the ceiling as she desperately tried to think of some rational explanation for the way Rafael had acted. She even questioned her own recollection of the night's events. She just couldn't wrap her brain around the notion that he actually had treated her the way he did, said the things he did, or left her there. She couldn't reconcile the selfish, demanding young man in the stadium with the kind and thoughtful person that she had come to know over the last few weeks; it just didn't make sense. Mindlessly, she changed out of her now rumpled dress and into a pair of sweats. She washed her face, hoping to rinse away the horror of the night before as well. The trauma to her psyche from last night left her feeling emotionally and physically exhausted.

When questioned, she told her family that she had a wonderful time at the dance. However, she ate little and spent much of the day locked in her room where, in her agitated state, she ripped off one or two of her acrylic nails and picked at the skin around her fingers until they bled. And when her brother tried to check on her, she quickly shooed him away, telling him that she needed to be left alone to do her homework. She also lied to Tessa when she called, insisting she was fine while at the same time reassuring her cousin that she would come to mass with her and sing with the youth choir that evening.

Tony had already started the rehearsal when Tessa and Alexis walked into church. He handed Alexis a music binder and asked, "It's your turn to cantor, right?"

She nodded and took it, even though she had no idea whether he was right or not. A minute later, Tony checked his watch and asked Jake if he knew where Rafael was. Alexis froze when she heard his name. When Jake shook his head, Tony informed the choir that he would play the guitar if Rafael didn't show up.

After Alexis went over her music, she looked toward the front doors of the church to see who would be saying the mass that evening. Father Bernal was dressed in green vestments as he waited in the vestibule with the altar servers and lector. Minutes later, Rafael hurried in through a side entrance of the church, opposite from where the choir sat, just as Father Bernal gave her the signal that it was time for mass to begin. She sat, immobilized, as Rafael quickly took his seat next to the piano and picked up his guitar. She overheard him apologize to Jake and Tony as he arranged his sheet music on the stand. Tessa tugged on her arm and said, "Hey, Cuz, Father Bernal's waiting for you."

Alexis slowly got up, walked over to the podium and turned to face the congregation. After inviting everyone to stand and sing the opening hymn, she looked at Jake and waited for her cue to begin singing. She briefly glanced at Rafael, whose eyes were on the sheet music in front of him. She told herself not to look in his direction unless she absolutely had to, as she didn't want to risk the possibility of breaking down in front of everyone. There was also a part of her that wanted to show Rafael that she was doing just fine even though that was the furthest thing from the truth.

Just after the homily, Tony reminded her that the song set for Presentation was going to be sung as a duet with Rafael on the guitar rather than as a congregational piece with the choir. She nodded and walked to the podium while Tony placed a microphone on a stand in front of Rafael.

When Rafael got the signal from Jake, he placed his fingers on the guitar and began to play. Alexis watched with rapt attention as his fingers caressed the strings. She admired the way he executed the music with such precision and feeling. They sang the refrain for a hymn based on a passage from the Book of John in unison the first time and in harmony thereafter. They alternated singing the verses. As their voices blended, she felt a connection to the music, to Rafael, and to God that made her wish that the song would never end. When it did, she sat down and felt more confused than ever.

Alexis gave Jake a hug during the giving and receiving of the sign of peace and was about to walk back to the podium when she saw Rafael extend his hand to her. She hesitated briefly, but then responded in kind.

He quickly grasped her hand in his and leaned toward her as he whispered, "Could I talk to you after mass?"

Alexis nodded then immediately withdrew her hand and returned to the podium for Jake's cue to sing.

As soon as the mass ended, Alexis closed her music binder and hurried toward the music room to drop it off with Tony. She felt an anxiety attack coming on at the prospect of having to face Rafael. She wasn't sure if she was ready to do that yet. However, her makeshift escape plan to exit the church without being seen was thwarted when she ran into him and Jake as they brought their sheet music and stands into the music room. Tessa walked in behind them.

When Tessa motioned for Alexis to come with her, Rafael turned to her cousin and said, "I can take her home."

Tessa pursed her lips as she glanced at Alexis, who slowly nodded her head. Her cousin reluctantly acquiesced to the offer. Still, Tessa looked wary as she slowly backed out of the room with Jake following on her heels.

Alexis' stomach was in knots. She stood by the door and waited for Rafael, who was talking to Tony about music for the Advent season. After he said good night to their choir director and a few of the other singers, he turned to Alexis, asked if she was ready to go, and walked with her to his car.

There was distinct chill in the air. Rafael offered to give Alexis his jacket but she politely declined. After he unlocked the door, he opened it for her before getting into the driver's seat. He started the engine, turned on the lights, and asked her if she had a preference as to what music she wanted to listen to on the way home. When she said no, he turned it on and set it to the Immaculate Heart radio station.

Rafael kept his eyes on the road and said little as he drove. The tension between them seemed to escalate in the silence. When he turned onto her street, she asked him to park in the dimly lit cul-de-sac rather than right in front of her house. She sat there and waited for him to say something after he had turned the engine off. Instead, he gripped the steering wheel and looked out the windshield. She thought that he was acting like he would have rather been anywhere else in the world but next to her. She decided to put him out of his misery and make a quick exit.

She had just turned toward the car door to open it when he said, "Alexis, I am sorry. I should never have left you alone like that."

Alexis' hands gripped the door handle as she tried to think of something to say. There were so many questions she wanted to ask and so much she wanted to tell him. Yet all the words she could think of seemed woefully inadequate to express the pain and confusion that she was feeling as a result of what he had said and done.

Finally, Alexis sat back in her seat and asked him, "So where do we go from here?"

"I don't know," he said almost to himself. "Hurting you is the last thing that I would ever want to do. Your friendship has meant a great deal to me."

The sound of the word *friendship* made Alexis flinch. That was not enough. Not anymore.

Alexis took a deep breath and said, "Is that all I am to you?"

"It is complicated, Alexis," he replied softly.

"Is there someone else?" As distasteful a prospect as it was, it was something that Alexis needed to know. *Better now than later*, she thought.

When Rafael shook his head, Alexis took another deep breath and then slowly exhaled in order to calm her increasingly frayed nerves.

She said, "Rafael, please talk to me. I can't read your mind."

Rafael gripped the steering wheel even tighter and closed his eyes for a moment before he said, "There is so much I wish I could tell you…"

He stopped in mid-sentence as soon as Alexis' lips touched his cheek. He turned his head toward her. His face was now only inches away from hers as their eyes locked onto one another. He leaned in to kiss her. She was surprised by how warm his lips felt, especially after last night. Her pulse began to race as he pulled her close and kissed her again and again. She didn't resist. She told herself that she wasn't going to do that this time.

Alexis moved onto his lap as Rafael moved his seat back and wrapped his arms around her. As his lips traveled from her face to her neck, she said, "It's okay. I'm not afraid anymore. I won't hold back this time, I promise."

Rafael moved his head back slightly and looked at her with a puzzled expression on his face as he said, "Mi querida, this is not the ideal place to be…"

"We could go somewhere else," Alexis offered.

"Why are you doing this?" he asked as he placed his forehead against hers and stroked her hair.

"Why not?" she asked as her lips found his. "I thought that this was what you wanted."

"I think it might be better if we take things a little more slowly," he suggested. "There is no need to rush into anything."

"That's not what you were telling me last night," she said, feeling slightly annoyed by what appeared to be his sudden change of heart. She looked at him with a perturbed expression as she said, "Is this your way of trying to get back at me for not doing what you wanted last night?"

"What do you mean?" he asked, looking confused.

"You know, after the dance. At the stadium, we…we…," she stammered.

Rafael's eyes widened as he grabbed hold of both of her arms and said, "What happened?"

"What do you mean 'what happened'?" she said. "You were there."

"How far did it go?" he demanded. "Tell me!"

Alexis pulled away from his grasp and blurted out, "Far enough."

She was angry and mystified by his behavior. *How could he possibly be angry with me?* He had been the one who initiated the whole thing.

"What's wrong with you? Do you think I'm making it up?" After Rafael shook his head, she added, "Then why are you acting like you weren't even there?"

"Because…I wasn't."

Alexis felt like she couldn't breathe as the import of his words settled in her mind. Sensing that she was coming close to having a meltdown, she quickly turned and reached for the door handle once again, opened it, and raced to her front door. She heard Rafael's door open while she fumbled in her purse for the house key. He caught up with her just as she put the key into the lock and turned it.

Rafael placed his hand on her upper arm and said, "Alexis, wait."

Alexis was shaking from head to toe in fury. Every muscle in her body felt tense as she cursed the tears that were welling in her eyes. She turned to him and shouted, "Do you really want to know what happened? I'll tell you. I gave you my heart and you threw it back at me. Just like you're doing now. Now leave me alone."

The front porch light went on as she turned back toward the door. Seconds later, Jeremy opened it and stepped outside.

"Take your hands off my sister," he said, glaring at Rafael.

Rafael immediately released his hold on Alexis' arm.

Jeremy stepped in between his sister and Rafael and said, "I think you'd better leave now."

Alexis saw Rafael looking helplessly after her. She shook her head at him and then retreated into the house.

After Jeremy closed the front door, she buried her face in her brother's chest and began to sob uncontrollably. Jeremy held her in his arms and said, "It's okay, Neneng. He's gone now. Does this have anything to do with why you've been upset all day? Do I need to speak with him?"

Alexis shook her head and assured him that his interference would not be necessary.

Later that night, Alexis picked up her cell phone and dialed Jake's number. When he picked up, she said, "Jake, remember that project that I talked to you about? I'm going to need your help. Will you do it?"

On Monday morning, Alexis hid in the chapel until the warning bell rang. When she ventured out, she found Rafael waiting for her by the front door of their class. She slowed her pace, hoping the final bell would ring before she got close enough for him to say anything to her. He took a step toward her and started to speak, but she cut him off with a shake of her head. She walked past him into the classroom and sat down. He followed behind and took a seat next to hers, looking despondent. His frequent glances in her direction during class made it nearly impossible for her to concentrate on Mr. Marquez's lecture. He did the same thing in their next class.

During lunch, Rafael sat so close to her that their arms and legs frequently touched. He also made a point of leaning toward her whenever she spoke to him. When he reached over and brushed a stray hair out of her face, Manuel acted like he was going to gag on his food while Danny and Tobey hid their faces in their hands as they fought the urge to laugh. Even Tessa had to look away. Jake, on the other hand, was the only one who didn't seem to find any humor in the situation.

After school, Alexis was tempted to skip her study session with Rafael but decided to go through with it since she knew that she needed to act as normal as possible in order to put her plan into action. She was already sitting down with her books sprawled out on the table when he came into the library and walked to his usual seat, directly across from hers. For a moment, he stood behind his chair and looked down at her. Instead of sitting down, he put his backpack on the table, pushed it toward an empty seat next to hers, and very deliberately walked around to her side of the table. He sat down next to her and took out his theology textbook.

A minute later, Jake came in. He scanned the room and then walked toward them. Rafael looked up and saw Jake just as he got to their table.

"What brings you to the library?" Rafael asked. "We usually don't see you in here after school."

"My cell phone's dead and I need to make a quick phone call," Jake said to Rafael and then turned to Alexis and asked, "Can I borrow yours?"

While she pretended to look for it, Rafael pulled his phone out of his back pocket and said, "Here, use mine instead," as he handed it to Jake.

"Thanks, man. I won't be more than five minutes."

"No problem. Any time."

After Jake walked out of the library, Alexis alternated between biting her fingernails and nervously tapping a pen on her textbook while waiting for Jake to return.

Rafael looked up from reading his theology textbook and asked her, "Is everything okay?"

"Sure, why do you ask?" she replied a little too cheerfully.

Although Rafael looked at her curiously, he said nothing more and went back to reading. A few minutes later, Jake returned and handed Rafael's phone back to him.

He said to Rafael, "Here you go. I guess I'll see you guys tomorrow then," and turned toward the library doors.

Alexis stood up as Jake walked out of the library and said to Rafael, "Hey, I gotta catch Jake. I just remembered something I needed to ask him. I'll be back in a second."

She sprinted out the door and spotted Jake heading toward the parking lot. He stopped and turned when she called his name.

Alexis was slightly out of breath when she caught up to him. "So, were you able to do it?"

"Yeah, we're in," he replied. She could tell that he was not at all happy about what he had just done.

Alexis tried to reassure him by saying, "Thanks for doing this for me. I know you don't agree…"

"No, I don't," Jake cut in. "If it had been anyone else but you who had asked me, I would've said no. I don't know what you're playing at, Alexis, but this is serious business. We could get in a lot of trouble for this."

"You said that there's no way he'd know we bugged his phone," she replied. "Anyhow, if I get caught, I won't let anyone know that you helped me."

"That's not the point, and you still haven't told me why you need to do this."

"I have a very good reason. Please, just trust me. I know what I'm doing."

"For both our sakes, I hope to God that you do," he said and then turned and walked away.

When Alexis got back into the library, she told Rafael that she wasn't in the mood to study and asked him to take her home. He nodded and quickly packed up his things. They said little as they walked to his car and almost nothing on the drive home. Still, she clearly got the impression that he wanted to talk to her.

After Rafael parked his car in her empty driveway, he turned to her and said, "Alexis, I don't know what to do. I want to fix what is wrong between us, but everything I have tried so far only seems to make you more upset."

"Sometimes I don't know what I want…or what's real," she said in small voice. "I'm screwed up, Rafael. I hear voices in my head. I have bad dreams. And if what you told me last night is true, now I'm hallucinating." She looked down at her fingers, which were raw and red, and then showed them to Rafael. "See these hands. I feel like this on the inside."

He took both her hands in his, looked down at them, and paused a moment before asking her, "Do you know what I see?" Alexis shook her head. "I see a beautiful girl with a beautiful soul."

"How can that be?" she exclaimed. "You should do yourself a favor and get away from me before I really crack up."

"Alexis, I am exactly where I want to be, and I will be here as long as you need me."

She was dumbstruck by his response. She was even more surprised by what he did next. He raised her hands to his lips and then, one by one, kissed each of her fingertips. When he was done, he cupped her face in his hands and gently kissed her lips. She closed her eyes and basked in the moment, despite the fact that the logical part of her mind was screaming for answers. *Did I imagine the whole thing? Is there some connection between what happened and all the other strange things that have been happening to me?*

Knowing that the house was empty, Alexis threw caution to the wind and asked him if he wanted to come in for a minute. She held his hand and led him to the living room. They sat down next to each other on the couch as she flipped on the T.V. He put one arm around her shoulder and used his free hand to tip her face up toward him. She shuddered with anticipation when his lips lightly grazed hers. He pulled her close as the intensity of his kisses increased. She wound her arms around his neck and pressed her body against his as she reveled in the sensations that he was awakening in her mind and body. *This*, she thought gleefully, *is what I dreamed it would be like.*

Alexis had no idea how much time had passed when they finally came up for air. *So much for house rules,* she thought with a slight tinge of guilt. As they sat on the couch with their arms wrapped tightly around each other, she touched his cheek and asked, "So why did you leave the dance without me?"

Rafael kissed her forehead and said, "I got a text from Mrs. Daniels, my host mother, right after we got off the dance floor. She told me that her mother had suffered a stroke and that the paramedics were on the way. Mr. Daniels was away on business. Her grandchildren were visiting from out of town, so I offered to come home early so she could get to the hospital as quickly as possible."

"How is her mother doing?"

"Better now. She is still in the hospital but should be well enough to go home in a few days. It was kind of you to ask." He kissed her again and then nuzzled her neck. "I felt really awful about leaving without telling you personally, but I couldn't find you and I had promised Mrs. Daniels that I would be at their house as soon as I could. Jake promised that he would get you home safely...I am so sorry, I..."

Alexis cut Rafael off with a kiss. He eagerly reciprocated with more of his own. She was just on the verge of losing herself again when she distinctly heard the sound of the lock to the front door turning.

She reluctantly pulled away and whispered, "Someone's coming."

By the time Jeremy opened the door, they were sitting parallel to one another with their eyes glued to the T.V. screen. He froze the minute he saw Rafael sitting on the couch next to his sister.

He looked at Alexis and said, "I guess you two were able to patch things up."

"Oh, yeah. We're great. Perfectly fine. Thanks," Alexis declared while Rafael smiled and nodded at her brother. "Mom said I could have him over. We've just been watching some T.V."

One look at Jeremy's face told her that he didn't believe her. She held her breath as he took a few steps forward and turned his attention to the screen. He glanced at his sister and said, "I didn't know you were interested in the mating practices of humpback whales. Fascinating stuff, isn't it?"

Alexis' face turned bright red; Rafael buried his face in his hands.

"Well, don't let me keep you from watching your show. I wouldn't want you guys to miss the ending." He then pointed towards the kitchen, adding, "I think I'm going to go and get something to eat."

To Alexis' great disappointment, Rafael made sure that they engaged in no further infractions of the house rules.

Even though things had definitely taken a turn for the better with Rafael, Lizzie's warnings about him still preyed on Alexis' mind. Asking him directly about her suspicions was clearly out of the question. Not only did she run the risk of permanently alienating him if Lizzie was wrong, but she also faced the possibility of alerting him to what she knew if Lizzie was right. She didn't think that asking her parents or Father Jim questions about Rafael or The Brethren was a viable option either, due to their close connection to Father Bernal. Thus, she was left with little choice but to seek out the answers to her questions from other sources.

Alexis knew better than to talk to Jake about their "project" at school. She knew that Tessa would not have approved of what they were doing and would have ordered them to stop immediately. She also didn't want to do anything to make Rafael suspicious. And so she was relegated to talking to Jake over the phone in the evening after Rafael dropped her off from school.

Jake agreed to meet with Alexis at her house on Thursday night and let her borrow an extra laptop of his to do some Internet research on her own, after she explained to him that she ran the risk of her parents finding out what she was doing if she used her own computer.

For people like Alexis who had grown up in the digital age, she was surprised to find just how far off the radar Rafael appeared to be. He told her once that he didn't have any social media accounts. When she asked him why, he explained that he neither had the interest nor the time to properly maintain those accounts and that he preferred to just contact people by phone or email. Her attempts to search for him on those types of websites confirmed what he had said to her. She also came up empty when she did word searches of his name, which only seemed to bring up information about every other Rafael Cordero in the world.

Alexis didn't fare any better when she tried to search for information about The Brethren. Like Rafael, it had no website or presence of any kind on social media websites. Although she did find several websites that listed The Brethren as one of many religious orders within the Catholic Church, she found that most of them provided little substantive information about it. She did, however, find one called CatholicConspiracies.com, which contained a few interesting pieces of information about it. It stated that The Brethren was a battle-ready army created in the twelfth century by the Church to fight the Devil and his forces on Earth. It pointed out that every chaplain of the Order was an exorcist and that all its lay members were skilled swordsmen and archers. The website also noted that The Brethren's statutes, membership, and assets were hidden from the general public. Although she got the impression that the information was written by a paranoid conspiracy theorist, she decided to email the website's owner, JJ Egger, anyway. To her great surprise, Egger promptly responded that he would be happy to help in any way he could and gave her a business address that just happened to be a few miles from where she lived. She quickly replied and made an appointment to see him on Saturday morning.

Alexis was a bundle of nerves on Thursday night. During dinner, she knocked over a full glass of water onto the dining room table and dropped her fork three times. Later that evening, she almost fell face first onto the floor after tripping on the edge of the Turkish rug in the living room. In response, Jeremy jokingly told her to go to bed before she really hurt herself or anyone else. She answered by playfully sticking her tongue out and telling him to mind his own business.

She opened the door for Jake when he arrived. She had told her parents that he was coming over to help her with a computer-based presentation that she was going to give at school and had gotten her father's permission to work in his study. After a quick hello to her parents and brother, Jake followed her into the room with his laptop in hand.

Alexis closed the door while Jake took the laptop out of a carrying case and booted it up. She sat down beside him as he logged on to the computer and then clicked on an icon leading to a webpage which only displayed boxes for inputting a username and password.

As Jake typed in the information, he said, "My dad's company uses this program to test how well its cyber security products work. When you asked me to help you, I remembered that he had a copy of this program installed in this computer. The only thing I wasn't sure about was how to install the program into the devices that would have the data you wanted."

"What made you choose Rafael's cell phone?"

"Ease of access," he replied. "Asking to borrow his cell phone is a lot less conspicuous than asking to use his laptop."

"So how did you figure out how to do it?"

"I gave my dad a couple of hypotheticals and he pretty much walked me through how to break into any electronic device and steal data. The great thing about this program is that it's virtually undetectable and can be installed in less than five minutes."

"Very cool," she said, looking at the computer screen.

Jake turned to Alexis and asked, "So what do you want to see first?"

"Let's pull up the websites he's visited," she replied as she leaned forward in her chair.

"You're not trying to see if he looks up porn sites, are you?"

Alexis frowned. "Just pull up the information and keep your comments to yourself, thank you very much."

"Yes, ma'am," Jake replied with a laugh.

Jake clicked on the domain name of a social networking site which led to the page of a user whose smiling face she immediately recognized. The only difference between this person and Rafael was his hair color and first name. Alejandro Cordero Alvarez. *So this is what Rafael's brother looks like*, she thought as she touched the screen and stared at his picture. Although she knew that they were fraternal twins, the resemblance between Alejandro and Rafael still took her by surprise. After noticing that his page had a link to a photo-sharing website, she had Jake click on that link. It led them to a page containing a slew of pictures of Alejandro with his friends and family. The most recent picture was posted in August and showed Alejandro standing in what looked like a vineyard with a dark-haired woman and a bearded man with gray hair. She assumed that they were the aunt and uncle that Rafael had mentioned to her in previous conversations. Many of the other pictures showed Alejandro smiling and laughing with friends. Surprisingly, the only picture she found of Rafael and Alejandro together on that website was an old one where they appeared to be about ten years old. The picture showed them standing side by side in their school uniforms. True to form, Alejandro was smiling with his arm draped around Rafael, who was stoically looking into the camera.

Alexis then asked Jake to show her the emails that Rafael had received and sent. She found out that he had two email addresses. One of them was a well-known web-based account while the other one had a domain name that she was unfamiliar with.

She had Jake pull up a free translation service on the Internet when she saw that all the emails from his web-based account were written in Spanish. After reading through a couple of these emails, she began to get a sense of who his friends and family were and what his life in Spain was like. These emails had opened up a window into a part of his life that she knew nothing about. She was disappointed to find that her name didn't come up in any of these emails. Given the current state of their relationship, she thought that he would have said something about her to at least one of his friends or family members. Based on what she had read, it was as if she didn't exist at all.

Her project hit a snag when Jake tried to bring up the emails from his other account. The only information that he was able to access was the number of emails sent and names of the sender and recipients. Two of the emails that Rafael had sent from that account were to Father Bernal. She also noticed that those emails were cc'd to three other exchange students at Mater Dei: Gonçalo "Gonzo" Morgada from Brazil, Vincenzo "Vinnie" Santini from Italy, and Akira Shigata from Japan. She remembered her cousin Joey mentioning the fact that he saw Rafael training with Akira and two others at his dojo. Now that she knew who the other two were, she wondered why he never interacted with them at school or bothered to introduce them to her.

"Why can't we see the actual emails?" Alexis asked.

Jake shook his head as he sat back and tapped his fingertips together. "I don't know. We should've been able to see that part of the email with this program," he said as he stared at the screen. "I'm impressed. He must be using some pretty state-of-the-art stuff."

"Is there any way to unblock these emails?"

"I'd probably have to use a software program that needs a powerful computer to break through the security measures that have been put in place," Jake replied. "My dad could probably do it, but I'd have to tell him why I need to unblock these emails. Another option would be to find some way to access my dad's work computer without him knowing about it."

Alexis nodded. She had no choice but to wait until Jake figured out what to do.

By the time Jake moved on to Rafael's texts, she felt like she had seen enough. It was late and she was feeling tired, frustrated, and disappointed. Over all, she had expected to learn much more about him than she did and found that the information she did learn had left her with more questions than answers about who he was and why he was here. *Maybe Lizzie's right,* she thought with a sigh. Otherwise, why would he be using the security measures he did for one of his two email accounts? And, if she was truly as important to him as he had indicated in recent days, then why had he not mentioned her to his family and friends?

After Jake had logged out of the website and shut down the laptop, he asked her, "So, when are you going to tell me why you're doing this?"

"Maybe Saturday," Alexis replied as she rubbed her eyes and yawned.

"Why Saturday?"

"I made an appointment to meet someone who might be able to help me learn more about a religious order that Rafael might be involved with."

"Do you want me to come with you?"

"I was just about to ask you that," Alexis said quietly as she walked out with him to the porch.

"What time do you want me to pick you up?"

"Nine thirty in the morning if that's okay," she replied as she looked through the window and saw her brother sitting on the couch in the living room watching T.V. "You didn't make any plans with Tessa did you?"

Jake shrugged his shoulders and said, "Nothing that I can't rearrange...But I gotta let you know that she's starting to get suspicious. She's asking questions."

"If she gives you a hard time, just tell her to come and talk to me."

"Don't worry, I can handle Tessa," he replied. "It's you that I'm worried about."

When they got to his car, Jake said, "I'll keep you posted on my progress on accessing those emails."

Alexis gave Jake a hug and said, "You're the best."

Jake smiled back at her and said, "I know, and don't you forget it."

CHAPTER 13—CONSPIRACY THEORIES

It was nearly nine thirty on Saturday morning as Alexis stood by the window, waiting for Jake to pick her up. Today was the day that she was going to meet JJ Egger, the Catholic conspiracy theorist she had met online. At best, she hoped that Egger might have some useful information about The Brethren that might help her understand what kind of threat, if any, its members posed to her. At worst, she would be forced to pursue other avenues to find what she was looking for.

Alexis jumped when she felt a tap on her shoulder. "Is everything okay? You seem kind of jittery," Jeremy said as he came up and stood beside her.

"No, I'm not," she replied, knowing perfectly well that he suspected she was up to something.

Fortunately, Alexis was saved from having to answer any more of her brother's questions by Jake, who had pulled into the driveway.

Just as she opened the front door to leave, Jeremy asked her, "So, where are you guys going?"

Thinking fast, Alexis looked at her brother and lied. "We're going to the music store on Third Avenue to look at some sheet music for our youth choir. Jake said that he saw some pieces there that might be good for us to include in our holiday repertoire."

"Oh…okay. Have fun then," he said. She smiled back at him and then ran out to Jake's car.

Alexis pulled out a piece of paper with Egger's address on it while Jake backed out of the driveway. The place they were going to was located in Bonita, California, a city just north of Chula Vista. After having driven north on Otay Lakes Road for a couple of miles, they turned left into a strip mall anchored by a grocery store and several mom and pop shops. The car clock indicated that they had gotten to their destination with ten minutes to spare.

Alexis and Jake walked up to the storefront of the address she was given and stared at the sign, which read *Comic Book World,* hanging from the front door.

"You've got to be kidding me," Jake said, frowning.

The theme from the 1960s version of the Spiderman cartoon blared from a speaker near the store entrance as they walked in. She looked around and saw store shelves lined with comic books and walls covered in comic book art and other superhero memorabilia. There was a single shelf filled with comic and sci-fi magazines near the front of the store and a long table lined with boxes filled with rare comics in protective covers in the back. The cash register was near the front and only one employee appeared to be on duty. The man, who had long, scraggly blonde hair and glasses, was sitting behind the counter with his face buried in a graphic novel.

Jake whispered, "I hope to God that's not the guy we're supposed to meet. If it is, we're leaving right now."

Alexis walked up to the cashier, cleared her throat to attract his attention and said, "Excuse me, but are you JJ Egger?"

"Who's asking?" he replied in a sarcastic tone.

"Look, there's no need to be rude," Jake chimed in. "She just asked you a simple question, okay?"

This is not going well, Alexis thought, and was about to ask again, when a shrewd-looking middle-aged man with a shaved head walked up to them and said, "What can I do for you folks today?"

The cashier responded, "Dude, the girl was asking for you."

"Ah," Egger exclaimed. "You must be Bonnie then."

"Yes," Alexis quickly replied as Jake gave her a questioning look.

Egger turned to Jake and said, "So, I guess that makes you Clyde." Jake looked like he wanted to strangle her. Her eyes pleaded with him to be patient.

Egger told the cashier that he was going to his office and asked Alexis and Jake to follow him to the back of the store. When they entered the room, they found that it was no bigger than a walk-in closet. It made Alexis feel claustrophobic. Egger walked around his desk, which looked like it was being held together with staples and masking tape, and sat down on a well-worn chair. He invited them to sit on black folding chairs layered with dust. Alexis discreetly swept her seat with her hand before she sat down and saw Jake do likewise.

Egger looked at Alexis and said, "What exactly do you want to know about The Brethren?"

"What can you tell us?" Alexis replied as she leaned forward in her seat. Egger sat back in his chair and eyed her curiously as he rubbed his hand under his chin.

"What's in it for you?" Egger asked.

"Well," she began, "like I said in my email, I have a friend who's been trying to do research on this religious order but hasn't been able to come up with much on her own. From what we saw on your website, you seem to have more information about The Brethren than any of the other websites we've looked at."

"Why isn't she here if she's the one who's so interested in finding out more about it?"

Alexis said, "She's really shy and…"

Jake interjected, "Sorry to interrupt, but can I ask a question?" Egger nodded. "How do we know that what you're telling us is legit? No offense, but you haven't exactly been making the best impression so far."

"Neither of you have to believe anything I tell you," Egger replied. "It'll be no skin off my nose one way or the other, but I guarantee that you'd be hard-pressed to find the information I can give you anywhere else."

"Who are your sources?" Jake asked. "Pardon my French, but how do we know that you're not just blowing smoke up our…?"

"Jake, please!" Alexis cut in.

Eyeing Jake, Egger asked, "Are you Catholic? Have you seen my website?"

Alexis could tell that Jake was on the verge of losing his temper. He responded, "Yes, if it's any of your business, I am Catholic. And, no, I'm sorry, but I haven't had the pleasure of viewing your website."

"That's too bad," Egger replied, "because I think it might open your eyes to what the Church is really all about. But then again, maybe you're one of those Catholics that likes to bury their heads in the sand and pretend everything's all right."

Alexis grimaced and prayed that Jake would not, for her sake, blow his top. She grabbed hold of one of his hands and gave it a squeeze in an effort to calm him down.

"And you, sir, have no idea who I am," Jake said hotly. "You have no right to presume what I think or don't think about my faith. The only reason I'm here is to make sure you don't screw her over. Is that clear?"

Alexis had no idea what to say or do next. Meanwhile, Egger kept his eyes steadily focused on Jake as he said, "Everything I put on my website is impeccably sourced. Sometimes those sources don't want to be known, and when that happens, I say so."

He then turned to Alexis and said, "Do you want to know what I've got on The Brethren or not?"

Alexis nodded. "Please excuse my friend. He's just trying to look out for me."

Egger pursed his lips as he put on a pair of glasses and turned his attention to the laptop on his desk. He said, "You won't find much on the web about The Brethren. This military religious order has been around as long as The Knights Templar, but its members don't exactly like to advertise that it exists. It tends to keep things very close to the vest, so to speak." Egger stroked his chin and asked, "Can you tell me again exactly why your friend wants to know about it?"

"She's been told that The Brethren might be interested in her somehow and she's trying to figure out why."

"Ah. I see," Egger said as he placed his fingers on the keyboard and started to type. A moment later, he said to Alexis, "The Brethren's official name within the Catholic Church is Ordinis Fratrum Crucis. The English translation of that name is Order of The Brethren of the Cross. It's a pontifical right order."

"So the local bishops have no jurisdiction over it?" Jake asked.

"None," Egger replied.

"How was it established?" Alexis asked.

"Like my website says, it was established by papal bull in the twelfth century. Its members are only accountable to the pope. It also has its own priests, who are also exempt from local control. It's not publicly known who its members are and, to my knowledge, their statutes and constitution are not open for public view."

"Who are they?" Alexis asked.

"Members of The Brethren come from all over the world, but a large percentage of them are from noble families in Europe, particularly Spain. It's headquartered in Madrid. I've also been told that its members have considerable wealth and influence within the Church."

"Why isn't there more information about it in the public domain?" she asked.

"Its members prefer to keep a low profile. As far as I know, it doesn't actively re-cruit and doesn't own many physical assets. Nearly everything is held in the name of the members. For example, you won't hear that it's running a school or sponsoring an event, but if you dig deeper, you'll probably find that the sponsors of the event or the school's benefactors are members of The Brethren."

"If it's all so secret, how come you know so much?" Jake asked incredulously. "How do you know your sources can be trusted?"

"There are people within the Church, both lay members and clergy, who don't ap-prove of The Brethren. They see it as an overly powerful and secretive society of men whose entire reason for being became obsolete centuries ago. Those are the people that seek me out and feed me information." He then said with a laugh, "I'd like to tell you who they are, but then I'd have to kill you. The last thing I'd ever do is compromise a source."

From the look on Jake's face, Alexis could tell that he wasn't at all amused by what Egger had said.

"Who are The Brethren, and how often do they meet?" Alexis asked.

"Its members work in every profession and sponsor sporting events like sword fighting and archery. Every member is taught how to use these weapons," Egger replied.

"Why swords and arrows?" Jake asked. "Why not use guns instead?"

"They don't use guns because they concluded that they don't work on the type of enemy they are trained to fight," Egger explained. "Bullets slowed but couldn't eliminate their intended targets. They found that only their specially fashioned swords and arrows had the power to send the Devil's beasts back to Hell."

"When was the last time The Brethren sponsored the kind of sporting event you just mentioned?" Alexis asked.

"The most recent event took place in Spain earlier this year. The Brethren called it The Trials. From what I've been told, this event title is very significant," Egger said as he reached for a bottle of water on his desk and took a sip. "The competitors in The Trials were hand-picked and were between the ages of 16 and 19. The challengers were weeded out by a process of elimination. In the end, only two competed in a concluding event called The Final Tasks."

"What are The Final Tasks?" Alexis asked.

"The Final Tasks test the last two competitors' physical prowess, mental agility, and skills with specific weaponry. The winner is the one who displays the highest marks in all three categories and is given the title El Arquero. In English it means The Archer."

Alexis recalled that the woman who had traumatized her after rehearsal had uttered the word "Archer" just before she released her. She also remembered her cousin Joey saying that the three exchange students Rafael trained with at his dojo called him that. As she sat there puzzling over this bit of information, Egger pulled out a CD from his desk drawer and inserted it into his laptop.

"This is a video of The Final Tasks. Not many outsiders know about or have seen it. Lucky for you, someone literally dropped off a copy of it on my front door." Egger turned his computer around and pressed the enter button. "Sit back, kiddos. This is going to blow your minds."

At first, the video showed nothing, but shaky footage of a dirt path leading to a glade. The full moon, which was set against a black starless sky, illuminated the landscape. The forward movement of the camera stopped when the cameraman reached the edge of a clearing. The camera panned the area, which was lined with men wearing white hooded robes with purple crosses embossed on the front. Her eyes widened when she caught sight of a familiar face in this sea of men.

"Can you stop the video right there?" she said as the implications of what she was seeing began to sink in.

Egger nodded and did as she asked. She blinked and looked again at the face frozen on the screen to make sure that her eyes were not deceiving her. She turned to Jake, who also leaned forward to take a closer look. Jake's jaw dropped as a glimmer of recognition spread across his face.

"Someone you know?" Egger asked.

"Yes," Alexis replied tentatively as she leaned back in her chair. "I know him very well."

Egger glanced at the screen and said, "Come to think of it, he does look somewhat familiar to me, too." His eyes roamed to Alexis' face and then back to the screen, adding, "And I do see a resemblance…"

"Can we go on?" she interrupted, averting her eyes from Egger's gaze. After a brief pause, he shrugged and pressed the play button.

The footage cut to the opposite edge of the clearing, where two young men dressed in white stood. Other than the fact that one of them was about two inches taller, nothing else distinguished one from the other. Their faces were hidden behind masks while their flexible and lightweight body armor outlined the contours of their lean, muscular bodies. The straps fastened to their bodies held short swords in scabbards and quivers filled with silver arrows and bows.

The competitors walked toward the middle of the open space in the forest and were met by a priest that she immediately recognized: Father Bernal. He laid his hands upon their heads and prayed over them as they knelt down before him. Afterward, he invited everyone in the glade to say *The Lord's Prayer*. The wooded area came alive with the chorus of male voices as they recited it in Latin:

Pater noster qui es in caelis
sanctificetur nomen tuum;
Adveniat regnum tuum;
fiat voluntas tua,
sicut in caelo et in terra.
Panem nostrum quotidianum da nobis hodie,
et dimitte nobis debita nostra,
sicut et nos dimittimus debitoribus nostris;
et ne nos inducas in tentationem;

sed libera nos a malo.
Amen.

The young men bowed their heads as Father Bernal made the sign of the cross before them and said, "*In nomine patris, et filii, et spiritus sanctum. Amen.*" In the name of the Father, and the Son, and the Holy Spirit. Amen.

At that point, the young men rose and a man dressed in a hooded white robe strode toward them. Egger pointed out to Alexis and Jake that the man, Hugo Molina, was the Grand Master of The Brethren. The competitors bowed to Brother Molina as he removed the hood from his head and raised his hand as a signal to the others in the clearing that he was about to speak.

"My brothers," Molina said in a commanding voice. "It is with a heavy heart that I greet each and every one of you this evening. Our Order was founded over a millennium ago for a very specific purpose. Since that time, we have remained vigilant, awaiting signs from the Lord that He is in need of our assistance. As you all know, that time has now come.

"It was only after much prayerful deliberation that I requested permission from the Holy Father to convene The Trials, which conclude tonight with The Final Tasks. These two young men standing before you represent the best of what was a very select group of competitors. Tonight, the title of El Arquero will be bestowed upon one of them."

Molina turned and spoke directly to the competitors. "This is a grave task that will be assigned to one of you. The risks are great and there is a very good chance that the one who is chosen may not survive his mission. So I ask you now, if either one of you feels that you are not up to the undertaking that may be set before you, please step forward now." Both competitors stood resolutely in place.

Brother Molina then said, "I wish both of you the best of luck and I look forward, at the end of this exercise, to be the first one to meet and introduce El Arquero to the rest of The Brethren."

He ended his speech by looking at each one of the competitors and saying, "Deus Tecum."

Each of them replied, "In Aeternam."

Alexis remembered these exact same words passing between her father and Rafael in her living room, right before the homecoming dance. She made a mental note of it and then turned her attention back to the video.

At that point, the camera panned to another part of the clearing, where a man in a black hooded robe stood apart from the others beneath a tree, holding a large black book.

Egger paused the video and pointed his finger at that man as he said, "He's a conjurer. The Brethren call him by his Latin name—adjurator."

"What is he doing there?" Alexis asked. "Why would The Brethren associate with someone like that?"

Egger smiled and said, "You'll see."

As the adjurator opened the book and mouthed the words of an incantation, the camera panned back to the competitors, whose taut bodies were crouched down in anticipation of an imminent attack from an as yet unseen enemy.

Alexis nearly jumped out of her seat when a gnarled hand suddenly burst from the ground and grabbed the taller boy's leg. He quickly unsheathed one of his short swords and slashed at the hand, which held his leg in a vice-like grip. It released him only after he had sliced off two of its fingers and tore a deep gash in its forearm. His respite, however, was short-lived as a large and grotesque-looking man-like beast burst forth from the ground. It wielded a large curved blade with its uninjured hand, while the other mangled limb oozed blood the color of tar. It swung wildly at its intended victim, who was struggling to get back on his feet.

"Nephilim," Egger said under his breath. "They're half man, half demon."

Alexis tried hard to make sense of what she was seeing. The Nephilim that was roaring and gnashing its teeth together on the screen was the stuff of fairy tales. And yet, she knew that the monster was not the product of a camera trick and was, in fact, as real as Jake and Egger.

She gasped as the Nephilim thrust its blade downward to strike at the taller boy's chest. The weapon, however, failed to meet its mark when the smaller, but swifter boy interceded by deflecting the blade with one of his own short swords. The Nephilim swerved and lunged at its prey, as the taller boy scrambled away.

From her point of view, the swifter boy appeared to be toying with the beast as he dodged and blocked its blade. She guessed that he was biding his time, waiting for the Nephilim to make a careless mistake, so he could then go in for the kill. Her eyes widened in surprise when, moments later, the taller boy came up from behind and slashed at the Nephilim's legs. As it fell to its knees, the other boy quickly wrestled the curved blade out of its hand and then sliced the beast in half. She gasped when the Nephilim's remains vanished into thin air as soon as it hit the ground.

As the camera moved back, it showed two four-legged, dog-like creatures with black fur and red eyes racing toward the competitors. These creatures reminded Alexis of the animal that had chased her in the trails.

She looked at Egger, who simply said, "Hellhounds."

Alexis started to cover her face with her hands when it looked as though one of the beasts was about to jump on top of the swifter boy. Her fear, however, quickly turned to amazement when she saw him thrust his short swords into the creature's belly as it tried to jump on top of him, causing it to flail and fall onto its side. He quickly finished it off with two more simultaneous thrusts of his swords into the creature's chest. It, like the Nephilim, vanished as soon it had taken its last breath.

The camera panned upward just as the taller boy was finishing off the other hellhound and showed six winged creatures hovering and screeching above the two competitors.

"Gargoyles," Egger informed them.

"My God," Jake exclaimed, looking ashen-faced.

The competitors promptly killed two of the gargoyles, which disappeared in midair with direct hits to the chest. She gasped as one of the winged creatures swooped down from behind and nearly sank its talons into the taller boy's back. That beast was followed by another, who grabbed the taller boy's arm, nearly ripping it off. He cried out in pain and then swung one of his swords at the gargoyle with his free hand in order to dislodge his nearly severed arm from the creature's grasp. The struggle continued for a few more horrifying seconds as the gargoyle tore at his back and legs with its other talon. The taller boy crumpled to the ground as soon as it let go.

While he lay prostrate, the swifter boy came into view. He shot two arrows at the retreating beast. The first one narrowly missed while the other hit it squarely in the chest, causing it to let out an ear-shattering screech before vanishing into thin air. The remaining three gargoyles let out deafening cries and dove toward him. He knelt down beside the taller boy and unleashed his arrows upon them in rapid succession. Within a matter of seconds, he had struck down two of them with deadly precision. As they disappeared from view, the last gargoyle pulled up. It circled and then dove toward him. He took aim and fired. The arrow hit its wing, causing it to veer onto its side as it fell to the Earth. He unsheathed his swords and plunged them into the beast's chest as soon as it hit the ground. It let out an ear-piercing scream as it too vanished into the night.

Suddenly, Alexis heard hundreds of men roaring in the background as a team raced toward the badly injured competitor. She watched the swifter boy stand close by, his chest still heaving up and down from exertion, as he continued to hold his blood-stained swords in his hands.

At first, she had found it somewhat surprising that it had been the smaller of the two competitors that prevailed in the end, but the more she thought about it, the more it made sense. What he lacked in size, he more than made up for with speed and agility. He also exhibited a fearlessness and grace under fire that was awe-inspiring. Of the two remaining competitors, she thought that he clearly deserved to be given the title El Arquero.

After the taller boy was tended to and carried away, Brother Molina walked toward the remaining competitor, who had remained standing in the middle of the clearing.

For the first time, the camera moved in for a close up shot of the young man. Although his face was covered by a mask, she immediately recognized the piercing blue eyes that were peering through the holes. She grabbed hold of Jake's hand; she felt like she couldn't breathe. From the look on his face, she could tell that Jake had recognized him too.

Brother Molina said, "You have fought admirably and well this night. You have shown us that you are worthy of the title that I am prepared to bestow upon you. Until tonight, your face has been hidden behind a mask. I ask you to remove it now so that we all may know who you are."

The young competitor kept his eyes fixed on Brother Molina as he said, "I pray that my efforts tonight in The Final Tasks have shown you that I am both ready and able to undertake the mission that you will entrust to my care."

Brother Molina put his hand on his shoulder and said, "By what name shall we call you?"

"Rafael," he said after he raised a hand to his mask and removed it. And with that, the video ended.

Alexis sat in her chair, trying to process all that she had seen. As he took the CD out of his laptop, Egger said, "It was the funniest thing. This video just showed up on my doorstep the day after I got your email. No return address, nothing to identify where it came from. All that was written on it were the words "The Brethren." It's almost like somebody knew that you had contacted me and wanted me to show this to you."

Alexis stared back at him. After what she had just seen, anything seemed possible.

"If you'd like, I could contact my sources and see if they'd be willing to answer any other questions about The Brethren that you might have," Egger offered. "If they agree to do it, would you like them to contact you directly?"

Alexis nodded and said, "Yes, please. Thank you so much. You've been very helpful."

"Good luck to you," Egger said as they rose from their seats and shook his hand. He closed the door behind them after they left his office.

Alexis felt like the world as she knew it no longer existed. She walked up and down the aisles of the store in a daze. Jake, who was standing stock-still in front of an anime drawing of a scantily clad woman, also looked slightly off kilter. A few minutes later, she wordlessly followed Jake out of the store.

When they got to Jake's car, they sat there side by side, and silently stared out the window. Alexis felt like her mind was on overload and was having trouble processing all the information she had just learned. In fact, there was actually a part of her that wished she'd never seen the video, that preferred being in the dark. Accepting the alternative meant admitting that two of the men she loved most were not who they seemed and, if Lizzie was right, might be a danger to her.

Eventually, Jake said to Alexis, "Are you okay?"

Alexis shook her head and said in a faraway voice, "I'm so sorry I brought you into this craziness."

"Alexis, we've been friends since grade school. Of course I'm going to be there for you if you need me." He paused a moment, then asked, "So what are you going to do now? Are you going to talk to your dad about this?"

"I can't do that," she replied. "You saw the video. He was one of the men in the white robes."

"What about Father Jim?" Jake suggested.

"Father Bernal's office is right next to Father Jim's in the parish hall. For all I know, he might be part of this, too."

"There must be *someone* you can talk to," Jake said.

And what about Rafael? What was she going to do about him? Scenes from the video flashed through her mind as the sound of someone knocking on the passenger side window made her jump. She turned toward the window and saw Rafael standing there.

Alexis panicked. She took a deep breath and tried to calm down as she reached out for the window switch. Her right hand shook as the window dropped down.

Rafael stooped over and leaned his arms against the car door and said, "What are you doing here?"

Alexis scrambled for a plausible answer that didn't involve telling him the truth. Nothing immediately came to mind. She felt her anxiety level rising exponentially with each passing second. She needed to think of something fast.

The answer finally came to her as she looked out the windshield and gazed at the storefront of *Comic Book World*. "Comics. Someone told me about that comic book place over there. I've wanted to check it out for weeks now. Jake was nice enough to bring me here this morning."

"Really? You never told me that. I could have taken you," Rafael said as his eyes flitted from Alexis to Jake.

"Jake's really into comics, too," Alexis quickly replied, turning to Jake as she said, "Isn't that right?"

For a second or two, Jake looked like a deer caught in the headlights, but he quickly recovered his composure and did his best to play along.

"Yeah, sure," he said as he shifted uneasily in his seat.

"Did you see anything interesting?" Rafael asked.

Alexis found his question rather ironic, considering the events of the last hour or so. She manufactured as sweet a smile as she could under the circumstances as she said, "No, not today. So, what are you doing here?"

"Grocery shopping," he replied. "I am here with my host mother, Mrs. Daniels."

"Well, don't let me keep you. I wouldn't want her to wonder where you are."

"Are you trying to get rid of me?" Rafael teased.

Alexis reached for his hand and squeezed it. "In what dimension would that even be a remote possibility?"

Rafael smiled and then kissed her. Jake broke up the idyllic moment seconds later with an uncomfortable cough. Rafael stepped back, offered a quick apology to Jake for his momentary lack of decorum and said to Alexis, "I will see you later."

Alexis instinctively knew that she couldn't let what she had just learned influence the way she acted. Things needed to appear normal...for the moment, at least. Rafael had just turned toward the grocery store when she called out to him, "Do you like monster movies?" He immediately turned around. She took a deep breath and continued, "There's a new one that just came out. It's called *When Monsters Attack*. I heard it's so awful it's funny. Want to see it?"

He laughed and said, "Why not? What time should I pick you up?"

"I gotta check the times," she replied. "I'll send you a text, okay?"

Rafael nodded, waved to Jake, and then headed toward the grocery store. Alexis' eyes remained steadily on him until he disappeared through the automatic sliding doors.

"Alexis, what are you doing?" Jake asked her as soon as Rafael was out of sight.

"That's just it, Jake," Alexis replied, feeling guilty and confused. "I have no idea what I'm doing or what to do next."

"Don't worry," Jake replied. "We'll figure something out."

Alexis raced up the stairs the minute she got home. She had just closed her bedroom door when her cell phone rang. Although the number didn't look familiar, she answered it anyway. It was a man's voice. He sounded old. When he asked for Bonnie, she knew that he had to be one of Egger's sources. The man said that he was a retired priest and asked her if she was interested in meeting with him to discuss The Brethren. She said yes, agreeing to meet him the next day, Sunday, at one o'clock in the afternoon at the Church of the Immaculata on the campus of the University of

San Diego. After she hung up, she checked the times for the movie on her computer and sent Rafael a text.

Alexis went back downstairs and was drawn to the living room by the sound of her mother singing and playing a Filipino folk song, *Dandansoy*, on the piano.

She sat down and leaned her head against her mother's shoulder until the song was finished and then asked, "Where's Dad?"

Lisa smiled and said, "He's in the backyard killing the plants again."

Alexis frowned. "Doesn't he ever learn? All he has to do is look at them, and then they start to wilt."

"You tell him that. I stopped trying years ago."

Alexis got up and went to the back yard. She found her father standing in front of a rose bush with shears in hand and a look of intense concentration on his face.

"Mom told me you were back here destroying the garden."

Eric turned to his daughter and smiled as he lifted his baseball cap off his head to wipe the sweat from his brow. "Ye of little faith. There's always hope. Even for someone with as black a thumb as mine."

Alexis walked over to the rose bush and bent down to take in the scent of one of the beautiful pink-tipped white blossoms in full bloom. She asked, "Dad, were you planning on going to USD tomorrow?"

"Just for a couple of hours," he replied. "I'm still trying to play catch up from all those weeks I spent in the Philippines. Why do you ask?"

"I was hoping to go with you, if you don't mind. I thought a change of scenery might help me concentrate on my studies a little better. I could just hang out on campus while you tend to your business stuff." He nodded and turned his full attention back to the rose bush. "Is it okay if we go after lunch? I was thinking of going from like one to four o'clock."

"Sounds good to me," he replied. "So, do you have any plans tonight?"

"Yeah, Rafael and I are going out for dinner and a movie. He's picking me up around six."

"I had a feeling you were going to tell me that," Eric said with a wistful look as he put the sheers on a nearby table and took his garden gloves off. "I'm really starting to miss those days when you thought that I was your knight in shining armor."

Alexis stepped forward and gave him a hug. "You'll always be my Prince Charming."

Eric mussed up the hair on the top of his daughter's head and said, "And you'll always be my little girl."

"Oh, Dad," Alexis said as she took a step back. A moment later, she asked, "Dad, have you seen much of Spain?"

"Madrid and Barcelona, mainly," he said, stiffening slightly. "You aren't making any plans to run off with Rafael, are you?"

Alexis rolled her eyes. "Rafael talks about his home sometimes. He tells me that his family has been in the winemaking business for generations and that they own a few vineyards. From the way he describes it, it sounds like one of the most beautiful places on Earth."

"There are many parts of Spain that are very beautiful. Maybe you'll be able to see that for yourself someday."

Alexis noticed a sudden change in her father's demeanor as he carefully placed his hand on a thick stem on the rose bush to examine it.

She cleared her throat and said, "Wasn't the conference you went to this past summer there?"

Eric flinched, nicking a finger on one of the thorns. He looked down at it as a tiny speck of blood formed where he had been pricked. He said to her, "Yes, it was."

When her father failed to elaborate, she asked, "What was the conference about?"

"Nothing you need to concern yourself with," Eric replied as he picked up the garden sheers, grabbed hold of the stem with the offending thorn on it, and snapped it off at the base. It was clear to her at that point that he was not inclined to continue with that aspect of their conversation, so she slowly and quietly backed away as her father grimaced and threw the stem on the ground.

It was nearly ten in the evening when the movie ended. As Rafael and Alexis walked through the crowded lobby, she asked, "So what did you think?"

Rafael looked like he was trying to find the most diplomatic way of answering the question. Finally, he said, "It was very…interesting."

Alexis laughed. "That bad, huh? What's the matter, don't you like monsters?"

"Well, not if they are green blobs that make your body disintegrate when they attack you." Changing the subject, he said, "Listen, I need to go wash my hands. They are a little greasy from all the butter you put on the popcorn."

Alexis smiled at him mischievously as she said, "Over-buttered popcorn and an awful movie. Aren't you glad you came?"

Rafael tipped her chin up with his hand and kissed her before turning and walking toward the men's room. She thought about how handsome he looked in jeans and gray polo shirt. It was nice to see him out of his school uniform, even though she thought that he looked good in whatever he wore. She also had to commend him for sitting through what was arguably one of the worst movies ever made.

When Alexis turned toward the glass doors of the theater, she saw two teenage boys holding up a third one near the entrance. As she moved closer, she realized that the third boy was Bobby. She walked outside to meet them.

Bobby smiled when he saw her approaching and said, "Well, if it isn't little Miss Goody Goody?" His two friends on either side of him laughed. "You know that's what *she* called you."

"You're drunk." Alexis thought that he reeked of more than just alcohol.

"Why thank you, Captain Obvious. Now can you please tell me something I don't know?" He peered at the theater marquee, then at her and slurred, "Did you go to the movie alone? You should've called me. I would have given you a warm body to sit next to."

Alexis replied, "Actually, my boyfriend should be out here any minute now."

Bobby's eyes widened as he said, "Wow. I'm impressed. So you finally bagged a guy. I didn't think it was in you. You were always so…uptight." He turned to one of his friends and said, "I dated her best friend. She told me all about her."

Turning his attention back to Alexis, he said, "So have you put out yet, or are you just teasing the poor guy?"

Alexis gave him an icy stare. "That's none of your business."

Bobby smiled back at her. "I got a Halloween party at my house next Friday. You should bring your man. I'll even let you borrow one of my rooms free of charge."

To her great dismay, he proceeded to turn his back to her and make kissing noises as he wrapped his arms around himself. His friends snickered.

"What makes you think that I would be even remotely interested in going to your party?"

Bobby's lips spread into a sly smile as he said, "You want answers, don't you?"

"What kind of answers?" she asked, intrigued.

"Don't play dumb with me, Alexis," he replied. "I know that you've been dying to know what I know about Avery."

"Is everything okay?" Rafael asked as he walked up and eyed Bobby and his friends with suspicion.

"Everything's fine," Bobby replied and then said to Alexis, "Isn't that right?" He then turned his attention to Rafael and said, "Alexis and I are old friends. I'm Bobby."

Rafael didn't appear to be even remotely convinced that they were friends. He stepped directly in front of Alexis and said, "Really? She has never mentioned *you* before."

Alexis started to panic as she looked over at Bobby's pals, who were puffing their chests in anticipation of a fight. Luckily, Bobby didn't seem to share their interest in mixing things up with Rafael.

"What's everybody getting so worked up about?" Bobby asked as he put a hand on each of his friends' shoulders. "It's all good, right?"

Alexis tried to diffuse the situation by shaking her head as she tugged on Rafael's right arm. Meanwhile, Bobby and his crew backed up a few steps and huddled together.

After a brief conversation, Bobby walked back to Rafael and said, "You'll have to excuse my friends. They can be a little overprotective sometimes." He added, "No hard feelings, man," as he held out his hand to Rafael.

At first, Rafael just looked at Bobby's outstretched hand like it was something distasteful, but Alexis' eyes pleaded with him to reciprocate. He hesitated a moment longer before reluctantly shaking Bobby's hand with a firm grip and an icy stare.

Afterward, Bobby stepped back and winked at Alexis as he said, "Maybe I'll see you next Friday," and then motioned for the others to follow.

When they were out of earshot, Rafael said to her, "What was he talking about?"

"He invited us to go to his Halloween party," she said. "I know that you're probably just dying to go."

"How do you know him?" Rafael tilted his head back and asked with a hint of derision in his voice.

"Bobby was Avery's boyfriend." Alexis saw a look of surprise form on Rafael's face as she added, "He's the reason she's gone."

Rafael moved closer and wrapped his arms around her waist while she rested her head on his shoulder. He said, "It doesn't seem possible that *your* best friend would be with anyone even remotely like him."

"She was having trouble at home. Her parents were fighting and I guess he filled a void. Like I said before, I kept trying to reach out to her, but she wouldn't listen…"

"I am sure you did everything you could to help her," he replied.

Alexis shook her head as she looked up at his face. "Sometimes I'm not so sure… I'm no saint, Rafael. In fact, I think that I'm as flawed as they come. I can't even help myself sometimes."

Rafael kissed her forehead and said, "Don't be so hard on yourself. You are a wonderful girl and I feel very lucky to have you in my life."

When they got to his car, he unlocked and opened the door for her. Before she got in, she turned toward him and lightly kissed his lips. He answered her kiss with a few of his own. As the minutes passed, she felt a mixture of panic, elation, and utter confusion as she tried to figure out his main motivation for being here with her now. *Is he here out of a sense of duty or love?* Her heart told her it was the latter, but the voices in her head said otherwise.

As their lips parted, Rafael looked down at her with a pensive expression. She got the feeling that a very heavy burden was weighing on him now. He kissed her again and then stroked her cheek with his hand as he said, "It is getting late. I should take you home now."

CHAPTER 14—THE BRETHREN

Alexis gathered her thoughts for her upcoming meeting with the priest as she rode with Eric up the curved road leading to the USD campus. She had no idea what she was going to say, but she hoped that he somehow would help her put the pieces of the puzzle that tied her father, Rafael, and The Brethren together. After what she had seen and learned in the last twenty-four hours, she was more determined than ever to find out what they were hiding from her…and why.

It was a little before one o'clock in the afternoon when Eric dropped Alexis off by a clover-shaped fountain in front of the Immaculata Church. He told her that he would pick her up in three hours. She felt a warm breeze brush against her cheek as she exited the car. She looked up at the clear blue sky and then at the fountain, which was shooting water up into the air like a geyser. She took a coin out of her wallet, closed her eyes, and made a wish before tossing it in. After opening the church's bronze doors, she stepped inside, glanced around, and sat down in a pew in the middle of the nave.

A few minutes later, a blonde-haired priest, who looked to be in his early thirties, entered through a side door, walked toward the altar, and bowed. *Is this the man I'm supposed to meet?* she thought nervously. The voice on the phone had sounded much older. Her hands gripped the back of the pew in front of her when he started walking in her direction. She held her breath when he looked over at her and smiled. Her hopes, however, were quickly dashed as soon as he walked past her.

Alexis checked her cell phone and saw that it was now five minutes past one. She had begun to worry that the priest had decided not to show up when she caught sight of a white-haired and frail gentleman, cane in hand, standing by her pew and smiling down at her.

"Are you Bonnie?" he asked in a fatherly tone. When she nodded, he held out his hand to her and said, "Good afternoon. I'm Father Michael Angelini. It's a pleasure to make your acquaintance."

Alexis shook Father Angelini's hand and slid over to give him room. His head and shoulders were bent over as he limped into the pew and slowly sat down beside her. He looked winded from the effort of moving as he took out a handkerchief to blow his nose. Still, she sensed the existence of a fire that still burned brightly within his old and infirm body.

"Thank you so much for coming and talking to me," she said.

"I was very eager to meet you as soon as I heard about your interest in The Brethren," Father Angelini replied as he placed the handkerchief in his pants pocket. "I understand that you have a friend The Brethren has taken a very keen interest in. May I ask how she came to believe this?"

"Umm…my friend…Mac was told that she's being watched by its members, but she doesn't understand why," she said. "She also thinks that there are people around her who know what's going on but are purposely keeping her in the dark. She needs answers and I was hoping that you might be of some help."

Father Angelini nodded and said, "I am happy to help you to the extent that I can. Although I am not a member, my position within the Church has afforded me, shall we say, special access to proprietary information about The Brethren. Very little is publicly known. Given its true mission, it is easy to understand why that is the case."

"From what I learned from Mr. Egger and his website, The Brethren's statutes and membership lists aren't open to the public. Why is that?" Alexis asked.

"It was established over a thousand years ago to fight the Devil and his minions on our physical plane of existence. Its mission is to guard the souls of people who are already, or will in the future, make a significant contribution to the life of the Church. These same people are, as you might suspect, prized targets of the Devil, as well. Members of The Brethren see it as their sacred duty to protect these people's souls from being captured by Satan. If that was your reason for being, would you want the public to know that?"

Alexis suddenly remembered the heated conversation that she had overheard between her father and Father Bernal about a girl whose soul was in danger of being damned to Hell. *Were they talking about me?*

"Is everything all right?" Father Angelini asked as a woman walked in from a side entrance and knelt in a pew not far from where they sat.

Alexis nodded, even though she felt far from fine, lowered her voice, and leaned toward him as she said, "Mr. Egger told me that Hugo Molina is its current Grand Master. Are you familiar with a priest named Juan Pablo Bernal?"

"Actually, yes," he said. "He is The Brethren's Head Chaplain and one of Molina's closest advisors."

"He's a good friend of another member of The Brethren, Eric Neil. Have you heard of him?"

"Isn't he a professor here? I haven't had the pleasure of meeting him personally, but I did know his father. Fredrick Neil was a fine man and a very well respected theologian. His passing was a great loss to the Catholic community."

Alexis felt a tinge of sadness as memories of her kind-hearted and jovial-natured grandfather briefly flashed through her mind. She asked, "Do you know if Fredrick Neil was also a member?"

"A member? Dear child, he was a Grand Master."

Although she was taken aback by the news, she pressed on. "How do you become a member?"

Father Angelini smiled. "You don't ask to become a member. They choose you. In many cases, membership has been passed down from father to son. Very few are invited in."

Alexis saw the woman in the pew rise and waited until she had exited the church before asking Father Angelini, "Have you heard of Rafael Cordero?"

He paused a moment before answering. She could tell from the look on his face that the name was not unfamiliar to him. She swallowed hard as she waited for his answer.

"The Cordero family has a long and distinguished history with The Brethren. Several members of that family were Grand Masters. In fact, Rafael's father, Javier, was being groomed to be The Brethren's next Grand Master when he died unexpectedly."

"Did you know that Rafael is here with Father Bernal?"

Father Angelini clapped his hands together as he said, "My God, so the rumors are true. The target is here."

"What do you mean by target?"

"The Brethren believes that a war against the Devil is imminent. If Father Bernal is here, that must mean that…"

"Javier Cordero's son is The Archer," she interrupted. "Have you seen the video of The Final Tasks?"

Father Angelini shook his head. "Mr. Egger is a resourceful man. I had no idea that he had such a video in his possession. I should pay him a visit and see this video for myself."

"In the video, I saw that The Brethren used what its members call an adjurator for The Final Tasks. Why would its members associate with someone who practices black magic?"

"The Brethren sees it as a necessary evil. If its members are to be prepared to fight the Devil, they need to know what to expect. Enlisting the services of an adjurator is the only way they can do that. Only someone who practices the dark arts can call up the fiends that inhabit the netherworld."

"How did you find out about The Brethren?"

"I am an archivist, among other things. Much of what I'm about to tell you is contained in documents in the Vatican Secret Archives. The Brethren also has copies of these documents at its headquarters in Madrid. The eyewitness accounts of its origins were primarily written by a priest, Father Francisco Moreno. There are also letters written by a noblewoman, Lady Isabella of the House of Antessa, which corroborate the priest's account of what transpired at the time The Brethren was established. It's a fascinating story. I've read and reread the accounts from that period so many times that I practically know it by heart."

"Please tell me. I'd like to know."

"The Brethren are part of a war that began long ago, when the Devil was defeated by the Archangel Michael and banished from Heaven for all eternity. From that point on, the Devil vowed to take as many souls away from God as possible. The Brethren is an arm of the Church that was specifically created to thwart those efforts."

"According to Father Moreno, it all began when a Spanish Duke from the House of Antessa was visited by the Archangel Michael. He informed the Duke that his daughter, Lady Isabella, who was betrothed to the King of Aragon, was in danger and urged him to seek assistance from the Holy See in order to keep her soul from being taken by the Devil. Numerous accounts stated that a great darkness befell the Duke's domain soon afterward. His crops failed, his people fell ill from a plague, and a neighboring nobleman, Count Lucian, raided his lands, taking advantage of the situation. The King sent an emissary to the Holy Father on behalf of the Duke in order to seek protection and safe passage for Lady Isabella from the Duke's castle in the Kingdom of Aragon to Vatican City until the danger to her had passed."

Father Angelini continued, "It was said that Count Lucian had sold his soul to the Devil in exchange for wealth and power. He also wanted Lady Isabella, who was renowned for her grace and beauty. He informed the Duke that he would enter into a truce if he agreed to give Lady Isabella over to him in marriage. She was locked away in one of the castle's towers shortly after the Duke refused his offer and was kept under constant surveillance. People were told that she had become ill; rumors spread that she had become possessed by a demon. The priest's account states that, in the days leading up to The Brethren's arrival at the Duke's castle, people heard unearthly screams at all hours of the night coming from the tower in which she was being kept."

"I wonder why she was considered such a prize…?" Alexis mused. "Do you know what she looked like?"

"There are no known portraits of her still in existence," the priest replied. "In Father Moreno's journals, he described her as having long, wavy brown hair, porcelain-like skin and brown eyes."

As Alexis sat and listened to Father Angelini, she couldn't help but compare herself to the apparently beautiful noblewoman, whose story he was relating to her. Based on Father Angelini's description, Lady Isabella was admired by her subjects and peers and sought after by many suitors. She, on the other hand, saw herself as an ordinary girl with one suitor whose true intentions were far from clear to her.

"Shortly after the King's emissary arrived in Rome, the Holy Father convened a Council which recommended that an army of knights be sent to assist the Duke," Father Angelini recounted. "After much discussion and debate, the Holy Father issued a papal bull establishing The Brethren and appointed Miguel de Montoya, a Count from the Kingdom of Aragon, as its first Grand Master. When Brother Montoya arrived by boat with a small contingent of men at the Port of Barcelona, the Bishop of Barcelona provided The Brethren with additional knights, squires and bowmen."

"What do you know about The Archer?" Alexis asked.

"Father Moreno wrote that the Archangel Michael also appeared to the Bishop of Barcelona and told him to seek out a young knight with exceptional skills with the bow and arrow. The angel informed the Bishop that this knight would be the one that would ensure Lady Isabella's safe passage to Vatican City. While Montoya and his men were en route to Barcelona from Rome, the Bishop convened a tournament. Young men of noble birth, primarily from the Kingdoms of Aragon and Castile, came to compete. The Bishop's eye quickly fell upon a knight who hit the bull's-eye and then split that arrow with a second one. It was at that moment that the Bishop knew that this was the one upon which the title of El Arquero should be bestowed."

"What was his name?" Alexis asked.

"Father Moreno's writings never refer to The Archer by name. Although Lady Isabella's letters mentioned the names of several of the knights who accompanied her to Barcelona, even her writings do not reveal his identity."

Alexis felt more and more confused as Father Angelini related the story of The Brethren's origins. If, as she suspected, history was repeating itself, then Rafael had to have been sent here to protect someone. *But who?* From what Lizzie had told her, the likelihood that it was Alexis was very low. If it wasn't her, then who was it?

"Bonnie?" Father Angelini asked with a curious expression on his face. When Alexis failed to respond to the unfamiliar name, the priest called her once again. "Am I boring you with too many details? I do have a tendency to ramble on. I forget that lay people don't have as much of an interest in all of this as I do."

"Not at all," Alexis replied. "Actually, what you've told me so far has been very helpful. Please go on, Father."

Father Angelini smiled and then continued his account. "By the time Brother Montoya and his army arrived at a hill overlooking the Duke's castle, they saw Count Lucian's forces amassing in a nearby clearing. Brother Montoya was taken to the Great Hall the minute The Brethren rode through the castle gates. The Duke begged him to take Lady Isabella away immediately. Brother Montoya ordered The Archer to gather a few men to whisk her away to safety that very evening."

Vivid images emerged in Alexis' mind as the priest related Father Moreno's detailed account of what occurred on the night The Archer began his journey to Barcelona with Lady Isabella. She pictured him racing toward the tower in which Lady Isabella had been locked away and then forcibly escorting her to the courtyard as she screamed and flailed in protest. It was like she could hear the sound of horses' hooves racing over the drawbridge toward the cover of a dense forest, the whoosh of hundreds of arrows flying into the nighttime sky as Count Lucian's forces attacked the castle and the screams of men as they fought and died in battle.

"Were they able to escape?" Alexis asked.

"Yes, but Count Lucian was never far behind. Father Moreno said that it was a grueling and perilous journey back to Barcelona. The situation was made more complicated by the fact that they discovered that Lady Isabella was possessed by the demon Baal. The priest recounted his several attempts to exorcise the demon from her body before it was finally cast out. He also alluded to the fact that The Archer's relationship with Isabella was a source of difficulty during their journey."

"Didn't they get along?" Alexis asked, sounding shocked.

"Not at first," Father Angelini said with a smile. "Luckily, the tenor of their relationship changed considerably by the time they reached the outskirts of Barcelona."

"Did they make it?" Alexis asked.

"Yes, Lady Isabella did. The Archer ordered two of his men to escort her to the Bishop's residence while he stayed back to engage Count Lucian in battle. She set sail for Rome the next day. Upon her arrival in Rome, she was taken to Vatican City. She stayed there until she gave birth to a son."

Alexis gasped. "A baby? Did she marry the King of Aragon?"

Father Angelini shook his head. "When news of her pregnancy reached the King, he immediately broke off their engagement. As a favor to the Duke, who was one of his most trusted advisors, he did so quietly and did not disclose his reasons. Fortunately, a Spanish Marquis from the Kingdom of Castile stepped in and offered to marry her. Both Father Moreno's writings and Lady Isabella's letters refer to the Marquis as Lord Rodrigo de Avila. He was the second son of the Marquis. He inherited his father's land and titles after both his father and older brother died. Lady Isabella settled in Avila with her husband and bore at least four more children that lived to adulthood."

"The oldest son, Francisco, became a priest and quickly rose through the church ranks. After being appointed to the College of Cardinals, he quickly emerged as a forceful advocate for reform. In fact, his efforts in that respect can still be felt to the present day."

"What happened to The Archer?"

"The records at the Vatican are incomplete. Various accounts indicate that Count Lucian perished in the battle on the outskirts of Barcelona, but there is nothing in the Archives regarding the fate of The Archer. Some say that the answer lies in documents that are solely in the possession of The Brethren."

"Were The Brethren called into service after that?"

"Yes, but it has not appointed another Archer, that is, until now, if what you've told me is correct."

Alexis asked, "Father Angelini, if my friend is the one that The Brethren is trying to protect, why wouldn't its members just tell her that? Why would they keep her in the dark?"

"There could be any number of reasons why they are choosing to hide this information from her."

Alexis' heart sank. *They must think that something is seriously wrong with me,* she thought as all the strange things that had happened to her flitted through her mind. Given these experiences, she couldn't blame them for holding such beliefs about her. Were these occurrences just a figment of her imagination or the result of forces beyond her understanding? Either way she looked at it, her prospects looked dim.

She swallowed hard and then asked Father Angelini, "To what lengths would The Archer go to safeguard the one he was sent to protect?"

"He will do whatever is necessary to eliminate all threats. So would every other member of The Brethren. They are pious men who are absolutely committed to their cause and are willing to sacrifice everything for the sake of their faith."

As Alexis pondered her fate, she came to a startling conclusion: If I'm not the one The Brethren seeks to *protect*…I must be someone that it sees as a *threat*.

The sound of Father Angelini's voice brought her back to the present moment as he said, "Although I have thoroughly enjoyed having this conversation with you, I'm afraid that I must be going now. It's getting late and I have other appointments that I must keep."

Alexis nodded and thanked him for his time. He stood up and placed his hand on her shoulder as she bowed her head. Given his outward appearance, the firmness of his grasp surprised her. He said, "Don't despair, Alexis, or let the darkness put out the light that shines inside you. Have faith and be assured that you will never be alone or forgotten." With that, he slowly made his way into the aisle and left her to her thoughts.

For a minute or two, Alexis sat there trying to make sense of what she'd been told when it suddenly dawned on her that Father Angelini had called her by her *real* name. She turned her head toward the main aisle of the church and found that he was nowhere to be seen. She started to panic since she was almost sure that she hadn't heard the doors open or close. She also thought that his physical infirmities would have made such a quick exit nearly impossible. Overwhelmed and bewildered, she sank back down in the pew as she contemplated the possibility that she had experienced yet another hallucination.

Shortly thereafter, she decided to confirm her suspicions about Father Angelini and sent Egger a text asking him if he had referred the man to her. Just as she had feared, Egger responded minutes later that he had made no such referral and had, in fact, never heard of the man.

Alexis felt like the world as she knew it had been turned upside down. She didn't know who to trust or what to believe anymore. She also had no idea what to do next or who to reach out to for help.

Alexis felt a lump in her throat as Eric pulled up to the fountain at precisely four o'-clock. She glanced at him as she got in and wondered if there were any other secrets he was hiding from her. She questioned how well she really knew him and wondered to what lengths he would go to serve his God. Although she recoiled at the thought of her own father harming her in any way, the facts as she now knew them suggested that such a scenario was more than just a theoretical possibility.

"So, were you able to get much studying done?" Eric asked.

"No, not really, but it was at least worth a try," Alexis replied as she pulled out her MP3 player and earbuds from her backpack, searched through her playlist, and picked a song. As she put the earbuds in, she said, "Dad, can you just drop me off in front of the church? Rafael will take me home."

He nodded as she slouched in her seat, closed her eyes, and lost herself in the music.

When Eric stopped in the church parking lot, Alexis gave her father a quick peck on the cheek and stepped out of the car. She rushed into the church and found that almost everyone else in the youth choir was already seated. Jake grabbed hold of her arm as soon as she walked over to the piano to pick up her music binder.

When she bent down to talk to him, Jake seemed agitated as he whispered, "We've got a major problem with your project. I need to talk to you after mass."

Just then, Rafael walked up with a guitar in hand and sat down next to Jake. He smiled at her as he slipped the guitar strap over his shoulder. She smiled back and then walked to the podium after seeing Father Jim give her the signal that it was time for mass to start.

The mass itself was uneventful. After Jake played the last chord of the closing hymn, Alexis went to the piano and stood by him as he organized his sheet music.

When Rafael went to put his things away, Jake said to her, "I think he found out that his phone was bugged. The program I installed hasn't been able to access any information for the last twenty-four hours and the links to the websites that he visited don't work anymore."

"How can that be?" she asked anxiously. "I thought you said that what you installed couldn't be detected."

Jake shook his head as he said, "I don't know what to tell you, but if he found out that he was being bugged, it's possible that he might be able to find out who did it…"

"If he doesn't know already," she interrupted. She thought for a moment and then said, "Is there a chance that maybe the program is just experiencing a glitch?"

Jake shook his head. "Not likely."

"We need to talk and come up with a plan," she said. "I'll tell Rafael that you're going to take me home tonight. I want to see for myself exactly what's going on."

"Don't you think he'll get suspicious if you tell him you're going with me? He was already looking at us kind of funny when he saw us together in the parking lot yesterday."

Alexis was about to respond when Tessa approached them. She put her arm around Jake and said, "You two are looking way too intense. What's going on?"

"It's Alexis' project," Jake replied. "We're running into problems and we're trying to figure out how to fix things, if that's even possible."

Alexis turned to her cousin and said, "Tessa, is it okay if I steal your boyfriend tonight? I really need his help." To her great relief, her cousin agreed without asking any questions.

Tessa said, "Rafael's waiting for you in the back and checking his watch like every couple of seconds." She winked at Alexis, adding, "I think he was looking forward to some alone time with his girlfriend. He's going to be very disappointed."

So am I, she thought as she turned to Jake and said, "I'll go back there and talk to him. Just wait for me by your car, okay?" Jake nodded as Alexis headed for the music room.

Rafael was putting some music in a file cabinet when Alexis walked in. He closed the drawer and moved toward her.

"A little birdie told me that you were getting antsy waiting for me back here," she teased.

Rafael looked at Tessa, who had walked in behind her, and frowned. Tessa shrugged her shoulders as she smiled back at him and gave her cousin a hug before leaving.

Alexis put her arms around Rafael's neck and leaned her forehead against his as she said, "Look, I need to work on something with Jake so, if it's okay with you, I'm just gonna hitch a ride home with him."

She felt his body stiffen slightly. She couldn't tell if he was angry, suspicious, or just disappointed by what she had said. His face was unreadable.

She moved closer and gently stroked his face with her right hand as she said, "You aren't angry with me, are you?"

"At you, never," he said, looking resigned. She felt a chill run down her spine as he took hold of one of her hands and brought it to his lips. He followed that up with a peck on the cheek and a whispered, "Buenas noches, mi querida," in her ear before exiting the room.

It was 6:40 by the time Jake and Alexis drove up to his house. Jake's father Martin, and younger brother Aaron, who were playing a video game together in the living room, smiled and waved to her as she passed by them on her way to the kitchen. She was also greeted by Jake's mother, who was busy making dinner. She exchanged pleasantries with Mrs. Lewis while Jake went upstairs to get his laptop.

When Jake returned, he motioned for her to follow him to his father's den. As soon as he closed the door and booted up his computer, he logged into the same program he had shown her a couple of days ago and clicked on the links that now led to nothing. She became particularly alarmed when she had him click on Rafael's brother's social media page and found that the profile had been deleted.

Afterward, Jake asked, "Did you get the impression tonight that he was on to what we were doing?"

Alexis shook her head. "Not really. He was acting like he normally does."

"So, what do you want to do now?"

"I need time to think. I'm still trying to sort out everything I learned from Egger and Father Angelini." She paused for a moment as she considered whether she could trust anything she had learned from the priest, given the fact that Egger had not referred him to her and, in fact, had never even heard of him. "I need more answers, but the problem is that the people who can give them to me can't or won't do it."

Jake shook his head as he put his hands on his hips and said, "You are in way over your head. You need help."

"I'll be fine," she quickly replied.

From the look on Jake's face, she knew that he wasn't buying a thing she had said. "You gotta promise me that you're going to be careful," he said. "Don't do anything stupid or reckless."

"I have to know the truth. I can't stop now."

"Is there anything else I can do to help you?"

Alexis shook her head and said, "If I think of something, I'll let you know. In the meantime, just do what you can to access those blocked emails and keep him from finding out who bugged his phone."

"I'll do my best," Jake said.

"I know you will," Alexis replied. "I think you'd better take me home. I've got a lot of thinking to do."

CHAPTER 15—CONFRONTATIONS

Alexis' anxiety level was at an all-time high by the time she arrived at school on Monday morning. Her recurring dream and Jake's news had left her bleary-eyed and emotionally spent. *If Jake is right,* she thought, *it'll only be a matter of time before Rafael will know who hacked into his phone, and when he does find out, what will he do?*

She and Jake exchanged worried looks when they met up with each other in the courtyard, but said nothing. When Rafael arrived minutes later, he sat down next to her and whispered in her ear, "How are you this morning, mi querida? I missed spending time with you last night."

Alexis let out a slow, unsteady breath as he gave her hand a quick squeeze. If Rafael knew or suspected that they had hacked into his phone, he wasn't letting on. She decided that there was little else she could do but keep up the pretense that nothing had happened until she and Jake could come up with a new plan.

A moment later, Rafael's phone beeped. When he pulled it out from his back pocket, she saw that it was new and panicked.

Alexis pointed and asked, "What happened to your old one?"

"There was something wrong with it, so I got a new one," Rafael replied as he put it back into his pocket.

Even though this explained why Jake wasn't able to access any new information, it still didn't explain why the links to the websites he visited no longer worked. She was certain that Jake was probably thinking the same thing as he sat next to her and pretended to check his own messages.

During lunchtime, Alexis found herself glancing surreptitiously at Rafael's training partners: Vincenzo, Gonçalo, and Akira. All four boys were strikingly similar in appearance, with lean, muscular bodies and short-cropped dark hair. They also carried themselves with a sense of grace and dignity that many of their slump-shouldered male peers lacked. Although none of them were more than six feet tall, she suspected that any one of them could have knocked down the largest defensive lineman on the school's football team without breaking a sweat. She wanted to know more about them and to learn what their roles were in the scheme of things. She also wondered why Rafael had never introduced them to her. Unfortunately, she was finding that her search for answers only led to even more questions, which left her feeling frustrated and confused.

Near the end of lunchtime, Tessa invited Alexis to go for a jog at Salt Creek Community Park after school. She readily agreed and told her cousin that she would meet her there at four thirty in the afternoon. She needed to clear her head and thought that a jog just might be what the doctor ordered.

The park was nearly deserted when Alexis got there. She felt a slight chill in the air even though the sun was still out and the sky above her was blue and cloudless. A cold gust of wind blew past her, sending her hair flying about and giving her goose bumps. She regretted not having worn warmer clothes but knew that there was little she could do about it now. So instead, she just hugged herself and tried to stay warm.

Alexis walked down a long staircase and passed a young couple walking their dog. Aside from that, she saw no one else. She made her way through a large grassy area to a cement bench facing one of two playgrounds in the middle of the park. It was unusually quiet for that time of day, which made her feel a little uneasy. After chalking up her fears to her overactive imagination, she decided to stretch to keep her mind off her worries while waiting for Tessa to arrive.

After Alexis finished warming up, she sat down on the bench, put in her earbuds, and turned on her MP3 player. She closed her eyes and turned up the music. She was listening to one of her favorite songs when she felt a tap on her shoulder. She assumed that it was Tessa until she opened her eyes and saw Lizzie's fiery red hair glistening in the sunlight. She pulled her earbuds out and smiled at her friend.

"Hey, Mac," Lizzie said with an impish grin. "Did you miss me?"

"What are you doing here?" Alexis asked. "You're not exactly an outdoorsy person."

"That comment shows just how little you know about me," Lizzie replied, pretending to look offended. Alexis wasn't fooled in the least. "So, have you learned anything new about you-know-who?"

"He does have a name you know," Alexis replied. "The hacking idea was a disaster, by the way. I got blocked within days of accessing the information on his cell phone. You're now two for two when it comes to bad ideas, if we count the library incident."

"My ideas were great. You just didn't execute them very well," she said as Alexis shook her head in disagreement. "What have you learned so far?"

"Just that his brother looks exactly like him and that he doesn't mention me or our relationship in his emails to friends and family."

"That shouldn't surprise you. Anything else?"

"Well, I also did some research on the Internet and met with two people who gave me a lot of information about The Brethren. One of them showed me an interesting video of something The Brethren calls The Final Tasks."

"What do you think is going on?"

"I'm still not completely sure," Alexis mused as she bit her fingernails. "I know that members of The Brethren are watching me and that Father Bernal, my father, and Rafael are part of that religious order. I also think that my mother and brother know something about what's going on, too. Still, I'm having a hard time squaring what I've learned about Rafael with the person that I know. Even though you told me that I shouldn't trust him, everything he's said and done so far makes me think that the last thing he would ever want to do is hurt me."

Lizzie sat down next to Alexis and patted her knee as she said, "Haven't you ever heard the phrase, 'Keep your friends close and your enemies closer?'" Alexis nodded. "Don't you see? He's probably lulling you into a false sense of security. He's drawing you in so he can keep a close eye on you. It also keeps him within striking distance if he thinks you need to be taken out of the picture."

As much as Alexis wanted to disagree with Lizzie's logic, she had to admit that her arguments made perfect sense under the current circumstances.

Alexis asked, "If The Brethren think that I'm a threat, then who are they trying to protect? He's always with me at school and he doesn't leave my side until he drops me off at home."

"Do you know where he goes or who he sees after he drops you off?" Alexis shook her head. "Didn't your cousin Joey tell you that he saw Rafael training with other people at his dojo? Has he told you about that yet? He could be doing anything, seeing anyone when he's not with you."

Again, Alexis could find no holes in Lizzie's argument. *She's right,* she thought. *So what do I do now?*

"Who else knows about what's going on, besides the people you've mentioned?" Lizzie asked.

"Just Jake, but he'd never say anything to anybody. He tried to help me think of people I could reach out to, but there don't seem to be any viable options at the moment. The ones I normally would go to either know about, or are closely connected to, The Brethren."

"Have you thought about fighting fire with fire?" Lizzie asked.

Alexis had no idea what point Lizzie was trying to get across to her. "What are you saying?"

"You're dealing with religious zealots, aren't you?" she said. "What are they most afraid of? The Devil…demons…dark magic…"

"What's your point?"

"You really need to get your head out of the sand and wake up! If these people are out to get you because of what they think you are or might become, then you might as well give them what they want. If they think you're a witch that needs to be burned at the stake, then you need to do all you can to arm yourself against them."

"The *them* you are talking about includes my father. He would never hurt me," Alexis protested.

"What did Abraham do when God asked him to sacrifice his son, Isaac?" Lizzie replied. "Your father is a devout Catholic and a member of The Brethren. Don't think for a minute that he wouldn't be willing to sacrifice you if he thought that was what God wanted him to do."

Alexis was beginning to hate herself for not being able to counter Lizzie's arguments with plausible alternatives, especially since Lizzie was, in essence, telling her that her father and Rafael would kill her if their faith demanded it. She felt like her head was spinning as she struggled to make sense of things.

"So what do you think I should do?" Alexis asked. "Do you know anyone that might be able to help me?"

A cat-like smile spread across Lizzie's face as she said, "What about Bobby?"

Alexis cringed at the mere mention of his name. "Besides being a complete jerk, he's next to useless. Anybody else?"

"Wait a minute," Lizzie said. "Don't be too hasty. I know for a fact that he dabbles in the occult. He just might be the person to help you out of this mess."

"Why would *he* want to help me?" Alexis replied. "We don't exactly have the best relationship in the world. In fact, it's nonexistent." *Then again, didn't he just invite me to go to his Halloween party?* Lizzie's eyes lit up as she told her what Bobby had said to her in front of the theater the other night.

"Perfect," Lizzie replied. "Take him up on his offer and see what happens."

"Rafael probably wouldn't want me go," she quipped.

"Your precious Rafael doesn't have to know. Make some excuse. Do something to get him out of the way."

Just then, Lizzie pointed to the top of the stairs on the east side of the park. Tessa had arrived. Lizzie said, "I'll see you later," and then abruptly stood up and walked away.

A few minutes later, Tessa sat down next to her cousin and asked, "Have you been waiting awhile? I'm sorry I'm late."

"Don't worry," Alexis replied. "I wasn't alone."

Tessa gazed at her with a quizzical expression and then took a quick look around the park. "Really? I don't see anyone within a mile of here."

Alexis, assuming her cousin was trying to be funny, pretended to ignore her comment and asked, "Are you ready, or do you need to stretch first?"

"I'm good," Tessa replied.

"Let's go then. My legs are dying to get moving."

On Tuesday, Alexis' school day was going smoothly enough until she got to gym class. Ever since the homecoming dance, things had gone from bad to worse with Anita. She seemed to take it as a personal affront that Rafael had chosen to be with Alexis rather than her. Most days, she did her best to ignore Anita's snide comments and spiteful glances, but she found it infinitely harder to do that when Anita and her friends mocked and ridiculed her within the small confines of the girls' locker room.

Alexis was changing into her gym clothes when Cecilia and Lea walked in. She groaned inwardly and sped up her efforts to get dressed and out of the line of fire. She felt their eyes bore into her as she walked past them to go to the assembly area where their gym coach, Jorge Jimenez, was waiting.

After a brief warm up, he directed all the female students to the soccer field and divided the class into two teams. Alexis volunteered to be a forward while Tessa was designated as the goalie. Anita, Cecilia, and Lea were on the other team, which suited Alexis just fine. When Coach Jimenez blew the whistle to start the game, Alexis quickly got control of the ball and kicked it down the field toward Cecilia, the other team's goalie. When she saw Lea and Anita running toward her, she passed the ball to an open teammate, who easily kicked the ball into the goal. Alexis deliberately gave her teammate a high five right in front of Anita before jogging back to the middle of the field for the kick off.

Alexis' team quickly regained control of the ball and once again raced down the field toward Cecilia. When the ball went out of bounds near the goal, Lea brushed past her and said, "You better watch your back, Alexis."

Alexis glared at her, but said nothing. Another girl on her team who had heard Lea, walked over and said, "Don't let her get to you. She's just mad 'cause we're winning."

Once the ball was again in play, Alexis nearly fell face forward when Lea swiped at her leg. Luckily, she braced herself with her hands before her face hit the grass. Coach Jimenez blew the whistle and called a time out. She quickly got back on her feet and told him that she was fine. Before the coach blew the whistle to resume the game, he reminded everyone that this was supposed to be a *friendly* game of soccer. *If only!*

It wasn't long before Alexis' team took control of the ball yet again. As she dribbled the ball down the field, she caught sight of Lea and Anita coming at her from opposite sides of the field. She sprinted forward just as they were about to crash into her, which caused them to collide into each other instead. Coach Jimenez again blew the whistle. While they were helping each other up, she came up to them and asked, "Did that hurt?"

They glared at her before walking away with their noses in the air. *Maybe,* she thought, *they've finally had enough.*

Alexis soon realized how wrong she was. Despite Coach Jimenez's constant admonishments, the pushing and shoving when the coach's back was turned got even worse. When the ball went out of bounds, Anita missed hitting Alexis square in the face by inches when she threw the ball back in. Minutes later, Lea elbowed her in the ribs and nearly knocked the wind out of her as they furiously tried to kick the ball out from under each other's control. Their struggle finally ended when Alexis accidentally tripped her. Lea landed hard on the ground and began clutching her right ankle. Coach Jimenez blew the whistle and called a time out, allowing Lea to be helped off the field by her teammates.

Anita's team managed to score twice before Alexis once again found herself in scoring position. The only thing between her and the net was Cecilia, who looked more interested in admiring her manicured nails than in protecting the goal. With one swift kick, she watched the ball fly into the air. Within seconds, she heard the bones in Cecilia's nose crunch as it smashed into her face. Cecilia let out a high-pitched scream as she covered her bloody nose with her hands. Coach Jimenez immediately blew his whistle and mercifully put an end to the game. After another coach came over and assisted Cecilia off the field, he ordered all of them to go to the locker room.

Alexis was taking off her shoes when Anita barreled toward her. Anita got right in her face and prodded her in the chest as she yelled, "Hey, what's your problem?"

"I don't know what you're talking about."

"You hurt Cecilia and Lea on purpose," Anita snarled.

"Soccer is a dangerous sport and sometimes people get hurt," Alexis replied calmly.

"Lea sprained her ankle because of you."

"We were both going after the ball," Alexis explained. "I could have been hurt just as easily as she was."

"What about Cecilia?"

"Is it my fault that she wasn't paying attention to where the ball was? She was supposed to be your team's goalie."

"I'm sure your precious Rafael wouldn't approve of what you did out there. I'd hate to be the one to let him know what just happened."

"So what are you gonna do, run and tell him? Do you really think he'd listen to you over me? I hate to break it to you, but that's not going to improve your chances with him which are, by the way, nonexistent. Like it or not, he's made his choice."

Alexis heard other girls nearby snicker as Anita's face turned purple with rage.

"I don't know what kind of spell you've put on him, but he's bound to snap out of it eventually," Anita replied.

"Wow," Alexis said as she shook her head in disbelief. "You really think you still have a chance with him, don't you? I knew you were vain, but I didn't think you were delusional."

Anita looked like a ticking time bomb that was about to explode. *Not a very pretty sight*, Alexis thought, feeling slightly amused.

Anita said, "I guess I was wrong about Rafael. I thought he had better taste in women. Apparently, he likes them plain and simple."

Alexis' whole body tensed up, as Tessa said from behind her, "Just walk away, Cuz. Don't take the bait. She's not worth getting in trouble over."

Tessa, of course, was right. She was now only minutes away from meeting Rafael and her other friends for lunch. *He's waiting for me,* she told herself as she took a deep breath and tried to figure out a way to step back from the precipice.

Unfortunately, Alexis sensed that Anita saw her hesitation as a sign of weakness and continued on with her offensive. "You're utterly forgettable. No one cares about you. Even *he* won't, once he goes back to Spain. Give him a few weeks away from you. He won't even remember your name."

"Jealous much? Why don't you just do everyone a favor and back off," Tessa said to Anita, as she put her hand on Alexis' shoulder.

Anita said to Alexis, "So, is your cousin going to be fighting your battles for you now that Avery isn't here to protect you?"

Tessa shook her head as she pleaded with her eyes for Alexis to just turn and walk away. Alexis gave her cousin a quick nod before turning her attention back to Anita. She knew that Anita wanted her to start a fight so that she could play the victim and vilify her. Although she was determined not to give Anita what she wanted, she was too angry to leave without getting in one last parting shot.

Alexis rolled her shoulders back and held her chin up defiantly as she said, "Rafael doesn't want you. He never has, and he never will. You can say whatever you want, but it won't change the fact that he chose me. I know it's hard for your overblown ego to accept, but you're just going to have to live with it."

After Alexis turned to walk away, Anita screamed out, "You think I don't know what you are? You're not like the rest of us. Tell me, how are your psychiatric sessions going? Are you still taking meds? Have you told him about that?"

Alexis went rigid as a few of the girls around them gasped and tittered among themselves. She slowly turned back around and saw Anita staring at her with a triumphant look on her face. She sensed that Anita was about to go in for the kill.

Anita said, "You can't hide who you are forever and, you know what, when he does find out what a nut case you are, he won't be able to run away fast enough."

Get her, screamed a voice in her head. *Smash that pretty little face of hers into the lockers.* She closed her eyes and tried to block the voice out, which only became more strident and insistent. *Make her pay.*

"You're nothing…nobody…live with that," Anita sneered.

Alexis felt something inside her snap when she opened her eyes and saw Anita smiling malevolently in front of her. She took a step forward and shoved Anita as hard as she could. She heard gasps and screams around her as the sound of Anita's body slamming into the lockers echoed throughout the room. Anita lurched forward and pushed Alexis back, causing her to stumble over a bench. Before she knew it, she was rolling on the ground with Anita, as they scratched, clawed, and pulled each other's hair. When she tried to get up, Anita kicked her in the stomach. She countered the attack by punching Anita in the jaw. Anita screamed and staggered back as blood flowed down from her mouth.

She's down. Kick her. Break her now, screamed the voice in her head. Just as Alexis was about to lose complete control, two coaches burst into the locker room and quickly reestablished order.

Alexis and Anita were told to change into their school uniforms and were then unceremoniously escorted to the administrative offices. She knew that word about her fight with Anita was probably spreading like wildfire around campus already and that Rafael and her friends would soon know what had happened. Too embarrassed and ashamed of herself to look anyone in the eye, she bowed her head and kept her gaze fixed on the ground all the way to the principal's office. She felt like a criminal who had been caught and was being taken to jail. It was, however, no less than what she thought that she deserved.

Alexis picked at the skin around her fingers as she sat in a chair in the main entranceway to the DePaul Center, waiting for the assistant principal, Karen Black, to call her back to her office. As she sat across the way from the receptionist's office, she got the distinct impression that the woman behind the desk was purposely avoiding eye contact with her. She peered down at her fingers and thought that they looked redder and rawer than ever before. At one point, Anita's grim-faced mother passed by, with Anita following close behind, arms folded and head bowed. She was holding her jaw and it looked like she had been crying. Alexis anticipated that she was likely to suffer a similar or worse fate when she was finally called into Ms. Black's office.

Alexis sat back and had just reached for the latest issue of *The Crusader* lying on a table next to her when Ms. Black appeared and asked Alexis to follow her. Her mother's office was immediately adjacent to Ms. Black's and, as they passed, she could see that the blinds were drawn and that her mother's door was closed.

"Take a seat," Ms. Black said in a very business-like manner. Alexis sat down, folded her hands in her lap and waited.

"You know why you're here, Alexis." She merely nodded in response. "Normally, the principal would be handling this, but, considering the circumstances, she delegated that duty to me." Ms. Black rested her arms on the desk as she leaned forward in her seat and said, "You know the rules. We have a zero-tolerance policy here at school when it comes to violence. Fighting of any kind is grounds for an automatic suspension of three days. During your suspension, you are not allowed to be on this campus for any reason and will be barred from participating in any school-related activities. I've been informed that your brother, Jeremy, is on his way to pick you up and should be here shortly. Do you have any questions so far?"

Alexis shook her head. Her mother was the principal. She, better than anyone else, knew that there was a rule against fighting and what the punishment would be. Aside from the three-day suspension, she knew that she was also looking at academic probation with the possibility of expulsion for any further offense.

She could only imagine what her parents were going to say and what type of additional punishment they were going to impose. She could picture the looks of extreme disappointment that would be on their faces and their shock at the idea that she would be capable of such behavior.

Alexis also wondered what Rafael and her friends might be thinking. She remembered the sound of Tessa's panic-stricken voice as she pleaded with her to stop fighting. She shuddered to think about their reaction. By giving in to her rage, she had proved Anita right and probably supplied Rafael with the irrefutable proof that she was indeed a lost soul.

A knock startled Alexis and brought her back to reality. She turned toward the door as it opened and saw Jeremy standing there. Although the expression on his face betrayed no sign of emotion, the look in his eyes told a different story. In them she saw a mixture of concern, frustration, and extreme disappointment. He turned to Ms. Black and said, "Good afternoon, ma'am. I'm here to pick up my sister."

"Very good," Ms. Black replied. "I'm just about ready to release her to you."

Jeremy turned to Alexis and said, "Are you ready?" She nodded and then looked away.

When it was time to go, Ms. Black said, "The school will be conducting a thorough investigation concerning the circumstances surrounding the altercation you were involved in this morning. You will have the opportunity to make a statement and provide any other pertinent information on your own behalf that would help us determine the most appropriate course of action to take. The findings will be reported to you and your parents at a conference that we will schedule within the next three school days. A determination as to your fitness to resume your coursework at this school will be made at that time. If you have no further questions, I will release you to your brother now."

Alexis kept her head bowed down as she followed Jeremy out of the room, down the hall, and out to the parking lot. As she stepped out of the building, she saw students walking to their next class and wondered if and when she would once again be among them.

They had just buckled their seatbelts when Alexis turned to Jeremy and said, "I don't want to talk about it."

"Fine," he replied flatly as he turned on the engine and put the car in drive.

Although Alexis' home was only ten minutes away from school, the tension she felt between her and Jeremy made the car ride home feel endless. Jeremy honored her request and said nothing. She, in turn, purposely turned her head toward the window to avoid any possibility of eye contact with him. *He'd never understand*, she thought. *How could he? He's the perfect son who never does anything wrong.* She, on the other hand, was far from being the perfect daughter. In her mind, the incident had created a dividing line between them that neither could cross at the moment.

When they got home, Alexis hurried into the house and up the stairs, closed the door to her room, and flung herself on the bed. It was about an hour later when Jeremy knocked on her bedroom door and called out her name. When she opened the door, he said, "They're ready to see you now."

Alexis nodded and followed him to their father's study. Jeremy opened the door and held it open for her. As she walked past him, he looked at her sadly before turning toward the hallway and closing the door behind him.

"Sit down, Alexis," Eric said in a grave tone.

A feeling of dread suddenly overtook Alexis as she dutifully complied with her father's request. She felt like a criminal awaiting sentencing. He was sitting behind his desk while her mother stood by the window. He looked grim and unsympathetic. She, on the other hand, clearly had a pained expression on her face. Alexis also noticed that her mother's eyes were slightly red and swollen.

Eric took off his glasses and rubbed his eyes. Although she was sitting only a few feet away, she had never felt more distant from him than at this moment. In all the years that she had been on this Earth, she had never felt afraid of him…until now.

Eric placed both his forearms on the desk as he leaned forward and said, "What you did today at school is inexcusable. We thought that we'd raised a daughter that knew the difference between right and wrong, who thought things through before taking any action…We're very disappointed in you."

"I know these last few months have been hard on you, anak," Lisa interjected, "but it doesn't absolve you of the obligation to make the right choices."

"When you don't make the right choices, you have to do whatever is necessary to make amends," Eric added. "Are we clear on that point?"

"Yes, Dad." Alexis had little choice but to agree. Although her parents had always dealt with her and Jeremy with a benevolent hand, there was never a doubt as to who was in charge.

"Good. The first thing we want you to do is to apologize to Miss Morales."

Alexis' eyes widened as her mouth flew open in disbelief. "You're joking, right?"

The stern expression on Eric's face told her that he was deadly serious. "Does it sound like we're joking, Alexis?"

"Anita was the one who started the fight in the locker room," she argued. "I had to defend myself. I had no choice!"

"You *always* have a choice," Eric replied. "You could have just walked away."

"You weren't there," she said, leaning forward in her seat. "You didn't hear all the awful things she said to me. I tried to ignore her, but she wouldn't let up. And when she called me a nut case, I just…lost it."

"Let me be very clear," he replied. "What we're telling you to do is not optional. It doesn't matter what Miss Morales may have said or done. Your actions and reactions are what concern us. You shouldn't have been involved in a fight. Period. From what we've been told, you purposely shoved Miss Morales and punched her in the face. You knew better and we expected more from you."

"But…"

"You made her bleed!" he said, cutting her off. She slunk back in her seat.

"Secondly, we've made arrangements for you to see your psychiatrist at least twice a week now."

Alexis rolled her eyes and said, "Those sessions are useless. How many times have I told you that?"

Eric said, "Given your current circumstances, you're in no position to argue with us."

"I'm sorry. I'm really not trying to be disrespectful…"

"Then don't be," Eric said curtly. "Lastly, you are not to go anywhere or see anyone without our permission or supervision."

"You're grounding me? For how long?"

"For as long as we think it's appropriate," he said.

"You can't do this!" Alexis said as she half-rose from her seat and gripped the arms of her chair to keep from losing all sense of control.

"That's enough, Alexis!" Eric replied.

"I don't get it. You just expect me to follow you, blindly, without asking questions. How am I ever going to learn to make the right decisions, when you won't tell me all you know?"

"You need to trust our judgment," Lisa said. "Sometimes less is more."

"You need to stop treating me like a child."

"Then stop acting like one," Eric replied sharply. "In addition, your access to the Internet is suspended as of right now. That goes for your cell phone, too."

Alexis started to protest, but the look on her father's face told her that the discussion was over. She was guilty as charged, and nothing she could say or do was going to change their minds or lessen the severity of her punishment. To them, she was a disobedient, disrespectful, and unstable child, who could no longer be trusted. Right then and there, she decided that if that was the child that they believed her to be, that was the child that they were going to get.

CHAPTER 16—HALLOWEEN

It was after four o'clock on Thursday afternoon when Alexis came home from a meeting with her parents and school representatives. She was told by the administration that it had concluded she was fit to be readmitted to school on Monday. They had based their decision on the fact that she had no prior history of violence, her psychiatrist's evaluation and treatment plan, and their investigation into the incident. Just as she anticipated, she was put on academic probation and was told that any further infraction would be grounds for immediate expulsion.

Alexis grabbed a book off the shelf in her father's study and went out to the porch swing in front of her house to read. It had been three days since she had had contact with anyone outside of her immediate family and she was beginning to go stir crazy. Her parents had made good on their promise to cut her off from all communication with the outside world and had not returned her cell phone or given her access to the Internet since the day she had gotten into the fight with Anita. She had no idea if anyone had tried to get in touch with her or had bothered to ask how she was doing. During that time, she thought of Rafael nonstop and wondered whether or not he missed her.

Alexis opened her novel and tried reading the first couple of pages. After having gone through the same sentence three times in a row, she closed the book and gave up. She looked out onto the street and saw inflatable ghosts coming out of pumpkins, jack-o'-lanterns, cobwebs filled with fake spiders, and tombstones aplenty adorning many of her neighbors' front yards. The sight of all the Halloween decorations reminded her that Bobby's party was tomorrow night. Knowing her parents would never let her go, she had to find a way to get out of the house without being detected and get hold of someone who would take her there. Besides, she had no desire to get behind the wheel. Asking Jake or Tessa was out of the question, since they knew that she was grounded. She also crossed Rafael off the list, knowing that he would never approve of her having any contact with Bobby. She scratched her head and then thought of… Tobey. *Didn't he say that he owed me one after I tried to defend him against Mateo?* She felt a rush of excitement course through her veins when she realized that she had found a possible solution to her problem.

With her parents at work and Jeremy asleep on the couch, Alexis seized the moment by grabbing the cordless phone from the kitchen and heading to the backyard, where she knew she wouldn't be heard. After quietly closing the sliding door behind her, she dialed Tobey's cell phone and anxiously waited for him to pick up. When he did, she could hardly contain herself as she said, "Hi Tobey, it's Alexis. I need you to do me a big favor…"

On Friday, Alexis played the part of the dutiful daughter to the hilt. Her parents were leaving for a Catholic theology conference in Los Angeles that afternoon. They reminded her that they would be gone until Sunday and that Jeremy would be in charge in their absence. *Perfect,* she thought, as she sat and ate an early dinner with them. When she asked about her cell phone and Internet privileges, her father told her that he would give back her cell phone and laptop before they left, but that she would not be allowed to go out under any circumstances or to have anyone over. She nodded in agreement, glad to have been restored some connection to the outside world again. If her parents suspected that something was amiss, they didn't let on.

As soon as her parents' car had backed out of the driveway, Alexis ran upstairs, closed the door, and turned on her cell phone. She immediately checked to see if anyone had sent her a text or left a voicemail. She spotted Rafael's voicemail message right away but lost her nerve and decided to check it later. After what she had been through this week, the last thing she needed to hear was what she feared might be a message from him saying that he was breaking up with her. She sighed and then decided to move on. She smiled when she saw that all her friends had sent her texts, too. She checked each one and was heartened by their words of support. After she sent a universal text to everyone but Rafael, telling them that she was fine and would see them at school on Monday, she spent the rest of the afternoon planning her escape.

It was around ten o'clock when the last of the trick-or-treaters stopped by. Alexis yawned and told Jeremy that she was going to bed. Her brother looked tired and weak as he lay on the couch in the living room watching T.V. Although he admitted that he felt warm and had a headache, he assured her that all he needed was some rest and ibuprofen, which she brought to him, along with a glass of water. Afterward, she headed upstairs to take a shower and pulled out her costume from the closet. Tonight, she was going to be Catwoman. She had bought it on impulse during one of her many treks to the mall with her cousin just before the homecoming dance. She slipped the black, skin-tight catsuit on and then applied her make-up. She put on a pair of sweatpants and a hooded sweatshirt over her costume and then peeked into Jeremy's room. When she didn't see him there, she went downstairs and saw that he was fast asleep on the living room couch. *The coast is finally clear*, she thought, relieved. She went back upstairs and sent Tobey a text, telling him to pick her up a block from her house. After staging the pillows on her bed to look like a body tucked under her covers, she turned off her bedroom light and quietly made her way downstairs. She had her backpack slung over her shoulder while holding a mini-flashlight attached to her keychain in one hand and her black high heel shoes in the other hand. She tiptoed out the front door in her bare feet and silently shut and locked it behind her.

The cold night air hit Alexis' body like a sledgehammer. She put on her shoes and pulled her hoodie up over her head and then walked toward the end of the street. She giggled aloud when she saw Tobey standing next to his car, dressed in a wild, bright blue costume, complete with antennae.

"Your chariot awaits my lady," Tobey said, bowing grandly.

Alexis shook her head and asked, "Just what are you supposed to be?"

Tobey smiled broadly as he said, "The Tick. Who else?"

He switched on the heat and asked for directions to Bobby's place when they got into his car. As they headed down the street, he asked, "How are you doing?"

"Better. You got my text, right? I get to go back to school on Monday."

"That's great."

Is it? she thought. "So what have people been saying?"

Tobey hesitated. "Everyone knows that you and Anita got into a fight over Rafael."

Alexis sighed. "How did *he* take the news?"

"We all found out at lunch time," he said. "Tessa told us everything. Rafael didn't say much, but I could tell that it shook him up pretty bad. I saw him talking to your mom by the DePaul Center after school that day, but I wasn't close enough to hear what they were saying. From what I could see, it looked like she was really letting him have it."

"What did Rafael do?"

Tobey shrugged his shoulders and said, "He just stood there and took it."

Alexis wondered why her mother never mentioned the fact that she had spoken to Rafael after her run-in with Anita. She was even more curious about what they had said to one another. Unfortunately, she knew that the likelihood of her getting any answers from her mother was slim to none.

"So tell me again why you're going to this party with me rather than with Rafael?"

"He wouldn't have taken me knowing that I'm not supposed to be out," she replied. "I also know that he wouldn't approve of where we're going."

"So you asked the guy you knew wouldn't say no," Tobey mused. "I should just turn around and take you home right now."

"Tobey, please. I have to go. This is important."

"Why is it so important for you to go to this party?"

"Bobby was Avery's boyfriend. He told me that he'd give me some answers about what was going on with her just before the accident if I showed up."

"I don't know, Alexis," he said. "I've got a bad feeling about this."

"We don't have to stay long. Besides, I'll be wearing a mask, and I don't think many people we know will be there. You don't have to worry about being seen with me."

"Alexis, I don't care about that," he replied. "It's you that I'm worried about. You're my friend. I just don't want you to get into any more trouble than you've already gotten yourself into."

"Don't worry," she reassured him. "Everything is going to be fine."

Bobby lived in an immense, Spanish-style house on top of a hill. Avery had once told her that the view from his place was spectacular and included the Bonita Golf Course sprawled out in the valley below. Cars were parked on either side of the street as well as in the winding driveway leading up to Bobby's house. They found an open spot along the street about a block away. Alexis got out of the car, took off her sweatpants and hooded sweatshirt, and left them in the car along with her backpack.

Alexis could hear music blaring from inside the house as she and Tobey walked up to the front door. Tobey nearly ran into a ghost hanging on the porch, which was almost completely obscured by the output of a fog machine. Nobody answered when she rang the doorbell. A screeching skull made them both jump just as she was about to put her hand on the doorknob. They walked in when they discovered that the door was unlocked.

The house was dimly lit and strobe lights hung from the ceiling in every room. Alexis felt the hair on the back of her neck stand up as soon as she crossed the threshold, but she just tried to shrug it off and told herself to stop being so paranoid.

Alexis spotted a group of people dressed like zombies standing near the door, asked one of them where the nearest bathroom was, and then left Tobey by the punch-bowl. As she locked the bathroom door behind her, she found the light switch and took a good long look at herself in the mirror. With her skintight costume and mask, she was sure that nobody would recognize her. Even if she ran into classmates, she certainly looked nothing like the demur Catholic schoolgirl they knew.

"Are you ready to party?" Tobey asked when she emerged from the bathroom.

Alexis smiled and asked, "Have I missed much?"

"Nah," Tobey replied as he took a sip of his punch and held up his cup, "You should try this, and the brownies are delicious."

"I made them myself," yelled an Asian girl dressed in an anime costume, trying to make herself heard over the noise.

Tobey grinned and shouted back, "My compliments to the baker." When the girl looked at Alexis, he quickly added, "We're just friends. My name's Tobey. What's yours?"

"Sayuri," she replied. "I like your costume. Are you a fan?"

"Totally."

Sensing that this was as good a time as any to extricate herself from Tobey, Alexis tapped his shoulder and told him that she was going to take a look around.

After being cooped up for nearly a week, being among a crowd of her peers felt liberating. Being masked added to the sense of adventure.

Alexis enjoyed chatting with random people who struck up conversations with her. She even took pictures with revelers dressed like the Joker and Batman, but politely declined invitations to dance from a drunken pirate and a Grim Reaper. Her heart stopped when she saw someone with a jet-black crew cut standing in a corner with his back turned to her. He was dressed like Robin Hood, with a bow and a quiver filled with arrows slung over his shoulder. A familiar ache filled the pit of her stomach as she tried to decide whether to run or to inch closer to see if it might be *him*. When he turned in her direction, she was both relieved and disappointed to find that it was not Rafael.

At that moment, she distinctly heard someone say, "Alexis?"

A feeling of dread came over Alexis at the sound of her name. Not wanting to give herself away, she casually turned around and pretended to be looking for someone else. She saw a thin, but muscular young man dressed in a black ninja costume looking at her. His face was largely obscured by a mask. He held out his hand and said with a noticeable Italian accent, "We have not been introduced, but my name is Vincenzo. You can call me Vinnie." It suddenly dawned on her who he was: one of the exchange students that Rafael trained with and a member of The Brethren.

Vincenzo said, "I go to school with you at Mater Dei. Aren't you Rafael's girl-friend?"

Alexis silently panicked, but outwardly kept her cool as she said, "I'm sorry. You must be mistaken. My name's not Alexis."

His eyes narrowed as he said, "Please forgive me. It is just that you look so much like someone from my school."

"No worries. I'd like to stay and chat, but I'm kinda in a hurry to find someone before I have to go…"

"Of course. Please do not let me hold you up. It was a pleasure to meet you…I am sorry, what is your name then?"

Alexis scrambled to think of a name. She blurted out, "Mac. My friends call me Mac."

"Good night, Mac. I hope you have a very nice evening," Vincenzo said with a bow before turning and walking away.

Alexis raced to the bathroom and slammed the door shut. She felt her heart pounding in her chest as she leaned against the door. She slid down to the floor and put her head between her knees. *What is Vincenzo doing here? Had Rafael sent him?* She remembered telling Rafael about Bobby's invitation to his Halloween party after their brief run-in with him in front of the movie theater last weekend. She highly doubted that Vincenzo believed her when she lied to him about who she was. If that was the case, she knew that it wouldn't be long before Rafael found out that she was there and came for her. She decided that she needed to find Bobby quickly, get whatever infor-mation she could out of him, and leave before Rafael arrived.

She forced herself to calm down and then went looking for Tobey, who was still deep in conversation with Sayuri about the demise of the comic book format. She walked up and told him that they weren't going to be staying much longer. He nodded and then quickly turned his attention back to Sayuri.

Alexis moved toward a sliding door which led to the backyard and walked through it. She saw groups of people coming in and out of a kidney-shaped pool and spotted Bobby hanging out in a Jacuzzi next to it with two or three other people.

From behind her, Alexis heard a familiar voice say, "What are you waiting for?"

She turned around and saw Lizzie, dressed like a medieval barmaid, standing be-side her with a beer in hand.

Alexis said, "You always have impeccable timing."

"Yes, and you, my friend, are wasting time," Lizzie replied. "Go over there and talk to him. I'll hang back and watch from here. Besides, I don't think Bobby would be happy to see me. Unlike you, I wasn't exactly invited…"

Alexis looked at Bobby, then back at Lizzie and said, "Maybe I should wait until he gets out of the hot tub."

Lizzie shook her head and gave her a friendly shove in Bobby's direction.

"Okay, here goes nothing," Alexis said as she slowly made her way toward him.

Bobby had just stepped out of the hot tub and was drying himself off when she stepped in front of him and said, "Hey, Bobby. Great party."

At first, Bobby wore a quizzical expression on his face as he cocked his head to the side and looked at her. A broad smile spread across his face a moment later when he realized who was standing in front of him. "Well if it isn't Miss Goody Goody. I can't believe you actually came."

"Don't be so surprised," Alexis replied. "I'm really not as much of a wallflower as you think I am."

"Where's your plus one?" Bobby asked as he walked over to a chair and put on a sweatshirt and jeans.

"If you must know, this isn't exactly his kind of scene."

"So, you ditched him. Nice," Bobby said as he reached into a cooler and took out a bottle of beer. He looked her up and down as he moved closer and said, "Nice costume. Want one?"

Alexis shook her head, but Bobby motioned for a friend standing next to the cooler to give her one anyway. He took it from his friend, opened it, and handed it to her. As she took it, Bobby clanked his bottle against hers and said, "Bottoms up!"

She slowly put the bottle up to her mouth. As the liquid touched her lips, she thought it smelled like gasoline and tasted worse. She made a funny face as she tried to swallow her first gulp. She said, "This stuff is awful. Why do people drink it?"

"They do it for the effect, baby. It loosens you up. Makes you feel less...uptight." Bobby put his arm around her and whispered in her ear, "Why don't we go somewhere a little more private?" She stiffened, but willed herself to relax as he took the bottle from her hand and set it down. She knew she had to at least pretend to be cooperative until she got what she wanted out of him. When he took her hand, she fought the urge to pull it away. As he led her back into the house, she noticed Vincenzo watching her from the other side of the pool. Her mind went into panic mode when she saw him pull out his cell phone just as she and Bobby stepped back into the house through the sliding doors. *Who is he calling?* At that point, Alexis knew that she was running out of time.

When they walked up to a table filled with drinks and empty cups, Alexis pulled her hand away from Bobby's and said, "Maybe this isn't such a good idea. I don't think Rafael..."

"Don't be a tease Alexis," he said. "I don't like it when people waste my time."

"I'm sorry," she said, trying to appease him. "I'm really not trying to be difficult, but you do know why I'm here."

Bobby said, "I never made any promises to you. I might, however, be willing to accommodate you...for a price."

Although Alexis wasn't exactly sure what that price was going to be, it didn't take long for her to realize where Bobby was going with this. "If it's what I think you're asking, the answer's no," she said, in a matter-of-fact tone.

"Don't flatter yourself," he replied. "There are plenty of girls here I could have if I wanted 'em."

"So, what do you want from me then?"

"Good question. I'll tell you when the time's right." Bobby turned his back to her and got two empty cups and filled them with soda. He was about to take a sip out of one and handed the other to her as he said, "This might be more your speed."

"Thanks, but I think I'll take the other one," she said, holding her hand out expectantly for the other cup.

He laughed. "You don't trust me, do you?"

"Do I really have to answer that question?"

He bowed and gave her the cup as requested and then touched his cup to hers as he said, "Cheers! Drink up."

Just as Alexis was about to put the cup to her lips, she saw a concerned looking Tobey staring at her from across the room. Although Sayuri was still trying to engage him in conversation, Alexis sensed that he was now completely focusing his attention on her.

"What's wrong now?" Bobby asked.

Alexis' gut told her to put the cup down, but she knew that she'd never get what she wanted if she did that. So instead, she just took a small sip. She relaxed when she found that it didn't taste like it had been spiked or tampered with.

"See, it's perfectly fine," Bobby said, smiling.

Alexis put the cup up to her lips yet again when a young man dressed in a toga walked up to Bobby to say hello. Minutes passed. She found herself growing more and more impatient as she waited for him to finish his conversation with Toga Boy. Her eyes constantly flitted to the front door. She prayed that Rafael would not burst in and insist that she go home before she'd had the chance to talk to Bobby.

Alexis had drunk a little more than half of her soda by the time Toga Boy walked off. Bobby turned to her and said, "So, are you ready to have that little talk of ours?" When she nodded, he added, "Good. Let's go upstairs then."

Although a part of Alexis knew that what she was doing was insane, another part of her reasoned that she needed to follow things through if she wanted to know why Avery had been so distraught on the day she died.

Tobey grabbed her arm as she walked past him and said in a slightly panicked voice, "Alexis, where are you going?"

"I'm just going upstairs to talk to Bobby for a little while."

"I don't think you should do that. Something doesn't feel right." Tobey clutched her arm and attempted to lead her toward the front door as he said, "Why don't you just let me take you home now."

"Let go of my arm," Alexis demanded as she tried to wrestle it away from him. Usually, she would have been able to do it easily but, for some reason, she was finding it much harder to do at that particular moment.

Tobey released her arm and said, "I can't protect you. If something goes wrong, I don't think I can…"

"I don't need anyone to protect me. I can take care of myself." Alexis looked at Bobby, who was waiting for her at the bottom of the stairs, and then back at Tobey. "And don't you dare call Rafael. I'll never forgive you if you do."

Tobey nodded and then slowly stepped aside.

"Who was that?" Bobby asked as she approached him.

"He's a friend of mine from school. He's just trying to look out for me. I told him not to worry."

Bobby shrugged his shoulders and then started up the stairs ahead of her. She stumbled on the first step. She caught herself on the banister and felt the room begin to spin around her a bit.

Bobby looked at her curiously as he extended his hand to her. She waved it away and said, "I'm fine," and followed him up the stairs.

When Alexis and Bobby reached the top, they passed two guys sitting against the wall drinking beer. One was wearing a black shirt with a skull on it while the other one was shirtless. She recognized them immediately as the same two guys that she had seen with Bobby in front of the movie theater. He gave each of them a high five as he walked by, telling them, "Don't let anyone up here, understand?"

Alexis followed Bobby down a darkened hallway to a room at the very end. He opened the door and let her walk in first. He flipped a switch and then closed the door behind him. The room had only a single lamp, which gave off very little light. He drew the curtains and then walked over to the full-sized bed in the middle of the room. He laid down at the head of the bed with his legs crossed in front of him and put his hands behind his head.

"So, what do you want to know?"

"Everything."

As Alexis' eyes became acclimated to her surroundings, she caught sight of a Ouija board propped up on his dresser. Books on witchcraft and demonology were stacked on his desk and pictures of pentagrams and circles with words and symbols written on them covered all four walls. However, the thing that disturbed her most was the sight of the upside down cross on the wall just above his bedroom door.

"Like it?" he asked with a smirk.

"Not really," she replied. "I see your parents at mass every Sunday. I'm surprised they let you keep this kind of stuff around."

"My parents aren't allowed in my room," he said decisively.

Bobby patted his hand on the bed and motioned for Alexis to come closer. She sat down at the foot of the bed instead. Her limbs felt weak and her stomach was churning.

"You all right?"

"I'm fine," she said again as she bent over and put her face in her hands. "So are you going to tell me anything or not?"

"Be patient," he said in an oily voice. "You don't look so good. Why don't you come over here and lie down for a minute."

"No th-thank you," Alexis replied as her ability to speak faltered.

Bobby grabbed her and said, "No, I insist." He pulled her toward the middle of the bed and then sat on top of her as he pinned her arms down. She wanted to push him off and run, but her body simply would not obey her commands to fight back.

"You want to know what happened to her. My friends and I took her up to San Miguel Mountain. We found the perfect spot and had a little party."

He smiled at her as he took his sweatshirt off. He lowered his body so that he was lying directly on top of her and placed his mouth next to her ear as he pointed to one of the pictures on the wall and said, "Do you see that pentagram? We drew one exactly like it out there and brought a turtledove with us and offered it up as sacrifice. The Master was very pleased."

Alexis' eyes widened in fear; Bobby laughed.

"What…did you…do to her?"

"He offered her the world in exchange for her…assistance. You'd think she would've been grateful, honored to do it." He moved back so that his face was directly above hers and shook his head, adding, "So what did she do? She freaked out and ran away instead."

"You're…sick!"

"Poor baby. Are you going to cry now?" he asked as he pulled her mask off and threw it aside. He brushed her hair out of her face and said, "Why don't you and I have a little fun? Who knows? You might even enjoy it."

He licked her ear and then dragged his tongue along her face until it reached her lips, plunging it deep into her mouth. The stench of the alcohol on his breath only worsened her nausea. As his hands reached for the zipper in the front of her costume, she closed her eyes and tried to disconnect her mind from what was happening to her body. All she could manage was a strangled cry as he pulled the upper part of her costume down. He ran his hands over her bare skin. Her stomach convulsed as the urge to throw up overtook her. Just then, someone pounded on the bedroom door.

Bobby swore as he sat up and said, "What is it? I'm busy right now."

"There's a guy downstairs asking for her," said one of his henchmen on the other side of the door. "What do you want us to do?"

"If it's the guy in the Tick costume, just tell him to get lost."

"It's not him. I think it's the guy we saw with her in front of the theater. He looks mad."

Bobby glared at Alexis. "I thought you said he wasn't going to be here!"

"Let me go," Alexis weakly slurred. "He'll kill you if he sees you with me."

Bobby quickly put on his sweatshirt, pulled her up off the bed, picked up her mask, and dragged her to the door. When he opened it, he said to his friends, "Take her downstairs, but make sure her boyfriend doesn't see her, and tell that friend of hers in the Tick costume to meet her at the front door."

Bobby thrust Alexis toward his friend in the black shirt, who put his arm around her shoulder. They had only moved a few steps when she heard the sound of footsteps bounding up the stairs. His friend opened a door directly across from Bobby's bedroom, shoved Alexis through it, threw the mask on top of her, and then slammed it shut. She slumped to the floor in a heap.

A minute later, she heard Bobby say, "Hey, man, what can I do for you?"

"Where is she?" Even though her mind was fuzzy, she would have recognized that voice anywhere.

"I'm sorry man, I don't know what you're talking about," Bobby replied innocently.

The next minute, she heard what sounded like a body being slammed into the wall.

"I said, where is she?" Rafael's voice was much louder now.

Bobby sounded like he was being choked as he said, "I told you, there's no one up here besides me and my friends."

"At least two people told me that they saw her come upstairs with you. If you don't tell me where she is right now, I promise you will be sorry."

Alexis heard Bobby cry out in pain as he said to his friends, "For Christ's sake, tell him where she is."

"She's in there, man," came the reply. Seconds later, she heard the door open and watched Rafael as he knelt down beside her.

His hand gently touched her face and then brushed the hair away from her eyes. "My God, what has he done to you?"

Alexis couldn't bear to look at him. She'd never felt so embarrassed or ashamed in her life. Wordlessly, he put the upper part of her costume back on and zipped it up before lifting her off the floor. He gently kissed her forehead as he cradled her in his arms and carried her through the door. She heard an audible gasp from Tobey, who was standing next to Vincenzo in the hallway. Even in her miserable state, she was elated to see them. Rafael was just about to hand her over to Vincenzo when she slowly stammered, "I think...I can stand...if you take my shoes off."

Rafael hesitated briefly before slowly lowering Alexis to the ground. She reached out for Tobey, who grabbed her by the waist and said, "It's okay. I got you." Rafael bent down and took her shoes off and handed them to Tobey. Although her legs felt wobbly, she found that she was able to stand with support.

When Alexis looked at Rafael's face, however, she instantly became filled with fear. With jaw set, eyes narrowed, and nostrils flared, he turned toward Bobby. His body went rigid as his hands clenched into fists. He was going to make Bobby pay for what he'd done to her.

Bobby was acting like a cornered animal as he stood by the door, with one foot in the room and one foot in the hallway. When Rafael took a step toward him, he retreated back into the bedroom and slammed the door. The lock turned just as Rafael put his hand on the door handle.

When Bobby's two friends started moving toward Rafael, Vincenzo said, "I really wouldn't do that if I were you."

Vincenzo needn't have bothered to warn them. The expression on Rafael's face when he glanced in their direction stopped them dead in their tracks. He stood in front of the door, putting one hand on the doorknob while flattening his other hand on the door itself. His eyes scanned it from top to bottom before he stepped back and drove the heel of his foot into the door near the doorknob. It gave way instantly.

After Rafael stepped into the room, Alexis lurched forward and nearly fell to the ground as she tried to move toward the now wide-open doorway.

Tobey looked exasperated. "What are you doing?"

"Somebody...please stop him," she pleaded, as she fought to get the words out. "He's gonna kill Bobby."

"So what? Look what he did to you!" Tobey replied.

Alexis frantically shook her head as she grabbed hold of Vincenzo and said, "Vincenzo...save Rafael please...before it's too late."

Vincenzo nodded his head, sat her down by the door and then walked into the fray.

When Alexis looked into the room, she saw Bobby holding a chair like a baseball bat in front of Rafael, who was standing just a few feet away from him.

"Stay away from me, man," Bobby screamed. "Or I swear to God I'm going to smash this over your head."

"Rafael, Alexis needs you," Vincenzo said as he came up behind Rafael. "Step back, brother, before it is too late."

Rafael kept his eyes locked on Bobby as he said, "Leave now, Vincenzo. This doesn't concern you."

At that point, Bobby swung the chair at Rafael. He easily deflected it as he leaned forward, grabbed hold of Bobby's arm with one hand and then punched him in the face with the other. The force of the blow caused Bobby to stagger sideways and lose his grip on the chair. Rafael kicked it away and was about to inflict another body blow when Vincenzo put him in a half nelson. Rafael escaped by dropping down and slamming the heel of his right palm into Vincenzo's chin. He shoved Vincenzo away and lunged at Bobby, who was racing across the bed to get to the door. Bobby had just cleared the bed when Rafael knocked him off his feet with a leg swipe. Bobby winced in pain as his right shoulder made contact with the wall next to the door. He slid down to the ground and then screamed when he looked up and saw Rafael glowering at him. Bobby's eyes were filled with terror as he cowered on the floor.

Just as Rafael positioned himself to inflict another blow, Alexis screamed in a halting voice, "RAFAEL, NO! PLEASE STOP!"

Rafael stopped, mid-swing, and turned to look at her while Bobby curled himself into a ball and cried like a baby on the floor. While he was thus distracted, Vincenzo came up from behind and put Rafael in a chokehold.

In a low, guttural voice, Vincenzo said, "I don't want to hurt you, brother, but this needs to end now. If you can't do it for yourself, then do it for her. She is begging you to stop," he said as his right arm continued to hold Rafael's neck in a vice-like grip. "She is safe now. Is that not all that matters?"

Alexis waited with bated breath for Rafael's response. She was afraid that he wasn't going to relent. When, moments later, he finally raised his hands in the air in surrender, she cried out in relief as the tears flowed freely down her cheeks.

Once Vincenzo released Rafael from his grip, Rafael dropped to his knees and hung his head. When he turned to look at her, she could almost feel the pain that was radiating from his eyes. It broke her heart. He then stood up and walked past her without uttering a single word.

While Bobby's friends rushed into the room, Vincenzo knelt down by Alexis. He put one arm around her waist and another arm under her legs and then lifted her off the ground as she buried her tear-streaked face in his chest. He carried her down the stairs and out the front door. Tobey followed close behind with her shoes and mask in hand. When they reached the end of the driveway, she asked Vincenzo to put her down. She braced herself against the hood of the nearest car to keep herself steady.

Rafael approached them from the street as the urge to vomit overcame her. He said to Tobey and Vincenzo, "You can go now. I will take her home."

Alexis shook her head and reached out for Tobey. He dropped her shoes and mask and caught her just as she threw up all over the front of his costume.

"Now I think *I'm* going to be sick," Tobey exclaimed as the stench reached his nostrils.

Alexis apologized and begged him not to leave.

Rafael pried her hands away from Tobey and pulled her back. Pointing at Tobey, she said to Rafael in a slow and deliberate voice, "I can't go with you…My things are in his car."

"I will walk with Tobey to his car and bring your things back," Vincenzo offered as he handed her shoes and mask to Rafael. Vincenzo put his hand on her shoulder and said, "There is no need to be afraid." He added, "You will be fine," as he looked over at Rafael, who nodded in response.

Alexis felt like an abandoned cub as she watched Tobey and Vincenzo walk away.

Rafael was about to pick her up and carry her to his car when she put her hands up and said, "I can stand…Just hold me steady."

Vincenzo returned with her backpack and clothes just as they got to Rafael's car. After he and Rafael stuffed all her things in the backpack, he said goodnight to both of them and then left.

Unable to endure the awkward silence that ensued, Alexis asked Rafael, "Who called you?"

"They both did," he said quietly. "I was already on my way when Tobey called me."

Rafael opened the car door for Alexis. When she hesitated, he said, "It has been a long night for both of us. Please just get in the car."

"Why did you come?"

"This is not the time or place for us to be talking about this," Rafael replied as he tossed her backpack into the backseat. "You are not well. I need to take you home... I should take you to the hospital."

"Don't you dare!" she said, panic-stricken.

"I don't want to argue with you."

"Then answer my question," she replied in as steady and firm a voice as she could muster.

"Why do you need to know now?"

"I need to know...what you're thinking...how you're feeling."

"This is not about what I think and feel. It is about you knowingly putting yourself at risk. What if I had not come? What would have happened to you then?"

"Tobey was there..."

"Tobey is a good person with a kind heart, but he can't protect you like I can."

"Or Vinnie..."

"You barely know him. He told me that you tried to convince him that you were someone else," he cut in. "Thank goodness he did not believe you."

Alexis suddenly felt light-headed. She closed her eyes and leaned her head against the car before carefully lowering herself into the passenger seat.

Rafael knelt beside her and said, "Why do you continue to put yourself in dangerous situations like this? Don't you realize how important you are or the effect of your actions on the people that care about you?"

"What about you?"

"What about me?"

"You've never said you loved me...not once."

The look of surprise and then puzzlement on Rafael's face baffled her. As far as she knew, she had made a perfectly true and valid statement.

He stood up and said, "Words don't mean anything unless you back them up with actions. The kind of love that lasts—that the Church teaches us to recognize—is more than just a feeling. Sacrificial love is a conscious act of the will."

"What's wrong with wanting to feel like you've been swept off your feet?"

"Feelings like that come and go. Real love is so much more than that. It requires hard work, sacrifice, and compromise. It is easy to miss, especially when you view love the way you do."

Alexis felt like she had just been slapped in the face. "I've heard enough...take me home."

Rafael bowed his head and closed the door. At that moment, the silence that hung between them suited her just fine. She was in no mood to be lectured—especially by someone her own age. She remained tight-lipped as he slid into the driver's seat and started the car.

As they headed to her house, she found that every bump and curve in the road made her still-sour stomach churn. It eventually got so bad that she had to ask him to pull over. She opened the door and threw up. When he again suggested that she go and see a doctor, she threatened to get out of the car and walk the rest of the way home. He gave up trying after she unbuckled her seatbelt and nearly fell into the pool of vomit she had just created outside the passenger door.

They continued on in stony silence. After Rafael parked his car near her home, he slung her backpack over his shoulder and, despite her feeble protests, carried her to the front door. As soon as he put her down, he held out the backpack to her. She reached in for the house key and, with a trembling hand, tried to put it in the keyhole. He reached out and steadied her hand with his own as she unlocked the door. Instead of saying thank you, she stepped inside the house without a backward glance and slammed the door in his face.

"Welcome back."

Alexis froze, knowing that she had been caught. She slowly turned her head toward the living room and saw Jeremy sitting on the couch, looking grim. She braced herself against the door and took a deep breath before attempting to engage him in conversation.

"Did you really think I wouldn't know that you'd left?" he asked. "I was this close to calling Mom and Dad and maybe the police. Where were you?"

"I went...to a Halloween party...with Tobey," she said very carefully, trying not to stammer.

"Are you *drunk?*" Jeremy asked incredulously.

Alexis nodded. She had neither the will nor the desire to tell him the truth.

"So, you were willing to risk getting grounded for life for a Halloween party?" he asked, almost shouting at her. He shook his head and reached for a glass of water. His hands trembled slightly as he raised the glass to his lips. "I don't know what to do with you. You shouldn't be taking risks like this—not with the way things are now."

"What do you mean by that?"

"Forget what I said," he replied as he ran his fingers through his hair. "It's late."

"Are you going to tell them?"

"I don't know. I haven't decided yet."

At that moment, Jeremy got up and almost fell forward as he swung his legs over the side of the couch. He placed his hands on the coffee table in order to break his fall. After steadying himself, he slowly sat back down.

"How are you feeling?" she asked, concern etched on her face. "You don't look good at all."

He said, "I think I'm in better shape than you are…I should be the least of your worries. Just go to bed."

"But…"

"Don't argue with me, Neneng. I'm still your kuya. Now go upstairs. We'll talk in the morning."

Although a part of her desperately wanted to tell her brother about what had happened to her and what she had learned about Avery, she knew that he was in no mood to hear what she had to say. So instead, she just did as she was told and clung to the wall as she gradually made her way upstairs. When she opened her bedroom door, she turned on the light and saw that the covers on her bed had been thrown back. She fell onto the bed and buried her face in a pillow. She was about to turn off the lamp on the nightstand when she saw her cell phone sitting on her desk.

Here goes nothing, she thought as she clicked on Rafael's message. "Hola Alexis. It is Rafael. Please give me a call when you can. Take care. I love you."

Alexis blinked a couple of times while staring at the phone. She looked at the date and saw that he had sent the message to her on Tuesday afternoon, the same day that she had been suspended for fighting. Days ago, he had said the very words she had just accused him of withholding from her. He'd said it despite what she'd done and whatever else he might have heard. He had even come to her rescue tonight, knowing that she had been grounded, and just stood there as she berated him for not telling her that he loved her when he *knew* that wasn't true. As she lay in bed, the scenario played out in her mind for the rest of the night like a nightmare from which she couldn't awake.

CHAPTER 17—LOOSE ENDS

Alexis woke up later than usual on Saturday morning and wiggled her hands and feet to make sure that everything was now in working order. Although she was thankful to be nausea-free and in full command of her limbs again, this knowledge did little to ease her very troubled mind.

She thought ruefully about how good she was getting at doing the wrong things and hurting the people she loved in the process. It also pained her to think about everything she was doing, intentionally or not, to drive Rafael away. She was sure that it was only a matter of time before he would ask to sever all ties with her and, when that happened, she knew that she would have no one to blame for it but herself.

When Alexis went downstairs, she found Jeremy sleeping on the couch with the T.V. on. While searching for the remote, she heard a meteorologist from a local news station predicting that temperatures around the county were going to drop and that dense fog would be setting in after sunset. She found the remote on the floor, picked it up, turned the T.V. off, and then laid it on the coffee table. She glanced at Jeremy and frowned. He didn't look well. She put her hand on her brother's forehead and found that he felt very warm. Although this concerned her, she decided to let him rest and wake up on his own. She was in no hurry to receive the lecture he was almost certainly going to give her, and she convinced herself that she would be better able to deal with that after she had gotten something to eat.

Alexis quietly backed out of the living room and went to the kitchen. She had just poured milk on her cereal when she heard a loud crash come from the hallway. She ran toward the commotion and found Jeremy on the floor by the stairs with shards of a broken vase strewn all around him. She rushed to his side to see if he was

189

breathing. Once she had confirmed that he was at least semi-conscious and had a steady pulse, she ran back to the kitchen, grabbed the cordless phone, and dialed 911.

Alexis did her best to stay calm as she knelt down beside her groggy and slightly disoriented brother and gave the operator her address. The woman on the other end of the phone was very reassuring and informed her that an ambulance was on the way. She listened carefully and did everything she was told. When Jeremy tried to sit up, she told him to stay put and rest.

She was racked with guilt as she held her brother's hand and tried to convince him that everything was going to be all right. She had left him alone and worried him needlessly by sneaking out of the house, even though she knew that he wasn't well. She was certain that he never would have done that to her.

When Alexis asked Jeremy what had happened, he said, "It was kind of a blur. I got up to go to the bathroom and started feeling dizzy in the hallway. The room started spinning and I think that I just tripped over my own feet. I knocked over the vase when I tried to brace myself with my hands."

"Did you hit your head on anything when you fell?" she asked.

"No, not that I remember," he said as he slowly reached back with his hand and rubbed the back of his head.

"Do you think that it might have something to do with the malaria you got in the Philippines?

"I don't know," he replied. "It's been a couple of weeks since that happened, so I thought that I was just coming down with the flu."

Alexis dutifully reported all this information to the 911 operator.

Shortly thereafter, she heard the sound of sirens coming down the street, followed by a knock on the front door. She thanked the operator, hung up the phone, and opened the door for the paramedics. She stepped back as the first responders assessed her brother's condition before putting him on a gurney and loading him into an ambulance.

Alexis tortured herself with "what ifs," "could haves," and "should haves" as she sat in the front seat with the ambulance driver and headed toward the nearest Catholic hospital. What if she had stayed home instead of sneaking out of the house? Could everything have been avoided if she'd just made a different choice? If she had stayed home and kept an eye on her ailing brother, would she be sitting in this ambulance now?

Alexis stayed by Jeremy's side as he was wheeled into the emergency room. She took a seat by his hospital bed after he had been checked in. She listened intently to her brother's conversation with the emergency room doctor when he stopped by to do a preliminary assessment, and she watched as the nurses took his vital signs and inserted an IV into his arm.

When a hospital attendant took Jeremy away for X-rays, Alexis called her parents and relatives to let them know what had happened. Even though Alexis assured her mother that Jeremy was awake and talking, Lisa told her that she would return immediately, but that her father would go ahead and keep a speaking commitment at the theology conference and then come to the hospital afterward. Aunt Cora arrived with Tessa half an hour later.

By the time Lisa got to the emergency room, Jeremy was back and his doctor confirmed what Alexis suspected all along: her brother had suffered a malaria relapse. Given his current symptoms and the severity of the first malarial attack, Jeremy's doctor recommended that he stay in the hospital for at least a few more hours for further observation in order to ensure that his condition was stabilized before being discharged.

After the doctor stepped away, Lisa tried to get Alexis to take a break and get something to eat with her aunt and cousin. She declined, insisting that she was fine, even though she was feeling exhausted.

"You need to take care of yourself," Lisa said more insistently after Tessa and Aunt Cora had left Jeremy's bedside. "The last thing we need is for you to get sick, too."

For the sake of keeping the peace, Alexis kept quiet despite her growing frustration with what she believed to be her mother's overbearing ways. More than anything, she wanted her mother to stop telling her what to do, especially now.

"So how was the conference?" Jeremy interjected.

"Good. Your father was going over his talking points for a panel discussion when your sister called," Lisa said. "Alexis told us that the doctor didn't think you were in any immediate danger. Your dad wanted to come back with me, but I convinced him to stay until after his panel was over. He's going to catch a two o'clock train from L.A. to San Diego. I'll probably ask your aunt to pick him up with my car so I can stay here with you."

Lisa turned to Alexis and said, "I think Tessa should take you home."

"Mom, I'd really…"

"Don't argue with me," Lisa said firmly. "Tessa can stay with you until we get home, and remember, no going out or having friends over. Are we clear?"

Alexis glanced at Jeremy, who gave her a knowing look. Lisa looked from one to the other and then asked, "Am I missing something?"

"No. Why do you ask?" Alexis replied.

Lisa turned to Jeremy and asked, "Did something happen that I should know about?"

"No," Jeremy said.

Just then, Lisa's cell phone beeped. She took it out of her purse and checked her text messages. She told Alexis and Jeremy that she was going to step out for a minute to call their father and let him know how Jeremy was doing.

As soon as Lisa had left the room, Alexis said to her brother, "Thanks for covering for me."

Jeremy replied, "I don't like lying to her, but I don't want to make things worse for you either." He paused a moment, then added, "Don't expect me to do it again."

Alexis nodded and said, "Don't worry, kuya. I won't do anything else to disappoint you."

"Neneng, it's not about disappointing me. It's about making the right choices for yourself. You're the one who's going to have to live with the consequences."

That was the problem. Even though Alexis tried, she never seemed to make the right decisions. And, as a result, she always ended up hurting the people she cared about most. As she looked into her brother's eyes, all she could think about was how much of a burden she was to her family and friends.

Alexis said, "Maybe you'd all be better off without me."

Jeremy looked stricken. "That's not true and you know it. I don't ever want to hear you say that again. Don't even think it."

Alexis was sure that Jeremy would have said much more if Aunt Cora and Tessa hadn't come back from their trip to the vending machine. She politely declined Tessa's offer of a bag of chips and told them that she needed to go to the chapel to pray for a little while.

As she turned to go, Jeremy grabbed her hand and said, "Remember what I told you." Alexis nodded as she squeezed her brother's hand and then left.

The chapel was completely empty when Alexis walked through the chapel door. She sat in one of the chairs in the front row and folded her hands in her lap. The room was quiet and still. Her mind, however, was in turmoil. She felt a single tear run down her cheek as the pitiless voices in her head taunted her. *Useless. Pathetic. Inept.* More tears fell as the voices got louder and more unrelenting. *You're a failure, a burden. You ruin everything you touch.* She buried her face in her hands as she recalled Anita's last words to her. *You're nothing…nobody…Live with that.* Within minutes, she found herself literally choking on her tears as they poured down her face. Her chest heaved up and down and her breathing became labored as the weight of her woes came crashing down on her. She had never felt so hopeless and alone.

As Alexis lifted her head from her hands and stared at the altar, she thought about the people she loved and how she had let each one of them down. She remembered

Avery's tear-streaked face and how she failed to stop her friend from getting into the car that turned into her coffin. She thought about the disappointment in her parents' faces when they grounded her for fighting and her brother's worried expression when she walked through the front door after sneaking out of the house to go to Bobby's Halloween party. Worst of all, she recalled how wounded and sad Rafael looked after he'd nearly beaten Bobby to a pulp because of her. She'd never seen him so angry or out of control, and she knew that it was her actions that had driven him to the breaking point. To top it off, she had acted like an ungrateful brat when all he had done was see her safely home.

Eventually, Alexis dried her tears with her shirtsleeves. It was clear to her what she had to do. She was going to absolve her father and Rafael of the burden of deciding whether or not she needed to be sacrificed for the sake of their cause. Although she knew that the act she was contemplating was a mortal sin, which would separate her from those that she loved in this world and possibly the next, she didn't see any other way out. She hoped that her family would forgive her and eventually move on with their lives. It also pained her to think that she would never again be able to look upon—and lose herself in—Rafael's beautiful blue eyes. He was a child of God who deserved to be with, and be loved by, someone other than a lost soul like her.

At that point, Alexis averted her eyes from the altar. She couldn't bear to look at it. When she considered whether or not God would still welcome her into His realm if she took her own life, she recalled the passage from 1 Corinthians 3:17 which said, *If any man destroys the temple of God, God will destroy him, for the temple of God is holy, and that is what you are.* Although she had been taught that God might forgive her for what she was about to do, such knowledge provided her with little comfort in her circumstance. Convinced that this was her only option, she just hoped that her resolve wouldn't falter when the time came to follow through on her plan.

As soon as Alexis walked out of the chapel, she pulled out her cell phone, clicked on the text message function and typed in Rafael's number.

Alexis wrote "Meet @ mhp 1:30 pm?" Meet at Mountain Hawk Park 1:30 pm? and then pressed the send button.

Less than a minute later, Rafael answered her text with a simple, "Yes."

When Alexis returned to Jeremy's bedside, Tessa came up to her and said, "Auntie told me to take you home. Just let me know when you're ready to go."

Alexis nodded in resignation. She wasn't going to pick a fight with her mother, especially now. She wanted her mother's last memory of her to be a happy one, since she knew only too well what it was like to have such a memory marred by a disagreement. Despite their frequent arguments, she would never wish such a fate upon anyone else.

Alexis walked over to her mother, who was standing next to Aunt Cora, and took her hand. Lisa, in turn, gazed at her daughter and furrowed her brow as she said, "Anak, you've been crying. Is everything okay?"

"I'm better now," Alexis replied with a weak smile. "Don't worry about me."

Lisa gently patted her cheek. "We're just going through a rough patch. Everything will work out in the end, you'll see."

Alexis put her arms around her mother and laid her head on her shoulder as she said, "I need to go now. Could you do me a favor and tell Dad that I love him and that I'm sorry?"

"He already knows that, *mahal*," she replied with an endearment in Tagalog. "You just get some rest and we'll talk more when I get home."

Alexis nodded, took a step back and then turned to Jeremy. She said to him, "Take care of yourself, kuya."

He motioned for Alexis to come closer. When she bent over to hug him, he put his arms around her and whispered in her ear, "Don't do anything stupid. Promise me."

"I promise," she lied. "I'll see you when you get home."

Finally, Alexis gave her Aunt Cora a hug before leaving with Tessa. When she and her cousin got to the hospital's parking lot, she said, "I need you to take me to Mountain Hawk Park before we go home." She gulped and her eyes started to tear up as she thought about what she was going to do.

"Why? What's wrong?" Tess asked, sounding alarmed.

"I'm meeting Rafael," she said in a choked voice. "I'm going to break up with him."

Alexis was relieved that Tessa steered clear of the subject of Rafael as they drove to the park. Instead, Tessa filled the time by letting her know what had happened at school while she was gone. She also said that everyone missed her and were looking forward to seeing her back in school on Monday. Her cousin also told her that she had heard that Anita had been stripped of her position in student government and, like Alexis, had been put on academic probation.

Alexis' anxiety level rose at an exponential rate as Tessa drove into the circular parking lot of Mountain Hawk Park. It didn't take long for Alexis to spot Rafael standing under a gazebo with his back toward her. He was wearing jeans, sneakers, and a long-sleeved, light blue denim button-down shirt. His hands were behind his back as he looked out toward the shimmering blue water of Otay Lake.

For a minute, Alexis just sat there staring at him from inside the car, unable to move.

Tessa put her hand on Alexis' shoulder and said, "Are you sure you want to do this?"

Alexis nodded. Her hands shook as she reached for the door handle. She felt like a bundle of nerves as she stepped out of the car and planted her feet on the pavement. Her resolve began to crumble as she took her first steps forward. She slowed her pace as the words that she had so carefully planned to say started to get jumbled in her head. Her legs felt like lead weights as she reminded herself over and over again not to let him get too close. She needed to get this done as quickly as possible and then leave. She knew that any delay carried with it the potential for complications. That was a scenario that she wanted to avoid at all costs.

Alexis stopped just short of the gazebo entrance and found herself gazing longingly at the handsome young man standing just a few feet away from her. Her heart ached to run to him, wrap her arms around his waist, and hear him say that everything was going to be all right. But her mind quickly squashed that idea with a stern reminder that there was going to be no happy ending for her. Not today. Not ever.

Despite everything that Lizzie had told her, Alexis knew deep down that Rafael truly cared for her. To what extent, she was not completely sure, but at least enough to hang in there when most other boys would have given up and left. That was, in fact, what she feared the most about meeting him: that he would not give up and would do everything in his power to change her mind. For his sake, this was an argument she couldn't let him win.

"Rafael," she said softly.

He immediately turned around and smiled at her tentatively. As they stared into each other's eyes, she knew in an instant that her intention to keep him at arm's length during this conversation was going to fly right out the window. He closed the physical gap between them in a matter of seconds. He placed one arm around her, pulling her close, and gently stroked her cheek with his hand. He kissed her forehead and then gazed down at her. As she looked into those startlingly blue eyes, she knew that she was in for an uphill battle.

Alexis' resolve dissolved completely when he leaned in and kissed her. Her pulse quickened as his kisses deepened. This certainly had not been part of her plan. Her whole body was now in active rebellion against the voices in her head, which were commanding her to pull away from him...now! Her arms countered by defiantly wrapping themselves around his neck as she pressed herself against him. He responded in kind by tightening his grip around her waist and kissing her with even greater fervor.

She felt like her head was going to explode as the voices screamed at her for giving in to him so easily. She tried reminding herself that he had lied to her by omission about who he was and why he was here. She also told herself that he was a loyal servant of the Church who would do anything and everything to protect and defend it, even if it meant sacrificing her in the process.

"Rafael, please stop," she pleaded as she gasped for air.

"What is it, mi querida?"

Alexis stepped back and shook her head when he tried to kiss her again.

"I don't have much time. I'm still on restriction and was supposed to go straight home from the hospital. Tessa was nice enough to bring me here to see you first. She's waiting for me."

"The hospital?" he said in a worried tone. "Are you okay? You should have let me take you last night…"

"No, no, it wasn't me. My brother collapsed this morning. I had to call 911, but he's better now. The doctors said that he suffered a malaria relapse and they want to keep him at the hospital until he's stable enough to go home."

Alexis sensed Rafael's relief that she had not been the patient. "I am very sorry to hear that his illness has recurred. I will pray for him."

"Thanks," she said and then put her right hand on his lips to stop him when he again tried to kiss her. "Please don't. We really need to talk."

He nodded and said, "I am very sorry about the way I acted last night. It was like something just snapped when I saw you lying there on the floor. I lost control. All I could think of was how much I wanted to hurt Bobby."

"He's a horrible person who doesn't care about anyone but himself," Alexis said. "I went to that party because I needed to know what happened between him and Avery just before she died."

"Did he tell you anything?"

Alexis bit her lip, which was quivering, and nodded. "He tried to get her to take part in some sick ritual involving black magic. He said that the whole thing really freaked her out."

Rafael closed his eyes. To her, he looked like he was trying to gather his thoughts and steady himself at the same time.

"The next thing I knew, Bobby was all over me. If you hadn't come…"

Rafael shook his head as he placed his hands on either side of her face and said, "Look what I did. I will never forget the fear I saw in your eyes. You probably thought I was a monster. I felt like one. I should have stopped. I knew better…Thank goodness Vincenzo was there to restrain me."

Alexis put her hand on his cheek as she said, "I wasn't afraid of you. I was afraid *for* you. I didn't want anything bad to happen to you because of me. I'm not worth it."

Rafael shook his head. "Yes, you are."

"Maybe you'd be better off with Anita…"

"Anita is a selfish and petty girl," he cut in. "You are nothing like her, and that is a good thing. You are loyal, kind, and courageous. Not many girls would have tried to take on a boy like Mateo to help Tobey. You have so much to offer this world and I cannot wait to see what God has in store for you."

"What good is all that if I keep making stupid decisions and hurting the people I care about?"

"People make mistakes," he replied. "God does not expect perfection."

"This isn't about God," she replied, as she moved further away from him. "This is about you and me."

"You are wrong, Alexis," he said. "It is always about Him. Every time you interact with another person, God is there. He lives and works through each of us, but He always gives us a choice about whether to follow Him or not."

"Rafael, I didn't come here to hear a theology lecture." Alexis knew that this was taking too long and that she needed to end things now.

"Why *did* you ask me to come here?"

This was the moment Alexis had waited for in their conversation, but as she opened her mouth to speak, she found that the words wouldn't come out.

"Do you want to know why I came?" Rafael interjected. "Because I missed you and couldn't wait to see you again. I also wanted to tell you that I…"

"Rafael, please don't say it," she pleaded with a vigorous shake of her head. "I can't do this anymore. This isn't working for me."

Rafael looked hurt and confused. "Why are you saying this?"

"Because I don't know who you are."

The expression on Rafael's face told her that he couldn't believe what he was hearing. "What are you talking about? Of course you know who I am."

"Do I? In the time that I've known you, how much of you have you really shared with me? What about what happened in the bleachers when we left the dance? You're hiding things from me; I know it. It feels like you don't trust me to know the truth."

Although she sensed that her words unnerved him, his demeanor remained calm as he asked her, "What do you want to know?"

"What should I know?"

"You're talking in riddles, mi amor," he replied. "How do you expect me to answer a question I do not understand?"

"You do understand, but you won't answer."

Rafael looked like he was struggling to figure out what to say next. Finally, he said, "I am so sorry. I have told you all that I can. There is nothing more that I can say to you."

"Who are you?"

"You know who I am," he said quietly.

"Who are you?" she repeated.

"Why are you doing this?" he asked, as he took a step toward her.

"WHO ARE YOU???"

He seemed to be at his wits' end. "I can't. I am sorry. I promised…"

"Who did you promise?" she demanded. "And why is keeping your promise to someone else more important than telling *me* the truth?" Both her heart and her voice were breaking as she said the words.

"Can't you give me a little more time?" he pleaded.

"To do what?"

"Alexis, please," he replied with a pained expression on his face. "Don't you know what you mean to me?"

"Tell me something, do your friends and family back home know about me?" Rafael's silence spoke volumes. "Why is that?" she asked as tears flowed down her face. "All my friends and family know about you. Why don't yours?"

"We can work this out together…"

"It's too late," Alexis said, shaking her head.

"It is never too late," he replied. "You can't give up on us now. I won't let you."

"I'm so tired," Alexis said, wiping the tears from her face. "Aren't you? I don't want to hurt you. You deserve better than that. Just walk away, let me go."

"I can't. We are bound together, you and I. It has been that way for me ever since I first saw you tripping on the curb before church. I wanted to run over and catch you, make sure you were all right."

"Rafael, please don't make this any harder than it needs to be. I know you don't agree with me, but I really think…"

"I will be there for you," he cut in, "no matter what you say. I am not going anywhere."

At that moment, Alexis realized that there was nothing else left to do but say goodbye.

"I have to go now," Alexis said, moving toward him. She gently placed her hands on either side of his face and gazed into what she knew for a fact were the most beautiful blue eyes she would ever see in this life. She swallowed hard when she saw a single tear roll down his cheek. She wiped it away with her thumb and then leaned in and tenderly kissed his lips one last time.

His tears now came faster as she slowly backed away from him. She could see that he was fighting to maintain his composure and sensed that he had no idea what to do next.

As soon as Alexis moved past the entrance to the gazebo, she stopped and said, "Please don't follow me." He nodded briefly then lowered his head and looked away. It was over.

Alexis turned and ran toward Tessa's car. She didn't look back. When she got there, she opened the door, got in, and began to sob uncontrollably. She waved off Tessa's attempts to comfort her. She didn't think that she deserved to be consoled after what she had just done. She motioned for her cousin to drive. At the moment, all she wanted was to get as far away from Rafael as she could.

Once they were in the driveway of her house, Alexis told her cousin that she needed some time alone. Tessa reluctantly agreed after Alexis promised that she would call her later.

When Alexis walked through the front door, she saw the shards from the broken vase still strewn on the ground. She shuffled into the kitchen and retrieved a broom and dustpan to clean up the mess. Afterward, she went back into the kitchen and got something to eat. When she had finished, she looked at the clock on the kitchen wall; it was almost three o'clock in the afternoon. It was time to go. She picked up her plate and empty glass and was about to put them in the sink, when the glass slipped and shattered on the floor. She bent down to pick up the pieces and cut her hand, leaving a deep gash in her palm. She became transfixed by the sight of the blood flowing from the wound. As if in a daze, she wrapped her hand in a towel, which did little to stem the bleeding. Still, she managed to sweep up the glass and then she headed toward the front door. She hesitated and then wiped her still-bloody fingertips on the wooden surface. When she opened the door, Lizzie was standing there waiting for her.

"Are you ready, Mac?"

Alexis nodded and closed the door behind her; she was ready to die.

CHAPTER 18—LOST

Father Bernal had just finished greeting the last of the departing parishioners from the five o'clock Saturday mass when he saw Rafael standing by the front doors of the church. The priest sensed that something was wrong by the troubled look on the boy's face, and motioned for him to come closer.

"I must speak with you, Father," Rafael said as he bowed his head.

"What's wrong? Has something happened?"

"I think I've lost her," Rafael replied, averting his eyes from the priest's face.

Despite Father Bernal's alarm at this news, outwardly, he remained calm. He said to Rafael, "Follow me."

What could possibly have happened between the two of them to have made him say such a thing? Although Father Bernal hoped that it was nothing more than a simple quarrel between two young lovers, the idea that it was something far more serious gnawed at him as they headed toward the sacristy. This was no ordinary couple. Far from it.

Father Bernal instructed Rafael to wait outside while he devested. As he removed his green vestments, he thought of how he had tried in earnest to dissuade The Grand Master of The Brethren from selecting the boy as The Archer. It was not that the priest doubted his fighting skills or devotion to his faith. He did, however, worry that the psychological scars from his parents' deaths had created an Achilles heel that might someday prove fatal to him or Alexis...or both of them.

After Father Bernal had put his vestments away, he asked Rafael to follow him to his office in the parish hall. As they walked silently out of the church, the priest looked at the boy and thought fondly of his parents. The boy had inherited his father's dignified bearing and his mother's stunning blue eyes.

In the days after Javier and Sofia Cordero's deaths, he had often wondered why God had spared the boy's life and what lay in store for him. When the call for competitors to participate in The Trials went out, it dawned on Father Bernal that this might be the work that God had called him to do.

After walking into his office, Father Bernal closed the door and invited Rafael to sit down. The priest leaned against his desk and fixed his gaze upon the boy, who had buried his face in his hands.

"Tell me exactly what happened." Father Bernal saw no point in beating around the bush.

"She broke up with me," Rafael replied as he lowered his hands from his face and sat back in his seat.

"Why?"

"We argued last night," Rafael said in an anguished voice. "Vincenzo called me yesterday evening and told me that Alexis was at a party and that she might be in trouble. When I got there, a friend of ours, Tobey, told me that a boy named Bobby had taken her upstairs. I went looking for her and I found her lying on the floor in one of the bedrooms. She was half-dressed and barely able to move or talk. I think she was drugged. I lost control; I went after the boy who did that to her. All I could think of was how much I wanted to hurt him."

Father Bernal's grip on the desk tightened considerably as he struggled to maintain his outward calm.

Rafael continued, "She kept pleading with me to walk away. If Vincenzo had not been there to stop me…I don't know what I would have done to Bobby."

My God, my God. This is much worse than I thought. Father Bernal closed his eyes, trying to gather his thoughts.

"Did anything else happen?"

"She was very upset and did not want me to take her home. Vincenzo convinced her that it would be okay but we argued after he left. She slammed the door in my face when we got to her house."

"Did you try to make amends?"

"She sent me a text this morning and asked me to meet her at the park," Rafael replied. "I thought she was going to give me another chance. When I first saw her, I was sure everything was going to be fine."

"What did she say to you?"

"She told me that she could not trust me…that I was hiding things from her."

"Did you tell her anything?" Father Bernal asked, worried that Rafael had broken the promise he had made to Eric and Lisa that neither he nor Rafael would tell Alexis about their true purpose in coming to San Diego.

Rafael shook his head. "Of course not, but I wish I could have."

"You know that is something we cannot do."

Rafael wrung his hands and then stood up and paced around the room. "I don't understand why Mrs. Neil is so resistant to the idea of telling her daughter the truth. All the signs are there. It would make things so much easier."

"Lisa loves her daughter," the priest replied gently. "She is doing what she thinks is best for her and we are duty-bound to honor her wishes."

"I tried to talk to Mrs. Neil after Alexis got suspended, but she would not listen to me," Rafael said as he stopped in front of his chair and faced the priest. "Father, is there any way you can talk to the Neils? They need to reconsider their position about what Alexis needs to know. They are binding our hands. I don't know if I can fulfill my mission under these conditions."

Father Bernal racked his brain, trying to think of some advice to give to this nearly inconsolable young man. He said, "I will do what I can, but you need to take a moment and think about your actions, too. Your feelings for her have clouded your judgment. This is exactly why I told you not to get too involved with her."

Rafael looked at Father Bernal with a pained expression. "I tried not to, Father. I did, but every day it got a little harder. Then one day I realized that it was not possible for us to be just friends anymore, not if I wanted to have her in my life. I told myself that everything I was doing with Alexis was for the good of my mission..."

"Was that true?"

Rafael shook his head. "At first, but it was not long after that that I realized that I had fallen in love with her. After that, I knew that I would do whatever it took to be with her."

"It's good to be aware of one's shortcomings," the priest said. Rafael bowed his head.

"Falling in love with her was the last thing I expected. If I had only known then what I know now, maybe I would have made a different choice and The Brethren would have chosen someone else to protect her." At that moment, Rafael looked Father Bernal squarely in the eye and said, "I am unfit and unworthy of the title El Arquero. You were right to discourage me from competing in The Trials. My presence here so far has done Alexis more harm than good. Maybe it would be better if Vincenzo took my place."

Although Father Bernal felt for the boy, he knew that Rafael's suggestion was completely out of the question. He said, "You were appointed because of your piety and fierceness in battle. Besides, you have already established a strong bond with her.

That is not something that can be replicated with someone else overnight. You are just going to have to go to her and try…"

"I can't, Father," he interrupted. "She wants nothing to do with me. I am probably the last person she wants to see right now."

"You can't give up on her. She needs you now more than ever."

"What would you have me do?" Rafael asked with growing frustration. "She needs someone she can trust. I am not that person. Not anymore." He sat back down in the chair and hung his head. "God has forsaken me."

"Stand up, boy!" the priest ordered. "And pull yourself together. You are acting like a lovesick schoolboy. If you can't do it for yourself, then do it for her."

"Forgive me, Father." Rafael said as he stood and faced Father Bernal. He looked like someone who was about to face a firing squad.

"I don't need your apologies," the priest said. "I need you to be the man that I know you can be and to do what you were sent here to do. What do you think your father would say if he saw you now?"

"He would be ashamed," Rafael replied, dejectedly, "and my brother, too. He should have been the one to compete in The Trials. Even I would have been no match for him."

"It is what it is. We can't turn back the clock and change what has already happened," the priest said as he placed his hand on Rafael's shoulder. "All we do have is the power to influence what may happen in the future." Rafael nodded in agreement.

Despite the fact that Rafael outwardly appeared to have regained his composure, Father Bernal sensed that the boy's mind and heart were still very troubled. It disturbed him to see this seemingly unflappable young man unraveling before his eyes. Just as the priest had feared, Rafael's relationship with Alexis had unleashed pent-up emotions in him that the boy was ill-equipped to handle. He also knew that there was little he could do but hope and pray that Javier's son had the fortitude to stay the course until the danger to Alexis had passed.

"This is not just about you and Alexis," the priest said. "The Archangel Michael sent us signs that led directly to her and told us that she was in need of our assistance. You are here to ensure that she will be given the chance to fulfill God's plan for her."

"But Father…"

"There is no room for equivocation," the priest said with growing impatience. "The title of El Arquero was bestowed upon you because we believed that you were the one that could defend her against the darkness and save her soul for God."

"Father, how can I save her if I can't even save myself?" Rafael asked in an agonized voice. "I feel so lost without her."

"IF YOU FAIL, SHE DIES! DO YOU UNDERSTAND? The Devil wants her for himself, and he will do anything and everything to have her. If that happens, the Devil will see to it that her soul will be beyond God's reach. Is that what you want?"

Rafael's entire demeanor immediately changed as he quietly said, "I would die before I would let that happen."

Father Bernal was about to respond when his cell phone rang. He took it out of his pocket and answered it immediately when he saw the name of the caller.

"Hello, Eric, what can I…" Father Bernal's face fell as he spoke to Alexis' father. Eric was urging him to come to his house as soon as possible. The news was not good.

Rafael looked panic-stricken as he waited for Father Bernal to finish his conversation with Alexis' father. The minute Father Bernal got off the phone, Rafael asked, "Why did Mr. Neil call you?"

Father Bernal tried to think of a way to tell Rafael what he had just learned without sending the boy over the edge. In the end, he decided that he had no choice but to tell him the plain, unvarnished truth.

"It is Alexis. She is missing."

It was clear from the look on Rafael's face that the news was another devastating blow to his already wounded psyche. For a moment, he stood in front of the priest in stunned silence before asking, "Do they have any idea where she might have gone?"

The priest shook his head. "No, but Eric told me that there was a short message on the back of the front door."

"What does it say?"

"Just two words written in capital letters: *SHE'S MINE.*"

"What's wrong, Father?"

"The words were written in blood."

The Neils were near the breaking point when Father Bernal arrived. He walked into their living room and found Lisa in one corner interrogating Tessa, who was on the verge of tears; Eric and Jeremy, on the other hand, were engaged in a tense conversation by the fireplace.

Eric approached Father Bernal and thanked him for coming and then motioned for the priest to follow him to the front door.

"We came home just past five thirty," Eric said. "Like I said over the phone, we had been at the hospital with Jeremy. We thought that Tessa had stayed with Alexis. I sensed that something was wrong the minute we parked in the driveway. We saw this as soon as we walked through the front door."

Eric pointed to the words written in blood on the back of the door and said, "When we didn't see her in the living room or kitchen, Lisa ran upstairs while I went to check the backyard and garage. I also looked around the house to see if she'd left any indication as to where she might have gone."

"Did you find anything?"

Eric shook his head. "We've been calling friends and family. We even filed a report with the police, but they won't take any action until she's been missing for more than twenty-four hours."

"When was the last time anybody saw her?"

"Her cousin, Tessa, told us that she dropped Alexis off here a little after two," Eric replied. "She convinced Tessa that she would be fine on her own. Nobody that we've been able to get hold of has seen or heard from her since."

"My parents searched the house from top to bottom," Jeremy chimed in as he joined Eric and Father Bernal in the entryway. "My aunt and uncle just finished knocking on our neighbors' doors to see if they saw her, but everyone so far has said no."

"Shouldn't you be resting, son?" Father Bernal asked Jeremy.

"Not until we find my sister," Jeremy replied. "The last time I spoke to Alexis, she told me that she thought that we would all be better off without her. I, for one, won't rest until I know she is safe at home."

Eric said, "We think that she either left on foot or was picked up by someone, since she hasn't driven since Avery died and her bicycle is still in the garage." He took a step closer to Father Bernal and said under his breath, "Jeremy told me that Alexis snuck out to a party last night and came back drunk. I haven't said anything to Lisa yet. I don't know if she could handle hearing news like that right now. Alexis' behavior lately has been completely out of character. This would kill her mother."

"Rafael told me what happened," Father Bernal replied. "I am sorry to be the one to tell you this, my friend, but I do not believe that your daughter was drunk. Rafael thinks that she was drugged by a boy at the party."

"WHAT!" Jeremy cried out while Eric stared at the priest in shocked silence. "What else happened?"

"Rafael found her in an upstairs bedroom, barely able to move and..." Father Bernal paused and looked away.

"For goodness' sake, Juan Pablo, what did he see?" Eric asked.

"Alexis was partially undressed...but Rafael was sure that he had interrupted the boy before anything could have happened to her. There simply had not been enough time."

Jeremy shook his head as he bent over and buried his face in his hands. Eric reached out and put a hand on his son's shoulder and then said to Father Bernal, "What did Rafael do?"

"He went after the boy. Luckily, Vincenzo was there to stop him before he was able to inflict any serious harm...or who knows what he would have done."

Rafael arrived shortly thereafter. Father Bernal noticed Lisa's face cloud over as the boy strode toward him. He quietly informed Father Bernal that he had made the appropriate preparations. He also told him that Gonçalo, Vincenzo, and Akira were on standby and that he had sent a message to The Grand Master, Brother Molina, to inform him of the situation.

The priest watched Lisa with a wary eye as she approached Rafael. The boy turned to face her just as she raised her hand, drew it back, and slapped him. He flinched, as the left side of his face reddened, but made no effort whatsoever to deflect or dodge the blow. In fact, it almost seemed as though Rafael thought that he deserved it.

"Lisa, what are you doing?" Eric exclaimed, as he rushed to put himself between his wife and Rafael.

Lisa attempted to push past her husband as she said through gritted teeth, "You have a lot of nerve coming here. You were the reason my daughter got suspended from school. If that wasn't bad enough, Tessa told me that Alexis was inconsolable after she met you this afternoon, and now, she's missing." She wiped her tears away from her face with her hands as she glared at him. "I thought you were supposed to help her, not make things worse!"

"Lisa, that's enough," Eric said. "Leave the boy alone. Screaming at him won't help us find her any sooner. I'm sure he's just as upset as the rest of us."

Lisa stepped back and looked at Eric with uncontrolled anger. "So, now you're going to defend him? How can you possibly do that? He's been nothing but trouble for her since the day she met him!"

"You know that's not true," Eric said wearily. "You remember what Alexis was like after Avery died. Rafael brought her out of her depression. He was there for her, and I'm sure he tried to help her as best as he could...Maybe if we'd told her..."

"You think it's my fault, don't you?" Lisa cut in.

"Don't twist my words, Lisa," Eric said.

"Go on. Just say it. I was the one who insisted that we not tell her." Aunt Cora and Tessa exchanged perplexed looks as Lisa glanced at each one of the men standing before her. She said, "I know that's what you're all thinking."

"Lisa," Father Bernal said in as gentle and compassionate a voice as he could muster, "This is not the time to lay blame at anyone's feet. We all care about Alexis and only want what's best for her."

Lisa's eyes flooded with tears and her voice shook as she asked Eric, "Why is this happening? Doesn't she know that we love her?"

Father Bernal's heart felt heavy as he watched Eric put his arms around his wife. Sadly, he thought there was little he could say or do to ease their pain. Despite his repeated warnings to Lisa about the dangers of keeping Alexis in the dark, she steadfastly refused to allow anyone to tell her daughter anything. And now, he feared that Alexis was in danger of losing her soul to the Devil because of their silence.

Just then, Father Bernal heard several car doors slamming. Tessa raced to the window and peeked through the curtains to see who had arrived.

"Jake's here with Manuel and Danny," Tessa said. "There are also a few other people from church out there. I'll go see if they know anything more."

Father Bernal put his hand on Rafael's shoulder and asked him, "How are you, my son?"

"I will find her, Father, and bring her home. I promise," he said with grim determination.

Father Bernal nodded and made the sign of the cross on the boy's forehead as he said, "God be with you, Arquero."

As Rafael headed toward the front door, Father Bernal quietly said a prayer for this young man who he firmly believed held Alexis' fate in his hands.

When Rafael stepped into the foyer, he became transfixed by the two-word note, written in *her* blood, on the back of the front door. The simple message, *SHE'S MINE,* left no doubt in the Archer's mind. The long-awaited time had come. He swallowed hard and moved in for a closer look as he thought about what she must have been thinking and feeling at the time she wrote those words. He stopped in front of the door and leaned forward, resting his forehead against it. He shut his eyes tightly together as he tried to ward off the pain and guilt he felt for letting her walk away from him earlier that day. It made him feel sick inside to think of what the Devil had in store for her. He stepped back and took a deep breath before placing his hand on the doorknob and turning the handle. He opened the door and looked up at the darkening sky, asking God to help him find her. He also prayed for the courage and wisdom to do what was necessary to keep Alexis from falling into the Devil's hands.

Rafael had just walked out the front door when he heard Jeremy call his name.

"Can I talk to you for a minute?" Jeremy asked as he walked onto the front porch.

Rafael said, "Of course," and moved toward him.

"I just wanted to start out by apologizing to you for the way I've acted toward you in the past," Jeremy said. "As for my mother, I hope you understand how upsetting this whole situation is for her. Normally, she would never say or do the things she did to you in there."

"There is really no need…"

"Yes, there is," Jeremy interrupted. "I misjudged you and was unkind to someone who was only trying to watch out for my sister. I don't know what happened between you and Alexis today, but I hope you don't hold any of it against her. She's acting on incomplete information and isn't thinking clearly…I guess we're all to blame for that."

"I don't blame her for anything," Rafael replied fervently. "The Devil has been playing with her mind and has filled her head with lies and distortions. I just wish I could have done more to help her see that."

"It's not too late," Jeremy said with conviction. "There's still time. Alexis is out there somewhere. She's lost, and she thinks that she's let us all down. She just needs the right person to get through to her and make her see things the right way. You were able to pull her out of the depression she was in after Avery died and I believe that you can help her see through the lies the Devil is feeding her."

"What makes you say that?"

"She loves you," Jeremy replied simply.

Rafael didn't know what to make of this statement, especially given what Alexis had said to him only hours earlier. Unable to reconcile the contradiction, he pushed it aside along with all the emotions that those words evoked within him.

"If you find my sister before we do, can you tell her that her family loves her?"

Rafael nodded. "Of course I will."

"If I were strong enough, I would've insisted on going with you, but in my condition, I know I'd just slow you down."

"Your parents need you here," Rafael replied.

Jeremy lowered himself onto the porch swing and said, "When you see her, don't hold back. She needs to know the truth about what's been happening to her. Tell her how you feel. Say it as often and as many times as you need to. Make her hear you. Understand?"

Rafael nodded again solemnly as he helped Jeremy to his feet. "I need to go now."

As he turned to leave, he heard Jeremy say, "Deus Tecum."

Rafael looked back and said, "In Aeternam."

Afterward, Rafael walked up to a group of people who were standing at the end of the driveway. The sight of Jake and Tessa standing with their arms around each other was painful for him to watch since it served as a stark reminder of just how empty his own arms felt without *her* in them. He brushed those feelings aside and told himself that wallowing in self-pity would be neither helpful nor productive in the present situation.

After Jake and Rafael exchanged greetings, Rafael asked him if he had heard anything new.

Sadly, Jake had nothing new to report. "Nobody's seen or heard from her. It's like she just dropped off the face of the Earth."

Danny and Manuel, who were standing next to Jake and Tessa, told him that they also came up empty after driving around the neighborhood, knocking on doors, and calling friends and acquaintances.

When Tessa turned to Manuel to ask him a question, Jake took Rafael aside and said under his breath, "We need to talk."

Rafael nodded and then walked with Jake until they were out of earshot of the others.

"I don't know where she is, but I might know *why* she's gone," Jake said nervously. "Do you remember the day you saw us in the parking lot in front of the grocery store?"

"Yes. Why do you ask?"

"We went there to meet this guy who told us all about The Brethren. He showed us a video of The Final Tasks. We saw you and her father in the video."

The news caught him completely off guard. *Dear God. She knows.*

"She thinks that The Brethren sees her as some kind of threat. She was afraid of what you or her father might do to her."

Rafael's eyes widened in disbelief at the news. "Why would she think that?"

"Why wouldn't she?" Jake replied with a shrug. "No one's told her anything at all, so she came to her own conclusions through other sources. She was desperate. She asked me to hack into your phone, and I did it...to help her. We couldn't see the emails on one of your accounts; she knew you were hiding something..."

"Why are you telling me this now?"

"When I found out she was missing, I broke down and told my dad everything. He helped me access the emails that you'd blocked and made a confession of his own: he told me that he was the one who designed the security program you were using."

Although Rafael knew that his phone had been compromised, he had not known who had broken into it. Now, he knew who had done it and why.

"Have you told anyone else about this?"

"No," Jake replied. "She made me promise not to say anything to anybody."

The situation was much worse than he had thought. Not only was Alexis being misguided by the Devil, she actually thought that he might harm her, too.

Rafael was thinking about what he was going to do next when the lights suddenly went out all around them. To make matters worse, he noticed that a dense and ominous fog was also rolling in, enveloping and concealing everything within it.

Tessa exclaimed, "What's happening?"

Jake shouted out to her, "The grid's probably down." He said to Rafael, "It happened before in 2011. If I'm right, it might be hours before SDG&E can fix it."

"Is there anyone you haven't been able to get a hold of?" Rafael asked Jake.

"Tobey hasn't been answering his phone, but I know his parents are out of town," Jake replied. "I don't know if he went with them or not."

"He is here. I saw him last night," Rafael informed him.

Jake and Rafael looked at each other as the same thought appeared to cross their minds.

"Do you think he knows where she is?" Jake asked.

"I am not sure, but I am going to find out."

The streets were dark and deserted as Rafael drove toward Tobey's house. He turned on his car radio and found that only one AM station was still on the air. The commentators on the news program were saying that the blackout was county-wide, that its source was currently unknown, and that no estimate could be provided as to when power would be restored. County and city officials were urging residents to stay indoors until the situation could be remedied, since no streetlights, including signals, were operational. That was a directive that Rafael knew he could not follow as long as *she* was missing.

As soon as Rafael arrived at Tobey's house, he rushed toward the front door and rang the doorbell. When no one answered, he knocked and then pounded on the door as he yelled Tobey's name. Next, he moved to the window beside the front door, cupped his face with his hands, and peered into a dark, empty room; nothing. Afterward, he stepped over to the side gate and looked over the fence. He was greeted by a very large, growling German Shepherd. He backed up a few steps and saw the *Beware of Dog* sign hanging from the fence. He wrung his hands and grimaced in frustration. *Where could Tobey possibly be?*

Rafael nearly jumped out of his skin when, moments later, his phone beeped. He pulled it out of his back pocket and felt his heart begin to race when he saw that it was a text from Tobey. The message read, "r u alone?" Are you alone?

He quickly responded, "Yes."

Tobey replied less than a minute later, telling Rafael to meet him at the skateboard section of Salt Creek Community Park in fifteen minutes. He looked at his cell phone and saw that it was already seven fifteen.

Rafael immediately texted back and asked if Alexis was with him. When Tobey failed to respond, he shoved his phone into his back pocket, ran to his car, and sped off. Although he now had a glimmer of hope that he might be able to find Alexis, he also sensed that he was running out of time. At this point, every second counted.

Rafael spotted Tobey's empty car as soon as he turned into the parking lot. He crossed himself, grabbed his backpack, and sprinted past the playground area next to the Community Center to a wooden fence that overlooked public tennis courts, soccer and baseball fields, and the skateboard park. He found that the incoming fog was obscuring his view of the grounds below. He ran down a dirt path that led to a short bridge built over a dried up creek and spotted a solitary figure sitting on one of the steps next to a railing in the skateboard area. Tobey stood up and stuffed his hands into the front pockets of his jeans as Rafael approached. He looked like he had just seen a ghost.

"Have you seen Alexis? Do you know where she is?" Rafael asked, trying to remain calm.

Tobey's eyes darted back and forth as he said, "Did you come alone?" Rafael nodded. Tobey took a step closer to him and asked, "You didn't tell anyone else that you were meeting me, right?"

He shook his head. "Of course not."

"*She* told me not to tell you anything, if you didn't come alone."

"Why would Alexis say that?"

"She didn't say that," Tobey replied.

Rafael was quickly losing patience with Tobey's riddles. He grabbed both of Tobey's arms and shook him. "Can you just answer my question? Everyone is worried sick about her!"

Tobey looked like he was on the verge of a nervous breakdown. He turned away from Rafael and started to cry.

"Why weren't you answering your phone?"

"Alexis asked me not to," he replied. "She said she'd leave if I told anyone that she was with me."

"How was she acting while she was with you?"

Tobey wiped the tears from his eyes and said, "Strange. She just walked in when I opened the door and then curled up on a recliner in my living room. She had a bloody towel wrapped around her hand, but she didn't say why. I cleaned and bandaged the wound, but she never said a word. She just sat there for a long time rocking back and forth."

"So she never spoke at all?"

Tobey shook his head. "I tried to talk to her, but she wouldn't say much...to *me*."

"What do you mean?"

"When I stepped out, I could have sworn that I heard two voices in the room. It freaked me out, and when I went back to check on her, the room felt…cold."

"Did you hear what she was saying?"

Tobey looked terrified. He shook his head as he said, "I must be going crazy. There must be something wrong with me."

"Tobey, you are not crazy. I need you to stay focused and tell me what happened."

He nodded, closed his eyes, and took a deep breath. "Around half past six, Alexis just got up and headed for the door. She wouldn't tell me where she was going. When I tried to stop her, she pushed me back and ran. I followed her on foot all the way to the pedestrian bridge by Otay Ranch High."

Rafael froze as he recalled Alexis' recurring dream. "What was she doing?"

"She was standing by the railing. I was afraid that she was going to hurt herself so I ran toward her. I was just a couple feet away when she told me to stop. She said, 'It's okay Tobey, Lizzie's here. Go home.'" More tears slid down Tobey's face as he said, "I tried to get closer but *she* got in my way."

"Who got in your way?"

Tobey nervously ran his fingers though his hair as he said, "It couldn't have been Lizzie. It's just not possible."

"Tobey, please. Who is Lizzie?" Rafael asked as he recalled Alexis mentioning that name before.

Tobey took his glasses off and wiped his face with his hands. "When Avery and Alexis were kids, they used to call each other by their middle names, Elizabeth and Mackenzie, Lizzie and Mac."

Rafael felt like the wind had just been knocked out of him. It made perfect sense for the Devil to use Alexis' best friend to get to her. He cursed himself for not having thought of that possibility earlier.

"What did Avery tell you?"

"She said that I needed to follow her specific instructions," he said, sounding agitated. "She told me that Alexis would jump right then and there if I didn't."

"Please try to calm down…"

Tobey nodded as he bent over, placing his hands on his knees and taking a deep breath. "She told me to tell you to meet me at this park just in case you didn't come alone. She said that she'd be watching. After I texted you, I got in my car and drove here as fast as I could."

"Did she say anything else to you?"

Tobey again nodded. "You have until eight o'clock to get to her."

Rafael took his cell phone out of his pocket once again to check the time. Fear gripped his heart when he saw that it was already past seven thirty. The pedestrian bridge was ten minutes away by car. He grabbed Tobey by the arm and said, "You need to take me to Alexis right now."

The combination of the fog and the darkness gave the area surrounding the pedestrian bridge an unearthly feel. Tobey parked his car on a side street and led Rafael, who had his backpack slung over his shoulder, to the ramp leading up to the bridge. He pointed his finger upward and said, "She's there."

Rafael felt a sense of foreboding as he looked in that direction. Although he could not see Alexis from where he stood, he felt her presence. He was also certain that she was not alone.

Rafael said to Tobey, "You need to go to her family and tell them where she is. Do you understand?"

Tobey nodded and said, "Is she going to be okay?"

"I don't know," he replied truthfully.

"Is there anything else I can do?"

Rafael put his hand on Tobey's shoulder and said, "Pray."

Tobey nodded, and then turned to go.

As Rafael stood at the foot of the ramp, he knew that this was the moment he had been preparing himself for since he had been appointed as The Archer. Before taking his first step onto the ramp, he took out his cell phone and sent a message to Gonçalo, Akira, and Vincenzo, telling them exactly where he was. If a demonic presence was lying in wait for him, he knew that he would need all the help he could get in order to send it back to Hell. He also wanted the others to be there to take over for him if he got seriously injured or died. Leaving Alexis defenseless was not an option.

Rafael crossed himself and started reciting Psalm 23 in his head as he headed up the ramp. *The Lord is my shepherd, I shall not want.* He had long since resigned himself to the possibility that he might not return home or live to see his eighteenth birthday. *Even though I walk through the valley of the shadow of death, I fear no evil, for You are with me; Your rod and Your staff comfort me.* The only thing he feared was losing her. He was prepared to storm the gates of Hell to protect and defend her. Ensuring that her mortal body and immortal soul were safe was all that mattered to him. This was a battle he knew he had to win, even if it cost him his life.

When he reached the top of the ramp, he recited the last lines in his head, as his eyes looked up toward the heavens above. *Surely goodness and loving-kindness will follow me all the days of my life; And I will dwell in the house of the Lord forever.*

From where Rafael stood, much of the bridge was obscured from view. A powerful gust of cold wind hit his body with such force that it nearly knocked him off his feet. As he steadied himself, he prayed that he would have the courage to face the evil that was threatening to take the life of the girl he loved, and the will to persevere no matter what the odds would be. As he took a step forward, he knew that the battle for Alexis' soul was about to begin.

CHAPTER 19—BATTLE AT THE PEDESTRIAN BRIDGE

Alexis had been on this bridge many times before in her dreams. It was exactly as she had pictured it. The fog. The darkness. Lizzie. The only missing piece of the puzzle was Rafael.

As she stood by the railing, the impenetrable fog and darkness made it almost impossible to see anything farther than her outstretched arms. The only sound she heard was the occasional howling of a coyote in the canyon below. The road beneath the bridge was deserted and the houses on the hills surrounding the bridge were pitch black. She had never felt so alone in her life.

Alexis had to grip the railing to stop herself from shaking. The hooded gray sweatshirt and black leggings she was wearing offered almost no protection from the bone-chilling cold. She wanted to get it over with, but Lizzie insisted that she needed to wait.

While looking down at the street below, she wondered what it was going to be like for her to die. She closed her eyes and imagined falling like a skydiver without a parachute, with her arms and legs spread wide. She thought about whether the force of the impact from her body hitting the ground would kill her immediately, or whether she would have to endure the pain for at least a few moments before her life slipped away.

Her eyes sprung open when Lizzie tapped her arm. With a wicked grin, Lizzie said, "He's here."

Alexis' grip on the railing tightened as soon as Lizzie uttered these words. She didn't need to say his name; it had to be Rafael. Her instincts told her to run, even though she knew that there was nowhere to go. Her heart pounded wildly in her chest as a thousand possibilities of what might happen when she saw him flashed across her mind. In none of these scenarios did he give her any indication that he cared about whether she lived or died.

"Alexis, are you there?" Rafael asked in a cautious tone.

The sound of his voice jarred her. She turned toward him but didn't see the outline of his body through the fog until he was just a few feet away from her.

Tell him to stop where he is.

Alexis called out to Rafael and said, "Don't come any closer." He froze in place.

"What are you doing here?" he asked gently. "Everyone has been so worried about you. It is so cold, mi querida. You must be freezing. Let me take you home now."

Alexis looked at him sadly and shook her head. "I'm not going home."

He took another step toward her. She moved back and said, "NO!"

Ask him to tell you who he really is.

Although she and Lizzie already knew the answer to that question, she was curious to see if he would finally admit it. At this point, she knew that she had nothing to lose by asking the question.

"I knew you'd come, "Alexis said. "That's why you were chosen. You never give up, do you?" Her anxiety level rose to a fever pitch as she prepared herself to ask him the next question. "Are you the one they call The Archer?"

After a brief pause, Rafael said, "Yes, I am."

"Are you here because of me?"

"Yes. I came here *for* you."

Alexis then asked him point blank, "Are you here to kill me?"

"What are you talking about?" Rafael said, sounding clearly alarmed. "Do you really think that I could ever hurt you?"

He's lying. Don't believe him.

"I was sent here to protect you," he said.

His loyalties lie with the Church, not you.

"Why should I believe you?" Alexis asked. "You've been lying to me since the day we met…if not directly, then by omission. If you're supposed to protect me, then why would you do that? Why couldn't you trust me with the truth?"

"I wanted to tell you," he replied, "but your parents would not allow it. Father Bernal told me that I had to honor their wishes."

"Then why are you telling me now?"

"Because you have a right to know the truth," he continued, his voice breaking. "You are here because we kept you in the dark. We let the Devil come into your life by not telling you what we knew. He has poisoned your mind, making you think that you don't matter and that your friends and family don't care if you live or die."

"Why me?" Alexis' mind couldn't comprehend why the Devil would take a particular interest in her, a Catholic schoolgirl, or why the Church would be so eager to defend her.

"Only God can answer that question. He sent us signs through the Archangel Michael. That is what led me to you."

You've heard enough. Cut him off right now.

She nodded and said, "I have to go."

"Alexis, you have got your whole life ahead of you," Rafael said, with a rising sense of urgency. "Nothing should end here tonight; not for you."

Alexis shook her head. "It has to. Don't you see? All I do is hurt people. I don't want to do that anymore."

"You know that is not true," he pleaded.

"Be happy," she said. "Tell my family that I love them and not to grieve for me after I'm gone. Goodbye, Rafael." She turned and ran.

"ALEXIS, NO!"

Alexis raced toward the part of the bridge where the height of the railing was only waist high and threw one of her legs over the side.

Rafael was just a few feet away from Alexis when she turned to him and screamed, "Stop right there, or I'll jump right now."

Rafael raised his hands in surrender and backed away.

"I am moving back," he cried out. "Now please, just climb back over the railing."

Do it now!

"Can't you give me just a little more time?" Rafael begged.

Suddenly, an entire chorus of voices seemed to be ringing in her ears. For an instant, she teetered slightly in the wrong direction, as her grip on the railing seemed to loosen of its own accord. Somehow, she found the strength to tighten her grasp and right herself before swinging her leg back toward the other side of the railing and slumping to the ground.

"Alexis, God loves you," Rafael said.

She shook her head. "He doesn't care about me."

"That is not true," Rafael replied frantically. "Don't let the Devil convince you that you don't matter to Him."

What are you waiting for?

Rafael continued, "Your brother told me to tell you that your family loves you and wants you to come home."

He's just trying to prey on your weaknesses...

"Listen to me," Rafael pleaded.

LISTEN TO ME!

Alexis covered her ears with her hands. She felt like her head was about to explode. She cried out, "STOP. PLEASE STOP!"

END IT NOW!

"Alexis, please don't go where I can't follow you. I would go to the gates of Hell and fight the Devil himself, but only you can choose to live or die in God's light."

*You're wasting time…*The voice seemed to grow weaker.

"Don't make me live in a world without you in it," Rafael implored her from where he stood. "I don't ever want to know what that is like. When I lost my parents, I wanted to die. I asked God why He took them and spared me. I promised myself that I would never let anyone get close enough to make me feel that kind of pain again. Then I met you. You made me *want* to feel again."

Alexis shook her head and said, "It's too late Rafael. There's no other way…"

"YES, THERE IS! Why can't you see that? You are not alone; I am right here."

"Go home, Rafael. There's nothing for you here."

"I can't," he replied. "Not without you."

As he said these words, the light from the full moon penetrated through the fog. Tiny droplets of rain touched her face as the fog gave way to rain. She was now able to see what, minutes earlier, had been completely shrouded by mist. She looked down at her hands and saw that her knuckles had turned white from balling them into fists. She knew that her life was at a critical crossroads. She had to make a decision now.

"Please look at me," Rafael implored.

Don't do it…It's a trick. The voice was weaker still.

"LOOK AT ME!"

Alexis felt her breath catch in her throat as their eyes locked onto one another. Rafael was no longer just a shadowy figure or a disembodied voice in the darkness, but a young man whose bloodshot eyes and tear-streaked face conveyed a depth of feeling for her that no words could have ever adequately expressed.

Rafael reached out to her and said, "Alexis, I love you. Stay with me, please."

Mac, don't do it. Barely a whisper now.

Alexis stood up and ran. To him. To safety. To love.

Rafael's eyes widened as she raced toward him. He caught her when her knees buckled and then wrapped her in his arms as they fell to their knees. She began to cry as the light drizzle turned into rain. He wiped away her tears with his hands and kissed the top of her head as she buried her face in his chest.

While lying safe in his arms, it suddenly dawned on her that God had been there the whole time. He had been there every time a friend or family member had answered her call for help or had taken the time to listen when she needed someone to talk to. Most importantly, He had sent Rafael to be her protector and counselor. He had been all those things to her and so much more. She couldn't believe that she hadn't seen that before.

Rafael kissed her tear-streaked face and her bandaged hand. He then took the wooden cross that was hanging from his neck and placed it around hers. He said, "Your soul belongs with God. Don't let the Devil or anyone else ever convince you otherwise."

Alexis recalled seeing the cross hanging in his locker when they first met and remembered its significance to him. She was, in fact, so taken aback by the gesture that she didn't know what to say or think. Her hands shook as she touched the cross and then looked up at his smiling face. To go from the depths of despair to extreme joy in so short a time was almost too much for her young heart to bear.

Rafael put his forehead against hers and held her hands in his as he said, "Pray with me."

She nodded, closed her eyes and waited for him to begin.

"*Sancte Michael Archangele…*"

"I know this prayer," she interrupted. "My Grandpa Neil used to say it when I was a child."

"Then say it with me now," he replied and then repeated the opening words of the Prayer to St. Michael. "*Sancte Michael Archangele,*"

"Saint Michael the Archangel," she repeated in English.

"*defendenos in proelio contra nequitiam et insidias diaboli esto praesidium.*"

"defend us in battle, be our protection against the wickedness and snares of the Devil;"

"*Imperet illi Deus, supplices deprecamur.*"

"may God rebuke him, humbly we pray;"

"*tuque, princeps militia caelestis, Satanam aliosque spiritus malignos, qui ad perditionem animarum pervagantur in mundo, divina virtute, in infernum detrude. Amen.*"

"O Prince of the Heavenly Host, by the power of God, thrust into Hell Satan and all evil spirits who wander through the world for the ruin of souls. Amen."

Rafael crossed himself and then looked at her intently as he said, "Alexis, we don't have much time."

"What do you mean?" she asked. "We can go home now, can't we?"

"God willing, I will see you safely home," Rafael replied in a solemn tone.

Just then, she heard the voice that had nearly driven her to an early grave.

I thought you were my friend. Why did you choose him over me? It seemed to have regained its strength.

At that moment, Alexis realized that whoever or whatever had been talking to her all this time hadn't been Lizzie at all. She also recognized that her ordeal was far from over. The Devil desperately wanted her soul, and Alexis sensed that he and his minions weren't going to let her go without a fight.

"I will never let any harm come to you as long as I am alive," Rafael said as he placed his hand under her chin. "I promise you that."

The sound of unearthly screeches and very large wings flapping just above their heads suddenly filled the night air, while a chorus of howls came from the canyons below. She looked up and saw two gargoyles circling above them, like birds of prey stalking their next meal. Still more of them perched themselves on the top of the suicide barriers on either side of the bridge. They all appeared to be waiting for a signal from their master that it was time to attack. She became consumed with fear as she recalled seeing these same beasts in the video.

"Listen very carefully," Rafael implored her. "Keep your head down and stay close to me. Don't worry, help is on the way. I will try to hold these things off as long as possible. If something happens to me, you need to run as fast as you can, and don't look back."

"I won't leave you; I can help."

"What I need you to do is live," he said earnestly. "I am not afraid to die. It was the bargain I made with God when I agreed to be your Arquero."

Alexis shook her head vigorously as the tears once again started to stream down her face. "I won't let you do this. My life isn't worth yours."

Listen to her Archer. Is she really worth dying for?

Was the demon now speaking to him too? she wondered. Rafael cupped her face in his hands and said, "Don't be afraid, mi amor. God is with you. No matter what happens to me, He will never leave your side."

Rafael stood up and squared his shoulders as he gazed intently at something just behind her. She didn't have to turn her head to see who it was. Although it looked and sounded like Lizzie, she now knew that, whoever it was, it was not and never had been the friend that she loved so dearly.

Rafael spoke first. "So, you are the monster that has been filling her head with lies."

"If that's true, then I'm in good company," the demon said in an oily voice. "You haven't exactly been truthful with her yourself, Archer."

"It is over," he replied. "She knows what you are now. You can't fool her anymore."

Alexis turned and saw the demon looking at Rafael like a gladiator sizing up his opponent. "So, you're the boy the Church sent to defend her. One would think that it would have had more sense than to entrust such an important mission to someone so…young."

"You have no idea who I am or what I am capable of," Rafael said, clenching his fists.

"I know you very well, Archer," the demon said in a condescending tone. "You were the warrior sent and blessed by the Holy Father himself. Your job is to defend this poor, unfortunate girl, but you're no match for me. You are mortal. I am not."

Rafael stiffened visibly at this obvious challenge. "You and your kind are vile and pitiless creatures. You prey on the vulnerable and feed off their fears. I am not afraid of you. God is with me, and your master will never have her soul as long as I live."

The demon laughed. "Ready your weapons, Archer. I don't want the Archangel Michael to complain that I sent you to your God tonight without at least offering you the opportunity to show off your skills. It will make my victory all the sweeter. But make it quick. It's time for you to die."

The demon was obviously relishing the idea of the battle to come and gave Rafael a moment to prepare. Alexis watched helplessly as Rafael took his backpack off his shoulders, placed it on the ground and opened it. He took out two short swords, secured a strap around his shoulders, and put the swords in their scabbards. He then placed the back strap of a quiver filled with arrows over his shoulder and secured the side strap. Lastly, he retrieved a curved silver object from his backpack and held it tightly in his right hand.

The demon looked at Alexis tauntingly. "You can still save him. I'll spare his life, if you come with me now."

"Don't believe him!" Rafael said defiantly. "He will kill me whether you go with him or not."

The demon replied, "Do you want this boy's blood on your hands? I know how much he means to you. It's not too late to save him."

"STOP LYING TO HER!" Rafael screamed as he unfurled the silver object in his hand. It took the shape of a bow. He quickly took an arrow from his quiver, placed the shaft on the arrow rest, and took aim at the demon's chest.

"Archer, would you really shoot down an unarmed and defenseless girl?"

"Tell us your name, demon," he commanded. "Tell Alexis who you are."

The demon paused, cocked his head and looked at Alexis as he said, "You know who I am. I'm your best friend."

Alexis shook her head. "I don't know who you are. Avery's dead. You're nothing but a warped monster that lies and twists facts to get what you want. I'm done listening to you."

The demon leered at Alexis as he said, "A monster? If I am it's only because your precious and loving God turned me into one." The demon took a step closer. "Do you want to know who I am? I am the Destroyer; I am lust and vengeance."

"Asmodeus," Rafael said.

The demon laughed and said, "Would you like to see what your precious God has done to me?"

Alexis watched in horror as two large horns burst forth from what once had been Lizzie's skull. The demon's hair shriveled away and his skin became like rotted flesh. He also bared his spear-shaped teeth as he sprouted a long whip-like tail and wings like a bat.

Rafael shouted, "Go back to Hell," and shot an arrow straight at the demon's chest. Asmodeus caught the arrow and broke it in two.

The demon roared in anger as he looked at the gargoyles perched above them and screamed, "KILL HIM!"

The gargoyles let out ear-piercing cries as they began their attack. The sound made Alexis feel like her head was about to split open. *The battle for her soul had finally begun.*

"ALEXIS, STAY DOWN!" Rafael ordered as he carefully aimed his bow at the two gargoyles swooping down on them. Despite the overwhelming odds that they faced, she knew that she was in the hands of a skilled warrior who would do everything in his power to keep her safe. Still, he was only one man against a multitude of winged beasts. The first two gargoyles quickly disappeared in a cloud of black dust, after being hit squarely in the chest with one arrow each. However, another came at him from behind and slashed his back with its razor-like talons. He winced as the gargoyle's claws pierced his skin. She cried out as blood began to stain the back of his shirt. And yet, he showed no sign that his injuries were slowing him down or hindering his ability to fight. The next time it attacked, he thrust his two short swords deep into its chest and sent it, like the others, back to the netherworld. He quickly sheathed his swords and picked up his bow and shot two more of the winged beasts down.

When Alexis looked up, she saw the last three gargoyles heading directly for them. Just as Rafael was about to shoot, she heard someone scream from behind her, "GET DOWN!"

Rafael looked back and then quickly pushed her to the ground. He crouched down beside her as three arrows whizzed past their heads. When she looked in the direction from which the arrows had come, she saw Vincenzo, Gonçalo, and Akira running toward them, armed for battle.

Just as the last of the gargoyles were brought down by Akira and Vincenzo, she heard the menacing growls of an untold number of beasts approaching them. Rafael ordered the other three to form a protective circle around her. All four had their bows drawn and ready when six pairs of red eyes emerged from the darkness.

"Hellhounds," Rafael said under his breath. "On my mark."

One of the four-legged hounds moved slightly ahead of the others. It stared at Alexis and had the same kind of menacing grin that she had seen the last time she had gone jogging alone on the trails. It bared its teeth and snapped its jaws, taunting her, and then charged toward them. A barrage of arrows greeted the hounds as they drew nearer. Three of them were brought down almost immediately by direct hits to the chest. The leader, however, seemed to be unfazed by the arrows that had pierced its side. Rafael ordered Vincenzo to guard Alexis, before crouching down and unsheathing one of his short swords. Akira shot two more arrows that struck the leader's leg and neck. Rafael leapt forward and grabbed its throat. He repeatedly thrust his sword into its chest until it fell to the ground in a heap and then vanished.

The remaining two hounds gnashed their teeth and howled at the sight of their pack leader's demise. One of them lurched forward, latching onto Akira's right leg, and began dragging him away. Rafael jumped on top of it and kept stabbing its neck until it released Akira's leg. Gonçalo finished it off by thrusting his swords into its chest. After one last gasp, it too, vanished.

Alexis realized that Akira was going into shock as he lay on the ground, bleeding from his leg wound. Thinking quickly, she removed his belt and used it as a tourniquet to slow the bleeding, while Vincenzo hovered protectively over her.

Meanwhile, Rafael shot two arrows at the last hellhound, which stumbled as it attempted to retreat. Gonçalo jumped on top of it and yanked it onto its side while Rafael finished it off. When it vanished, they both turned and ran back toward Alexis and Vincenzo. Asmodeus, however, reappeared on the bridge and blocked their path. Vincenzo pushed Alexis back as the demon's powerful tail swept across the width of the bridge, knocking him to the ground. Vincenzo cried out in pain when the demon grabbed his arm and hurled the young warrior against the railing. At the same time, Gonçalo and Rafael jumped over the demon's tail and rushed to Alexis' side.

Rafael turned to Gonçalo and said, "I am going to try and distract it while you get Alexis off this bridge."

Alexis did not want to leave him, but knew that her presence was only hampering his efforts to end this battle and, in the process, putting them all in greater danger.

Gonçalo said to Rafael, "You must be the one to end this, Arquero. You are the only one who can defeat him. She will be safe with me, I promise."

Rafael nodded and gave Alexis a reassuring glance before turning to face Asmodeus, who had just commandeered Vincenzo's swords.

Rafael and Asmodeus circled one another with swords drawn. The demon struck first. Alexis was horrified yet mesmerized by the ferocity with which Rafael and the demon fought one another. The sound of their swords clashing time and time again rang in her ears.

It wasn't long before Alexis realized what the demon's strategy was. He was going to wear Rafael down and kill him slowly, before her eyes. Although she knew that he was a skilled and able-bodied fighter, she could see that he was becoming fatigued and that the accumulated nicks, cuts, bruises, and overall trauma to his body were beginning to take their toll. Asmodeus, on the other hand, seemed to be operating on boundless energy.

Alexis' heart stopped when the demon's powerful foreswing sent one of Rafael's swords flying out of his hand. As Rafael ran toward it, she pleaded with Gonçalo to intercede. He looked at her gravely as he shook his head and said, "El Arquero would never forgive me if I left your side."

Just then, Alexis heard Rafael scream, "Get her out of here NOW!"

Gonçalo grabbed Alexis' arm as they ran toward the south side of the bridge, using every ounce of energy that they had left. They had almost made it to the top of the ramp when she heard the demon roar. When she turned and looked back, she saw Asmodeus vanish in a cloud of black smoke. Rafael, whose back was to her, fell to his knees as he bent forward to catch his breath. *Is it over? Did he defeat it?*

A glimmer of hope began to rise within her. Maybe now, she thought, she would get the chance to tell him she was sorry and make amends for everything she'd said and done to hurt him. However, the look of sheer terror on Rafael's face when he turned to look at her told her that something was horribly wrong.

She heard him yell, "NO!" as he jumped up and started to run toward her.

When Alexis turned her head back toward the ramp, she saw Asmodeus standing directly between her and her means of escape. She could smell the stench of his fetid breath bearing down upon them as he stepped between her and Gonçalo. She turned and tried to run toward Rafael but got swept off her feet by the demon's tail. She put her hands out in front of her to break her fall. She winced when the right side of her body hit the ground. She was struggling to get back on her feet when the demon's tail struck her body again with such force that the pain nearly sent her into shock. It felt like she had just been lashed by a massive whip. She turned her head just in time to see that his tail was swinging toward her yet again. She was certain that she wouldn't be able to take another hit.

Alexis closed her eyes and braced herself for the next—and possibly fatal—blow. To her surprise, it never came. Instead, it was Asmodeus who roared in pain. When she opened her eyes, she saw that Rafael had chopped the bottom half of his tail off and was now driving his short swords deep into the gaping wound. The demon retaliated by snatching both swords out of The Archer's hands and throwing them aside. Rafael reached out for Alexis and pulled her away from Asmodeus' immediate grasp while Gonçalo engaged the demon with a frontal attack. They scrambled to their feet and were running in the other direction when they heard Gonçalo let out a blood curdling scream. She turned her head just as Gonçalo slumped to the ground.

Rafael yelled for her to run when he saw that the demon was bounding toward them. She sprinted forward, but realized a split second later that he was no longer at her side. She looked back and saw Rafael standing directly in the demon's path with his bow drawn. His arms were shaking as he shot the last two arrows in his quiver. The demon dodged one and batted the other away. He then shoved Rafael roughly to the ground as he headed toward his ultimate prize. Grabbing hold of Alexis, he dragged her, kicking and screaming, to the far end of the bridge.

Alexis looked up at the night sky and prayed that her death would be quick and painless, but quickly forgot her own peril when she saw Rafael, bloody and bruised, crawling toward her on his hands and knees. More than anything, she wanted to tell him that it was okay to rest his battered body and stop fighting. She knew in her mind and heart that he had done everything humanly possible to save her soul and that he faced certain death if he continued to fight. Yet, there he was, inching his way toward her. She knew that he would never give up.

Alexis hated the thing that was holding her captive and the pain and suffering the demon had caused to the four young men who had risked their lives on her behalf.

When Rafael had crawled within striking distance of them, Asmodeus looked down at him and said, "You've lost, Archer. Your men have fallen, your weapons are gone and your body is broken. *SHE'S MINE!*"

Rafael slowly stood up and reached for something in his back pocket. From where she stood, it looked like a small vial. He unscrewed the lid and then looked up at Asmodeus defiantly and said, "Let her go."

The demon laughed. "Why would I do that?"

"Because," he said as he flung the clear liquid in the vial at the demon's face, "in the name of God, I command you to do it."

The demon roared as the liquid seared his face. *Holy water.* He released Alexis from his grasp and writhed in pain. Seizing the moment, Rafael grabbed Alexis and pulled her away. She fell backwards as Rafael stepped in front of her and took out a small cross from his other back pocket, which he jammed into the demon's forehead.

As the demon doubled over, Rafael turned his head toward Alexis and screamed once again, "RUN!"

Asmodeus lurched forward and tried to grab Alexis as she got to her feet. Rafael rammed his body against the demon's arm to block the attempt. He was now using the only weapon that he had left; his body. When the demon lunged at her a second time, Rafael once again inserted himself between them. This time, the demon slammed him against the rail. She uttered a strangled cry, as Rafael fell, unconscious, to the ground.

Asmodeus moved closer to Rafael and then sneered at Alexis as he said, "So this is the mighty warrior that God sent to defend you? Look at him now. Have you ever seen anything more pathetic?"

Alexis felt numb as she gazed at Rafael's nearly lifeless form. She looked around and saw that the three others who had come to her aid were also lying on the ground, badly injured. She was now alone and defenseless against this monster.

And then, from out of nowhere, a sudden peace, unlike any she had ever known, came over her. As the demon loomed over Rafael, it became crystal clear to her what she had to do. Without saying a word, she leapt toward Rafael and covered his body with her own.

Alexis looked at the demon defiantly and said, "Rafael is everything that you can never be. And in spite of your attempts to drive me away from God, The Archer helped me to see through your lies." She ran a finger across Rafael's cheek and said, "He beat you at your own game," and then looked at Asmodeus, adding, "You're the one that's lost. God loves me; Rafael showed me that. And because of him, you'll *never* have my soul."

Asmodeus moved a step closer and raised his arm, as if he were about to strike, when Alexis said in a voice devoid of fear, "If you're going to kill him, you'll have to kill me first. If you do, St. Michael will take us straight to God and you'll be left having to explain to your master how you let his prize slip through your fingers."

"She's right, demon," said a familiar voice from behind her. "She'll never go willingly with you now." It was Father Bernal.

The priest's words were followed shortly by the sound of her mother screaming out her name as she came running toward them, followed by Martin Lewis, Jake's father. Alexis also saw her own father, Eric, standing next to the priest, along with two other men with their bows drawn. When she looked in the opposite direction, she saw at least four other men coming from the other side of the bridge, bows in hand.

Alexis saw the terror in her mother's eyes as she beheld the demon standing over her daughter and Rafael. Asmodeus leered at her parents and then laughed at her mother's horrified face as he transformed himself back into Avery's likeness.

The demon turned to Father Bernal and said in a girlish voice, "Tell Brother Molina and the Holy Father that you may have won the battle tonight, but you won't win the war. The Master will take her soul. Mark my words."

Asmodeus then looked down at Alexis and said, "I underestimated you. But don't worry, we won't make that mistake again."

Alexis glared at the demon and said, "Go to Hell."

Asmodeus smiled at her and said, "With pleasure," and then disappeared into the darkness.

Once the demon had vanished, Alexis looked down at Rafael, who was still lying unconscious on the ground. She leaned forward and kissed his forehead. *He's so still,* she thought as she let the tears come. Although her body ached from the blows the demon had inflicted, the pain from her physical wounds was nothing compared to the emotional anguish she felt as she gazed at Rafael lying there, battered and lifeless.

Alexis gently touched Rafael's cheek and said, "Don't leave me," and then lifted her eyes up to the heavens as the rain splattered on her face. "Please God, don't take him away from me now."

Eric knelt down beside her and tried to pull her away from Rafael. She cried out frantically, "No, Daddy. NO! I can't leave him. I won't go."

"Alexis, I'm so sorry," Eric said, fighting back tears. When Alexis looked up at her father, the full force of the physical and emotional trauma she had just endured suddenly closed in on her. She felt dizzy and lightheaded. As she began to lose consciousness, she whimpered, "Daddy, Rafael's hurt. Please help him. Help them all."

CHAPTER 20—NEXT STEPS

Alexis heard the sound of sirens blaring and felt the occasional bump in the road as she slowly regained consciousness in the back of the ambulance. As soon as she arrived at the hospital, the paramedics lowered her gurney to the ground. They were whisking her through the sliding doors of the emergency room when she saw three of her injured protectors being brought in ahead of her. She also caught sight of several of the men that had arrived on the bridge with her parents, as they huddled around Father Bernal. Once inside, she spotted one more ambulance pulling up to the emergency room entrance just before the double doors shut, blocking her view of the reception area and beyond. She closed her eyes and said a prayer, knowing that it held Rafael.

Ironically, Alexis found herself in the same area of the hospital that Jeremy had been assigned to only a few hours earlier. It was a large room with rows of beds separated by curtains. From her limited vantage point, she tried to see if she recognized a familiar face in one of the other beds. She grew anxious when she realized that none of the others were there. Then again, their injuries had all been far worse than hers.

Knowing that there was little she could do for any of them now and fearing the worst, she gave herself over to her care providers. She spent the next few hours with her parents at her side, as hospital personnel ran tests and continued to monitor her at set intervals.

Alexis could think of nothing except Rafael, but the memory of his unconscious body lying on the ground kept her from even uttering his name or asking her parents if they had any idea about how he was doing. The fact that no one volunteered any information only heightened her fears that he had suffered severe or even fatal injuries. It did not, however, take long before her need to know the truth won out.

She looked at her father, who was sitting beside her in a chair, gathered her courage, and asked, "Dad, is Father Bernal here?"

"Yes, he is," Eric replied. "Why do you ask?"

"Has he said anything to you about Rafael or the others?" Alexis asked with a slight tremor in her voice.

"I saw him briefly while you were getting X-rays," he said in a measured tone. "He told me that Gonçalo, Vincenzo, and Akira are doing well and should be able to go home within the next few days."

"What about Rafael?" Alexis asked as she braced herself for her father's answer.

Eric gently placed his hand over hers and said, "His injuries were more extensive than the others. He lost consciousness after he was thrown against the railing. Unfortunately, Father Bernal still isn't certain about his prognosis."

Although Alexis was relieved to know that he was still alive, she worried about the long-term consequences of the injuries he had suffered. The idea that he would come out of this ordeal physically maimed, and possibly emotionally scarred, troubled her greatly.

Lisa, who was standing next to Alexis' bed, lowered the rail. She sat down next to her and put her right arm around her daughter's shoulder.

"He's going to be fine, honey. You'll see," Lisa said reassuringly.

"I wish you could have seen Rafael on the bridge tonight," Alexis said as she looked into her mother's eyes. "He was amazing. The Brethren would have been proud of The Archer they chose for me." She turned toward her father and said, "He did everything he could to protect me. The whole time we were out there, he never once thought of himself. He didn't stop, even when he was so badly hurt that he could barely move. In the end, when he had no weapons left to fight with, he tried to shield me with his own body."

"I wouldn't have expected anything less…and from what I saw, you did the same for him," Eric replied solemnly.

"Did you know when Rafael was chosen that he was going to be sent here for me?"

Eric shook his head. "I didn't find out until I saw Father Bernal with him at church. Father Bernal wanted to break the news to your mom and I in person."

"Why didn't you tell me?"

"Would you have believed us if we did?" Eric asked.

Lisa sighed. "It was my fault. I wanted to be sure that there was no other possible explanation for what was happening to you. Everyone was honoring my wishes." She bit her lip, adding, "After you got suspended, Rafael came up to me and begged me to tell you what was going on, but I wouldn't listen, and then I blamed him when you went missing."

Her father interjected, "I should have insisted that we tell you. You had a right to know. I promise, from now on, no more secrets. When you're up to it, I'll tell you everything and what I think we might be up against, okay?"

Alexis nodded and then asked her father, "Do you think that I'll be able to see Rafael tonight?"

"Maybe tomorrow," Eric replied. "I don't think he's in any condition to see anyone right now."

"Your father's right," Lisa added. "Besides, you need your rest, too."

Just then, the doctor walked in and gave her some good news; she was going to be discharged soon. He had concluded that her fainting spell was primarily due to anxiety and emotional stress, and the X-rays showed that she had suffered no breaks or fractures. After the doctor had gone, she asked her father how much her care providers knew about what had happened to her. He leaned in and quietly informed her that the true nature of her injuries was only divulged to those who cared for her on a need to know basis, and that such information would be kept confidential; she thought as much. Besides, she didn't think many people would believe it anyway.

Although Alexis was happy to be going home, she felt a slight pang of guilt when she thought of the other four people who had been on the bridge with her. She was certain that none of them would be released tonight.

She was sent home with a mild sedative and directions to follow up with her primary care physician. It was nearly dawn when her parents pulled the car into the driveway. She walked up the stairs and went directly to her room. Once there, she flopped onto the bed and quickly lapsed into unconsciousness.

Alexis woke up close to noon the next day. Sunlight was pouring in through her bedroom window as she opened her eyes. As she stared up at the ceiling, she heard the sound of dogs barking and children laughing as they played just outside her open window. *They sound like they don't have a care in the world,* she thought wistfully.

Thankfully, it had been a night of dreamless sleep...the first one she could remember in a long time. She was also grateful to have come out of her ordeal relatively unscathed. Still, she felt far from ready to face the day. Her body was sore and her mind numb from the previous day's events. Nevertheless, she knew she owed it to Rafael, Gonçalo, Vincenzo, and Akira to not wallow in self-pity, and so she swung her legs over the side of the bed and got up.

After freshening up and getting dressed, Alexis heard voices coming from downstairs. She headed toward the dining room, where she found Jeremy and her parents sitting at the table eating lunch.

Jeremy got up immediately and hugged her. Although she thought that he looked better today, he still seemed frail and a little unsteady on his feet. He smiled at her and asked, "How are you doing this morning?"

"Better now," she replied as she put on a brave face for his sake. The last thing she wanted to do was burden him with the details of her minor aches and pains, especially after the emotional roller coaster ride she had put him through, in addition to his own ordeal from the day before.

Alexis sat down next to Jeremy, who passed her a plate full of freshly baked rolls. She took in its scent as she picked one up and felt its warmth in her hand. Her stomach growled at the sight of the feast set before her and she eagerly filled her plate with chopped steak, vegetables, and steamed rice.

After Alexis had taken her first few bites, she noticed that the room had become quiet and that all eyes were on her.

Eric spoke first. "How are you feeling?" After Alexis, with a mouthful of food, mumbled that she was okay, he said, "There are some things your mom and I want to discuss with you."

She wiped her mouth with a napkin and said, "What do you want to talk about?"

Lisa said, "It can wait until after lunch. There's no rush."

"Now is as good a time as any."

Eric sat back in his chair and paused briefly before he said, "Father Bernal told us about what happened to you at Bobby Lane's party. What he did was despicable and we're going to see to it that he's punished to the full extent of the law."

Although the thought of Bobby behind bars appealed to her, the repercussions of taking the steps to make that happen gave her pause.

Eric continued, "When you're up to it, we want to take you to the police station and file a report."

Alexis shook her head. "I can't do that."

"Why not?" Jeremy asked. "After what he nearly did to you, he needs to be punished and put away. The sooner the better."

She said to Jeremy, "It's not that simple. If I press charges against Bobby, he's going to turn around and come after Rafael and have him charged with assault and battery; I just know it."

"Who's to say that he won't do that anyway? Besides, you can't let him get away with what he did to you," Jeremy argued.

"It's not about letting Bobby get away with anything," she replied. "If he does go after Rafael, then I will go to the police. But I won't force his hand by making the first move. I don't want Rafael to get into trouble for trying to protect me."

"We can discuss this later, when you've had the chance to get more rest and think things over," Lisa offered.

"I'm not going to change my mind," Alexis said firmly. As far as she was concerned, the subject was closed. But in the back of her mind, she knew that she might need to take some steps to make sure Bobby wouldn't press charges against Rafael in the future.

Alexis then asked her father, "Do you think you could take me to see Rafael after lunch? He might be well enough for visitors by now, and I'm sure he's wondering where I am."

Her parents exchanged furtive glances. She immediately sensed that something was amiss.

"Is Rafael all right?" Alexis asked as she put her fork down. "Did something happen to him after I went to bed?"

Eric shook his head. "We heard from Father Bernal this morning. He says that Rafael is doing better. It's just that..."

"What?" she asked as she started to rise from her seat. "TELL ME!"

"Please sit down," Eric said.

She looked at her father suspiciously, but did as he asked. He leaned forward in his seat and said to her, "Alexis, Rafael has asked that you not visit him right now."

Alexis stared at her father in disbelief. "Why?"

"Father Bernal didn't tell me why," he said slowly. "He just asked me to convey the message to you."

"Why would Rafael say that?" she demanded. "There's got to be something you're not telling me."

Eric shook his head again. "I told you last night that I wouldn't keep anything from you. I honestly don't know any more than what I've just said," he added gently, "but if that's what Rafael wants, then I think you need to honor his wishes."

Alexis felt her cheeks flush as she pounded her fist on the table and said, "You're lying to me again! He would never say that!"

"Alexis, please..." Lisa pleaded. She stood up and started to move toward her daughter, but stopped when she saw the withering look on Alexis' face.

"If you won't take me, I'll drive there myself," Alexis insisted.

"Neneng, be reasonable," Jeremy interjected. "You're in no condition to be going anywhere, and besides, you haven't driven a car in months."

"I don't care," Alexis said, as tears begin to well up in her eyes. She looked at her mother and said, "If Dad got into an accident, wouldn't you do anything and everything to be by his side? There'd be nothing anyone could say or do to keep you away from him."

"Honey, you're talking about a completely different kind of situation," Lisa replied, in a futile attempt to try and reason with her daughter.

"NO, I'M NOT!"

Jeremy put his hand on his sister's shoulder and said, "You need to calm down."

She spun around and said to him, "You don't know what happened between us!" She looked at each of them, adding, "None of you could possibly know what we have been through together. He told me that he loved me. He promised that he would stay with me even if it meant that he would lose his life. We are bound together in a way that none of you will ever understand."

Alexis wanted to scream and was finding it extremely hard to maintain some semblance of self-control.

Jeremy asked his father, "Is there any way Father Bernal could talk to her and give her some more information? After everything she's been through, I think she deserves to know why Rafael doesn't want to see her."

Eric nodded. "I agree. I'll call him right now."

Her father got up from the table, took out his cell phone, and dialed. Time seemed to stand still as she anxiously waited for the priest to pick up on the other end of the line. She clasped her hands together and started to pray when she heard Eric finally speak. Although she listened intently to her father's side of the exchange, she was unable to discern the gist of the conversation between the two men.

After Eric hung up, Alexis' eyes widened in anticipation as he said to her, "Father Bernal is scheduled to hear confessions at four o'clock this afternoon and then celebrate the five o'clock mass at Corpus Christi afterward. He said that he will be at the church by three to speak with you."

"Thank you," she replied weakly as she stood up to face him.

Eric placed his hand under her chin and said in a halting voice, "There's nothing I wouldn't do for you."

"I know, Dad," she replied as she wiped away her tears with a napkin.

Eric took hold of her hands and gave them a squeeze. "You'll get through this, and we'll be with you every step of the way."

Alexis said, "I don't want anyone else to get hurt because of me," as she looked at each one of her family members.

"Our lives are in God's hands," Eric said. "We live and die according to His timetable, not our own."

Lisa added, "We'll all be okay. You just need to focus on taking care of yourself."

Alexis knew that her mother was right. She looked at her now lukewarm plate of food and tried to eat. After a few bites, she gave up and excused herself from the table. Her head was throbbing. She walked to the front porch, sat down, put her head between her knees, and did her best to block everything out. All she could do now was wait.

It was just a little before three o'clock when Lisa dropped Alexis off in front of the church. As she walked through the front door, she dipped the tips of her fingers in the holy water font, made the sign of the cross, and entered the main body of the church. She scanned the room for Father Bernal, but didn't see him. She walked up the main aisle and then genuflected before entering a pew near the sanctuary. She sat down and took one more look around before lowering a kneeler to pray.

As Alexis gazed up at the large cross behind the altar, she thought about everything that had happened and the challenges that lay ahead. She was terrified of the possible consequences to her friends and family because of her situation. Her biggest fear was that someone else that she loved would get hurt…or die. Silently, she began to pray.

Alexis thanked God for bringing Rafael into her life. He had been her beacon of light in the darkness and a voice of reason in a world that often made no sense. He was also her first love and best friend. As she stared into the face of the crucified Christ, she prayed for Rafael's complete recovery and asked God to help him find his way back to her.

She wasn't quite sure how long she had been praying when she heard the sound of Father Bernal's footsteps coming toward her. She sat back and turned to the priest, whose eyes were bloodshot and surrounded by dark circles. Although his face looked drawn and haggard, it was readily apparent to her that he was still in full command of his faculties.

"Thank you for coming," Alexis said as she slid over to make room for him.

The priest returned her greeting with a slight smile as he sat down next to her and said, "Your father said that you needed to talk to me about Rafael. He was very insistent."

Alexis' pulse quickened at the very sound of his name and she found herself struggling to rein in her chaotic thoughts. She blurted out, "How is he doing?"

"As well as can be expected," Father Bernal replied. "He has a concussion, fractured ribs, and a broken arm. When he was first brought into the hospital, he required surgery in order to stop the internal bleeding. The gashes in his back were another issue. He is lucky to be alive." Alexis looked down at her hands. Father Bernal looked at her sympathetically and said, "Don't blame yourself for what happened. He would be the first one to tell you not to do that."

Alexis nodded. "How is he feeling?"

"It is hard to say," the priest said. "From what I have been able to observe, he seems to be doing well enough. He has a high threshold for physical pain. He is also very guarded when it comes to his feelings. He has been that way ever since his parents died. He shut people out and locked his heart away where no one could touch it. That is, until he met you."

She bit her lip and nodded. A moment later, she asked, "When do you think he'll be released from the hospital?"

"His doctors are hopeful that he will be well enough to go home in two weeks," he replied cautiously. "He is young and strong, and his body is very resilient. I am almost certain that he will be able to come through this without any long term complications."

"Does he get many visitors?"

"I have been there twice, and his host family has kept a constant vigil at his bed-side," he said. "They are very kind and loving people."

Alexis agreed, having met them on several occasions at church. Although it pained her not to be at his side, she was relieved to hear that he was not alone and re-ceiving support from people who truly cared about him.

"Does his family in Spain know what's happened to him?"

"Yes, I contacted them myself. They talked about coming here, but I convinced them that it would not be necessary for them to do that."

Alexis thought of how upset his aunt, uncle, and brother must be, especially since they were so far away. She couldn't help but feel guilty for being the source of their pain. After a moment of indecision, she decided that it was time to ask him the ques-tion she had come here for. "Father, why doesn't he want to see me?"

The priest leaned forward and placed his chin in his hands. He seemed to be carefully considering what he was going to say next. Finally, he said, "It is not that Rafael doesn't want to see you. He is in the process of making a very important deci-sion and believes that he needs some time and space from you to do that."

"What decision?"

"He is trying to decide whether or not a transition would be in the best interest of the mission."

Transition? Panicked, she asked the priest, "What are you saying, Father?"

"At this point, he doesn't know if he is physically and mentally able to continue on as your Arquero."

Alexis was stunned by his revelation, which confirmed her two worst fears: that her ordeal was far from over and that Rafael was leaving her.

"Father, how can he even think of stepping down now? You aren't actually considering replacing him, are you?"

"The decision is not up to me," he said. "Only he knows whether he can still do what he was sent here to do."

"What will happen if he chooses not to go on? Would The Brethren conduct The Trials again?"

The priest shook his head. "The Grand Master would likely appoint one of The Guardians who came along with Rafael to replace him."

"Who would that be?" she inquired.

"Vincenzo," he replied.

"What about Rafael's brother, Alejandro?"

Father Bernal shifted uncomfortably in his seat as he shook his head and said, "That is not possible." Although she wondered why that was the case, she decided not to pursue the issue.

"What would happen to Rafael?"

"He could choose to stay and support Vincenzo or go home. That would be up to him."

The thought of Rafael leaving was more than Alexis could bear. To her, he was irreplaceable. "He can't leave," she pleaded. "You have to let me talk to him. None of the others can take care of me like he can."

"Alexis, you must be patient," he said. "You are, at once, the source of his greatest strength, as well as his greatest vulnerability. In order for him to continue, he has to be sure that he can balance the two. Give him a chance to think things through. He cares for you a great deal and only wants what is best for you and the mission."

As Alexis tried to process what Father Bernal had said to her, she realized that the only thing she could do now was wait and see what Rafael's decision was going to be. Knowing that there was little else to be said on that topic and with nothing to lose, she decided to ask the priest some other questions that had been troubling her mind.

"Father, why me?"

He replied, "The answer to your question will only be revealed to us in time, but this much I can tell you now. Less than a year ago, The Brethren received word that the Archangel Michael appeared to a young girl in a remote village in Nigeria. He told her that the time for The Trials was coming. A few weeks later, we learned that he appeared to an old man from a very small fishing port in Peru. He told him that the Devil had targeted a young woman. Then in March of this year, we heard that he appeared yet again to a cloistered nun in California. He told her that the young woman was in San Diego. Based on this information, we convened The Trials. Finally, in

May, he appeared one last time to an elderly woman in a mountain village in the Philippines. He gave her your name."

"Of course, we did not just accept these signs at face value when this information was related to us. We investigated the backgrounds of each of these people, searched the Internet and other databases, and conducted interviews to see if someone was trying to perpetrate a hoax on us. In each case, the individuals that had been visited by the Archangel Michael had little or no ability to access the Internet and had no ties to organizations or persons who would be capable of doing such things. Most of them were in remote parts of the world and lived simple lives. In fact, none of them had ever even heard of The Brethren or of each other."

"Do you have any idea what is going to happen next?"

"We have the accounts of what happened the last time The Brethren appointed El Arquero centuries ago," he replied. "But there is no guarantee that things will unfold as they did then."

Alexis nodded. "Father Bernal, are you going to see Rafael tonight?"

"Yes," he said. "I am going to go to the hospital to see all four of them after mass."

"They were so selfless and brave," she said quietly. "It's hard for me to believe that my life was worth their sacrifice."

"They all volunteered to come," he said. "They knew what price they might have to pay in order to keep you safe."

Alexis shook her head as she said, "Why would people who don't even know me risk their lives to save mine? And just how many more lives might need to be jeopardized on my behalf if this isn't over yet?"

"We are here because we take it on faith that you have an unknown, but vital role to play in the life of the Church. As to your other question, we will bring as many resources to bear as necessary to ensure your safety until the threat has completely passed. No more, no less. As long as you are in immediate danger, we will be here for you."

Alexis then asked the priest if he would tell them thank you for her and give them her best. She also asked if he would relay a special message to Rafael. Father Bernal readily agreed.

"Please tell him that I'll be praying for him," she said. "I'm actually going to start a novena to Saint Raphael the Archangel for him tonight."

"The patron saint of healing," he mused. "Excellent choice. I am sure that he would appreciate that very much."

Their conversation ended shortly thereafter. Alexis again thanked Father Bernal for meeting with her on such short notice and for giving her some insight as to Rafael's mindset. For his part, Father Bernal wished her well and urged her to contact him whenever she felt the need. As the priest walked toward the confessional booth, she stood up and exited the church through a side entrance and met her mother, who was waiting for her in the car.

Despite her parents' misgivings, Alexis insisted that she was ready to go back to school on Monday, as planned. Although she dreaded the possibility of being stared at and whispered about by her fellow students, the idea of spending another day at home alone with nothing but her thoughts to occupy her mind was an even less appealing option. She pointed out to her parents that she had already missed one week of school. She argued that any more time off would only make it more difficult for her to catch up before the end of the semester. She also told them that her friends would be there for her. In the end, her parents relented, provided that she agreed not to overtax herself and to go to bed early. She gladly accepted those conditions and spent the rest of the day anticipating and preparing for her return to school.

On Monday morning, Alexis walked into the kitchen and sat down at the island to eat breakfast. She ate slowly as she watched the local newscasters discuss the power outage on Saturday. Although they mentioned some instances of looting, the newscasters said that little out of the ordinary occurred as a result of the blackout. *If only they knew.*

As Alexis scooped up her last bite of oatmeal, Lisa sat down next to her and said, "If you're really not up to going to school today, just say so. You don't have to put on a brave face for us. We're perfectly okay with you taking more time off if you need it."

Alexis shook her head. "I already told you that I'm ready to go back today. You, Tessa, and all my friends will be there. I'll be fine."

"Then we'll need to get going in ten minutes," Lisa informed her. "I've got a conference call this morning that I need to prepare for."

"That's fine," she replied. "I'll be ready."

Alexis turned to her father and asked, "Have you heard anything more about Rafael or the others?"

"Not anything more than what I've already told you," Eric replied as he took a sip of coffee from a large mug.

When Alexis saw Lisa put her purse on the island and take out her car key, she asked her mother, "Is it okay if I drive?"

Lisa glanced at Eric, who nodded his assent, and then handed it to Alexis. "Sure, why not?"

Alexis stared down at the key for a moment before gripping it tightly in her hand and heading to the garage. Lisa opened the garage door while Alexis got into the driver's seat, buckled in and adjusted the rearview mirror. Taking a deep breath, she slid her hands over the steering wheel and put the key into the ignition.

"You ready?" Lisa asked as she got in. Alexis smiled at her tentatively as she started the car and heard the engine roar to life. She was as ready as she'd ever be.

After months of excuses, she was once again behind the wheel. As she drove through the familiar tree-lined streets of her neighborhood, she appreciated the fact that her mother had let her drive so readily and had kept any concerns she may have had to herself.

After Alexis parked the car in the faculty parking lot, her mother said, "Keep your chin up. If you need anything, you know where to find me."

Alexis, once again, assured her mother that she was fine. She got out of the car with her backpack in hand and headed straight toward the courtyard.

As she walked among the other students, her spirits dampened slightly. She had always felt like a fish out of water. Slightly off. Set apart. And yet, she never gave up trying to find a way to fit in. Now, she sensed that the gulf between her and her peers was wider and more unbridgeable than ever. None of them would ever know about what she had been through or what it was like to walk in her shoes; not that she would have wished that fate on any one of them.

When she walked into her first class of the day, theology, she keenly felt Rafael's absence. It was the same in every class that they shared together. Thankfully, her friends stayed close and formed a supportive cocoon around her throughout the school day. Anita, who also returned to school that day, evidently wanted no more trouble and gave her a wide berth.

Alexis eagerly anticipated the return of Rafael and the others. It was not, however, until the latter part of the week that they started to trickle back in. She saw Akira from a distance as she headed to her English class, and then spotted Vincenzo wearing a cast on his right arm and a brace on his ankle during lunchtime.

She walked up to him and asked, "Vinnie, can I talk to you a minute?"

"Of course," he graciously replied. He excused himself from his group of friends and held out his hand, which she firmly grasped with both of hers, as she helped him to his feet. Once they were no longer within earshot of his friends, he asked her, "How are you?"

"Shouldn't I be asking you that?" Alexis replied.

"You have been through more than any of us ever will," he said. "You look well."

"Physically, yes. Do you know when Rafael and Gonzo will be coming back? I saw Akira this morning but I haven't gotten the chance to speak to him yet."

"Gonçalo should be back in school tomorrow." He paused a moment, then added, "Unfortunately, I am still not sure whether Rafael will be coming back at all."

Alexis' heart sank. "Have you been able to speak to him?" She couldn't bear to hear the words, *at all,* but she decided not to press the matter until she was able to finally talk to Rafael face-to-face.

"I went to see him right after I got discharged," he said. "He told me that he is feeling better."

"What are you telling your friends when they ask about what happened to you?"

"I have told them that Gonçalo, Rafael, and I were in a car accident on Saturday night." He leaned closer to her, adding, "No one, except those of us involved, will ever know what really happened."

"What about the gashes on Rafael's back?"

"If anyone asks, we've been told to say that he fell into some brush after he got out of the car."

"So what is Akira's story?"

"He had a run-in with a wild animal on the trails."

"I see," she said. She paused and looked down at her feet as she said, "So, I heard that you might be in line for a promotion."

Vincenzo sighed as he stuffed his left hand into his pocket. She got the sense that this was not a situation that he was particularly comfortable with or happy about. He said, "Believe me, I would like nothing better than to have Rafael continue on as your Arquero."

"I hope you know how grateful I am for all that you and the others have done for me," she replied. "I wouldn't even be standing here if it wasn't for you. It's just that…"

"I am not Rafael," he interrupted. "You don't have to explain, you have a very special bond with him. Anyone with eyes can see how much you care for each other."

"Then why would he even think about leaving?" she asked a little too loudly.

"I wish I could tell you that," he said.

At that moment, Alexis noticed that some students were looking in their direction. She blushed as her whole body tensed from the unwanted attention.

Vincenzo frowned as he watched her and asked, "Are you okay, Alexis?"

She shook her head. "I'm so sorry. I'm talking too loud and making a scene. People are staring at us."

"Let them," Vincenzo replied firmly. "Do not worry about what other people think or say. They have no idea what you have been through. All that matters in the end is whether or not you have lived your life in accordance with God's will. He has a special plan for you. We should know soon enough whether or not Rafael will be part of that plan."

"I think about him all the time," Alexis said as tears began to well in her eyes. "I pray for him every day. There's so much I want to say to him, and I'm just so afraid that he's going to leave before I can do that. I can't even begin to imagine not having him in my life."

"If it is any comfort to you, all of us have encouraged him to stay. I know for a fact that even Father Bernal has told him that. It would benefit no one, especially you, if he left now."

"Can I ask you something?"

"Absolutely," he replied.

"Did Rafael send you to Bobby's party?"

"Not exactly," he said slowly. "He did tell Father Bernal about you running into Bobby at the theater and suggested that it might be a good idea for one of us to go to the party. But it was Father Bernal who made the decision and asked me to go. It was just a precautionary measure...we really did not think that you would be there, especially after you got suspended."

Alexis nodded and said, "Not one of my better decisions, as it turned out...but I'm glad you showed up. You better get back to your friends. I've kept you from them long enough."

"Please feel free to come and talk to me, Gonçalo, or Akira whenever you need or want to. We are here for you, too."

"Do you or the others have any plans for next Saturday?"

"Not that I know of. Why?"

"I'm going to have a party at my house."

"What is the occasion?"

"My birthday. My parents are going to have some friends and family over to celebrate. It's going to be later in the afternoon, around five o'clock. It would be great if all of you could come."

Vincenzo smiled and said, "Well, happy birthday in advance. How old are you going to be?"

"Seventeen," she replied.

"Would you like me to tell Rafael about it?"

She looked at Vincenzo expectantly and asked, "Do you think he would come?"

"I can't make any promises, but I will certainly let him know about it," he replied.

"Thank you, Vinnie."

"You are very welcome, Alexis."

At that point, one of his friends called out to him. Alexis said, "I hope you can make it to my party."

"Of course I will come. I am sure Akira and Gonçalo will be there too."

As Vincenzo walked back to his friends, Alexis could barely contain her excitement at the thought that she might actually get to see Rafael once again. She also hoped that maybe, just maybe, if he was still undecided, she would get the chance to convince him to stay.

CHAPTER 21—SEVENTEEN

Alexis woke up on a gloomy Saturday morning to the pitter-patter of raindrops striking her window. She rubbed her eyes and yawned as she sat up in bed. An envelope with her name on it was propped up against the lamp on her nightstand. She grabbed it, tore it open, and took out the card inside. The front of the card said "Happy Birthday Sister" and had a picture of a big brother holding his little sister's hand. She opened it and found seventeen dollars inside, along with a handwritten note from her brother. "Smile and be happy. So proud to be your kuya. Never forget how much you are loved. Jeremy." She smiled as she stood the card up on her nightstand and got out of bed.

She went directly to the bathroom to freshen up. After splashing cold water on her face, she gazed intently at her reflection in the mirror. The pressure of people's expectations weighed heavily on her mind, especially with respect to those who had put their lives at risk for her. She hated the idea of disappointing them. And so she vowed to do whatever she could to make sure that their sacrifices would not be in vain.

The smell of bacon, eggs, and fresh baked bread filled the kitchen as she walked in to a chorus of voices singing "Happy Birthday." She smiled as she tried to mirror the upbeat mood of everyone around her.

When breakfast was over, Alexis volunteered to go with her mother to get party supplies and food for her birthday celebration that evening. Afterward, she met Tessa for lunch. She struggled not to let her eyes glaze over as her cousin rattled off all the things she had planned for them. In typical fashion, Tessa shuttled her from store to store until the *perfect* party outfit and matching accessories had been found.

It was three o'clock in the afternoon by the time Alexis and Tessa returned to her house. Preparations for the party were already in full swing as they walked through the front door. Her mother, Aunt Cora, and Nanang were in the kitchen preparing food while the men were busy cleaning and decorating the house. Tessa decided to help out in the kitchen while she opted to go to the living room to see if she could lend a hand there.

Alexis could hear Uncle Turing barking orders like a drill sergeant to Jeremy and her cousin, Joey, as she walked into the room. Her uncle looked like a king on his throne as he lounged on the couch while Jeremy and Joey moved furniture, set up chairs, and put up decorations.

Jeremy rushed to her side and whispered, "Is it a sin to think about doing bodily harm to your uncle?"

Alexis was barely able to hide her amusement. "Probably. That would most likely fall under the category of a mortal sin."

Jeremy sighed. "Oh well, I guess I'm going to have to go to confession then. I was doing so well, too."

Alexis hid her face with her hands as she repressed the urge to laugh and then looked at Uncle Turing, who was micromanaging Joey as he hung a "Happy Birthday" sign on the fireplace. She said to Jeremy, "Looks like you're not alone. I think Joey's about to blow a gasket."

Jeremy nodded in agreement. "So, how old are you again?" he teased.

"Seventeen," she said proudly.

"Wow, you're practically ready for that senior citizen discount."

She stuck her tongue out at him. He winked back at her.

When Alexis asked Jeremy if there was anything she could do to help, he said, "Nah, we're almost done here. Besides, you're the birthday girl, remember?"

"Where's Dad?" she asked.

"He's in his study. He had to make a phone call, or at least that was his excuse," Jeremy said as he nodded toward Uncle Turing.

Alexis patted her brother on the back and said, "Good luck. I think I'll go find him."

She walked over and opened the door to her father's study. He was sitting behind his desk sifting through some papers. He smiled at her as she walked in. After having gone through a brief period of discord, she was relieved that the rift between them had largely healed. Each night, he had taken the time to update her on what he knew and patiently answered every question she asked. As far as she could tell, he had held nothing back.

After a few minutes of playful banter back and forth about how he had managed to escape Uncle Turing's clutches, she asked him if she could borrow his car. He handed her his keys on the condition that she not go alone. She agreed and told him that she would ask Jeremy to go with her.

When Alexis went back to the living room, Jeremy jumped at the opportunity to escape and gave Joey a secret nod of condolence as they walked out the door. When he asked her where they were going, she told him that she wanted to visit Avery's grave. After a quick stop at the grocery store for flowers, they headed to the cemetery.

Alexis felt apprehensive as she drove into the memorial park. This was the first time she had come here since the funeral. She followed a winding road, parked in front of the chapel, and then walked silently with Jeremy across a well-manicured lawn lined with markers. She thought bitterly about how Asmodeus had disguised himself as her best friend and manipulated her into thinking that the only viable solution to her problems was to take her own life. In retrospect, she felt foolish and naive. Although Avery's death had left her in a vulnerable state, she should have known that her best friend would never have given her such counsel or knowingly put her in such grave danger.

When Alexis reached Avery's grave, she was overcome by an overwhelming sense of grief and loss. Jeremy put his hand on her shoulder as she closed her eyes and took a long, slow deep breath. As she bent down to place the bouquet of flowers beside the marker, he offered to wait for her by the car. When she nodded, he turned and walked away.

Alexis looked down and began to trace each letter of Avery's name with her finger. A—she remembered a five-year-old Avery coming up to her in the school playground and asking her to play, VE—and how a ten year old Avery stood up to Anita when she tried to bully her, RY—and, finally, a fourteen year old Avery dragging her onto campus and telling her how great things were going to be on their first day at Mater Dei.

Alexis looked up at the sky and noticed that it was getting dark. Time was running out. *It's now or never,* she thought to herself. She bowed her head and folded her hands in front of her to say goodbye to her best friend.

"I miss you," she said quietly. "There isn't a day that goes by that I don't wish you were still here." She looked at the flowers lying beside the marker and said, "I hope you like them. I got the assortment. I remember how you could never decide which kind you liked best."

"I'm sorry I didn't come to see you sooner. It was really hard at first. I didn't want to believe that you were gone." She paused as she thought about what Bobby had told her. "I wish you had been able to confide in me. I know what Bobby put you through, and I've been thinking about what you said to me just before you took off in your car. I didn't understand what you were trying to tell me then…but I do now.

You kept saying, 'He's watching' and, 'not safe' over and over again, and right before you took your keys out of my hand and got in the car, I remember you telling me, 'Stay away. I don't want to hurt you.' You were trying to protect me, even then, weren't you? Just like you always did."

"I kept thinking about all the mean things we said to each other. It really hurt to know that I'd never get the chance to tell you I was sorry…that I didn't mean it… but it made me feel better when Father Jim told me that you're in a place where no one will ever be able to hurt you again. Hopefully, I'll see you there someday."

Alexis closed her eyes and reached for the wooden cross around her neck.

"Please help me get through this," she cried out to her friend. She tightened her grip on the cross as she said, "A very special person gave this to me. You would have liked him a lot. Sometimes I think I love him so much that it hurts inside, but he might be going away soon and I don't know what's going to happen to me if he does."

Alexis let go of the cross, then folded her hands in front of her and asked her friend, "Could you do me a favor and pray for me? Put in a good word with the Big Guy upstairs and ask Him to pull a few strings for me with Rafael if He can, okay?"

At that moment, Alexis felt a hand on her shoulder. "Are you ready to go?" Jeremy asked. "It's already past five. Everyone's going to be wondering where you are."

Alexis nodded as she touched Avery's marker one last time and then stood up and said, "I think I've said everything I needed to say to her for now. Let's go home."

Only a single streetlight and a few porch lights illuminated the darkened street in her neighborhood as Alexis drove up to her house. She recognized most of the cars parked along the street and quickly noted that Rafael's was not among them. Although she felt disappointed, she told herself not to give up hope just yet.

Since the driveway was already filled with cars, Alexis parked on the street. As she and Jeremy stepped onto the porch, she heard the sound of music and animated voices coming from inside.

Tessa opened the door just as she reached for the doorknob and said, "You're late." She took Alexis' hand and dragged her up the stairs. When Alexis opened her bedroom door, she found that the cream-colored babydoll dress and black leggings she had purchased for the party were already laid out on her bed. With her cousin's help, she quickly changed into her new outfit, retouched her makeup, and pulled her hair back with a black band. Once she had gotten Tessa's seal of approval, she headed back downstairs.

Alexis was halfway down when the doorbell rang. Jeremy, who was standing near the door with some of his friends, opened it. She was thrilled to see Akira, Gonçalo, and Vincenzo walk in. She hugged each one of them and smiled when she saw Akira blush. A moment later, she caught sight of Father Bernal standing near the kitchen doorway. He returned her friendly wave with a broad smile as he strode toward her. He greeted her with a warm handshake and wished her a happy birthday.

"Thank you for coming," she said to them all. "I'm so glad that you were able to celebrate my birthday with me." She looked from Vincenzo to Gonçalo to Akira to Father Bernal and said, "It means a lot to me to have nearly all of you here."

Father Bernal looked at her curiously and said, "What do you mean by *nearly* all of you?"

Alexis' cheeks flushed as she said, "Father, I..."

The priest said, "I came out here as soon as I heard you had arrived. I brought a guest with me. I hope you don't mind."

"Of course not," she quickly replied.

"He is in the kitchen. I have to warn you though, my young friend is not quite himself yet," said the priest solemnly. "You see, he just got out of the hospital today, but when I told him about your party, he insisted on coming. From what I can tell, he is very eager to see you."

She blinked a few times and then stared at the priest with a mixture of shock and surprise. Her mind raced, as the realization that Rafael was in the next room began to sink in. She could barely contain herself as she said, "If you'll excuse me, I think I need to greet more of my guests."

Alexis thought her heart was going to burst. She stopped at the doorway and looked in. The kitchen was just as packed with people as the living room. She immediately spotted Rafael in the crowd, sitting on a stool at the island with a cast on his arm. Her face, however, fell as soon as she saw who he was talking to. She shook her head as he tried to carry on a polite conversation with, of all people, Uncle Turing. It was a fate she wouldn't have wished on her worst enemy.

At first, Alexis just stood in the doorway and stared at him. Rafael didn't notice her, as he seemed to be focusing all his attention on what Uncle Turing was saying. Even with the large number of people in the room, it was easy to hear Uncle Turing's pronouncements. His voice was at least three decibels louder than everyone else's. *Does he think that Rafael is hard of hearing?*

"So, you're the Spanish boy who's been dating my niece?" Uncle Turing asked with a smug look on his face. Rafael nodded and was just about to respond when Uncle Turing added, "Did you know that the Philippines was a colony of Spain for more than three hundred years? Magellan was the one who discovered it. Your country brought us your language, architecture, and religion. That's why so many of us are Catholic."

"Yes, I learned about that in school," Rafael replied politely.

With a glint in his eye, Uncle Turing leaned forward in his seat and said, "And do you know what the natives did to Magellan when he came to the Philippines?"

"If I remember correctly, I believe that they killed him with a poisoned arrow."

A wide grin spread across Uncle Turing's face, as he picked up a butter knife and sliced into a roll of Pan de Sal and slathered it with butter. He pointed the knife at Rafael as he took a bite and said, "They cut his nuts off. Ha!" Uncle Turing slapped his knee, laughing at his own joke. "They cut him to pieces. I guess they didn't like what he had to say."

Rafael smiled slightly, picked up a glass of water and took a long sip. Afterward, he reached for a piece of Lumpia and was about to put it in his mouth, when Uncle Turing asked him, "Have you eaten much Filipino food?"

He shook his head. "No, not really, but I would like to. The food on this plate looks delicious. Your wife was kind enough to prepare it for me."

Uncle Turing pointed to the food on Rafael's plate and said, "Has my niece told you about some of the more exotic dishes we eat?" When Rafael said no, Uncle Turing said, "Have you heard of Dinuguan or Balut?"

"No, should I have?"

"Dinuguan is meat cooked in pig's blood. The blood turns brown when you cook it. Sometimes we call it chocolate meat. It's actually one of Alexis' favorite dishes." Rafael swallowed hard and looked slightly queasy. "Balut is a hard-boiled egg with a duck embryo inside. You really should try it sometime."

Alexis decided that this was the perfect time to rescue Rafael, before Uncle Turing made him want to swear off Filipino food for all eternity. She stepped up to the island and said, "Uncle Turing, Rafael's not going to want to eat any of our food if you keep scaring him like that."

"I was doing no such thing," Uncle Turing protested, as he looked to Rafael for support. Alexis, however, sensed that Rafael was no longer focusing on her uncle. She felt his eyes on her and, in particular, on the wooden cross that she was wearing around her neck. She instinctively put her hands to her face, as her cheeks began to flush.

Uncle Turing, for once, was speechless. He turned to Aunt Cora, who was standing just a few feet away, and motioned for her to come closer. When she did, he leaned toward her, covered his mouth with his hand, and said in an overly loud whisper, "Cora, I think I hear violins playing."

At first, Aunt Cora gave him a questioning look, but once she realized what her husband was doing, she followed that up with a swat on the head and threats, in Tagalog, of further bodily injury if he said or did anything else to embarrass his niece.

Alexis was mortified. However, the sight of Rafael's amused smile did much to ease her concern about her uncle's antics. She asked him if he wanted to join her on the front porch to get some fresh air. He gladly accepted her invitation and took her hand as she led him out of the kitchen.

She felt multiple sets of eyes on them as they passed by the living room. Thankfully, no one tried to stop and engage them in conversation before they reached the front door. She desperately wanted to talk to him alone. When they stepped out on to the porch, however, they ran right into Manuel and Danny.

"Happy birthday, Alexis," the boys said in unison as they walked up the driveway.

"You look good, man," Manuel said as he shook Rafael's hand.

Danny quickly added, "How are you feeling?"

"Much better, thank you. It is good to see you both."

"I guess we'll be seeing you back in school on Monday, then," Manuel said. He looked at Alexis and winked as he said, "You were definitely missed. Do us all a big favor and try to be more careful on the road next time."

Rafael nodded and then looked at Danny, who asked, "So, did your car get totaled?"

"Uh…no. It has been repaired. Just like me."

"You guys," Alexis chimed in, "everyone's here. You really should get inside and get something to eat. There's so much food in the kitchen."

Manuel looked at Danny and said, "I think she's trying to get rid of us."

Just then, Tessa opened the front door and motioned for Manuel and Danny to come inside.

"Don't get your panties in a bunch, Tessa," Manuel said. "We'll be in, in a minute."

"Now!" she ordered.

Manuel gave Tessa a mock salute. "Yes, ma'am. Like I just said, we'll be right there."

"Manuel Gonzalez, don't make me come out there and get you."

"I think we'd better go inside," Danny said as his eyes darted from Tessa to Manuel. "Tessa looks really mad."

Manuel replied, "You're not afraid of a girl, are you?"

"You betcha. Her brother, Joey, isn't the only one in her family that practices karate. Tessa has a black belt. I'll see you inside. You're on your own, man."

Manuel made a face and stuck his hands in his pockets as he turned to follow Danny into the house. He looked at Rafael and Alexis and said, "We'll catch you guys later," and then gave Danny a nudge and pointed toward the window, as they walked through the door. Danny responded with a sly smile and thumbs up.

Tessa helped hasten their retreat by pulling them the rest of the way through the door and slamming it shut.

Rafael leaned against the porch railing and shook his head as Alexis said, "I'm so sorry. I don't know what's wrong…"

She stopped speaking mid-sentence when she spotted two familiar faces peeping through the curtains. Rafael had noticed Manuel and Danny, too, as they smiled and waved vigorously at them. Seconds later, Tessa appeared behind them. She grabbed them both by the hair of their heads and yanked them away from the window. Alexis was speechless.

After a moment of silence, Rafael said, "*You* have some interesting friends."

"No, they're *our* friends," she replied, as she boldly took a step closer to him.

Knowing that she had her work cut out for her, the short distance that now separated them provided her with little comfort. She also knew that she had no time to waste. At this point, every second counted.

"How've you been? I've been so worried about you."

Rafael kept his body turned toward the door and averted his eyes from her gaze as he said, "I am sorry. I just needed some time alone to think things through. It is hard for me to think clearly when I am with you."

"Have you made a decision?" She gripped the railing with her right hand and tried to read his face as she waited for a response. His silence unnerved her. She looked away, desperately wanting to maintain her composure. She made the split-second decision to ask a second question, despite the fact that he had not yet answered her first one.

"Are you leaving me?"

Rafael took a long, deep breath before answering. Again, without looking at her, he said, "When I came here, I was given a complete report about who you were and what you were facing. I made a solemn vow to The Brethren that I would do everything humanly possible to protect you from harm." He turned his face toward her, adding, "But, from the moment I saw you, I felt a connection to you that no one could have prepared me for. I started to let my emotions cloud my judgment. It caused me to make some bad decisions."

She shook her head as she looked into his eyes and said, "You saved my life…"

"Those bad decisions drove you to that bridge," he said as he clenched his jaw. "It was only by the grace of God that I was able to stop you from jumping."

"I didn't jump," she argued. "You kept me from doing that. You're the reason I'm still here."

"You give me too much credit. I was lucky. The Devil will not make the same mistake twice. He is cunning, and I am afraid that he will use our feelings for each other as a weapon to get to you. I don't want that to happen. You are too important…"

Alexis reached for the wooden cross that he had given her and held it out to him. "The night you gave this to me, you promised me that you would stay. You can't leave me. I won't let you go."

Rafael turned his body toward her and took a step closer. "Alexis, listen…"

"No, you listen to me. God chose *you* to be my Archer. He did that for a reason. It was His will that brought you to me. If you are as loyal a servant as you claim to be, then you know that you have to finish what you started. You don't have the right to walk away now."

Rafael nodded. "You are right. I don't," he said slowly, "but when I think of how close I came to losing you, I just…"

Alexis moved closer and looked up at him. "I'm right here, and I'm not going anywhere. I'm going to be fine as long as you're with me."

She noticed his eyes soften as he said, "I need to tell you something."

Alexis feared the worst. She pleaded, "What do I have to say to make you hear me?"

Before she could utter another word, he touched her face with his hand and then leaned in and kissed her. A moment later, he whispered in her ear, "Will I have to keep kissing you to get you to stop talking?"

"Well, I guess I'd better keep talking then," she answered breathlessly.

He smiled and said, "You are a stubborn, frustrating girl."

"But you love me anyway. I heard you say it. You can't take it back now."

He placed his forehead against hers and said, "God help me, I do." He kissed her again and again.

"So does that mean you're staying?" she asked as his lips moved from her mouth to the side of her neck.

"Why else would I be here?" he whispered in her ear. "I would have told you so five minutes ago if you hadn't kept interrupting me."

They both laughed. He looked at her and said, "Father Bernal told me what you did when Asmodeus was about to kill me."

"You tried to do the same for me," she replied as she laid her head on his chest. It comforted her to feel his strong heartbeat, especially after what he had just been through.

He nodded and said, "Still, that was a very brave thing you did."

"What else was I supposed to do?" She felt him flinch when she touched the scars on his back from the gashes left behind by the gargoyle's talons. "I wasn't about to let you die."

He kissed her again, trying his best to embrace her with the cast on his arm. "You saved my life, too. My family told me to tell you how grateful they are."

"They know about me?"

"My aunt and uncle have always known about you, and now my friends do, too." Alexis' eyes widened in surprise as he said, "I told them all about this beautiful American girl and how she has completely changed my life."

"Really?"

"I can show you the emails if you would like." Alexis shook her head. He added, "You won't even need Jake to hack into my phone to see them this time."

"I'm so sorry, I…"

"Don't be," he interrupted. "I pushed you to do that by not telling you what you deserved to know."

After they kissed yet again, she said, "Don't ever leave me. Promise?"

Rafael looked into her eyes as he said, "I can't stay away from you. I love you too much."

She felt almost giddy as she let his words sink in. She put her arms around his neck, looked up at him and replied, "I love you, too."

Alexis couldn't have thought of a more perfect way to end her birthday. She was safe and happy in the arms of a young man that she loved more than anything else in this world. To her, that was all that mattered.

Reveling in their happy moment, Rafael and Alexis didn't notice the streetlight across the street go out.

The Devil, who was once again an old man in tattered clothes, stood underneath it in the darkness and glared at the happy couple. He spat on the ground and dug his hands into his pants pockets as he tried to think of what he could do to ruin their idyllic moment. He wasn't alone. Standing next to him was someone whose mere presence filled him with hate and loathing. Still, he knew that he had little choice but to endure the white suited gentleman's company.

After a few minutes of silence, the Devil turned to the Archangel Michael and said, "That was a fine bit of theater you pulled off at the Immaculata. You know, I think I prefer seeing you as a frail, old priest."

The Archangel smiled. "What choice did I have? Asmodeus outdid himself appearing to Alexis as a homeless woman, her best friend, and even Rafael. Luckily, she was able to see through the facade."

"Yes, but not before he had nearly taken her virginity which, by the way, she seemed more than willing to give away."

"Alexis sensed that it wasn't really Rafael," the Archangel replied calmly. "Asmodeus was only able to replicate Rafael's body, not his soul."

"She's not foolproof."

"She knows the truth now," the Archangel said. "He's told her everything."

"Has he really?" the Devil inquired.

"He's told her everything she needs to know…for now."

The Devil smiled as he contemplated his next move.

The Archangel looked over at Rafael and Alexis and said, "They make a lovely couple, don't they?"

The Devil laughed bitterly. He hated to admit defeat, especially when the one standing next to him was most likely the architect of the loss he had recently suffered. He said, "Asmodeus was a fool. He underestimated the strength of their bond. I will not make the same mistake."

"What makes you think that you can succeed where Asmodeus failed?" the Archangel inquired. "Wasn't it pride that led to your fall?"

The Devil sneered, "Love is a volatile emotion, especially among the young. It brings out certain desires, which they will be hard-pressed to resist. You have no idea how much I'm looking forward to watching their relationship implode. When it does, she *will* be mine. It's just a matter of time."

"He loves her unconditionally, and he will die for her without so much as a second thought, if it becomes necessary," the Archangel said evenly. "If that happens, there is no way that He will let you succeed."

"The Archer will fall," the Devil said defiantly, "but not before he's broken her heart to such an extent that she'll be begging to be released from her misery, and I'll be there, waiting for her with open arms."

"You won't win."

"We'll see about that, Michael. We shall see…."